Copyright © 2022
Published by DOWN ISLAND PRESS, LLC, 2022
Beaufort, SC
Copyright © 2022 by Wayne Stinnett
Library of Congress cataloging-in-publication Data
Stinnett, Wayne
Vodou Child/Wayne Stinnett, Stewart Matthews
p. cm. - (A Jerry Snyder novel)
ISBN: 978-1-956026-43-6 (eBook)
ISBN: 978-1-956026-44-3 (print)
Cover and graphics by Aurora Publicity
Edited by Marsha Zinberg, The Write Touch
Final Proofreading by Donna Rich
Interior Design by Aurora Publicity
Down Island Press, LLC

If you'd like to receive my newsletter, please sign up on my website:
WWW.WAYNESTINNETT.COM.
Every two weeks, I'll bring you insights into my private life and writing
habits, with updates on what I'm working on, special deals I hear about, and
new books by other authors that I'm reading.

The Gaspar's Revenge Ship's Store is open.
There, you can purchase all kinds of swag as well as autographed
copies of Wayne Stinnett's books.
WWW.GASPARS-REVENGE.COM

Visit Stewart Matthews's website at
WWW.SMWRITES.COM

Also By Wayne Stinnett

The Jesse McDermitt Caribbean Adventure Series

Fallen Out
Fallen Palm
Fallen Hunter
Fallen Pride
Fallen Mangrove
Fallen King
Fallen Honor
Fallen Tide
Fallen Angel
Fallen Hero
Rising Storm
Rising Fury

Rising Force
Rising Charity
Rising Water
Rising Spirit
Rising Thunder
Rising Warrior
Rising Moon
Rising Tide
Steady As She Goes
All Ahead Full
Man Overboard
Cast Off

The Charity Styles Caribbean Thriller Series

Merciless Charity
Ruthless Charity
Reckless Charity
Enduring Charity

Enduring Charity
Vigilant Charity
Lost Charity
Elusive Charity
Forced Charity

www.waynestinnett.com

Also By Stewart Matthews

The Cready Marsen Mystery Series

Repo Man   The Captain

The Detective Shannon Rourke Series

Chicago Blood   Chicago Lies
Chicago Broken   Chicago Creed
Chicago Betrayed

The Barrett Mason Series

Matador   Ghosts
Tyrant   Wardogs
Jackal   Red Star

www.smwrites.com

Courage doesn't always roar.
Sometimes courage is the quiet voice at the end of the
day saying,
"I will try again tomorrow."

—Mary Anne Radmacher

Virgin Islands

Anegada

Tortola

St Thomas — Road Town

Virgin
Gorda

Puerto
Rico

Charlotte
Amalie — St John

Vieques

Anegada Passage

. Sombrero

Dog I   Anguilla

The Valley

Sint Maarten   St-Martin

St-Barthélemy

St Croix

Saba

St Eustatius

St Kitts

Basseterre

Nevis

Barbuda

Antigua &
Barbuda

St John's

Redonda   Antigua

Caribbean Sea

Montserrat

Plymouth

Guadeloupe Passage

Grande
Terre

0   km   100

Basse Terre
Guadeloupe

Basse-terre

Marie-
Galante

18°N

16°N

64°W

62°W

CHAPTER ONE

Oualichi, known today as St. Martin
November 11, 1493

S mall, bright-colored birds, some with ornate plumage, chittered and peeped as they flitted from branch to branch in search of berries and tiny insects. Larger birds screeched and squawked in the higher branches, and off in the distance, waves could be heard washing up on a sandy beach. They were pleasant and familiar morning sounds to anyone who lived among them.

The night was over. Macuya's tormenting vision was gone.

The morning sounds awakened him, and he'd lain in bed trying to figure out what the vision meant. Finally, he sat up, looking out through the doorway, as if expecting his vision to appear again.

There were no predators on the island, so there was no need for a door. The house was round and sturdily built, with low, outside walls made of logs and poles anchored deep in the ground, and a high, conical thatched roof constructed of palm fronds woven together with sturdy, fibrous rope made by several women of the village. The roof was open in the center to let smoke escape from the cook fire.

It was just becoming light outside—the soft, gray dawn of a new day. Besides the birds, Macuya could hear children already at play and men working. He stretched his arms over his head and yawned.

Macuya was the village *kasike*, accepting the title from his father, who had died a year earlier after a terrible fall. His grandfather had been *kasike* before that. The duties of the village *kasike* were mostly symbolic, leading the people in ceremonies to appease the *zemis* in times of famine or other disasters. Aside from that, he led an uncomplicated life.

His wife Yuiza lay beside him, still asleep, their baby suckling her as he also slept. The baby had been sick and had cried much of the night, with both parents fawning over the boy child, afraid for the worst.

Rising quietly, Macuya went outside to relieve his bladder, then retrieved his *guaiuko* from inside and fitted it around his waist. He was planning to go to the cliffs to spear the fish that accumulated in the pools around the rocks, and he would need the protection the rough fabric provided, even if it was uncomfortable against his manhood.

"Where are you going?" Yuiza asked, rising slightly and holding the child to her breast.

"To get fish from the pools," he replied. "The early light is best. No shadow is cast on the water. How is he?"

Yuiza stroked the baby's head with her free hand. "Better, I think. His breathing is becoming normal."

"That is good," Macuya said, relief in his voice. "I will be back before *Guey* is high overhead. You rest."

"He kept you awake also," Yuiza said, her dark, knowing eyes searching his.

2

The infant was their second. A girl child had been born to them, but she had died before the night spirit, *Karaya*, had become full-faced a second time. The boy child had been a gift to them from the fertility goddess, *Ala Bey*, and Macuya and his wife were again happy when he was born.

"Yes," he said, smiling back at her. "But the child does not suckle from my breast. I will be fine."

"You had the vision again," she said, gently laying the baby beside her and rising from their bed.

Macuya turned and stared through the open doorway. "Yes, it was very vivid."

"Was it the same as before?"

For several of *Karaya's* nightly cycles, Macuya had been visited in his sleep by some dark figure, warning him of impending doom. Just what it was, the vision didn't tell him. But this morning, just like many others, he'd awakened feeling something terrible was about to happen.

He turned, gathered up his fishing spear, and made his way through the village, toward the mountains that still blocked *Guey's* light. Other men of the village greeted him and more than one were also carrying fishing spears and traps.

The people of Oualichi lived mostly on fish and cassava root. They also grew maize, groundnuts, and yams, but fish and cassava were their main staple. The harvest had been plentiful, and the fishing was always good.

When he and two other men arrived at the tidal pools beneath the cliffs, they split up randomly, as their fathers had taught them, and their fathers before them. Whatever the men caught would be cooked by the women of the village and eaten by everyone, or dried and stored for later. Each fisherman had his favorite place and method. Some set traps and retrieved them each morning, others went out in boats, luring larger fish to the surface and spearing them with long, weighted poles. Macuya and the men he was fishing with, like their fathers before them, preferred stalking along the rocks with shorter spears.

Macuya held his ready, arm cocked, holding the spear close to his ear as he slowly waded toward the rocks, under which he knew fish would be hiding. Sure enough, as he moved closer, a large fish came out to see what the two stalk-like things were that were moving toward his lair.

With lightning-fast reflexes, Macuya thrust his spear before the fish could move to either dart away or hide deeper under the rock. He pinned the great fish to the bottom as it thrashed in the shallow water. Once it was still, Macuya grabbed it by the gills and, keeping the spear embedded in the side of the fish's head, lifted it out of the water and splashed back to shore.

"What is that?" Guamá, one of the village elders asked.

Macuya tossed his catch on the beach, then turned to look where his friend was pointing.

His eyes went wide and his mouth fell open. On the horizon, silhouetted by *Guey* and the bright sky, were a large number of sailing *canoas*, but they were much larger than any Macuya had ever seen, with many billowing sails. The tops of the masts were decorated with long, colorful strips that fluttered in the light *hurican*. The front and rear of each were built much higher than in the middle.

Macuya instinctively moved toward the safety and concealment of the rocks, calling the other two men to do the same. As the great *canoas* drew closer, Macuya climbed the rocks for a better view.

4

"I have never seen such large *canoas*," he said to the two men below him.

He could see men moving about, their bodies covered from head to toe in dazzling costumes. They gathered to one side of each of the great *canoas*, pointing toward the island. The massive vessels even dwarfed the large *piragua* the village had built from a single massive log when Macuya was a boy. It was owned collectively by all the villagers, and still used as the villager's primary means of trading with other lands.

"What are they?" Yuquibo asked.

He was younger and had yet to travel away from the island with the trading *piragua*.

Macuya counted the ships. When he'd counted all *pólu* fingers on both his hands, he started again, mumbling under his breath, "*Pólu-hek, pólu-ká, pólu-kún, pólu-kóbix, pólu-kóbre, pólu-piruá, pólu-akarát.*"

"Are you sure?" Guamá asked.

Being one of the village elders, Guamá was one of the few who was permitted to question what Macuya said. He respected the man and had learned much from him, as well as from his own father.

"Yes," he replied, as he continued to watch, the feeling of impending doom so strong in the pit of his stomach he could almost taste it.

"That is more than all our *canoas* together."

Macuya didn't need Guamá to tell him that. The village barely had *pólu canoas* they could put in the water at any one time. The Taino people of Oualichi were mostly planters and coastal fishermen, so rarely strayed far in their small boats. From the high mountains, a desolate island could be seen far in the distance. He'd visited it once, but it was too rocky and had no drinking water. Only those who went out with the trading *piragua* had ventured any farther.

"Who do you think they are?" Yuquibo asked, when Macuya dropped to the sand beside them.

"I do not know," he said quietly, then looked toward Guamá.

The older man looked up at him. "It is they," he said. "Do you remember when *Guey* was at its lowest point in the sky during the last purification?"

"Do you mean the trading *canoa* that came, and the men spoke of a terrible massacre?"

"They called themselves spah-nish," the elder said. "They killed men and boys and took many slaves and wives."

"They are stopping!" Yuquibo said, taking several steps into the water.

Macuya looked out through the gap in the rocks. The giant *piraguas* were lowering their sails, except one. The lone vessel came closer as the three men watched, safely concealed by the surrounding cliffs.

"We should warn the others," Guamá said.

"Yes," Macuya agreed. "Go to the village and warn the people. Yuquibo, go down to where the *canoas* are kept on the shore and call the men in. I will watch these strangers from the shore and move toward the village."

Guamá nodded. "I will have all the men meet at the cove with the fishermen."

Macuya stopped him as he turned to go. "Tell the men to bring their bows and spears, Guamá."

Once the two men left, Macuya crossed the shallow pool, then climbed over the rocks that held the water and fish in after the tide receded. From there, he could see the great *piraguas*. One was moving closer to the coast, so he did his best to conceal himself from them.

Fortunately, there were many large rocks along the coast, often forcing him into the water to go around them. So, he was able to watch the visitors from safety the whole time. Only the coves on the side of the island where *Guey* disappeared had long stretches of soft sand.

Macuya moved slowly, keeping an eye on the thing with the colorful sails. The others were too far away to discern much detail, but he could easily see the men on the nearer one as it came closer. When it finally turned, it was close enough for Macuya to see the men's faces, many covered with frightening-looking hair.

He let the sailing *piragua* get ahead of him before he came out of his hiding place to race across the sand to the next rock. If he'd had his bow with him, the hairy-faced men would be within range. But he'd never killed anything more than fish and an occasional bird. He wasn't sure if he could.

Finally, as it neared the long point that protected their cove from storms, the closer *piragua* turned and began sailing toward the others. As it neared them, they too began raising their sails to catch the *hurican*.

Macuya was able to move faster as they sailed away and quickly reached the trail that led across the rocky point and down to the cove where his village was. From the top of the jagged promontory, he paused and watched the large sails grow smaller and smaller, as the hairy strangers continued away from his island.

He decided they were the danger that the spirits had been trying to tell him about. If each *piragua* had as many men on them as he'd seen on the one that came close, then they would outnumber his entire village many times over.

7

Macuya knew nothing of where the hairy strangers had come from, but just from their numbers and the size of their vessels, they came from a land with far more people than were in all of the islands.

The men were gathered at the edge of the water, fishing *canoas* pulled up on the sand. Guamá and another elder came toward him.

"We saw them leave," Guamá said. "The danger is over."

"For now," Macuya said, wading out into the water with his spear. "But I fear they will return. And I also fear that there are more of them than there are stars in the sky."

CHAPTER TWO

Marigot, St. Martin
November 6, 2022

The back office of Billy Pearce's church was not a sacred place, but it looked like one. All the religious trappings were there—crosses, candles, leftover sacramental wine in an old water bottle, weeks-old eucharist in a zip lock, a framed picture of The Virgin and her baby Jesus on the wall.

There was even a picture of His Holiness Pope Francis, but Billy's church was not Catholic as far as Shara Bradley was aware. She'd once asked him about that Pope picture, and he'd shrugged and said he was a good dude, so why not have his picture back here?

Seemed a fair argument to make.

Shara looked from the Pope's picture—the one where he was against a slightly-clouded, pure-blue sky, giving a wide, open-mouthed smile, and waving at all the good Catholics of the world, and probably even a few heretical onlookers, while he rolled by in his clear-sided, bulletproof car—to Billy.

Billy was a white man. He had eyes the color of bay water and his skin was tanned and crinkled in all the right places, and even if his hair was long and greasy and was slowly, but surely, washing back from the shore of his forehead, Billy still looked good. A lot of women thought so, Shara knew. She'd heard them talk outside of service.

He might've sworn he was thirty, but Billy looked fifteen years older than any thirty-year-old white man she'd ever met. There weren't a lot, but she'd been stuck in enough hotel rooms at the Mer du Mélasse resort over on the east side of St. Martin doing her homework while Mommy cleaned to know a thirty-year-old white man from a forty-five-year-old one.

Anyway, it didn't matter. Billy looked good, he had money and, most importantly, he needed Shara's help.

She did his books.

She was *currently* doing his books; she sat in front of the desk she'd helped him take from an insurance office that closed five years prior. It wasn't stealing, exactly–nobody missed the desk. It had been sitting in that empty ruin of an office for years before she gave Billy the idea that they could take it.

When they finally worked up the nerve to break in and haul the desk home, Billy, always efficient, always looking out for a good bit of something to have, also noticed a matching filing cabinet and two identical office chairs, so they took those things too.

Shara wasn't entirely sure taking that many things from the abandoned office was the right thing to do—she'd only mentioned the desk on a lark, but Billy firmly believed The Lord provided for those who sought to provide for themselves. And it all looked pretty good in the formerly unfinished office in Billy's church, which, apart from that old desk and filing cabinet and chairs, had a brand-new safe about the size of a cooler, which Billy kept under his desk.

"Can you hand over de American tens, Billy?" Shara motioned toward a small stack of US bills. She'd already sorted the donations—

Euros into one section, US dollars into another, and guilders in yet another. Then the various currencies were sorted and stacked by denomination.

He slid the money across the desk toward her, then lifted up his hand, and as soon as she laid her fingers on the stack of bills, dropped his over hers.

Shara met his eyes in the dim light. His were like two pearls floating in the air, beautiful and mysterious, and almost irresistible to her. She couldn't stop herself from getting closer, rising a couple inches out of her chair, leaning over the money and the ledger.

His lips locked onto hers and she closed her eyes. Billy's hand came to her shoulder, then began to slide downward, across her blouse, almost like a reflex. Aside from money, the man only ever had one thing on his mind—and it wasn't a half-bad idea. What if Shara closed the ledger, then climbed on top of the desk, lay across the money and spread her legs for him under the eyes of The Virgin and the Holy Father?

Ah, but there was work to be done. And she didn't like the way the Pope smiled at her when she had her shirt off.

Shara bobbed her shoulder, moving her clothed tit out from under Billy's hand and opened her eyes... and Billy was already pouting. Old as he was, he had the temperament of a pigtailed third-grader who didn't get a pony for Christmas.

But she knew how to keep him in check. Shara hooked her fingers into the collar of his undershirt and pulled his face close to hers.

"You know I got to get dis work done," she said softly.

"I know," he admitted. "But, baby, what's the world without a little lovin'?" He pecked her lips. "You just look so damned sexy sittin' there, runnin' numbers the way you do. How's a man s'posed

11

to stay away from a woman as temptin' as you?"

Shara giggled and gave him a peck in return. Then, she let him go and sat down in her chair.

"I'm runnin' numbers for you, Billy," she reminded him in her sweetest voice. "And you know I got to do this job to get a good recommendation before I apply for schools."

"You know that rec's comin' from me," he said with a grin. "I'll trade favors."

"Aw yah, lawd!" She threw an eraser at him and laughed. She knew the kind of favors Billy wanted to trade with her, and she'd *just* turned one such proposal down.

"You make me wish I was a senior in high school again," he said. "Just so I could follow you. Nineteen was a good age for ole' Billy Boy—that was when I figured out that I had a callin' to take care of, and plenty of girls to meet along the way. Maybe a few too many. Plenty who broke my heart, but I can't be too sore about it. They led me to you, even if you're goin' away and leavin' me on my lonesome."

"I won't be gone forever," Shara said. "I know my work 'ere is important as anyt'ing I could do."

"That's right," Billy said with a grin. "And I'll be here waitin' for you, sweet darlin'."

She felt her cheeks flush. He might've been a preacher, but Billy still had wildness in him. She'd seen it right off, back when they'd met at a Wednesday night youth group he'd put on. He played guitar and charmed the girls and made all the boys look at him with envy. Billy could've taken nearly any Christian woman on St. Martin, but he'd chosen Shara.

He sat back in his chair, and then opened a desk drawer and out came his dark velvet bag with his weed and bowl inside.

12

She counted the tens and scratched the totals into the ledger while he pinched off a bud and packed it into his bowl. He lit it, then caught her watching him as he inhaled. Billy lifted his eyebrows as he finished his hit, offering it to her.

"I tol' you I got to finish de numbers. You don't want to make another late payment to Mr. Desir, do you?"

Billy smiled, and smoke wafted out from his perfectly straight teeth.

"Little Miss Taskmistress," he said. "I don't know where I'd be without you, baby doll."

She eyeballed the weed.

"What?"

"You keep smokin' dat stuff when dere's work to be done, and even wid me around, you ain't gonna do your best work for de people. I seen de boys who smoke all day, and dey all workin' down at the market, sellin' Chinese T-shirts to tourists. You're better den dat. You got an important message to spread, Billy, and a lot of folk around St. Martin need to hear it before it's too late."

While she talked, he re-lit the bowl, inhaled, and held his breath until she was finished. Then he let the smoke go in a long exhalation.

"And this helps me spread it," he said. "You know about the bad thoughts in my head, baby—you didn't forget about that, right?"

"No, I didn't forget," she said.

"The herb keeps my receptors open and clear so I can tune in to the Lord's message—it keeps the devil out of my head."

"It slows you down, too, and you got a lot of bad folk out dere wishing you harm. Dey ain't gonna stay deir hands while you in here, wastin' time."

"You callin' me lazy?" he asked in a jarringly serious tone.

13

Shara's attention was drawn from the ledger to the sharp, thin line of Billy's mouth. He'd done this before—snapped into a seriously bad mood at a moment's notice. He looked like a different person when his easy smile was hard to come by.

"I didn't mean not'in' like dat, Billy," she said, trying to recover. "It's just dat I know you got all dis *potential* in ya. The power to be a great man, a great leader, is within ya and I love ya, and I want to see dose great t'ings come true for ya."

He stayed quiet and stared at her.

Why did you open yo' mouth, she silently berated herself. Why did she nag him? Couldn't she keep sweet like a good woman, do her work, and support a great man?

Then his lips cracked, showing his teeth. He was grinning again.

"I'm kidding!" he said. "I know you care about me and all that, Sweet Pea. But the weed's gotta stay for now. I really, really need it. Without it, things are all cloudy in my head, and I just can't pick up The Word, ya know?"

He picked up the bowl and lit it.

"Sure, Billy." Shara breathed, while Billy sucked another wad of smoke into his lungs. She went back to the money, sliding the ten-dollar bills away, then pulling the fives nearer.

"Truth is," he said, exhaling smoke while he talked, "the weed is like my brand, okay? I can't be like the other holy men out there. I have to stand out, I have to be somebody memorable, because all the people coming to me aren't here because they want another Catholic, or Baptist, or Vodou service. They want to be here for new ideas and bold direction, so I pretty much *have* to do it all differently, and weed helps me do it.

"I get what you're saying," he continued, "but if smoking grass makes me a little lazy, so be it. Slowing down and really listening to

14

His message might be good for all of us."

He lit the bowl again and pulled heavy on the smoke.

"You're right," Shara said.

He was always right. If he wasn't a little crazy, she wouldn't have come to see him in the first place, and she definitely wouldn't have slept with him. She went back to adding the fives into her running count. At least for a second or two, until she felt Billy's knuckle gently lift her chin up.

His face was in front of hers and before she could react, he kissed her. He opened his mouth, and she tasted the pungent smoke, felt its dryness slipping over her tongue and into her lungs, then felt Billy's other hand slip into her shirt and up the front of her chest.

Shara let Billy feel for a moment, then pulled back and blew the smoke into his face.

He laughed so hard, he had to fall back into his chair. He rolled away, grinning, ash falling from his bowl onto the floor.

"I love you, little girl," he said, scooting forward. He pinched off another bit of weed and began pressing it into the bowl. "Now tell me how those numbers are looking."

"Right now, you're already $833 ahead of this month's expenses. You're lookin' plenty fine, Billy."

Billy reached over the ledger and scooped up the thin stack of seventeen five-dollar bills she'd counted, then put them in his pocket.

"How much am I up again?" he asked.

"Seven-hundred and forty-eight," she answered.

Billy winked at her. "Shara, I think I see a very nice dinner in our future. First of many, I believe."

Shara batted her eyelashes at him. "Is that all?"

"Tonight's the future," he said. "After that, I just about picture you going to—which school was it you wanted to study at?"

"Florida State," she said.

"I see you right there, Florida State, sitting at the fifty-yard line every Saturday, taking it in," Billy said. "But when it's time to work, you, little girl, get your work done and you do it so well, all your professors notice, and all the other students get jealous."

She put her elbows on the desk. "Tell me more."

"Every boy on that campus is gonna come after you," he said. "But I'll make sure they don't even get to sniff your perfume, because not a single one of them is worthy of your beauty, which is to say nothin' of your intellect and your dedication."

He spun around in the chair as he continued. "I'll call you every night and we'll talk until we both fall asleep at three in the morning, and your girlfriends will always ask, 'Shara, who's that on the phone you're always gabbin' with?' You'll just smile and shrug, and they'll never know nothin' you don't want them to."

Shara closed the ledger. She stood up from her chair and slowly walked around the front of his desk to the back, holding eye contact with Billy all the while.

"Little girl," he said with a grin, "women have been burned at the stake for glances half as salacious as the one you're giving me now."

She picked up his packed weed bowl and his lighter, and she put her lips to it and lit it.

Billy's eyes lit up while she inhaled.

She held it in until her lungs cried for mercy, then blew the smoke into his face once again. Breathing in through his nose, he vacuumed every bit he could.

When he let the smoke go, he grabbed Shara by the hips and rose up out of his chair. He pressed against her, making her back into his desk.

"Wait, wait, Billy," she said.

"Oh, I can't wait anymore! You're gonna give me a heart attack!"

She turned around, picked up the ledger, then turned back and smiled at him. "Just one second." She set it inside the open safe beneath his desk.

Then, when she meant to turn back toward Billy, she saw inside his open desk drawer, and froze on the thing that should not have been there.

It was a small clay jar, about the size of Shara's fists if she pressed them together, painted black and marked with the *veve* of Ogun with white chalk. To see it put a chill right down her neck.

When she looked up at him, ready to cuss him out and call him crazy for keeping that cursed thing all the time, she lost all train of thought as he smiled his sly smile. She felt his hips pushing into hers and the tingling started to take her over.

Billy shut the drawer.

She threw her arms over Billy's tight shoulders and let him push her backward onto the desk. Money went falling off and all her neatly organized piles of it were destroyed.

He wasted no time, kissing her, pushing his hands up beneath her shirt and whispering things that should not even be thought within fifty feet of a portrait of the Virgin Mary.

Then, the lights went out.

"Christ Almighty!" Billy swore as he came off Shara. She heard him shuffle in the darkness, then a desk drawer slid open and a few seconds later a candle came on.

"I thought they fixed the goddamned grid!" he said.

Behind Shara, out in the chapel, the front door crashed open.

"Billy?" She bolted upright.

17

He still had his pants on, but his shirt was half off, with one arm out of the sleeve. He quickly jammed his arm through it, went to the old filing cabinet, and pulled a gun out.

He didn't answer her. He was checking to see if the thing was loaded.

"Billy!"

"Hush up!" he whispered.

Billy went to the door and cracked it open, looking across the chapel.

"Who is it?"

"Just shut the fuck up and get your head down," he whispered harshly.

Shara obeyed. She slid off the desk, fixing her bra and shirt and stooping low, while she moved to the front corner of the office.

"Who is it?" she asked quietly.

"Don't see anyone," Billy answered. As he looked out through the crack in the doorway, a scratch of light went down from his forehead, across his nose and to his lips, which he licked. It must've been the streetlamp across the way, coming through the front window. Reflections moved with his eyes like tiny beads of light as he studied the chapel on the other side of his office door.

Billy slowly turned his face toward her. "No matter what you hear, stay back," he said.

Shara nodded.

Slowly, Billy opened the door. He only needed a few inches until he had enough space to get his thin frame out into the chapel.

Shara didn't stay put. She hurried over to where Billy had been standing. Her pupils were wide open, and they found just enough light for her to see Billy's figure—a dark shadow against an even darker background. She watched as he crept through the pews,

18

holding his gun about the level of his belly, ready to shoot.

"I heard you come in," he said to the darkness. "You people think you can scare me off by fuckin' with the power?"

No answer.

Something clattered to the ground to the right. Billy quickly spun and fired.

For a split second, she saw Billy's body light up from the gun, but her eyes were soon overwhelmed by her ears. The sound was louder than anything Shara had ever heard. She squeezed her eyes tight and pressed her palms to the sides of her head as ringing zipped through her skull, then echoed away a few seconds later.

She blinked until she thought she saw Billy, now up near the altar. She heard a book hit the ground to her left, Billy yelled and fired again, and the sound of the gunshot hit Shara hard enough to make her flinch.

While she blinked away the flash from the pistol, she heard Billy cry out in a long, shrill sound. Her mind went back to years ago, to the bulls having their throats cut, bucking and bleeding and screaming like children while the drums beat, and the others called out to Ogun for his blessing and guidance.

She saw a shadow flash in front of Billy, then sensed it turning to her.

Shara slammed the office door closed. She slapped the deadbolt and Billy screamed again; she ran under the desk while Billy's screaming turned to gurgles and gasps, and then the church's front door opened and closed again and there was no more sound from Billy. She knew—she knew.

Billy was dead.

CHAPTER THREE

St. Thomas
Monday, November 14, 2022

Hearing odd-sounding footsteps on the dock, I looked up to see a man with a barely discernible limp walking toward my boat. I recognized him instantly, set my scuba regulator aside and got up from the table where I'd been working on it.

"So, the wayward son has returned," I said, as DJ Martin started along the finger pier beside my boat.

"Hey, Dep! How's it going?"

"Is that all I get?" I said, moving toward the steps in the starboard sugar scoop. "You disappear completely for half a year, and come back to me with a simple, 'Hey, Dep' now?"

He stopped beside the bottom of the steps and looked up at me. He'd changed. DJ had been a mess when he'd disappeared off Armstrong's radar back in April: he was overweight, wheezing, crippled for life from an IED, usually drunk, and for all I knew, dabbling in one kind of drug or another.

The DJ Martin standing before me had lost a lot of weight. Or more precisely, he'd reallocated that weight, turning fat into muscle.

"Hey, man, a conversation's gotta start somewhere, right?" he said, removing his sunglasses and squinting up at me in the bright morning sun.

"No phone call or text?" I asked, starting to get a little hot, and it had nothing to do with the tropical sun on my neck. "Not even a note on the door saying, 'Gone fishing' or 'Picking up chicks.'"

"I'm not here to make excuses or get a talkin' to, man. And I'm definitely not gonna stand down here cranin' my neck."

I hadn't heard from DJ since he'd simply sailed away from a debriefing in April at Armstrong Research's shipyard on North Bimini. We'd closed a big pharma case in Puerto Rico a year earlier, then drew a couple of less glamorous ones, which we nonetheless solved, though the results didn't dazzle the intended beneficiaries. Or Colonel Travis Stockwell, head of security for Armstrong Research, and our handler.

Nobody at Armstrong knew where he'd gone either. We both worked for their Mobile Expeditionary Division, but we weren't exactly employees. We were ARMED field investigators, under contract for one dollar a year.

He was the second of ARMED's investigators to disappear in as many months. At first, I was worried, but after talking to a few others, I'd learned that "burnout," whatever abstract concept that was, was fairly common, and field operatives had a habit of disappearing for a couple of weeks or months. Management expected it and some of the more seasoned handlers in support and logistics didn't even bat an eye; they just scrolled to the next operative's name on the list.

Still, it was troublesome not knowing if or when DJ was going to return. Not even the tech people aboard *Ambrosia*, Armstrong's floating data center, had any idea where he might have taken his unannounced, unplanned sabbatical.

I was tempted to march down the steps, get on his level and tell him to continue his long walk on that short pier. I'd had a string of steady successes all through the summer with my wife, Alicia, who was becoming a real investigative asset, thanks to a tenacious attitude and a kinder, more client-friendly demeanor than I.

"Come aboard," I told him instead. "But you can leave your bag. You won't be staying long. Alicia and I are going diving."

"No, we're not," Alicia said, coming out of *Wayward's* saloon as DJ came up the steps. "Hello, DJ. You're looking well—it's so good to see you!"

I couldn't tell if she felt as cold about DJ's return as I, and was better at hiding it, or if she was genuinely happy to see his scraggly-goateed face.

"We're *not* diving?" I asked her. "Then what're we doing, exactly? Because we are certainly not going to drop everything at a moment's notice to entertain DJ."

"Don't listen to him, DJ—truth be told, Jerry's been a little worried about you."

"I have not," I stated flatly, which was a bald-faced lie that Alicia knew better than to believe.

"He's got a damned funny way of showing it," DJ said.

"He does," Alicia agreed, then turned to me. "Jerry, *we're* not diving, because you're going to take DJ diving. You two can hash it out on the bottom of the ocean."

DJ grinned at her. I just threw my hands up in exasperation.

An hour later, ~~as we approached the~~ waypoint on the chart plotter, I throttled back on the engine and brought our rented boat down off plane. Alicia and I had picked up this particular eighteen-foot center console for the week, with the idea of checking out some dive sites on the lee side of St. Thomas, the island we lived on. The engine and wind noise had prevented any more talking between DJ and me during the ride around the island, other than one- or two-word shouts or a gesture.

"A mooring ball?" DJ asked, looking around.

"Mooring balls prevent reef damage," I replied.

"That's cool, man. I just thought we'd go see something a little more off the beaten path, ya know? Away from all these other people."

It being a Monday, there was only one other boat, and it was on a ball at the far end of the dive site.

"We don't all have a compulsive need to slip away from other people whenever we like," I said. Which was a tad wide of DJ's objection, but on the journey to our diving spot, I'd had plenty of time to think to myself, and my

24

thoughts liked to curveball my words at inopportune times.

DJ leaned on the gunwale, arms crossed, weight distributed evenly on his good leg and the prosthetic. Dark, wraparound sunglasses hid his eyes. "I get the hint, Dep. Say what's on your mind."

"It didn't bother you that people were worried about you? Why couldn't you call, DJ? Or send an email or a carrier pigeon—just *something* so Alicia wasn't up all night worrying?"

I turned away and snagged the mooring ball's line with a boat hook, then connected the bow line to it with a carabiner.

"Oh, so it was Alicia doing all the worrying?"

"You know, Charity Styles vanished not long after you did," I said, changing the subject. "And nobody's heard from her either."

"Charity's fine," he said flippantly.

"And you know that exactly how?"

"Look man, between me and you, when I was off doin' my thing, I ran into her up in North Florida and the two of us hung out for a while."

He *hung out* with Charity. I began to suspect DJ's AWOL stint wasn't as off the cuff as he claimed.

"Small world," I said.

"I know what it sounds like, Dep, but there wasn't any planning to it. We just happened to be in the same place at the same time."

"Uh-huh," I grunted, as I pulled my buoyancy compensator out of my dive bag and slid it onto one of the

25

tanks. "So, two Armstrong operatives disappear from different parts of the world, and you just bump into each other in North Florida?"

"Shit, man, I was more surprised than anybody else," he replied. "First time I saw her up there, Charity pulled her piece on me, and you know her rep—she was ready to blow my brains out."

He was right. Charity Styles wasn't known to talk her way out of misunderstandings. Now, more than being upset at him, I was curious to hear how DJ had survived.

"And so, you decided to stick around with her? Why?"

"Oh, it wasn't nothing personal. She said she liked me— she just thought ARMED had sent me after her."

I stopped tightening the first stage on the tank and looked over at him. "Why in the world did she believe Armstrong would do that?"

"Remember after we busted that big party in PR?" DJ said, as he fitted my spare BC over another tank.

"The bust that kept us from being terminated."

"Terminated?" he said, scoffing. "You make everything sound complicated, Dep. They can't *fire* us. We're not employees."

He was right about that. Armstrong's field investigators and covert operatives were paid for their time, but it was a pittance compared to what a private investigator could make in the private sector. ARMED recruited people who were financially secure and wanted to make a difference without money being an issue.

"You know what I mean," I retorted. "Why would Styles think ARMED was chasing after her?"

26

"Eisenstein didn't hang himself whacking off," DJ replied.

One of the subjects of our investigation into big pharma had committed accidental suicide in his bathroom by putting a noose around his neck in the shower. I learned later it was a delightful little hobby called auto-erotic asphyxiation.

"What do you mean?" I asked, opening the valve on my tank. "We were both there. There wasn't anyone else in his room and nothing was disturbed, and I believe that particular act, by definition, is done alone."

"Charity had been there before we got back from the party," he said. "She caught Eisenstein with that underage bartender."

I raised an eyebrow at DJ. "You're saying...?"

"Yup."

"And she staged it to look like..."

"A solo adventure into the wider world of onanism," DJ finished.

"What a way to go."

"That shitbag deserved worse," DJ said.

"You're not wrong."

"Remember the liquid soap smeared on the outside of the bathtub?"

"What about it?" I replied, thinking back to the discovery of the body.

He'd been an overweight man, flabby and pale-skinned. He'd been found hanging by his neck, a towel wrapped around it and the shower head and his toes just inches from the bottom of the tub. His hands hadn't been

27

tied and he'd still had an erection. I knew from attending post mortems as a cop, that it was normal, so thought nothing of it at the time.

"She made him stand on the edges of the tub and covered his legs with the liquid soap, then she turned the water on and he slipped. She told me how he'd started to strangle himself, clawing at the knotted towel around his neck while she watched him die."

I shuddered. Killing was one thing—DJ, Charity, and I were all military vets and we'd all seen combat, as had most of Armstrong's investigators and virtually all of the operatives. Killing a man in the manner DJ described and waiting around for the victim to slowly die was bordering on insanity.

"DJ, I'm not above admitting how much Charity Styles frightens me," I said. "Did she tell you all of this about Eisenstein?"

"Yeah," he replied. "And I'm telling you in confidence."

I looked over at him as he pulled his shirt off. He'd lost several inches around the middle and was a lot bulkier through the chest and shoulders.

"It's not a story I plan to inflict upon anyone else," I said. "Did she ask you to keep it a secret?"

"Not exactly," he replied, struggling to get the fin over his prosthetic foot. "She told me about it when she was under emotional duress."

"Oh, so you slept with her."

"Ha, ha." He got the fin on, then sat back and secured the BC's straps around his waist. Finally, he looked up at me with a sly grin. "And, Dep, a gentleman doesn't tell."

Then he pushed himself up onto the gunwale with his arms and one good leg, and rolled backward off the boat, making a large splash. I hurried and pulled my own straps tight, then got up on the opposite gunwale, checked behind me, and fell backward.

When I righted myself underwater, I looked around and saw DJ on the other side of the boat. He hung motionless in the water column, fins dangling, and hands clasped nonchalantly in front as he looked back at me. The prosthetic looked strange in the water, covered in colorful stickers from places he'd been, but apparently it was of no consequence in the water. The foot part of the contraption had the full range of motion of a human foot and his amputation was below the knee, so he was even less awkward underwater than on land.

I swam forward on my side of the boat, and he followed on his, and when we met at the line going down to the mooring anchor, we gave each other the okay signal and began our descent.

Communicating underwater was limited to a few hand gestures or what could be written on an erasable slate. Long time buddies develop even more signals. But DJ and I had only dived together a handful of times, and with the idea of DJ Martin and Charity Styles together taking up quite a bit of headspace, I couldn't figure out hand signals on the fly. In any case, I resolved to put their budding relationship completely out of my mind and just enjoy the dive.

Thatch Cay was an island just off the northeast tip of St. Martin, about a thirty-minute boat ride from my and Alicia's house. At least in the powerful center console. Aboard my catamaran, *Wayward*, it'd be a good day's sail. We'd heard stories of the tunnels and arches there—the remnants of lava tubes formed back when the island was born—and I'd wanted to dive them for some time.

We swam toward the first arch, and it was obvious DJ was more comfortable in the water than I'd remembered. We'd been partners for over a year, but if we weren't on an assignment, we didn't hang around together very much, and none of our assignments so far had involved scuba diving.

There was an abundance of sea life all around the towering arch, with dozens of colorful fish darting in and out of little crevices among the corals and sea fans. DJ pointed out a blue angelfish as big as a platter. We followed it through the arch and came to the first tunnel.

Red-hot, molten lava had once flowed out of the tube, cooling into basalt rock, and breaking apart as it came into contact with the water, which it vaporized instantly in a dance of steamy bubbles and fracturing black rock. Erosion had broken the fragile rock into sand over time, leaving only the tubes to show that this had once been a volcanic island.

It actually still was, but La Soufrière Volcano hadn't even belched any smoke in 120 years.

Suddenly, a large bull shark flashed past us, its pectoral fins pointing straight down, a sure sign that it was agitated. In open water, the shark turned abruptly, as if confused, and went straight toward DJ.

I had no time to react or do anything as the shark rolled and took DJ's foot in his mouth. I watched in horror as my partner grabbed his leg behind the knee and began beating on the shark's snout.

As quickly as it happened, it was over, and the shark was gone.

DJ started toward the surface, a wild panic in his eyes. One fin was mangled and of little use. It was then that I realized the shark had grabbed his prosthetic, which slowed my heartbeat a little.

But DJ was still going up too fast.

My training kicked in and I was on him like a shot, grabbing him in a bear hug and wrapping my legs around his, while dumping the air from both our BCs. With only one fin, his wild dash for the surface quickly became a slow sinking.

I grabbed his head and forced him to look at me. I blinked my eyes three times, hard and slow, then a pause followed by slow, fast, slow blinks. I knew DJ knew Morse code. I was telling him OK with my eyes, as my hands were busy trying to keep him under control. He'd become freakishly strong since he'd left.

He tried to turn his head, but I wrenched it back as we hit the sandy bottom and toppled over. I blinked the code again, then I saw reasoning in his eyes. He scanned the water behind me with his eyes, then looked directly at me and returned the OK code.

I released him and pointed a thumb toward the surface, while motioning downward with my other palm facing down—slow ascent.

He nodded and turned his head and body in a full circle before punching his auto-inflator button a couple of times to get neutrally buoyant.

I did the same and together, we slowly started to kick toward the surface, releasing a little air from our BCs as it expanded. We hadn't been down long, no more than ten or twelve minutes, and we'd only been at a depth of fifty-two feet when we hit the bottom in a tangled heap. I checked my dive computer as we neared twenty feet and there wasn't even a safety stop indicated, but I got DJ's attention and tapped my console containing an air pressure gauge, compass, and my dive computer. I held my right hand palm down over two fingers, similar to a timeout signal, letting DJ know we were going to do a two-minute safety stop.

He nodded his understanding of what I was telling him, and we both moved close to the mooring line and adjusted our buoyancy to remain at fifteen feet. He checked his console, then shrugged and showed it to me. His computer didn't indicate we should do a safety stop either.

I just shrugged my shoulders back at him.

Facing each other, with the encrusted mooring line between us, we both looked all around. I just wanted DJ to go through the normal procedure, to judge his panic level.

He seemed calm and I could tell by the bubbles from his second stage exhaust ports that his breathing had slowed to normal.

After two minutes, I feigned checking my computer again, then jerked a thumb upward.

DJ spat his second stage out when we broke the surface and laughed. "I bet that bull's gonna have one hell of a toothache."

I joined him in laughing as we swam to the back of the boat. "At first, I didn't know which foot he'd grabbed."

"I didn't either!" he shouted, as we pulled our fins off and tossed them aboard. He held one up. "I think I owe you a new fin, Dep."

I looked at it in disbelief. The fin had two distinct bite marks—one about three inches up from the tip and slightly to one side, and the other completely engulfing the foot pocket and almost severing the strap. If it had been the other foot, DJ might have ended up a double amputee. Bull sharks have the strongest jaws of any fish of comparable size, including the great white—almost a ton of bite force.

"Well, you can't dive with just one," I said, shrugging out of my BC and climbing aboard.

"Sure you can," he replied, as he handed his BC up to me. "I probably did a few dozen dives before getting Patty."

"You named your prosthetic?"

He climbed up awkwardly, not putting much weight on the mangled-looking contraption. Had it been a real foot, DJ's ankle would have been broken, at the very least, and all the little bones of the instep crushed. It was bent inward and what little weight he was putting on it was on the side.

"Gonna spend the rest of my life with her," DJ said with a shrug, as he sat down and began rolling the rubber cuff down over his knee. "I have a spare, but I've fixed this before." He pulled it off the stump of his lower leg and inspected the damage. "I was staying with this island girl down in St. John named Tildy O'Shea and she had one of those fancy alarm systems in her house."

I sat opposite him and as he worked on the prosthetic, I started breaking down our gear, wondering where this was going and what kind of island woman would live in a house needing an alarm system.

"Anyway," he continued, "she had these double French doors that let out onto this real pretty patio with all kinds of native flowers and vines. Anyway, when we'd go to sleep, I always propped the leg against the door."

"What's that got to do with naming your prosthetic?"

He looked up and grinned. "Whenever you opened any of the exterior doors, the alarm's keypad would announce which door it was."

"Makes sense," I offered. "If someone's breaking into my house and I'm there, I'd want to know where they were coming in from."

"Exactly," he said, loosening a small screw at the base of the broken contraption. "So, in the morning, I'd hop out the bedroom door for a smoke and to put this on. When I opened the door, the alarm would say 'patio door.' Get it?"

I just looked at him puzzled. "Not in the least, man."

He snapped a rod back into place and held his prosthetic up, testing the ankle joint. "Her name is Patty O'Doure. It's Irish, just like Tildy."

"You named your pegleg 'patio door?'"

"It's spelled with a U and has an E at the end. Patty..." he paused..."Oh Door."

I hung my head, shaking it slowly.

"What, Dep?" he asked, putting his stump back into the sleeve and tugging it up. "Ya think it's odd to name it?"

"No," I replied, looking up at him. "It all makes perfect sense—we name our boats and our cars—but we don't name inanimate objects after another inanimate object." I picked up his mangled fin by the tip, which was held in place only by the rib on one side. "It'd be like saying you killed Boat, here. Anyway, I don't think we'll be diving any more today."

"Too bad," DJ said, standing and testing the fake foot. "It looked like a pretty cool dive. How far back do those tunnels go?"

"No idea," I replied, starting the outboard. "Can't find a lot of information, but I've heard people say some of them are interconnected and could run for miles."

CHAPTER FOUR

We idled into Yacht Haven Grande, DJ and I both laughing. Alicia and I kept our Majestic 530 catamaran there mostly because it was close to our house—just a short trot up the hill. We were also keeping the center console there, tied off to our sailboat. So far, management hadn't said anything, and it was only a week.

As I turned into the wide fairway between our dock and the next, I saw Alicia sitting in *Wayward's* cockpit with a man.

"Holy shit," DJ muttered, also noticing them. "It's Stockwell."

Alicia saw us and rose, then Travis Stockwell stood up beside her, turning to face us. With his close-cut silver hair and steely demeanor, Stockwell looked ready, at any moment, to force DJ and me into consecutive rounds of physical training up and down the Saint Thomas hills until we keeled over dead. Knowing Stockwell, he'd resuscitate us and then force us to finish the workout to his satisfaction.

"I knew he'd come sniffin' around eventually," DJ said, standing next to me at the leaning post.

"I'm sure he simply ran into us by chance," I replied. "Get the bowline ready."

Stockwell moved over to the side deck and started forward. "We didn't expect you back until noon," he called out over the fairway.

I turned sharply to the left, kicking the stern around, then shifted to reverse and quickly spun the wheel the other way. "We had a run-in with a shark," I said, as I backed the boat into the other half of the double slip.

With *Wayward* on an inside slip, there wasn't room for any kind of large boat in the empty slip, but the Mako fit nicely. That might be why marina management hadn't said anything about keeping it there.

"A shark?" Alicia said, concern in her voice as she came out onto the side deck.

DJ tossed Stockwell a line, and after shifting to neutral, I stepped over and handed the stern line up to my wife. "He only wanted a quick nibble of DJ," I told her. "Nothing to worry about."

"I can't say I wasn't expecting you, Colonel," DJ said, standing in front of the T-top. "Just didn't think you'd be here so soon."

Stockwell finished tying the line to a cleat on *Wayward's* toe rail and stood, looking down at DJ, dark, wraparound sunglasses hiding his eyes. Not that his face would be readable without them. Though in his late sixties, retired Colonel Travis Stockwell seemed as if he'd been chiseled from solid granite, and his eyes were just as steely gray, giving away nothing of what the man was thinking. He was six-two or so and close to two hundred pounds, all lean muscle.

"Good to see you again, Sergeant Martin," he said, his voice that of a three-pack-a-day smoker—somewhere between a growl and a gravely rasp, but he didn't dare dull his physical prowess with cigarette smoke.

"Mind if I ask why you're here on my boat?" I asked him, stepping up onto the gunwalel, then up to *Wayward's* deck.

"You weren't at your house when I went there," he replied, his flexing jaw muscles and moving lips the only indication he *wasn't* actually made of rock. "So, naturally I came here, and your wife was gracious enough to invite me aboard for a cold iced tea."

DJ climbed up, one foot at a time, not quite trusting the damaged prosthetic.

Stockwell noticed and looked down at it. DJ had managed to get his shoe back on over the damaged "foot" part, which was made of hard silicone encasing a curved titanium blade that gave it some springiness, like a real ankle and toes.

"What happened?" Stockwell asked.

"The bull shark tried to snack on my foot, sir," DJ replied. "All it got was a mouthful of Patty—my prosthetic, I mean."

Stockwell slowly took his glasses off and looked down. "Damaged?"

"Just Patty's foot," DJ replied. "It's still functional, but my prosthetist would be pretty sore at me if I kept using it.

Lucky for me I've got a replacement foot and a whole separate prosthetic stowed in my duffle."

"Good," he said, then turned and fixed me with those steely eyes. "I have an assignment for you two."

"For us?" DJ asked.

"Koshinski called," he replied. "She'd received a communication from Styles saying that you were on your way here."

"Yeah, um," DJ stammered. "I figured I should mend the bridge here first, Colonel."

"Aww!" Alicia turned her head toward me. "Did you hear that, Jerry?"

"And is it mended?" Stockwell asked, turning back to me.

"Yes, sir," I replied for both of us.

"Good. Can we go inside?" he asked Alicia.

"Of course, Travis," she said. "Please come in."

Once we were all settled in the spacious saloon, Stockwell explained that a confidential informant on the island of St. Martin had contacted his operative and asked for a favor. The favor went all the way up to Jack Armstrong, himself—CEO of Armstrong Research, which had been a true oil exploration company all through the '80s and '90s, right up until the attacks of 9/11. Armstrong's headquarters had been in the North Tower of the World Trade Center. Jack's wife had been one floor below the corporate offices, dropping off their son at daycare when the first plane hit, obliterating their lives in an instant.

"That's all this assignment is?" DJ asked, after listening to Colonel Stockwell's summation of the event.

"What?" Stockwell barked.

"St. Martin's over a hundred miles away, Colonel. And I'm guessing the operative this CI usually goes to with information lives on or near there. Am I right?"

Stockwell stared at DJ for a moment. "That asset is unavailable."

"So, it gets passed down to us?" DJ asked. "Doing small-time work to repay a favor?"

"That's correct, Martin," Stockwell said. "And if you continue to ignore the company when you are called upon, you'll continue to get assigned details like this. It's a murder investigation. Normally, that's totally outside of what we do, but in this case, Mr. Armstrong decided to make an exception."

"What else can you tell us about the contact?" I asked, trying to divert Stockwell's attention.

"He's a native St. Martiner," Stockwell replied. "Or *Saint-Martinois* in French. He lives with his father just outside Marigot, a harbor town on the west side of the French half of the island."

"Who is he?" Alicia asked, working at her laptop. "I mean, what does he do there in Marigot?"

"He runs a small Vodou congregation," Stockwell replied.

"Wait...what?" DJ interrupted. "Did you say voodoo? Like zombies and shrunken heads and stuff?"

41

"You watch too many late-night movies," Alicia scolded him. "Vodou is a religion practiced by millions of people all over the world."

"He's a bit of a conspiracy nut," Stockwell said. "I looked over all his communications with our Leeward Island operative and he goes off on long tangents at times, but his information's been good, and we pass it along to the appropriate authority."

"So, why not this time?" Alicia asked, looking up from her screen. "What's different about this murder?"

"The informant, Pierre Noubon, believes he's onto something bigger than just the murder of a preacher." Stockwell sighed and looked down. "St. Martin is so disconnected from where our work usually happens. It just doesn't have a lot of high-level corruption, terrorist activities, or even drug smuggling. It just sits out there in the corner of the Caribbean, a destination for the rich and famous. I'll be straight with you: I just don't think this Noubon character is worth taking seriously. But it came from Jack, himself."

DJ stood up and looked down at Stockwell. "So, lemme get this straight, Colonel. You're giving us a small-time murder investigation, requested by a conspiracy nut who we shouldn't take seriously."

Stockwell's eyes fixed on DJ's with laser intensity, not the least bit cowed by the younger, stronger bull attitude.

"Shit rolls downhill, DJ," Stockwell growled. "And who better to carry out favors than two guys who need to get back into my good graces? For whatever reason, Jack thinks you're an asset. But I'm still the one who hands out

42

investigations before real operatives go in and blow shit up. Until you two knuckleheads start showing me some initiative, *investigators* is all you'll ever be."

It was known among most of the investigators that there were a few who didn't just investigate—people like Stockwell, Charity Styles, Jesse McDermitt, Deuce Livingston, and a handful of others. I'd met a few of them and those I'd met were all from military spec-ops backgrounds. They not only uncovered the garbage of the world, they also personally took it out. All sanctioned by an invisible thread of a tie to the Department of Homeland Security.

I glared at DJ. "I've had a string of solved cases while you were gone." Then I turned to Stockwell, ready to ask why I was being punished for DJ's misdeeds.

I didn't even get a chance to say anything.

"I don't care, Snyder," he said in a low, even tone. "You're guilty by association."

Alicia and I both gave DJ the stink eye, but I knew we were both feigning it. She was glad he was back, and truth be told, so was I.

"Chip will be your liaison," Stockwell said. "There's a communication from him on your Metis tablet with an attached file. I suggest you familiarize yourself with the police report, bio information about the victim, and crime scene photos while you're on your way to the Leeward Islands."

The multi-encrypted technical interface system, or METIS, was Armstrong Research's own invention. It connected all ARMED assets, including ships, planes, ground vehicles, and personnel, on an as-needed basis. Headquarters in New York could connect in real time to check any ship's navigation or mechanical systems, communicate with operatives in the field through ARMED satellites in geosynchronous orbit, or connect those operatives, investigators, IT personnel, or anyone within the organization for instant direct communication, or even direct a physical asset, like remotely taking control of one of Armstrong's ships. In Greek mythology Metis was a wise counselor, the keeper of all knowledge, the first wife of Zeus, and mother of Athena. An appropriate name for the system and its devices.

Stockwell got to his feet. "I'll be going. I expect a preliminary report on your arrival the day after tomorrow."

"The day after..." I began. "With all due respect, Colonel, that's a one-hundred-and-thirty-mile crossing."

"That's why you have until Wednesday," he said, heading toward the sliding door. "Just let me know that you arrived and didn't sink your pretty boat."

He disappeared into the cockpit and down the sugar scoop.

"Well, this is bullshit," I said. "We were looking forward to a relaxing week of diving."

"It's only a twelve-hour sail," Alicia said. "Maybe we should tow the Mako."

"And Gilligan only went on a three-hour cruise," I muttered.

"Good idea," DJ agreed. "It might come in handy."

"It just feels like busy work to me," I grumbled. "Even Stockwell doesn't think there's anything more than a simple murder. The only reason we've been assigned to investigate it is to placate an informant." I looked over at DJ. "And as punishment."

CHAPTER FIVE

The reports didn't give us much more information than what Stockwell had already told us, but we took turns reading it all out loud and discussing each item as we prepared dinner. We decided to just stay aboard and get an early start in the morning. We kept enough of anything we might need on the boat to last several days, and if we thought of anything we might need from the house, Alicia wrote it down.

"Yeah, just let the filet slide into the pan," DJ said to Alicia, as I made a couple of notes. "There's less of a splash and it doesn't disrupt the fish."

I looked up. "Disrupt the fish?"

He turned and grinned. "It's been through a lot, Jerry. A hook, or maybe a spear, then a knife. The soul of the fish lives within its flesh as well as its mind."

"Do what?" I asked, as Alicia tried to stifle a laugh.

"I didn't know you were so spiritually aware, DJ," she said, gently twisting a pepper grinder over the filets in the skillet. "When did this start?"

"You remember that fake itch I used to have?" he asked, as he slowly diced celery.

Alicia nodded. "In your missing foot?"

"Yeah," he said, looking up as his hands continued to work the blade. "It's gone. A friend of Charity's did it. A sound healer."

"A friend of Charity's?" Alicia asked.

"Charity Styles is who DJ's been with for the last few months," I interjected. "Though it was completely by chance."

He glared at me. "That's right, Dep, just like I said."

Then his demeanor changed, and he actually smiled. "She's a very complicated woman and I've learned that I'm more complicated than I thought."

"I've always thought you were a very complex person, DJ," Alicia said.

He turned toward her and smiled, then glanced down at the fish in the skillet. "When you turn them, use the tongs and squeeze from the sides."

"Like this?" she asked, demonstrating.

"Yeah," he replied. "Gently." He turned and absently continued cutting vegetables without looking up. "I left a part of me back there on that street in Fallujah. Not just my foot, but a part of my soul. Charity helped me find it."

"How?" Alicia said, gently turning the thick grouper filets.

"We went for a sail," he replied. "You know her boat's almost a hundred years old?"

"No," I replied. "I've seen it before but had no idea."

"The keel was laid in 1932 in Neponset, Massachusetts," DJ explained. "She was built by George Lawley and Sons Shipyard, who were these yacht- builder guys who went on for like seventy years and five generations. It was built from a design by this famous naval architect, John Alden. But Charity has *Wind Dancer* all wired up with modern instruments and computer navigation. She turned all that off and showed me how to sail by watching the wind and water, and it was like, spiritual, man."

"How far did you sail?" Alicia asked, plating the fish, one by one.

"That first time, down to Tampico."

"Wait... what?" I set the METIS tablet aside and got up to help them set the table. "From North Florida to Tampico, Mexico? That's gotta be a thousand miles."

"Took me six non-stop days of sailing her to get there," he said, putting a salad bowl on the table. "Charity said the computer could have done it in five."

"You?" I asked, holding a chair for Alicia after she'd brought the platter of fish to the table. "She let you sail her boat alone?"

"Well, she was there," he said. "And we stood alternating watches, but all the plotting and planning was up to me."

"You sailed across the Gulf of Mexico in a ninety-year-old wooden boat," Alicia said. "That alone sounds like an adventure."

"There's a lot of time to talk," he said, taking a bite of the fish. "Mmm, this is good. And a lot of time to think. Charity's been where I've been, man."

I started to say something, but he stopped me.

"I know, I know, you've been in the soup, too."

"I was going to say that I've never experienced what you and she went through," I said. "Trained for it? Sure. Went into enemy territory alone? Yeah." I paused and looked across the table at DJ. "But people like you and Charity, McDermitt, Livingston, Whitaker, Barkley... You *faced* the enemy and didn't back down."

He looked across the table at me, surprised. "What about when you were a cop, Jerry? Different kind of enemy, maybe. But just as dangerous. Maybe more so."

"What's she like?" Alicia asked. "I've heard stories but only met her once. Well, twice, but that first time on *Heart and Soul* didn't count. I didn't know who she was."

DJ took another bite and shrugged before swallowing. "She's cool," he said. "Wicked sense of humor, super smart, and a good listener."

"You sound like you're talking about an ugly second-cousin you want to pawn off on a drunk friend," I said. "You could say that about anybody."

He put down his fork and tented his fingers. "That first night, I tried. I mean..." he glanced over at Alicia and shrugged again. "Well, she is smokin' hot, right?"

Alicia grinned, her eyes twinkling. "And she shot you down?"

"Major flames," he said, nodding. "It was a cold ride back to the hotel after we took out the bad guys. Same room—separate beds. But we decided to get some sleep before driving back to Apalachicola."

"But you ended up staying with her for some time?" Alicia pressed.

DJ's eyes shifted from Alicia to me. "We ended up falling on the floor between the beds, both screaming in horror from different nightmares."

"Oh, my—" Alicia started.

DJ shook his head quickly. "No, no, it was a good thing, man. I'd had that nightmare for years and that was the first time I had someone to cling to. Later, she said the same thing."

"Later?" I asked.

"The next day," he replied. "We did sleep together that night—like actual sleeping. We were both fully clothed and it was after several hours of talking. She's the most mind-blowing woman I've ever known."

Alicia smiled. "You're in love with her!"

DJ laughed, nearly choked, then laughed even harder. "In love with Charity Styles? No, no, no. You don't understand. No mortal can be in love with her. Want her? Absolutely. Even worship. But she's so far out of my league, it's like she's some goddess on Olympus looking down at a poor fisherman."

"If you ever slept with her, she'd probably eat your head like a praying mantis," I said.

"Jerry!" Alicia cried out. "I'm sure she's a very nice woman!" Then she turned to DJ. "And I'm sure you were a perfect gentleman."

"It was either that or die," I said.

Alicia glared across the saloon at me.

"Don't get too mad at him, Alicia honey." DJ heaved a heavy sigh. "Before I met Charity, Jerry would've been right, but man, I've changed. My values are different now.

51

And believe me, nobody's more surprised to hear me say this than I am. But gentlemen don't talk about things like that."

Alicia and I exchanged glances. He had changed.

We discussed a few things over dinner about the assignment, then turned in early, to be rested for a long crossing. I wanted to leave just after the high tide two hours before sunrise. That would make our arrival an hour before sunset, and we could probably still check in with Customs.

Alicia had awakened before me and started breakfast. She'd handed me a full mug as I passed through the saloon, and walked out into the cockpit. It was quiet in the marina and the wind was light. But I knew once we got out of the lee of the high island, we'd encounter steady easterly winds, almost on the nose in the direction we wanted to go.

I sat down at the helm and turned on the Navionics and weather instruments to try to figure out the best way from the Virgin Islands to the Leewards. On a map, it's a straight line, but I'd quickly learned that nothing on a boat is done linear. There were submerged obstacles like reefs or the ships that ran into them, currents, wind, sea state—a million things that could and often would alter a plan several times while underway.

"'Sup, Dep?" DJ asked, stepping out into the night air.

"Plotting our crossing," I said, bringing up the Windy app on my phone, and moving the map center around to get an idea of the winds between where we were and where we were going. "Looks like for most of the day, the wind's going to be a few degrees south of due east."

"Sucks for you blow boaters," he said, taking a seat next to me and looking at the charts. "I'd just head out the channel and turn left toward Marigot."

"Unfortunately, that's the exact direction the wind is coming from."

He watched the short loop on my phone for a moment. "Looks like it'll turn slightly more northerly in the afternoon. You could head up the Francis Drake Channel toward The Settlement and by the time we get there, the wind will be starting to change."

"Or take advantage of it now to get a little farther south."

He nodded. "Yeah, and outside The Sisters there won't be as much deflection."

I laid in the first waypoint twenty miles southeast of St. Thomas. "We'll make our first tack here, about sunrise."

"Good idea," he agreed. "No prickles to run into out there."

"Prickles?"

"A little kid on a sailing channel I follow on YouTube," he said, as if that explained everything.

"A kid?"

"He's only three," DJ said. "They live on a sailboat and he was pointing out things on the chart plotter like his daddy does, you know, the little sandspur-looking things they use on nautical charts to show coral heads."

"We don't want to hit any prickles," I said, placing a second waypoint about forty miles to the east-northeast of the first. "Noonish. We'll keep an eye on the wind and when it starts to change, we can move this closer or farther."

"And from there, straight to Marigot," he said, adding the third waypoint. He tapped the edge of the chart plotter next to the total distance display. "Hundred and thirty miles... Against the wind. How fast is your boat again?"

"Beating to windward isn't for the faint of heart," I said. "We should be able to make better than ten knots, which'll give us more of an apparent wind angle, almost on the beam."

He glanced at his watch. "Sunset's in fourteen hours."

We ate quickly, and while Alicia secured things in the galley, the only chore we'd left until morning, DJ and I got the boat ready. I started the engines while he released the spring lines. By the time we were ready to get underway, Alicia was finished below.

With the two of them standing in either pulpit to watch out for "prickles" or any other crunchy things in the night that I couldn't see, we threaded our way south out of Long Bay and into the Caribbean. A waning half-moon sat halfway up the eastern horizon as a guidepost.

Alicia took the helm and turned us into the wind so DJ and I could unfurl the sails. Then we turned southeast and shut off the engines as a steady fifteen-knot wind quickly brought our speed up. The wind would increase once the sun was up, and our second leg would be at a much better speed.

Just a few miles out of the bay, with my back to the lights of Charlotte Amalie, the vast expanse of the night sky came alive. I set the autopilot and we readied ourselves for the long crossing. Getting there before Customs closed would be great, but if we didn't, we could always check into the French side the next morning. I knew after a twelve- or fourteen-hour sail, we'd all be exhausted anyway.

CHAPTER SIX

Oualichi
November 16, 1493

After the hairy strangers left, life quickly returned to normal in the village. The people went back to their regular activities, catching fish along the shore, hunting birds and small animals in the forest, tending the cassava plants, and laughing and talking around the fire as *Guey* dropped lower in the sky at the end of the day.

Many didn't believe Macuya had seen hairy-faced men. Only their *ao'n* and the small animals they were trained to hunt had fur on their face. The people didn't come right out and say it, out of respect for his title as the village *kasike*, but he could see it in the eyes of many of the people. Still, the men who'd gathered on the beach had seen the strangers' great sailing *piraguas* and believed Macuya when he said there were more men on them than there were people on the island.

Guey had crossed the sky five times since the strangers came and on three subsequent nights, *Karaya* was accompanied by Macuya's dark nightly vision. He was almost certain the visiting spirit was warning him of the hairy-faced men he'd seen. He knew they would return one day.

As night became day, Macuya rose from his bed, having been given a name for the child by *Ata Bey*. Yuiza was awake, gently stroking the fine hair on the infant's head.

"He will be called Guababo," Macuya said, rising from the bed.

"Guababo?" she said, as if tasting the word on her tongue. "Yes, it is a strong name, and he will grow to be a strong leader like his father."

Macuya and Yuiza had known each other for as long as either could remember. When they were small, they'd been cared for together by the women of the village and their mothers were close friends who worked together, spinning the puffy white flower of the *sarobei* on *husos* to make yarn and rope. Others wove the yarn into fabric to make blankets and ceremonial clothing. He remembered his mother telling him how he'd helped to teach Yuiza to walk when he was already running.

Suddenly, shouting men could be heard in the distance, and Macuya went outside to see what was going on. Yuiza followed him.

"Take Guababo," he said, fearing the return of the hairy-faced men. "Gather the other women and children and go to the caves."

He went back inside and gathered up his fishing spear and war axe, as Yuiza quickly bundled the baby in cloth and went out, calling to the women of the village. As an afterthought, Macuya went back inside and retrieved his *cachucha*, adorned with long red, blue, and green feathers. He fitted it onto his head, then hurried back out to find the other men gathered at the edge of the village, looking through the trees in the direction of the cove.

"The fishermen went to the cove at Guey's first light," Guamá said, as more shouts and guttural screams could be heard in the direction of the cove.

Their only strength lay in their numbers—Macuya knew that—and nearly half the men of the village were already at the cove. It appeared a terrible fight was being waged.

Macuya looked around. Each man with him had a spear, bow, club, or axe. "To the cove!" he shouted, leading the way at a trot.

Running out onto the sand, Macuya drew up, stunned by what he saw before him. The men from the village were being set upon by a force of men, far greater in number than their entire village. Rafts of *canoas* were pulled onto the sand all around, and a horde of them were still paddling ashore.

Caribs! Macuya realized.

Everywhere he looked, one of his friends was being beaten, stabbed, or ripped apart by several men whose faces were painted white. They were a fearsome sight and in numbers Macuya knew he and his men could not stop.

His mind reeled as his men charged at the interlopers, only to be overwhelmed and taken down. He swung his war axe at a man, but missed. Then he felt a sharp blow to the back of his head and he went down onto the sand as all around him, his friends were slaughtered.

The last thing Macuya saw as darkness closed over him was Guamá being held by four men as a fifth one swung a large axe.

Guamá's head fell at Macuya's feet, and then everything went dark.

He had no idea how much time had passed, but at one point, Macuya could hear the terrible screams and cries of his people. He tried to lift his head but couldn't. Then a wave of nausea passed over him as he began to feel the pain.

Macuya blacked out once more.

When he next woke, someone was pouring water over his head and smacking his face. Dozens of men yelled and whooped around him and beyond that, he could hear terrible sounds.

Someone pulled his hair, lifting his face, as seawater was thrown in his eyes, stinging them open and causing him to gasp.

The men around him walked away, laughing, and Macuya realized he was bound to a tree, tight ropes pulling his arms straight back. He lifted his head and slowly opened his swollen eyes.

It was dark, but there were a number of fires burning. Around him lay the broken and mutilated bodies of several of his people, men he had hunted and fished with. Men he'd either known all of his life or all of theirs. He could see no boys, no girls, and none of the village's women.

He turned his head toward the sound of the crashing waves and knew he was not at the cove anymore. Blinking his eyes, he was not even sure if they were still on Oualichi. He suddenly realized they were on the desolate rock where nobody ever bothered to go but was only a short distance away in a sturdy *canoa*.

There was little on the desolate island—no wildlife except birds of the sea and lizards, few plants, and the soil was too rocky to grow cassava. Why had they been brought there? Why was he still being allowed to live?

He heard laughter and screams of pain. When he turned his head, he saw several men holding the young fisherman, Yuquibo, who was seated in the sand. Another man stretched one of Yuquibo's legs out over a fire, putting a foot against his hip to pull the man's leg into an unnatural position. The young man's tormented screams split the air as the Carib warriors cooked his leg.

More screams came from behind him on the beach, the screams of women. The men who had started eating Yuquibo's leg after he'd

60

died from the pain quickly got up and went running toward the beach behind him.

A Carib moved toward him. He could tell the man was one of the leaders, if not the *kasike* of the tribe. His face was painted white, with two black stripes running down each side, the inner one across his eyes. He yelled at Macuya, but he didn't understand the words.

The commotion behind him grew closer and the Carib's face in front of him drew up into a cruel and hideous smile.

Suddenly, the rest of the Caribs came rushing past him in small groups, dragging the women and young girls of Macuya's village with them toward the fires.

Macuya was forced to watch as the women of his village were violated, the Caribs becoming more and more violent as the night wore on.

"Macuya!" he heard Yuiza scream in anguish.

He turned his head and saw Yuiza struggling against two men pulling her from a *canoa*. The two men dragged her toward the man Macuya thought was the leader. Their infant son, Guababo, was nowhere to be seen.

"Do not harm her!" Macuya managed to scream. "Please," he sobbed.

The Carib *kasike* looked over at him, and the cruel smile returned to his face. Two men forced Yuiza back onto a large, flat rock and the *kasike* fell on top of her, stabbing her in the chest over and over.

The *kasike* stood and came toward the stunned Macuya, holding the bloody knife out in front of him.

"A miserable curse to any man who comes to this island!" Macuya screamed just before the Carib knelt and began sawing through his leg with the bloody knife.

CHAPTER SEVEN

November 16, 2022

The crossing had been enjoyable and uneventful, but completely exhausting. Alicia filled out all the entry forms online for French Customs and we were processed pretty quickly when we'd arrived an hour before sunset. She'd also arranged a slip at Marina Fort Louis, an upscale marina in Marigot Bay, on the lee side of St. Martin. We'd managed to get *Wayward* in her slip and tied up without falling in, and had spoken to the evening dockmaster. He'd told us we could see the boss in the morning, so we went to a nearby restaurant instead of cooking. By the time we got back to the boat, the sun had just set, and all three of us literally collapsed in our cabins.

I was up early the next morning and sent a message to Stockwell that we'd arrived without incident and had cleared into the country the night before.

I'd wanted to bring Alicia along to make her a more integral part of our team, but Stockwell had insisted that only DJ and I were to conduct the investigation. She wasn't happy about having to stay aboard *Wayward*. But she could be a big help with intel—quicker than Chip in some cases.

"You boys be careful," Alicia said. "No fighting."

"Yes, ma'am," DJ said and put his arm over my shoulders. "I'll take good care of your man. Next time you see him, he'll be better off than when you left him, probably nice and clean and happy, maybe with a meal in his belly if he keeps his attitude in check."

Alicia laughed and went back inside, leaving us on the dock.

I turned around, facing the beige-and-powder-blue Fort Louis Marina Welcome Center. "You're in a fantastic mood."

"It's a beautiful day, Dep," he said as we walked toward the cubical building sitting at the intersection of the eastern side of the main hexagonal dock, and the walkway to shore. He slapped me on the back. "We're back together in a tropical paradise, lookin' for a killer—why would I be excited about what we're doing?"

I shook my head as I reached for the door. We walked in and were greeted by a blast of cold air and a man behind the counter. The name tag on his crisp, white shirt read Guillaume. He asked which vessel we'd arrived on, then I prepaid him for ten days' dockage with electricity.

"Where you boys 'eadin' today?" Guillaume asked.

"We're checking out Marigot," DJ answered. "Maybe the market, maybe a restaurant or two. Probably a couple nightclubs later. Neither of us is a planner, so we like to go wherever the moment takes us."

Guillaume grinned and plucked a couple pamphlets from the holder next to the register.

"Well, we're 'appy to 'ave folks of all different stripes 'ere on de island. Enjoy ya'selves and don't worry 'bout not'ing and nobody bad comin' up on ya."

He gave DJ the pamphlets and I narrowed my eyes on him. Nobody bad coming up on us? Was there a problem with muggings on the French side of St. Martin?

DJ returned Guillaume's smile as he accepted the pamphlets.

"Well, aren't you just a big ole' sweetheart?" he asked. "You know how we can get a ride to a friend's house in town?"

"In Marigot?"

"Yes—" DJ turned to me. "What's the address?"

"One second." I unlocked my phone and shuffled to the notes I'd jotted down during our meeting with Stockwell and during the trip over. "It's Voy-ee 38, roo du Hollandey?"

My French was not passable.

"Oh, Hollande. Yeah, yeah, yeah," Guillaume's ear was apparently tuned to understand the butchered French of American tourists. "I got a friend who can take ya. Man's outside wid a silver Toyota, he'll give ya a good deal."

"Thanks, partner," DJ said.

We took the east exit out of the welcome center and started up a hundred feet of dock. The dock eventually led to a parking lot at the foot of the hills on which the ruins of Fort St. Louis stood.

DJ dropped the pamphlets the clerk had given him into a trash can. I caught a quick glimpse of one, and I saw a man in a pink Speedo on the front drinking and laughing with other men in his company.

"There's our Toyota." DJ nodded toward a late model Corolla, flat gray like a shark's back. It was parked along the curb, with a white-haired old man leaning up against it, staring at his smartphone.

"Hey!" DJ shouted. "You know the guy in the welcome center?"

The white-haired man looked up from his phone. "Guillaume?"

"Was that his name?" DJ asked me.

"It was," I said.

65

"Yeah, that's our guy," DJ said as we approached the driver.

He asked us where we were going, and I gave him the address, which he understood after I repeated myself three times, omitting the sounds of different consonants on each attempt.

Five minutes and ten euros later, DJ and I were outside a tin-roofed house with a big, knotty tree in front and a low, half-overgrown stone wall around the quarter-acre lot.

"I'm getting pretty gnarly vibes from this place, Dep. Like, the bad kind of gnarly."

To DJ's credit, Pierre Noubon's house did look straight from a *Texas Chainsaw Massacre* flick. The stucco on the edifice was cracked in several places, the front door was weather-beaten and discolored, and there were tiny burlap bags hanging from the branches of the big tree.

The bags were about the size of a man's fist and at best guess, there were more than fifty, less than a hundred.

"That tree ain't native to here," DJ said.

"Are you an arborist now?" I asked. "Is that what you and Charity got up to?"

"It's a kola tree," he said. "Came from West Africa."

"How the hell do you know that?"

"I seen 'em when I was a kid, Dep," he said softly. "My neighbor used to have one out back that everybody said was cursed. When I was a kid, that thing was backed up to my bedroom window and sometimes when I went to bed, I used to hear it howling at night when the wind was blowing just so.

"Anyway, this old lady neighbor of mine used to take the kola nuts and bottle 'em into a drink and hand 'em out to all of us—the neighborhood kids, I mean—but she was a crazy old bat and everybody thought the drinks were cursed or poisoned, so we just dumped the shit out."

DJ looked at the tree as if he thought the branches were going to grab him by the neck and pop his head off his shoulders.

"Are small burlap bags part of the curse?" I asked.

"Not that I remember."

I opened the wooden gate and walked toward the tree. The first bag I came across was about eyeball height and it smelled like something earthy but sharp, like rotting mint leaves or a bundle of basil. I cupped my hand under the bag, lifting it gently. The thing was maybe a couple of ounces and when I moved it, it crinkled like dried leaves.

"Don't mess with it, man!" DJ said.

"Why not?"

"You don't know what's inside that thing or what it'd do if you touched it. Could be like poison ivy or something!"

I didn't think DJ was worried about me acquiring a rash so much as he'd picked up a case of the heebie-jeebies, given the B-horror movie aura radiating off Pierre Noubon's property.

"Well, DJ, creepy as these little bags are, I'll take your advice and end my investigation here. I'm sure Armstrong would appreciate us keeping it to one job at a time."

"Hey, good idea, man," he said, still outside the gate.

"Shall we go knock on Mr. Noubon's door?"

He raised his eyebrows and stared at me, silently granting me permission to do it all myself.

"Come into the yard, DJ."

He did. After a second or two. Slowly. Fake foot first, tapping the ground like a bad landmine detector, and when he was confident the tree's malevolent energy wouldn't possess his flesh, he stepped forward with his good foot.

I waited for him under the shade of the kola tree.

"Everything shipshape?" I asked him.

"Yeah, man. I just—" He cut his eyes from mine to the tree as he walked nearer. "You ever look at something and get an uneasy feeling and you can't figure out why? Like you're gonna puke or pass out or let your butt go?"

"Never in my life," I said.

"You're lucky, Dep."

"You misunderstand. I've had that feeling, but I always know why," I said, trying to follow his sight line into the branches. "In your case, I think it might be a little neighborhood lore coming back to haunt you."

He cleared his throat. "Yeah, probably that."

"What do you say we go talk to Mr. Noubon now?" I put a hand on his shoulder, reassuring him that we were grown, rational men, and the days of supernatural kola nut trees and crazy old ladies were long behind us. "If things get dicey, I think we can probably outrun the tree."

DJ pulled his attention from the tree, looked at me and nodded. "A'ight then."

We continued the short trek across Pierre Noubon's yard to his front door. After mounting the steps, I stood on the small porch and rattled the knocker. My knock was answered, not from inside the house, but by something growling in the overgrown bushes beside the front step. Then it hissed, and a separate hiss came in rejoinder.

I peered down. Through a small gap in the bush, I saw three cats. One small and black, the other two large and tan. The two big ones had the little guy cornered up against the foundation, and his tactical situation appeared untenable.

I knelt down, reached straight in, and grabbed the little guy by his scruff, life-lining him out. I lifted him up until the two of us were face-to-face.

"I didn't take you for a cat person," DJ said.

The cat and I studied each other carefully. His pupils narrowed from circles to slits, and his ears went up. The little guy had a pink scar across the top of his snout and was missing part of an ear but didn't seem to mind one bit that I'd clamped my hand onto the excess skin across the back of his neck.

"I'm not a cat person," I said, checking the knob and finding it unlocked.

"The cat looks like it's a Jerry person," DJ answered. "We goin' in?"

I nodded, lowering the cat into my other hand, and pushed the door open with my elbow. We walked into a small front room with a cat jungle gym taller than me. The thing was infested with them—cats, I mean. It was all flicking tails and big eyes and pulled-back ears when DJ and I walked through the front door. There must've been a half a dozen cats staring back at us from the jungle gym, and maybe that many more scrambling for cover elsewhere in the front room.

Remarkably, the house didn't smell like a litter box. It smelt like the bag I'd checked in the tree branches out front—earthy, spicy, yet stronger than patchouli. Even so, I could feel my sinuses beginning to clog.

The front room held more than a harem of cats and cat accessories. There were bookshelves and a scratched-to-hell easy chair. The bookshelves held books, of course, but also wooden figurines, candles, small, air-tight jars that, in the dimness, looked to hold everything from sticks to leaves to rocks and dust.

Colorful fabrics had been tacked to the walls in various places, some of them woven tapestries of human figures dancing among random objects like a trumpet and a mirror, a pair of snakes twisting around each other and meeting at the nose—and other solid-colored, sheer fabrics that hung loosely here and there like streamers.

"Noubon's got some kind of pad here," I said. "I could do without the cats, however."

"You don't like cats, Dep?" DJ stepped around me and further into the room. He reached for a calico napping on the easy chair, which woke the thing before DJ even made contact. The cat rubbed the tips of his fingers with the top of its head. "I love little kitty cats, man. They're troublemakers, through and through. And they're cute. Don't you think they're cute?"

I lowered the black cat in my hand. When I let go, it didn't scurry off, but sat down near the tips of my shoes and neatly tucked its tail around its paws, looking up at me curiously.

Then I sneezed, and it jumped.

"Oh, shit, I get it now," DJ said. "You're allergic."

My hands started to itch. I rubbed my palms on the leg of my jeans, but that didn't kill the itch. My eyes watered and I sneezed again.

"You wanna get out of here, man? I bet I could talk to Noubon and find out what we need to know to get us started."

"No," I said, holding back a sneeze. "No, I have" —I let the sneeze go— "I have a job to do."

"Who's that?" a man's voice called from somewhere deeper in the house. Noubon.

"Mr. Noubon? We're here from Armstrong," I called back.

"Armstrong!" he replied. "Ya' boys sure do work fast."

"Yessir." I sneezed.

"We're looking for Pierre Noubon," DJ said. "Is this his house?"

70

"It is!" he said.

I walked behind DJ. We turned from the front room into another. It appeared to be a study of some kind, with a desk and more bookcases packed similarly to what was in the front room.

The only window was blocked by a heavy tapestry, but lit candles on the desk and the bookcases, and a spill of light from the doorway to our right provided enough light to see.

All around us, the walls were thick with colorful, sheer fabrics and woven tapestries. Half looked similar to those in the front room, and half appeared to be of Catholic saints. I recognized a portrait of St. Francis from an old statue one of my dad's friends kept in his clubhouse garden. The other portraits, in various sizes and hanging at various heights along the walls, were a mystery to me.

An array of handmade drums were lined up along the wall to my left—opposite the door DJ and I were heading toward. The biggest came to my belt line, the smallest the size of a conch shell.

"Alright man, I know I said I got a bad vibe out in the front yard," DJ said, looking around the room. "But I'm feelin' this place. It's peaceful. It's got like, a real, sit-quietly-and-use-your-brain thing going on. You picking up the energy here, Dep?"

The little black cat rubbed up against my legs and I sneezed again.

"No," I said.

"That's too bad, man. You're missing out on all kinds of good, healing rays, you know? Stuff that might get you to quit coughing and sneezing if you can open up your mind and accept it inside you."

We proceeded to the next room, where the windows were open, letting in sunlight and a breeze that swayed the colorful fabrics. There were also more bookcases, tapestries, and drums here, as well as assorted furniture, including a pair of couches facing each other

71

across a coffee table at the center of the room. On the coffee table were candles, jars holding separate quantities of dust, herbs and oils, and a human skull that had some kind of pattern drawn across the crown in red paint.

The breeze crossed my cheeks. I closed my eyes, took a deep breath, and unlocked my nostrils.

"Pierre Noubon?" DJ asked.

I opened my eyes to see DJ to my left, beside an old man sitting next to the largest window. At first glance, I'd thought he was an easy chair.

Noubon, it turned out, was older than Stockwell had mentioned—he had long, ash-colored dreadlocks, and pupils to match—Noubon was blind. His face was thin, with a strong jaw and thick eyebrows. Most noticeable, however, was that Pierre Noubon was wheelchair-bound. He calmly sat with his hands atop a cat sleeping on his lap, as if waiting for someone other than DJ and me to walk in.

CHAPTER EIGHT

The room was dark and shadowy, no lights on that I could see. But then, what need would a blind man have for lights?

"Mr. Noubon," I said. He didn't answer. He didn't even look in my direction.

DJ clapped his hands in front of Noubon's face and didn't get a single twitch out of the guy.

"What the hell is going on with this dude?" DJ asked. "Is he catatonic?"

"Maybe he's dead," I said. "The voice we heard could've been gas escaping his lungs."

Noubon drew in a deep snort and then let it go gently. He was snoring.

I walked over and tapped his shoulder. "Mr. Noubon?"

He didn't react.

"I think this old man's completely whacked out of his head," DJ said. "He's taking a nod, and we're standing around playing grab-ass."

"Probably drugs," I said.

"Got to be," DJ said. "I saw a man on fentanyl fall asleep in his car at a gas station while he had a lit acetylene torch in his hand. He only woke up when a drop of melted steering wheel landed on his knee, and he started howling like a banshee."

"He was talking to us thirty seconds ago," I said.

DJ shrugged. "Maybe it ain't drugs. Could be he's old and fell asleep."

"Gentleman," a voice said from behind us—the same voice that had answered us earlier.

I turned around to see a younger version of the old man in the wheelchair. Same length dreads, same clean-shaven, strong jaw, but with dark brown eyes and a welcoming expression on his face.

"Pierre Noubon?" I asked.

"I see you met my fadder, Marcel." Noubon's voice resonated deeply through the room, with a kind of speech-moving-the-stone quality that must've had every ear hanging on his words.

"Man's a hell of a heavy sleeper," DJ said.

Suddenly, behind us, a peel of laughter burst out. Marcel—the old man—was doubled over and looked like he was going to spill face-first out of his wheelchair. DJ turned around, facing him, and looking displeased.

"What the hell, man? You were awake the whole time?"

He was cackling too hard to answer.

"Tru all dese years, my papa los' a few t'ings, but nevuh his sense of humuh," Pierre said, coming around me. He took his father and pointed him toward the couches, and the cat on Marcel's lap jumped off.

"Da boyee," Marcel said through a laugh and the heaviest accent I'd ever heard in the Caribbean, "'Da boy, he tot me asleep!'"

"You fooled him, Papa," Pierre said, as he stopped Marcel next to one of the couches. "Now don't go laughin' into a fit."

"No, no." Marcel wiped a tear from his eye before he motioned toward us. "Dese two dem?"

"Yes. De two men who gonna help us."

"Dey cursed."

Pierre locked the brake on his father's chair, then turned to us and gestured for DJ and me to join him on the couches.

"Cursed, are we?" I asked.

"Don't worry about what Papa say. De man was an *oungan* almost his whole life, and at his age, his mind slip back and fort'. He call two of de cats cursed last night, and tried to kiss his breakfast dis mornin'."

"What's an *oungan*?" I asked.

"A priest of Vodou," Pierre answered. "Papa been doin' it, long as I remembuh. Before we left Port-Au-Prince and all de while I was doin' my bad t'ings as a young man. When I stopped breakin' de law about fifteen years ago, I took after him, same as he did his papa. He taught me all de t'ings I know 'bout speakin' to de *loa*, servin' dem, and servin' de people here."

When I finally sat down, a cat yelled out, and I popped up. I thought I'd sat on one.

"It's awright," Pierre said, nodding toward a closet behind me as he took his seat on the couch opposite us. "I got two in dere all morning, and it sound like dey finally makin' up wit each uddah. I apologize for de timin'."

"Not a problem," I said, as I barely held back a sneeze while settling next to DJ on the couch.

"Cats don' agree wit you? I hear you snifflin' and sneezin' in de front room." Pierre pulled out a tray from beneath the coffee table, then set it on top. "I got somet'ing to help, if you wan' it."

The tray held a carved, wooden pipe, some light green herbs in a small bowl and box of matches.

"I'm, uh... not a smoker," I said.

75

"It ain't dis," he said, as he pinched some of the herbs from the bowl and dropped it in the carved pipe, then packed it down with a wooden rod.

"It's a tonic. I can give it to you when we done talkin'. You drink it before you go in a place wid cats, and you won't sneeze once, you won't sniffle at all—dere won't even be a single tear in yuh eye."

"No, thank you."

"It's plenty safe now. I used it on all kinds of folk 'round here, and it won't make your skin itch when you stop takin' it, like de pills you buy at de corner store dat come from a factory. You know dey do dat on purpose—once you stop takin' de pill, you feel like you're burnin' from de inside out, so you say 'oh, I gotta keep goin' with dat every day. I got to take me pill and I don't want to feel like dat ever again!' And, you go back to de store and buy some more, and more, and more, and you be a consumer fo life. You see?

"All kind of t'ings dey do like dat," he said. "Just shove all kinds of pills down your t'roat, mon, and put drugs in de food to make de children cry for more, and why? Dem want control of you, mon! Control yo mind, yo body, sure, and yo spirit too, mon. But not me— I'm here to help people. I want to make de people feel better, mind, body, spirit, all of it."

And so the conspiracy theories began.

From what I had seen in his house, I got the impression that Pierre Noubon probably had half a dozen herbal remedies for any given sickness, and likely none of them were in any danger of being sold over the counter at a typical drugstore. Maybe they'd find a place in a back-alley shop or an old lady's bathroom cabinet, however.

Regardless, I would not ingest, inject, smoke, or apply anything he gave me. I knew herbal and natural healers have been around for thousands of years before even rudimentary science, but I didn't know anything about the man except that he had a sketchy past and might have strong opinions about reptilians at the UN.

Noubon took a match out of the box, lit his pipe, and puffed it while he lay back on the couch.

"Anyway," he said. "You two boys come from Armstrong?"

"We did," I said.

"What your names?"

"Jerry Snyder," I said, then motioned toward DJ. "That's DJ Martin."

"Good to meet you both." He released ringlets of smoke from his mouth.

"I'm wonderin', man, since you seem to know a thing or two about medicine and the like—you got anything that can help with bad dreams?" DJ asked him.

I shot him a look of disapproval. This wasn't a visit to the spirit healer; we were here on business.

"I don't want shrooms or anything like that," DJ said, half as a defense to me, and half as a filter to Noubon. "Just something to make my dreams a little milder."

"Ah, yes, I understan', I do," Pierre said, bouncing up from the couch.

DJ rubbed his hands together.

"You seen war, have you?" Noubon asked as he trailed smoke over to the bookcases against the wall to our right.

"Yessir," DJ replied. He plopped his fake leg up on the table, hiking his pant leg up. "Seen too much of it."

Marcel stared at the titanium rod that held DJ's "foot" to the stump of his lower leg and laughed riotously.

"Yes, I know how Mr. Armstrong like his people trained up

before dey come to him." Pierre was sifting through glass jars on a bookshelf. "All dem guns and bombs and blood. T'ings not good for a person to see. T'ings dat fracture a man's mind, even if his body ain't broken."

I squeezed my hand into a fist and asked, "Mr. Noubon, I'd hate to be a bother, but we're short on time— what can you tell us about the murder?"

"Murder?"

"Yes, the reason we're here." I answered Noubon but looked disapprovingly at DJ.

"You're gettin' down to business, I see," Noubon said. "It is as de police report tells. One man, Billy Pearce, stabbed in his church. And a girl, Shara Bradley, gone missin'. If you really short on time, you should go back to de report—I'm sure it be a much quicker way of gettin' what you need dan talkin' to an old *oungan* and his papa."

"The police report was thin on details," I said.

"A course, a course. Dat's how it go now." A gaggle of jars clinked together as Noubon shifted from one shelf to another. "Mr. DJ, dese dreams, are dey fearful dreams?"

He nodded. "They scare the hell out of me, at least. I woke up piss-soaked at least one time and sweatin' every other time."

TMI, DJ.

"Problems wit your kè. As I tot."

"Mr. Noubon, can we stay on task for a minute?" I asked.

"We on task," Noubon said.

"That's debatable, but fill in some details about the case, then?" I asked. "Where can I find the crime scene, or who else should I talk to about it?"

"Pearce kep' a chapel not far from here, over on Concordia, and dat is where it happened to him. I'll give you de address before you go. As far as udder folk to talk to" — Noubon turned toward us, grinning wide, apparently having found the jar he needed— "I been t'inkin' bout dat for a time. You should start wit de girl's mama."

"Any particular reason why?" I asked.

"My fear is de girl, Shara, she not dead, but gone missin'." He loped around the back of the couch.

"As in, kidnapped?" DJ asked.

Noubon puffed his pipe and nodded his head. "A sad t'ing to say 'bout me own home, but St. Martin seen a lot of bad t'ings happen lately, and dat girl missin', dat is—"

Noubon was cut short by his father.

"Ohhhhhh—" he moaned. His blind eyes rolled back into his head, and no sooner had Noubon stood up and tossed the glass jar from the shelf onto the couch than foam began to bubble from his father's lips.

He was having a seizure. I shot to my feet and held DJ back. "Don't touch him!"

Noubon sprinted for the door we'd come through, and I pulled the coffee table with its sharp edges away from Marcel. The last thing I needed was losing more time from tending to an old man with his head split open.

Within seconds, Noubon was back, running with a disposable plastic cup in hand, sloshing clear liquid on the floor.

"Pierre," Marcel rasped. He was coming out of the seizure, at least enough to speak. He reached for his son.

"Here, Papa, here." Noubon grabbed his father's hand and put the cup in it. The old man drank immediately.

"What is that?" I asked as Marcel gulped it down.

"Valerian root tea," Noubon answered. "It calm de tête—de mon's head, I mean."

79

Marcel emptied the cup in a few seconds, then held it out for his son. "I t'ank, boy."

"Yes, Papa." He said, taking the cup and setting it on the coffee table. He then went back to his father and stroked his forehead. The old man started to lean back in his chair.

"Res' now, Papa," Noubon said.

"De boys, to Oualichi," he said sleepily. "B'fore anuduh die. DJ, Jerry, destroy de *govi*." He'd sunk low enough that his head rested against the back of his wheelchair, and he drifted off to sleep.

"What did he just say?" I asked.

Pierre shook his head. "Can't say I know."

"Well, what's a '*govi*'?" DJ asked.

"A *govi* is part of how we care for our family after deat'. It a clay jar." He nodded behind us, and I swiveled to see a row of colorful clay jars sitting atop a long shelf, ranging in size from an apple to a melon. "After a relative die, and dey complete deir journey to *Ginen*, de jar holds deir *gwobonanj*."

"What's that? Their ashes?" DJ asked.

Noubon sucked on the pipe, thinking, then carefully released the smoke.

"No, not ashes. A person have two parts to deir spirit. De *tibonanj*, which is de personality, what you might call consciousness, and also a line keepin' his body connected to his divine shadow, de *gwobonanj*. When you dream, it is yo *gwobonanj* wanderin'. And when yo body die, it is de *gwobonanj* dat live on. When de body die, de *tibonanj* is judge by *Bondye*, and de *gwobonanj* travel under de sea, to a place called *Ginen*, where de *loa* are—all de spirits dat we worship and ask fo' guidance from and give ourself to on occasion.

"One year and one day after yo' deat', a person's *gwobonanj* return from *Ginen*, and de family mus' give it a place to rest within a

80

govi, or else be cursed by de person's roamin' spirit."

Pierre rested his hand on his father's forehead. "It is a common ceremony—every Vodouist has had to care for a *govi* for one family member or anudduh til it is destroyed by an *oungan* or a *manbo*—dat what we call a woman priest. We destroy a *govi* so de *gwobonanj* can res'. Papa must've done it a tousand times. He livin' in de pas' again."

"Hmm. Interesting," I said. "So, you want us to find a murderer and a missing girl. But why us?"

Pierre raised an eyebrow at me. "You are about your business, Mr. Jerry."

"He's just that way," DJ said. "You might love Jerry eventually, but you'll definitely hate him first."

"Why you?" Pierre asked me. "Why de highly trained and experienced members of Armstrong Research, who do t'ings like take down terrorists and bust up de drug rings? Why have you look at a murder of a nobody and a kidnappin' of a nobody on a nowhere island?"

"Took the words right out of my mouth," I said.

"See what I mean?" DJ chimed in.

Pierre smiled at me.

"Armstrong owe me a favuh," Pierre said. "De trut' is, de police are handlin' backlogs from all de t'hings dat happen during Irma. Dis side of de island was almos' los' after de hurricane, but we, all de peoples who live here, and who love St. Martin, band togedduh and are tryin' to rebuild, but rebuildin' takes work, and work takes men to do de job.

"Our problem now is we don't have enough men to do all de jobs dat need doin'. Sometimes, what de police t'ink are de less important jobs don't get done at all. It de same old story of de men at de top not carin' 'bout what happen to de people at de bottom. So

81

long as dey get rich off our sufferin', dey don't care 'bout a t'ing dat happen to us, so long as dey can keep us distracted from findin' de trut'.

"Dat why I wan' you gentlemen to go solvin' crimes against nobodies."

"Distracted from the truth," I said. "You think there's some kind of conspiracy going on? And that conspiracy has caused the police to willfully ignore crimes on St. Martin?"

"I t'ink human nachuh is what it is, and I do not expec' to see justice for a man like Billy Pearce, who half de island hated, and de oduh half despised. De powers-dat-be would as soon sweep it all under de rug and preten' it nevuh happen."

"But not you," I said.

"I won't be ignorant of what happen here, but to be clear. I detested Billy Pearce too." Noubon tried to puff his pipe to no effect. He eased back to his spot on the couch and then upended his pipe over the tray, tapping out the ash. "He was a mockery to fait', a cynical person at his bes', and a malicious presence at wors'."

"But you still want to burn a favor with Armstrong to find his murderer."

"Yes," Noubon said. He'd set his pipe aside and had the jar of whatever for DJ on the table now, with the lid unscrewed.

I looked at DJ, getting a feel for what he thought about Noubon's seemingly illogical wish to consume what was a very valuable favor. DJ shrugged at me and scratched his head.

I put my attention back to Noubon, and at the same time the cat I'd saved out front of the house hopped onto my lap and I sneezed.

"I can still give you dat remedy, Mr. Jerry." He had a pinch of the stuff for DJ, moving it from the glass jar into a zip lock baggie.

"Pass," I said to Noubon. "We're on our way out the door,

anyhow. First, to the church where we'll see if there's anything the police missed about this girl. Once we're done checking the scene over, I'll speak to Shara Bradley's mother. Can you get me in contact with her?"

"Of course," Noubon said. He zipped the baggie and held it out for DJ. "Put a sprinkle of dis in boilin' water before you go to sleep, and while it boil, inhale de fumes. Help if you put a towel over de back of yo' head to keep de vapors from escapin'. After a few minutes, you have de most blissful sleep you ever had."

DJ took the baggie and held it up to the light. The stuff inside looked like dried pieces of thick grass, green as a lime rind.

"Can you tell us where the church is, exactly?" I asked Noubon.

"Yes, Mr. Jerry." He stood up and motioned for us to follow him back the way we'd come in.

"And the girl's mother," I said.

"Yes, I imagine she at de resort where she work, call de Mer du Mélasse. I'll call some folk 'bout where Shara's mama is, but don' worry 'bout it takin' yo' precious time—you hear from me before lunch time."

DJ and I followed Noubon out of the room.

"Good," I said. "Moving quickly can mean the difference between apprehending a murderer and not."

"Oh, yes, very important," Noubon said, as we passed through the study. "But I wonder if you gonna hear what I hear 'bout dis whole t'ing with Billy."

"You heard something?" I asked. "Would you be so kind as to share what you heard with me?"

"I can tell you," he said, "but I t'ink dis de sort of t'ing you not gonna believe 'til you come to realize it yourself."

What the hell did that mean?

"Mr. Noubon, we've all gone through a considerable amount of trouble to be here—and I'm including you in that statement. Withholding information is counterproductive."

Noubon stopped in the front room, then shrugged. "I s'pose you de type a man who won't leave 'til I say what I know."

"I am," I said.

"He definitely is," DJ confirmed.

"Yes, I believe it." Noubon looked from me to DJ and back again, clearly pondering something. "What d'ya know about a duppy?"

"A what?"

"It's a type of... spirit," he said. "De type what kill a man."

CHAPTER NINE

The sound of my shoes on the cracked concrete and DJ's asymmetrical footfalls, echoed off closed up storefronts.

"Jesus, DJ!" I muttered as we looked for the church. "Pierre Noubon brought us all the way out here on a ghost chase."

"You're mixing metaphors, man—it's goose chase or ghost hunt."

DJ and I had left Noubon's house, going up the street, then taking a right at the next intersection onto Rue de Concordia. The street was packed with two-story, boxy buildings constructed of brightly painted concrete, with steel blinds across the outsides of every window.

"Stockwell is probably in Bimini, laughing his head off at the thought of us playing Scooby-Doo," I said.

"Noubon's daddy put a chill in me," DJ admitted suddenly.

Great. Now DJ was getting spooked over Caribbean ghost stories told by paranoid old men.

"Do tell," I said, hoping he wouldn't.

"What he said about a little jar, and that we were cursed, and all this talk about a ghost?" His eyes met mine, then bounced away and studied a palm tree ahead. "It's all bullshit anyway, isn't it?"

"Of course it is. And Stockwell knew that," I said. "But I suppose it doesn't matter, does it? The assignment may be bullshit, but it's still an assignment, and every assignment is a test of our fitness for duty."

"We ain't in the service anymore."

"You know what I mean," I said. "It seems likely this investigation is more about the proverbial shit rolling down the hill, but that's what you get. You, of all people, can't complain about a test of loyalty, or a test of your skills, or even a test of your patience. You came back to Armstrong, DJ. You'd made a clean break, and you could've kept on going, and nobody would've looked for you, but you turned around anyway, and this is what we all get."

I expected him to say something back, maybe half an explanation, or a wisecrack, or even a dirty look, but DJ made no effort to respond, only keeping his eyes forward and keeping pace with me until he spotted the entrance to the church—not that it resembled a church at all.

"That's us," he said, jogging ahead.

DJ stopped at a storefront identical to a million other strip mall spots back in the States. Like the other buildings, this one was concrete with steel hurricane shutters across the pair of long, large glass windows on either side of the door, and I could've been convinced it wasn't a church at all, but a modest tax attorney's office, or a place to drop off dry cleaning.

But, sure enough, the numbers over the door matched the address Noubon had given us.

The door itself was criss-crossed in crime-scene tape and had a letter-sized piece of paper stuck at eye level. This official notice from the Marigot Gendarmerie Brigade—the local, French equivalent to the police—was written in French, but I figured it was all the usual stuff about no one entering the church by order of one magistrate or another.

"Lockpicks?" I asked DJ.

He pulled on the door's handle, and it came open, ripping some of the crime-scene tape.

"You don't gotta be all that clever if you're lucky," he said as he went in.

I followed him.

The church was dark, lit only by slices of light coming through the hurricane shutters, and the smell of spicy-sweet incense that, in my lifetime, I'd only caught a whiff of at Our Lady Queen of Angels.

Suddenly, I was a bored kid, standing in pews, looking at the bubbling baptismal fountain next to Father What's-His-Name while he led the adults through the chorus of *Roll Out the Barrel*—the rare, joyous Catholic moment, and probably the reason why I remembered it.

In this jolt of memory, I also recalled my father's face, stoic but singing, and Arlen, two rows ahead, pretending to conduct the imaginary polka band while definitely beaming and probably belting out the words.

That was my only surviving memory of Catholic church, along with telling on some kid in Sunday school for throwing a candy cane at me.

I came out of my past when the lights flicked on, revealing a hybrid between a Catholic Church—the gilded candle stands, the purple cloth with gold crucifix tapestry straight ahead—and a mom-and-pop Caribbean restaurant. I liked the old fishing net rumpled in a nearby corner.

The previous Pope, Ratzinger, smiled at me from the chapel wall, and beside him were framed posters of palm trees, of the backs of people in white robes holding hands, and a copy of an old painting of the Virgin Mother holding Baby Jesus.

There were half a dozen pews, but also a scattered mishmash of steel chairs, wrought iron chairs, bar stools, wood chairs, wicker chairs, beach chairs, and anything else that could have been reasonably scavenged from a roadside or dumpster or abandoned building in St. Martin.

Ahead, the altar appeared to be a cabana bar, repainted white and decorated with golden crucifixes. On top of the altar lay a purple cloth runner, a copy of the Holy Bible on a pedestal, and a fake palm-frond-wreath candle holder.

"Holy shit." DJ was ahead and to the right, between the frontmost pews, looking at the floor. "Man, you gotta see this, Dep. I think that poor bastard was drained of all his blood right here. I don't envy Billy Pearce, that's for damned sure."

"We're in a church, DJ," I said as I came closer. "Language."

"Oh shit, right. Sorry, man."

DJ stood beside a large blood stain in the blue-gray industrial carpet. Judging by the size of it, he was right to assume Billy Pearce had been exsanguinated.

"That's as big as any I saw in Newport Beach," I said.

"Didn't know a man's body could hold so much."

I crouched down and looked through the area adjacent to the stain. A pair of well-used barstools were ahead, against the wall, the altar was about five feet to our left, and the front door about forty feet to my right. From my vantage point, I saw no bloody handprints, fingerprints, long smears—say from a limb dragging over the ground, in an attempt made by Pearce to drag himself away—or any other sign that he'd struggled or tried to move from this spot.

"Probably the assailant hit a major artery and that was that." I stood up and brushed a cat hair off the knee of my jeans. "Not the

88

worst way to go. You'd black out quickly and never know you were dead. Pearce probably wasn't aware he'd been stabbed but for a handful of seconds."

DJ grimaced. "Wouldn't the police report say if an artery was hit?"

"No, that's a determination for the coroner to make," I said. "Whether or not the coroner has even seen Pearce's body is beyond my knowledge, but from the way Noubon described law enforcement on this side of St. Martin, I'd hazard a guess Pearce would be lucky to be on a slab in a cold room somewhere, and not simply left in a ditch."

I turned to my left and looked at the altar. A thin line of blood had spattered across the front, and it seemed to me that whoever did this had stabbed Pearce with a fair bit of momentum.

"Then again, Noubon believes a ghost killed Pearce," I said.

"Be the first time I ever saw something like that," DJ added. "But man, all I know is I know nothing, right?"

As I turned and walked toward the altar, I heard DJ's footsteps going the opposite direction.

"Who's to say?" he began, his voice echoing off the walls. "Could be evil ghosts walking around this world, and they're so few and far between, I just ain't seen one yet. Shit, I mighta been part ghost for a time there, what with that phantom itch on my foot. And if I had a foot that was a phantom, why can't a man's whole body be phantomized?"

I let DJ talk while I searched around the altar.

"You know," he continued in a low voice, as if talking to himself, "they say a ghost comes from tragedy, or from someone who has unfinished business in the world. Might be that phantom itch of mine was the unfinished business of my toes. They sure got blown off

89

in a hurry, and I never did get to say goodbye before they were taken off somewhere and burnt in a pit, probably."

Behind the altar, I found a shell casing. I carefully knelt down, pulled out my phone and the flash went off when I took a picture.

"What's that?" DJ asked.

"Cartridge casing," I said. "Either a forty Smith and Wesson or nine-mil."

"Oh, okay," DJ said, then resumed his meandering. "You ever think all those ghosts that haunt people are just mad? And if they are, what're they mad about? I s'pose if my foot was itching because of unfinished business, a ghost could have their whole body itchin'. Imagine that, Dep—itchin' without a body, I mean. And, like my foot, if you don't got a body to scratch, that itch ain't goin' away easily."

I looked all around the floor around the altar, then looked over to where the dried blood was, trying to envision the scene.

"But you know," DJ said, stooping to look under another pew, "seeing as they're walking through walls and the like, a ghost might just think he or she can relieve the itch by rubbing against a wall, but they can't, can they? So they're cursed to wandering around, looking for a ghostly tree to rub their back against or some kind of spirit medium or psychic with a good set of fingernails."

Other than the shell casing, the altar appeared clean. I looked for my next investigative target.

"Or maybe a ghost *can* rub against a wall, but only certain walls. Shit, might be a haunted house is only haunted because there's a rough little part of a ghost wall, or a ghost interior stud that hits the spot just right for some poor widow who was murdered by her new husband to get her land. Maybe the wall's the only place that itch can get scratched, so she don't *want* to leave."

Not seeing or hearing anything in the chapel that warranted

sticking around, I proceeded toward the only door on the eastward wall. DJ was almost nose-to-nose with Pope Ratzinger's portrait, his back turned to me.

Behind the door, I found an office. I left the door open, so DJ wouldn't feel like I wasn't listening and get all pissy, which was a sure way to keep him going twice as long as he would have otherwise.

"All that little widow is doin' is walkin' back and forth all day in the attic from one good scratch post to another. Or maybe not. Maybe she leaves the house every day, lookin' for somewhere new to go, but she's cursed to going back to the ghost wall when the itchin' gets unbearable, so she just can't get too far."

I flicked on the light. A messy desk in the middle of the room drew my attention first, and then the scattering of various forms and denominations of currency that were commonly used on St. Martin.

If all this money was left behind, it seemed this murder likely wasn't someone trying to bump off Pearce to get at the church's collection plate.

"I mean, imagine bein' in that position, Dep." DJ said. "Every day for two hundred years, you try walkin' as fast as you can, hopin' there's some kind of portal or way out of this itchy, ethereal prison you find yourself in, but you never can get to it, no matter how fast you go."

Next, I went to the filing cabinet behind the desk. It was unlocked, but mostly empty, except for some old utility bills.

"And you know in the back of your head as you take every step, you're just gonna have to turn around and head to that rickety old house eventually because at a certain point that itchin' gets so bad, your body's on fire. You know?"

I turned around and carefully looked over the rest of the room. "It's all about an itch, huh?"

There was a small, open safe under the desk, and what appeared to be a record book of some kind sitting on the top shelf.

Pulling it out, I dragged the desk chair closer, but stopped when it felt like one of the wheels was stuck on something. So, I pushed the chair back and sure enough, a wheel had been dragging a small pebble. Or I thought it was a pebble at first. When I looked closer, I realized it was a human tooth. A gold tooth.

I wanted to take it, but didn't have any evidence baggies to put it in. I looked around the desk for a suitable holder for a gold tooth, and the only thing that made sense was a dollar bill. So I used it to pinch the tooth off the ground, then folded it as best I could to keep the tooth from falling out, and put the whole thing in my pocket.

"Wouldn't that make you feel sore?" DJ asked, as he wandered past the open door to God-only-knows where else. "Being trapped like that? Itching all the time? Wouldn't that put you in a mood to wail and curse the living? They can scratch whenever they want, the smug sons of bitches! They don't know how damned good they got it! And—"

DJ suddenly stopped. "Oh shit, I think I found somethin'."

"What?"

"You got a screwdriver or something?"

"Left my toolbox on the boat," I said.

"Okay, it's a flathead screw I gotta undo, so you got a knife? Something flat like that?"

I considered handing DJ the tooth, which appeared to be an incisor, before I slipped a quarter off the desk and marched it out to him.

"It'll do," he said. DJ used the edge to twist two screws off a vent cover high on the wall. I wasn't sure why he thought he'd found something until the cover came off, and a couple rolls of cash spilled

92

out—and those only seemed to be a fraction of the rest of the neatly rolled and stacked bills in the vent.

DJ whistled.

"Quite a find, Dudley," I said.

He reached into the vent, then came back with three separate rolls. One was US five-dollar bills, and the other two were euro fives and twenties.

"Probably a thousand bucks in my hand right here." He stepped back and craned his neck to see in the vent. "Looks like, I dunno, fifteen or twenty more rolls of bills up there, so I'd guess there's as little as six thousand, or, shit, up to twenty maybe. Only real question is why it's still up there, but I guess you could assume the guy with the knife didn't know about it."

"I have a theory Pearce's killer didn't care about the money at all," I said.

"Why's that?"

I pointed through the open office door. DJ saw the cash sitting on top of the desk.

"If I'm killing Billy Pearce for money, the first place I'm checking is his office, and even if I'm in a terrible hurry, I'd see all that cash sitting on his desk."

DJ squashed his lips together, then popped them apart. "So why do you think Billy Pearce was killed?"

"Noubon said he didn't have many friends. And what were his words exactly? That Pearce made a mockery of faith? Sounds like Noubon knew Pearce was in this business to take money out of his followers' pockets, and I'm willing to bet Noubon wasn't the only man on this island that thought so. A time like this, in a place like this, Pearce probably left more than a couple people penniless."

"Probably so," DJ said, eyeballing the open vent. "Question is, what do we do with it?"

"We leave it," I said. "I've got two GPS trackers back on *Wayward*. Let's see if we can hide one in the middle of a roll of bills and we'll keep an eye on it. If it walks, we'll follow it and find somebody who can answer a few of our questions."

DJ nodded. "Good thinkin', Dep." He stuffed the rolls of cash back inside the vent, picked up the cover, and using the quarter once again, tightened the screws.

While he did that, I returned to the office desk and opened up the ledger I'd found in the safe.

All the numbers were here—income, expenses, gross profits—notably there was nothing to do with charity or donations, and most of the expenses, aside from utilities and rent, went to payroll. I would've bet there was only one person on the payroll at this church.

But the numbers weren't the only things here. There were doodles too, like anime eyes, cute little hearts, puppies and kittens, and other little touches like Billy's name scrawled in long, bubbly cursive. As I turned more pages, I saw more doodles, including another name scrawled in that same loopy cursive script: Shara Pearce, née Bradley.

It seemed to me that Shara had been keeping Billy's books. She also had an active, and romantic, imagination.

The police report said Billy was forty-two, and Shara was seventeen, but apparently, he didn't mind the age gap. I started to wonder if she'd killed him and fled—maybe he was unfaithful to her, or it was simply a lovers' quarrel spiraled out of control—but if she went on the run, wouldn't she know about the money in the vent? And if not that, surely she'd have taken the cash sitting out in the open. Though I didn't have a hard time believing a kid her age would panic and run without—

94

The front door opening broke my train of thought.

"*Qui es-tu?*" a deep, male voice asked.

"Ohhh—hey, officer," DJ answered, and I popped up from the desk and headed out to the chapel. "I'm just looking for the can, is all."

The cop was a white guy, a little under six feet tall with a bald head, a sharp chin, a sharp nose, and a cutting look in his blue eyes. He'd frozen in the front door, holding it open while DJ was backed up against the wall, and thankfully, the vent cover was back in place.

"You are not permitted to be here," the cop said in accented English. "Did you not see the sign on the door?"

"Sign?" DJ looked to me. "You see a sign?"

The cop wasn't buying it. DJ was just going to get us in more trouble—I had to tell him the truth.

"Officer, we came here because—"

"Shit, bro, I already told the man!" DJ wobbled over to me; an effect made all the more real by his prosthetic leg. "We was lookin' for the goddamned shitter. Ain't you people on this island got public terlets around?"

DJ leaned on me, and his head circled ever so slightly, which was a real nice touch, but I knew the cop would see through it. We were going to be detained and delayed and maybe accused of murdering one, if not two, people. The idea of being arrested, especially for a crime I didn't commit, was thoroughly unappealing.

We were screwed.

"You two gentlemen should leave now," the cop said.

I almost hesitated. Almost.

DJ and I both had the good sense not to argue with a man in uniform. And frankly, in this line of work, you learned to take the breaks offered you without thinking too hard or second-guessing the whys or the hows.

"Sorry, officer!" I said, draping DJ's arm over my shoulder. We split.

Outside the church, DJ kept up his drunken gait, leaning on me as we walked westward.

"How in the hell did that work?" he asked. "We were done, man. We were cooked! I was thinkin' about punchin' that cop in the mouth and runnin' all the way back to *Wayward*."

He looked over his shoulder, then took his arm off me and stood up straight.

"We never would've escaped on a cat the size of *Wayward*," I said. "We couldn't outrun a sea cucumber."

"Good thing we didn't have to!" He flicked something gold into the air and caught it. "Lucky us!"

"What the hell is that, DJ? Did you take money from that vent?"

He grinned at me, then slipped something onto his pinky. He held it up for me.

DJ's pinky was now sporting a thin, flat, gold ring with what looked like a piece of raw iron where a gem would normally have been set.

"Found it on the ground between a couple of the chairs," he said. "I don't think whoever lost it is going to come back for it. I mean, shit, aside from the cops, nobody's going back to that church—probably not even us. Pretty unique looking, right?"

"I'm planning on going back," I said. "And someone else may come back for that hidden cash. You should hand that ring over to the police. It may be an important piece of evidence."

"All the more reason why I should keep it," he said. "This little ring might crack our case open, and if it don't, I got me a nice little souvenir. Besides, the cops left all that cash, so it don't look like they're investigatin' real hard."

CHAPTER TEN

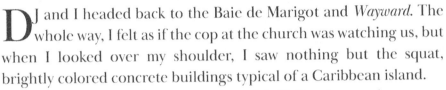

DJ and I headed back to the Baie de Marigot and *Wayward*. The whole way, I felt as if the cop at the church was watching us, but when I looked over my shoulder, I saw nothing but the squat, brightly colored concrete buildings typical of a Caribbean island.

When we got to the intersection with Hollande, my phone rang in my pocket, and I pulled it out. It was Noubon.

"Mr. Jerry, I got my contact all ready at Mer du Mélasse. But before he introduce you to Shara's mother, Mary, he want to meet you, and he got to do it now. Can you boys be at de service entrance of de resort in t'irty minutes?"

"Where is it again?" I asked.

"'De Nort'eas' corner of St. Martin, across de water from Pinel."

"We're down the street from Pearce's church," I said. "How long does it take to get to the resort from here?"

"I t'ink about twenty minutes by car, so you bes' hurry along."

I stepped off the curb to cross Hollande, picking up the pace, then looked over my shoulder and motioned for DJ to hurry up.

"We don't have a car here," I said. "So, where can we get a cab?"

"No real cabs on de island, so to speak. But I'm sure you can go to a restaurant or a store nearby and ask somebody working dere to get you a ride. Dey do it all de time for tourists."

"I suppose we'll have to work with the tools we're given," I said. "I'll call you later."

"Hold on, Mr. Jerry!" Noubon said. "Don't hang up yet. You gotta understan' dat going to de Mélasse can be a sensitive t'ing for some folks. So, when you get a ride, if de driver ask you why you goin' dere, it's very important you make sure dey t'ink you a tourist, and you on yo way to de resort to try de rums you heard so much about, and dat's all. Unuhstan'?"

"Why would going to a tourist resort on St. Martin be a sensitive topic?"

"I told you, boy—St. Martin in de t'rall of powerfully evil forces. Dey don't want outsiders lookin' at dis and dat and asking questions about what dey shouldn't a seen."

"I forgot the police and government are out to get us—and ghosts too," I said.

"Good for you to keep in min', but it don't stop dere. People be watchin' all de time. Common folk," he said. "Dey gonna be at de Mélasse, and dey might be as vicious and treacherous as anybody you ever fin'."

I'd talked to Pierre Noubon twice, and already his paranoia was grating on me. If Stockwell really intended this assignment to be a test for me and DJ, he'd picked one that was certainly putting me through my paces.

"So, I'll keep my purview to rums," I said.

"Dat would be de wise t'ing to do," he said. "When you meet my man at de Mélasse, you got to do exac'ly as he say. Don' go wanderin' off, or you might end up in de wrong spot and get killed. And be careful who you seen wit and who you talk to along de way."

"I always try to be as selective as possible," I informed him, and hung up.

I had already crossed the road and was waiting out front of the liquor store directly across from Rue de Concordia when DJ galloped up the curb and to my side.

"Alicia checkin' in on ya?"

"Noubon," I said. "His contact is waiting for us at the resort. He said we should be careful about who we talk to along the way, that there are spies and bad people all around us, and that if anyone asks, we're going to Mer du Mélasse to check out the rums. I guess it's popular with tourists."

"Seems a fair cover," DJ said. "You think maybe he's a little extra careful when nothing calls for it?"

"If a bird crapped on his head, he'd be on the lookout for spy satellites."

DJ nodded in agreement. "Guess we should figure out a way to get over there, man. I'm not opposed to hoofin' it, but I think that might take us more time than we've got."

Just as DJ said that, a late model Ford pulled to the curb. The rear door opened, and a pair of women hopped out, but before they went into the liquor store, one circled around the front of the car and slipped the driver some money.

"No need, DJ."

The driver had just let his foot off the brake when I waved at him, and he jerked to a stop. He reached across the front passenger's seat and rolled the window down.

"Lookin' for a ride, my frien'?"

I leaned toward the open window. "How quickly can you get us over to Mer du Mélasse?"

"Fifteen or twenty minutes," he said.

"Good, because I need good rum and I need it fast."

I opened the rear passenger door and hopped in, DJ took the

seat next to the driver.

"Twenty bucks cover it?" DJ asked.

"That be fine, indeed, sir." The driver eased off the brakes and we were on our way.

We went northward, following the road past the edge of Marigot and into a place where the houses thinned out, but did not completely disappear into the scrubby, green hills.

"I don't pick up many tourists in de part of Marigot where you boys been," he said.

"Yeah, me and my friend got a little turned around looking for the can," DJ said. Then added, "the bathroom, I mean. Y'all ain't got too many that's easy to find."

The driver nodded and looked at me in the rearview mirror. I smiled at him when our eyes met, and I thought of what Noubon told me about being careful.

"You two stayin' at de Mer?" he asked me.

"We're rum hunters," DJ said. "Been all around the Antilles lookin' for a good bottle or two, and apparently the stuff at the Mer has a reputation, so we had to come check it out."

I was worried DJ was putting too many details into our cover story, but the driver seemed to be buying it.

"Truly, my frien'?" The driver was beaming. "Which one dey talkin' 'bout out dere?"

DJ didn't know and couldn't answer. He tightened his face and looked at me.

"Neither of us can remember the exact name," I said. "It's a dark—that's all we know for sure."

"Yep, we're gonna have some huntin' to do when we get to the bar," DJ said.

The driver was satisfied with that answer. He took us the rest of the way, and recommended a couple of things to see, some places to eat, and that was about all he had time to tell us on the short trip.

The resort itself, a long, four-story, white building with a red, clay-tile roof, didn't look anywhere near as foreboding as Noubon had tried to make it seem. The way he talked, I expected shady men with earpieces and sunglasses to lock onto our car as soon as it pulled into the drive.

Instead, I saw plump, sunburnt tourists in beachwear wandering in and out of the front door of the place. Almost to a man—and woman—they were drunk off comped mixed drinks made by locals who were likely paid pennies on the dollars of what they deserved.

I hated these places. Where was the adventure? Where was the excitement? Even if you were interested in neither and needed some serious peace and quiet, I could think of two dozen beaches within a days' sail that would be more calming than what was surely an overpacked beach on the far side of the Mélasse.

We pulled up the big, circular drive and stopped near the front doors. DJ handed the driver the twenty plus a five for a tip, and he cheerfully thanked us.

"Thanks for the lift, man," DJ said as he opened his door and got out.

As I slid across the backseat to exit, I noticed the driver glance at DJ's pinky finger—at the stolen ring on it.

Saying nothing, I hurried out and the driver pulled away with a smile and a wave goodbye.

"You need to pull that thing off right now," I said quietly.

"My lucky ring? Why?" DJ recoiled his hand, as if I'd try and snatch the ring right off his finger.

"The driver was looking at it, DJ."

"So what? I looked at it too. It's different."

101

"Be smarter than that," I said. "Marigot isn't exactly a bustling metropolis. The whole island's only eight miles long. That driver might know every person on this island, including the guy that ring belonged to. He might think you stole it off his friend, and if he does, what do you think he may do?"

"It ain't that ser—"

I laid my open hand on DJ's chest, stopping his thought.

"It *is* that serious. Maybe that man doesn't do anything, but what about the next person we come across? Keep that thing on, and we're looking at either another run-in with the cops—and I think we've pressed our luck enough there—or we'll find ourselves in the middle of a group of pissed-off locals asking us questions we can't answer."

DJ sighed and pulled the ring off his finger. He twisted it between his thumb and forefinger, doting over it like it was a Spanish doubloon and I'd just told him to toss it back into the sea.

"Put it away for now," I said. "You don't have to get rid of it."

He nodded.

Normally, I wouldn't let him keep stolen property, but anything we took from the crime scene in Billy Pearce's church might become evidence later, like the tooth I found.

As I led the way to the service entrance, I put my hand in my pocket and touched the crumpled dollar with my fingers. Through the paper, I felt the tooth inside it like a little shard of porcelain.

Instead of going in the main door, we rounded the northeastern corner of the resort, looking for the service entrance. I locked eyes with a bald man in a resort uniform, smoking a cigarette with one hand, and holding a side door open with the other.

"Snyder?" He said my name like a croak.

"That's me," I answered.

He jutted a chin toward DJ. "Who's that?"

"My partner," I said. "We work together."

"The old man didn't say a word about two of ya." The way he put his hand on the handle of the door, he must've considered turning around and forgetting about the whole thing. Then he sighed and waved us closer.

"Don't touch a thing when we go through storage," he said. "I know you people comin' from off the island like to lift whatever ain't bolted to the ground and walk off with full pockets like you ain't done nothing wrong. Comes outta my paycheck when you do that, you know?"

I looked at DJ, who grinned sheepishly, then we went inside. I wasn't clear on how he expected DJ and me to take anything from the storage room, as the only things I saw were shrink-wrapped towels and bedding, and we buzzed through the room so quickly, we couldn't have snatched anything, anyway.

Still, I didn't say anything. Griping wasn't conducive to meeting our objective and completing the mission.

He led us into a narrow hallway, where a line of food carts along the left-hand wall waited. Up ahead, steam poured out of a doorway that must've led to the kitchen.

"What is this?" DJ asked. "Some kind of workers' hallway?"

"The resort prefers the guests don't see us walkin' around doing our work whenever possible. They say folks don't like thinkin' about work when they on vacation, and it ruins the pristine image they tryin' to put forward when sweaty men and women are pushin' food carts and cleanin' carts up and down the hallway. I say we wouldn't be so unpresentable if they saw it fit to share more with those of us who don't match their beliefs."

"Match their beliefs?" I asked. "How do you mean?"

He didn't answer me. When the hallway branched, he turned left, and led us outside. There, we came to a set of steps. He went down, and I stopped at the top to reconnoiter the beach situation, which was worse than I could've possibly imagined.

Not only was it overcrowded; they were also blasting music through loudspeakers, and from our slightly elevated position I saw the bar in the middle of it all with hundreds of people swarming around it like ants on an old piece of pineapple.

"Look at that!" DJ clapped me on the back as he stepped past me and trotted down the steps saying, "Who says this job don't have any fringe benefits?"

DJ slipped behind a pair of women walking past the bottom of the stairs in matching thong bikinis. They were headed toward the bar. "Fringe benefits, Dep!"

"Stay with the mission," I called after him. I moved quickly down the steps but had to immediately sidestep a drunk weaving around in the sand, sloshing his neon-blue drink everywhere.

Ahead of me, DJ double-timed it to the pair of bare butts and had them laughing about something from the first word he'd offered.

I kept on his tail as best I could, but a resort worker with a tray of drinks knocked into me, and even I would have a momentary lapse in concentration when a shower of frozen mix drinks dropped onto my shoes.

"Oh, sir! Sir, I am so sorry!" the woman carrying the tray said as she picked herself up and brushed sand off her uniform shorts. It appeared she'd escaped the worst of the spill, with only a little on her bare knees and ankles.

"It's fine." When I looked ahead of me, DJ had disappeared in the crowd around the bar. I kept walking.

"Sir, did I spill on you?" she called after me.

"No, no, totally fine!" I waved her off and looked down at my shoes, which were now shades of splotchy blue and pink under the sand sticking to the moisture.

I waded into the thicker part of the crowd, dodging and bobbing around drunks and people screaming to be heard over the thumping island music. The further I went, the more I doubted I'd find DJ, let alone Noubon's contact, who'd vanished off my radar.

Then, the crowd miraculously parted, and I saw DJ near the bar, receiving a lei from one of his thong girls. Didn't they realize St. Martin was some six-thousand miles from Hawai'i?

DJ saw me coming and his eyes went wide.

"He-ey! Dep!" he yelled over the music. He had an arm around each girl. "This is Trinnie, and this is Raquel!" He nodded at each of them in turn.

"He's with me, girls," I yelled back. Then, I grabbed him by the shirt and pulled him into the crowd. I led DJ through and didn't let go of him until we had cleared the mass of people around the bar and were standing in front of Noubon's contact, who waited for us beside a small house on the beach.

"The two of ya done playin' around with the women?" he said with a grin. Then he jerked his head backward, toward the small house. "You want to talk to Mary Bradley? She's in one of the private villas, cleanin'. Just look for the one's that's open."

"Thanks," I said, releasing DJ's shirt and handing the guy a twenty.

Half a dozen small, identical beach houses were arranged in a line before us, and a cleaning cart was parked on the small, concrete porch two doors down.

I started toward it and checked behind me to make sure DJ was following.

"I'm still here with you," he said.

We continued, eventually turning onto the porch and peering through the open door to see a tall woman in the hotel uniform taking leftover crab leg scraps from a breakfast bar and dropping them into a trash bag.

I knocked, and she turned like I'd shot at her.

Mary Bradley had the sun-scorched, creased skin of a working-class woman who had to have been on the brink of exhaustion. But there was a strength about her, something I perceived on instinct at first, until I looked closer at her bare forearms. Doing something as simple and easy as pinching a ripped and broken crab leg between her thumb and forefinger revealed lean muscles in her forearm that testified to either rigorous athletic training or decades of working with her hands. I assumed it was the latter.

"Sir, I'm not done with de cleanin' just yet," she said to me. "D'ya mind givin' me a couple more minutes?"

"I'm actually not the person staying here," I said as I pushed open the door and DJ and I stepped inside.

"Okay, if ya come to use de bat'room, I'm sorry, but ya can't. Ya can either use de ones on de beach, or in de lobby, or go back to yo' room."

"No, I'm actually here to—"

"Sir, if ya was wantin' a tour, ya need to talk to de concierge in de lobby. Ya can't go bargin' into odduh people's rooms."

"Mary," I said, which paused her before she cut me off again. "Did you know a man named Billy Pearce?"

Slowly but surely, the mention of Billy's name curled her fingers around the crab leg until she held it in a fist. "Why would ya come in 'ere and say dat name to me?"

106

"Because we're looking into Shara's disappearance, and he's the last man she was seen with."

Mary shook her head and pursed her lips like she wanted to spit on me, then thought better of it. She picked up the trash bag, threw the crab leg inside, clapped the crab bits off her hands, then snatched a towel out of her back pocket and wiped at her fingers like she was trying to take the skin off.

Even this unremarkable bit of movement hinted at the muscles beneath Mary's uniform shirt. Fabric bunched and rippled around her shoulders and her biceps and as she smacked her lips, clearly disgusted with me, her neck flexed and relaxed.

"Are you an athlete, Mary?" I asked.

She narrowed her eyes and cocked her head, obviously confused by my line of questioning.

"What dat got to do wid anythin'?" she asked. "Did you come here to talk 'bout me or 'bout my daughtah?"

"Shara," I said.

"Uh-huh." She looked me over once more, then went to folding a stack of napkins on the bar. "I wondered when de govuhment would finally get 'round to sendin' de specialists dey promised." She laughed bitterly and leaned an elbow on the bar. "Well, go on, den. Ask me yo' questions."

"We're not with the government," I said.

"We're freelance troublemakers, actually," DJ added. "But we've also solved a problem or two."

I gave him the stink eye, then went back to Mary. "Ma'am, we want to find Shara, too. We work for a private organization and were hired by a local named Pierre Noubon."

She cocked her head away from me and wrinkled her brow. "Noubon? That old *oungan* in Marigot? Why would he want to help me or Shara?" Then she turned away, back to the napkins. "I got too much work to do 'round here, and I don' got de time to put up wit' de friends of a crazy old man."

I edged closer to Mary, putting my hand on the bar, but leaving a few feet of space between us.

"I can't say why the man wants what he wants, Mary, but he *does* want it. Noubon is very sincerely looking for your daughter, and we wouldn't be here if he weren't," I said. "So, please indulge me."

Mary shook her head. "Nobody can help me."

"I read the report from the Gendarmerie," I said. "In my professional opinion, they're careless and they've done a shitty job and they've done a terrible disservice to you and Shara. We've already found quite a few things they've missed."

"What dey miss?"

I looked at DJ.

"We found a whole stash of money up in Billy Pearce's church," DJ said. "Seemed funny to Jerry and me that it just so happened nobody found it. And, if it was a little innocent mistake, what else was missed?"

Mary stopped folding napkins and frowned. She didn't fully trust us yet, but with a little good will, I knew I'd have a chance at getting answers to basic questions about Shara—who she was as a person, who she hung around, and, most importantly, what exactly was the nature of her relationship with Billy Pearce?

"Ma'am," I said, "we aren't here to take advantage of you. We haven't, and won't, ask for a dime. Frankly, neither my associate nor I need it. All we want is to have a few questions about Shara answered, and if you never want to see us again, you never will."

She rubbed an eyebrow and lowered her head, hiding her face from us, but when her shoulders started to shake, I saw a tear splash down on the bar top.

"Shara," she said, her voice hitching, "was never an easy chil'. From de day she was born, she kep' me up all hours, cryin' and screamin' and no matter what I give her, it nevah calm her."

"People never speak about how difficult it is to be a mother," I said.

"Yes. Shara was always nasty to me. Wit uddahs she could be sweet and helpful and dutiful, but aroun' me, she grew into a fierce, strong-willed little girl, always gettin' into trouble and disobeyin' me. I t'ink she blame me for her fadduh never bein' around, t'inkin' I told de man off because I'm a she-banshee who can't bow to no man, but I always wanted to protect my precious baby, to honor her, to keep her safe from all de bad t'ings I know's out dere in de world, wantin' to take a sweet girl and twist her into somet'ing evil."

Mary squeezed her fists tight, and the steely muscles showed through both her taut forearms. "Den she fell in wid Preacher Billy."

"He was a cheat," I said.

Her eyes turned to me and widened. "Like you wouldn't possibly know, bein' from elsewhere. De man not only took my girl from me, and took people's money, he took de very souls out dere bodies and sent them off de wrong way, and he did it all to make money off folk that knows little more dan sufferin' dese las' few years. It's a wonder nobody up and killed him a long time ago."

"Mr. Noubon told us Billy Pearce had a lot of enemies on St. Martin," I said. "Do you think someone would kidnap her to get to him? Did Shara ever mention anything about people threatening him? Did she ever feel threatened?"

"My daughtah hardly ever spoke to me." Mary clenched her fists tighter. "Not over de las' year, unless I go and track her down like she

109

some long-los' stranger, like I didn't birth her and spend years of my life raisin' her right. Even so, I heard some t'ings."

"When was the last time you talked to her?"

"Las' week." A bitter frown crossed Mary's face. "I went down to Billy's church with food for her and him, and even as I handed over de whole pot of callaloo, she had de nerve to treat me like I was an old blin' woman, beggin' at de market for her change. All because Billy was in his office, screamin' at Mr. Desir again."

I exchanged glances with DJ.

He took the lead.

"We heard Billy Pearce ain't the only hustler coming to St. Martin." DJ said. "Was Desir working with him?"

Mary laughed. "You might say he is. After Irma, all dem small-minded men like Billy Pearce know dey can eat off de good fait' of desperate people, so dey been poppin' up like weeds. Dat Joseph Desir is an aid to de French Prefect, and de rumor was, he been shakin' Billy down for money to keep his little church goin'. Dat night I went to de church to see Shara, Desir came after Billy hard."

"What'd he do?" I asked.

"Shara didn't tell me hardly not'in' of Billy's business, but from what I know about Mr. Desir, he probably ask Billy for more money. He came out de church with a bloody lip swearin' he gonna do all kind of nasty t'ings to Billy."

Bingo, bango.

"Know where we can find Desir?" I asked.

"Man owns a spot in Grand Case, right at de intersection of Boulevard de Grand Case and Rue des Écoles. It ain't marked wit no sign, but it's a big blue and white buildin', and you'll know it by de golden trumpet over de door," she said. "If he ain't dere now, probably someone dere know where he be."

"How will we know him?" DJ asked.

"Mr. Desir be short—about my height. Mus' be he maybe fifty years old, wid short, gray hair and a gold toot' right in de front of his mout'. De man look obzocky as any I seen. You go to his club, you gonna spot him, easy."

"We'll find him," I said.

With that, Mary Bradley turned and wrapped her arms around me. My spine popped and I had to work a little harder to draw a breath. I started to work away from her, but then I thought of Alicia and how she was so good at getting in with people, and what she'd do in this situation. So, I hugged Mary back and felt her sob quietly into my shoulder.

"Don't go breakin' a mudduh's heart, unnuhstan' me you? And be careful wid yourselves. Mr. Desir be a dangerous man and dat place in Marigot ain't fit for outsiders."

"We'll be careful," I said.

"You got to find my little girl and bring her back to me, safe."

"I will," I said.

"We will," DJ added. "You can count on that."

She looked at him, still holding on to me. "T'ank you, both."

CHAPTER ELEVEN

Headed back the way we'd come, DJ was quiet, with a troubled look on his face, completely ignoring the crowd on the beach, even the two girls who'd latched onto him on our way in. They both smiled at him from the bar, but he was oblivious.

"It's good to see you're focused on the mission," I said to him.

He looked over at me questioningly. "Huh?"

"You didn't seem to notice your two new friends smiling at you."

He turned around, but they'd already disappeared into the crowd. "Oh, them?"

Then he turned forward again. "I'm telling you, Dep—getting old, the first thing to go is the lingo, man."

It was my turn. "You think you can't keep those two women interested in your conversation?"

"No, man, I'm not even thinking about that."

We came to the steps leading up to the workers' hallway in the Mélasse, and trotted upward.

"What's on your mind, Dudley?"

"It's 'obzocky.' What the hell kinda word is that?"

I pulled open the door ahead of us, letting DJ enter first. The hallway was much as we'd left it—empty, except for a few carts of room service and fresh linens.

"It's EC English," I explained. "Here in the Eastern Caribbean, it refers to a person who is particularly ugly or strange-looking. Disheveled."

"So we're looking for a really ugly, bald, short, gray-haired guy with a gold tooth next."

"With the general level of attractiveness around St. Martin, I think our person of interest should be fairly easy to find," I replied.

We were making our way through the narrow back hallway like a pair of criminals when I heard someone call my name. "Jerry?"

I froze.

"Oh, shit," DJ said as he turned to look.

I recognized the voice. It went through me like a hot needle, and I felt my insides starting to burn. I was beginning the process of convincing myself I didn't hear what I just thought I'd heard—that it was wafting rum fumes clogging my brain, or, maybe without my knowledge, at some point this morning, my lips had come in contact with an errant toad.

Then the voice reasserted itself.

"Jerry Snyder?" It was closer and it belonged to Arlen Burkhart.

I turned slowly, facing my fate. He was at the head of a group of four men; all of them, including Arlen, were dressed like members of a corporate retreat. His loose, red shirt with colorful mandalas was open down to his breastbone, and his dark hair was slicked back from his face. Since I'd last seen him at the Hildon corporate headquarters in Puerto Rico, he'd grown a close-cropped beard.

"Gentlemen, if you'll pardon me just a moment—I'll catch up with the rest of you shortly," Arlen said to the other three. They turned down a perpendicular hallway as he continued to come toward me.

"Ain't that just a sonuvabitch?" DJ asked quietly. "Want me to stick around or get gone?"

"I've got it," I said.

DJ clapped me on the shoulder before moving toward the exit.

"My word, Jerry, what a small world it is!" Arlen said as he came closer. "I never expected to find you here, but what a delight it is to see your face again. What is it that brought you here to the Mélasse?"

"That's my business," I said.

"Well, I certainly don't mean to pry!" He laughed. "Where's Alicia? Are you staying here? I'd love to sit down and catch up with the two of you, if you've got time in your schedule—*Heart and Soul* is anchored out past Simpson Bay, on the Dutch side, and I picked up this new chef from Kingston who can do wonders with just about any bit of fish or crab or what-have-you that can be found out here. You have to try his food, and if you'll have him at the table while you eat, he'll sit and charm you with all kinds of stories. The man's just an absolute delight." He paused, looked me in the eye, and smiled warmly. "It is so good to see you."

Arlen's smile made me want to puke. I wanted to break his teeth. I wanted to grab him by the collar of his shirt and haul him back to the States and throw him in front of a judge for murdering an innocent man on his private island. To hell with Shara Bradley and Billy Pearce and Armstrong and whoever else—Arlen Burkhart was a cancer, and it was up to me to stop his growth.

"Alicia's not here," I said. "We're not staying here."

"Oh," he said with disappointment. "That's too bad. Well, are you free at all this week? I could use your expertise in a... business matter."

"I'm booked," I said.

115

And, thinking I'd had enough Arlen to last the rest of this year, I tried to turn away, but he started to say something again, and I made the mistake of not walking down the hall like I'd never heard him. I stopped, keeping my back to him.

"Jerry, son, I know we have a rough history between us, and I know I have things to explain to you," he said. "But does it always have to be this way? Can't you find it in your heart to accept that I am a changed man who is trying to make amends for all the wrongs of his past? Can't you give me a chance to do that for you?"

"What amends?" I asked, turning back to him.

He balked, clearly offended. "Did you want specific examples?"

"Sure."

"There's The Burkhart Foundation for starters," he said. "After Irma, we helped the French government identify small business owners in need of capital and gave out interest-free loans."

"Interest-free loans for small business owners? How magnanimous of you," I said. "And where did the capital for these loans come from, Arlen? The money you earned from shorting Hildon stock? Or did it come from the profits you made after buying all those drug patents off Hildon when they went under? You remember those patents, don't you? The ones you bought and then jacked up the price on? Or did the funds for the Burkhart Foundation come from the proceeds of mob-sponsored real estate deals?"

Arlen grabbed the back of my neck. For a split second, his grip was tight, like I was a puppy pissing on his shoes just to embarrass him. Then his fingers slackened.

"Jerry, you can't hold onto a grudge against a person forever. We're all human, we *all* make mistakes, and what can we do but try to be better persons as we move on through our lives? You can't keep throwing all that back in my face," he said. "Not forever."

"You're right, Arlen," I said. "However, I know you're not better. I know that you can't help who you are, no matter how badly you want to change. I know what you did."

He raised his eyebrows. "What did I do, Jerry?"

"You killed a man. On your island."

"No—"

"You shot him twice in the back of his head."

He paused, gawking at me, then blinked, playing confused. "Where on God's green Earth did you hear a rumor like that? And what in His name leads you to believe I actually did such a thing?"

DJ. And I trusted his word over Arlen's without question. But I wasn't going to throw my partner's name to a wolf like this man.

"You can't lie to me anymore," I said, turning my back on him. This time, hopefully for good."

I walked outside and found DJ waiting for me.

"You straight, Dep?"

I kept walking. "We've got work to do, DJ."

CHAPTER TWELVE

DJ paid for a ride westward to Grand Case. We arrived among storefronts, boutique restaurants and art galleries, all looking brand-new. Grand Case seemed more tourist friendly than Marigot, or, at least, it looked more capable of separating vacationers from their money.

The driver dropped us off at the intersection of Boulevard de Grand Case and Rue des Écoles. A boxy, two-story building painted powder blue on the top floor and white below sat at the northeastern corner of the intersection.

DJ and I walked around until we found the west-facing door with the trumpet mounted over it.

"Just like Mary said," DJ remarked. "Man, maybe we oughta put her on payroll. Gettin' a straight answer out of a person like her, havin' gone through what she did, is kind of a remarkable thing, ain't it?"

"Let's not get ahead of ourselves," I said.

Faint music pushed out from behind the door. It wasn't the typical drum and bass stuff I expected from a club in a tourist town like Grand Case, but something more frenetic, bordering on incoherent. From outside the building, it sounded as if they'd trapped a herd of wild animals inside.

I opened the door, revealing a dark foyer devoid of any bouncers or hostesses. There was only the music, which now blasted out at us, and a carpet of thick, gray smoke, which unrolled down the front step. It was almost as if DJ and I had opened the mouth of a great beast and were now invited to hop onto its tongue to begin our journey down its throat.

"You smell that, Dep?" DJ sniffed the air, then grinned. "Smells like a good time. Smells like somebody got a few cousins from Jamaica over to visit."

I did detect a few notes of ganja among a bouquet of both spicy and earthy scents.

"I know you're a flower child now and your third eye is practically winking at me every time I look in your direction, but we're here to work," I said, starting inside.

DJ followed me in, then shut the door behind us. We were in near darkness, or so I thought until my eyes adjusted and I saw a hint of red light spilling out from a wide doorway ahead and to the left.

The longer we stood in this small foyer, the more details started to come into focus. This room was about twice as wide as DJ and I, shoulder to shoulder and about ten feet deep. Other than a staircase going up to a door that had been boarded shut, we could try the closed door to our right, or follow the music ahead and to our left.

We followed the music to a barroom teeming with people and with air thick enough to taste.

The crowd moved under the power of a large band of drummers playing on a slightly elevated stage. There were probably half a dozen men and women beating drums of various shapes and sizes, with a few more people in the audience clapping against drums small enough to hold in one hand while they gyrated around the room hooting.

Everyone seemed to be dancing around a large post in the center of the room, twirling and bobbing around it like a maypole. But when a pair of bodies shimmied apart, I saw flames dancing inside a brazier next to the pole. I watched for a moment, and noticed the brazier was crewed by a pair of women fanning the smoke. One of them tossed in a handful of leaves, and the flames stretched above the heads of the dancers before crouching low again. The drummers beat furiously in response to the fire, and a fresh wave of smoke erupted to the ceiling.

No one appeared to take notice of DJ and me. Whatever they were doing, they were wrapped up nice and tight in it. I figured if we were inclined to do so, we could've taken to the stage and beat on a few drums ourselves without a majority of the participants noticing.

Instead of inserting myself in the proceedings, I walked to the bar, which was on the right-hand side of the room. It was made of smoothed concrete and lit with multi-colored rope lights. It had a big mirror behind it and stylish- looking glass shelves with hardly a bottle upon them. The bar appeared to belong inside this room more than... whatever it was DJ and I were witnessing. Nobody seemed to be working it, but there was a stack of plastic cups and a trio of small teapots on hot plates at the end opposite me.

I picked out a teapot, poured a sample into one of the cups.

"You got to be shittin' me." DJ was beside me, talking straight into my ear, so that I was sure to hear him over the drums. "Don't drink that, man!"

"Not on your life," I said. I sniffed the cup. The liquid smelled bitter.

Then a young man came dancing at me, off-balance. I was ready to catch him by the neck and knock him out when he dropped to his hands and knees, scrambled beside me, and put his head to a bucket near my feet. He vomited.

"What the hell did they give that kid?" DJ asked, reaching for the cup. I let him have it. Whatever was inside, I didn't want it.

He sniffed it and his head reared back.

"Shit, Dep, that's ayahuasca tea," he said. "What the hell would they go and do something like that for?" He slid the cup on the bar, then grabbed me by the shoulder, pulling me close. "Worst time I ever had was 'cuz of ayahuasca. I thought the devil was chasin' after me, and I ran about twenty-three miles over, I dunno, three or four hours, totally trippin' out of my head. Lucky me, I was in the salt flats, and all my buddies had to do was follow my tracks until they found me passed out in a heap."

He shivered and shook his head. Then, when he opened his eyes, they lit up. DJ was looking past me, out the door.

"What is it?" I started to turn my head.

"Don't look!" DJ said. "It's him!"

"Desir?" I asked. "What's he doing?"

"Talkin' to somebody on a phone, I think," he replied. "Just lookin' through the room—now he's leaving."

"Give him a five-second head start," I said. "Then I'm going to count to five and follow you."

DJ nodded. His eyes shifted around the darkened room while he counted silently, then he was off. Like my partner, I counted to five before leaving the ruckus behind and slipping out the front door.

The light outside was overbearing, but the relative quiet of cars on the boulevard and wind coming off the beach across the way was a welcome change. I looked left, then right, and I saw DJ hobbling around the corner of the building immediately to the north.

I followed.

Soon, I found myself in an open-air market. DJ slipped past a lady selling handcrafted jewelry off a blanket spread on the ground and I picked up the pace. I met up with him around a set of folding tables with handcrafted candles of all shapes, sizes, and colors.

Ahead of us, Desir turned off the main drag and into an alleyway.

I tapped DJ's elbow.

"Hang here," I whispered.

"Yep," he answered. He picked up a green candle and sniffed it, then sputtered a cough. "Holy shit!" I heard him say as I closed toward the mouth of the alleyway. Whatever DJ followed that up with was lost in the sound of people browsing through the market.

I buzzed past the alley's entrance and peeked in. I saw Desir and another young, wiry-looking man in red, loose-fitting clothes that strongly resembled a toga standing among the trashcans and discarded boxes one expected to see in an alley.

I continued to the nearest stall, where a woman dressed in a white cap, white flowing blouse, and matching white skirt sold jars of powders and leaves like the stuff Pierre Noubon had all over his house.

In the alley, Desir said something that made the other man laugh, and when he threw back his head, sunlight hit his neck, highlighting a machete tattooed below his jaw.

"Looking to cure a particular ailment, sir?" the woman in white asked me. Her voice was like a warm blanket, and she had a pleasant, welcoming smile.

"Not me," I said. "Not yet."

I turned my eyes back to the alley just in time to see Machete Tattoo hand Desir a letter-size envelope. I knew a cash handoff when I saw one, and any doubt was removed when Desir peeked into the envelope and a US bill flapped free. He tucked it back in and put the money in his pocket, beaming, showing a gap where a front tooth should've been.

I thought of the gold tooth in my pocket.

Desir came out of the alley first. I turned my back, picked up a mason jar of minced, browned leaves and glanced DJ's way. He and I met eyes and he gave me a subtle nod. When Desir passed by him, DJ fell in right behind, shadowing him.

"Sir, unless you're trying to find a quick way to get yourself pregnant, what's in that jar isn't going to do you any good," the woman in white told me.

"I'm considering my options," I said.

She laughed. "Well, if you decide to keep to the path you're on, I have powdered maca root straight from the Andes. It'll make any man very potent."

Machete Tattoo was coming out of the alley now. He moved like a stray dog with a fresh cut of beef, checking every angle to make sure no one was coming his way.

The woman in white picked up on how carefully I watched him.

"You don't want to look too closely now," she said. "That one there is no good. Lots of trouble tied to him."

A step or two outside the alley, Machete Tattoo was stopped by a teenager, who asked him something I couldn't hear. Machete Tattoo folded his hands and smiled, then turned his face to the sky, shut his eyes and touched the boy's forehead with his thumb. He muttered something only the two of them could hear, then opened his eyes and looked in my direction.

He came toward me.

"Excuse me, bruddah," he said, as he reached around me and plucked a leaf off a thin branch laid across the woman's booth. He

124

winked at her, and I, having seen the man all of two minutes, already wanted to punch him in the nose.

"Is he a regular of yours?" I asked her.

Her face was tight. "No, he's very much not."

Machete Tattoo went back to the teenager, took the kid's hand, turned his palm up and pressed the leaf to it. Then, he closed the kid's fingers around it and kneaded his fist, grinding the dried leaf.

He spoke loudly in French. I didn't understand a word of it, but it seemed to attract some attention from the other people in the market, including the woman in white.

"You don't have a single idea what you're talkin' about, boy," she called to Machete Tattoo, and the chatter in the market slowly died off. "Ain't one *loa* in all creation that hold dominion over the rest of them."

Machete Tattoo kept his hands on the boy's, but otherwise stopped what he was doing and slowly turned an eye to her

"So you believe," he said.

"I believe you been brainwashed," she said. "And I believe you'll be paying me for that jatropha leaf you took. Don't waste good medicine on your nonsense."

I didn't understand what exactly they were fighting over, but the word "nonsense" seemed to get Machete Tattoo's full attention. He dropped the kid's hand and slowly walked over to the booth, and the whole market appeared to have paused and watched him.

"You're temptin' some ver' pow'ful t'ings," he said quietly to her.

I didn't think anyone else could hear him talking—I was the closest person to both of them, and I barely could.

"I'm not afraid of a confused man serving a corrupt woman who never has shown her face to the people here," she said. "Whenever your daughter wants to come to Marigot, you let her know where I am. I might be afraid if I see her, but probably not."

"Do not fear her," he said. "Fear what she bring." Then he turned around and faced the small crowd that had gathered.

"We fight for all de people of St. Martin," he said with his voice raised to a minister's oratory. "Believers and non-believers, alike. The righteous will lead us all to freedom from de bonds of white colonialism" —he nodded toward the woman in white— "and their avatars on our island."

A couple people in the crowd shouted their approval.

He turned to me and pointed, and it was then I noticed the thin gold ring on his index finger, and the way the light dulled against the small iron ingot set inside it. Was it his ring DJ had found?

"Your people will no longer hold dominion here," he said. "Like de slaves of yesteryear, we are de chosen children, protected by powers beyond understandin', and we will lead a great victory over you and the ills your French and Dutch ancestors pushed upon ours."

Mom was Italian; Dad, German.

"We will not bow to cultural hegemony! We will not be de vassals of your corrupt government! Dose days are gone and de most powerful of de *loa* will usher in a new era of freedom, prosperity, and morality for St. Martin!"

A bigger slice of the crowd cheered for him.

"De Daughter's words—" he continued on while the woman in white grabbed me by the shoulders.

"You should go," she whispered. "Nothing good will come to you by staying here."

"I get the feeling nothing good will come to anyone by *him* staying here." I nodded toward Machete Tattoo, who was ranting on,

126

shouting, and raising his fist, which prompted some in the crowd to raise a fist too.

"I'd like to talk to him," I said.

"What do you think you can say to him now? You think you can have a chat with him about how you aren't a cog in the great white colonial machine?"

She had a fair point.

"What's his name?" I asked.

"It doesn't matter," she said. "You're safer not knowing."

"I don't care about safe," I said. "I care about getting my job done."

She eyed me suspiciously. "Whatever your job may be, sir, I can't think you'll do it after these people beat you to death."

I guess she had a point. A couple people in the crowd of about two dozen were giving me extremely disconcerting looks.

I turned my back and started to walk away, and a big cheer came up from the crowd. I looked over my shoulder and I think they were cheering because I was leaving.

"At least tell me your name," I called back to the woman in white. "So I can thank you." *And also find you later and ask you more about what just happened.*

"My name is not important," she said as she pushed me back in the direction I'd come from.

I didn't like leaving information behind, which it very much felt like I was doing. But what were my choices? Dig my heels in, cross my arms and refuse to move until someone answered some of my questions? Were names and answers worth catching generations' worth of owed beatdowns from the mob that formed before me?

I walked off. And, while doing so, I checked the booth where I'd last spotted DJ. The only people I found were a tourist couple sniffing herbs and sneezing and the man running the booth.

"Seen a guy with a long goatee and a fake leg?" I asked him.

"No English," he said through a smile and a thick accent.

I walked past the old man and to the next group of booths. I saw locals and tourists alike browsing through T-shirts and handmade jewelry, but no DJ or Desir.

If DJ'd followed Desir elsewhere, I had little chance of finding either of them.

The other direction, I saw Machete Tattoo giving out another blessing, with the crowd still near him. I shook my head.

Then, I heard a crash.

DJ and Joseph Desir spilled over a folding table, cracking it in half and knocking handmade jewelry into the street, onto the sidewalk, and at the backs of women screaming and running like they'd been shot at.

What a mess.

I ran over to help my partner, but by the time I got there, DJ had the smaller, rounder man pinned.

"I got him, DJ. Ease off!" I said as I grabbed Desir's arm to take control of him.

DJ rolled off, keeping a hold on Desir's other arm. We both tried to raise him to his feet, but Desir was limp as a ragdoll.

"Mr. Desir," I said to no response. The guy had a bloody nose and a gash above his eye leaking all over, including onto the jewelry. "Think you might've handled him a little too roughly, DJ?"

"Oh, I'm fine, Dep," he said. "The man only tried to stab me, but I'm dandy."

I checked DJ over. He wasn't wounded—just sweaty and pouting with a silver ear stud lanced into his forearm. I reached over Desir and pulled it out. "Don't steal from the locals."

I tossed it toward the biggest pile of scattered jewelry on the ground.

At the same time, Desir moaned. He was coming to, and I felt it was my responsibility to check him out to make sure he was lucid enough to talk to us. A nearby patio with a few chairs stacked in a corner looked like a fair triage station, and—if all went well—makeshift interrogation room.

"Who's payin' for all dis mess?" an older man said, sifting through the pile of jewelry on the ground, trying to sort the good from bad. "It took me and my whole family mont's to make all dese t'ings!"

"We'll pay for it all," DJ said. "Right, Dep?"

Desir stirred. His feet scrabbled on the ground but couldn't find their balance.

"Of course, but we'll need a minute, sir." I jerked my head toward the patio. "Let's sit him down a minute."

"Man, we can't just—"

Desir moved again; he was probably trying to say something, but only gibberish game out.

"Let's go, DJ."

DJ didn't want to go, and I knew leaving this old merchant here with a mess wasn't right, but what was I supposed to do? There was a murderer on the loose.

"We're coming back," DJ said to the old man.

"Of course," I added. "Damages will be paid in full."

We walked across the street and over to the covered patio with Desir mumbling the whole way. Then we plopped him down into a dusty wrought iron chair.

"Man left a whole trail of blood," DJ said, nodding in the direction we'd come from.

I wouldn't call it a trail so much as a series of dribbles, but DJ was right if his point was that Desir had made a mess.

Lacking a first aid kit, I'd have to find something else. Maybe a piece of Desir's own shirt, or somebody's sock, but as it turned out, neither was necessary. An old cleaning rag had been left on a table nearby. It didn't look like anyone would miss it, so I took it, slapped it against my leg a few times to beat as much loose dust off as I could, then pressed it to Desir's forehead.

He howled like a stuck cat. Good to see he was regaining consciousness, even though his eyelids were still nearly shut.

"Put your hand on that," I told him. "Hold it to your forehead."

He did.

"Now, Mr. Desir, I'd like to ask you a few questions," I said, standing in front of him.

Slowly, he opened the one eye not covered by the dirty dishrag. Desir looked up at me towering over him and blinked a few times. He was pissed, understandably, but he was compliant, staying in his chair.

Then he groaned and doubled over.

"Shit, boy!" he said. "You cracked my head open."

DJ slapped the back of Desir's head, and the man sprang upright in the chair.

"You're lookin' alright to me, friend," DJ said. He reached over Desir, then pinched the corner of the envelope of cash sticking out of his front pocket and snatched it away.

"That's my money!" Desir said.

"Yeah?" DJ flipped open the envelope and took the stack of cash out. "How'd you earn it?"

"It's from my mother's estate," Desir said.

"Uh-huh." DJ said as he started passing the bills between his hands, one at a time, counting them to himself.

"I suppose that man with the neck tattoo you met in the alleyway was your lawyer," I said. "Strange that you wouldn't meet him in his office."

Desir glared at me.

"Thirteen, fourteen, fifteen." DJ counted bills aloud. "A lot of money here to pass off in an alleyway, Joe. Kinda careless, really. Ain't you worried about the wrong person seein' you with all this cash? What if, I dunno, a pair of bad guys got it in their heads to go and mug you?"

"You're holding a government official hostage. You two gentlemen realize that?"

"We know who you are, Mr. Desir," I said. "And I'm sure the Prefect's office and the newspaper would love to know what kind of official government business you've been working on here at the market. But they don't have to know, so long as you're cooperative."

Desir sighed and adjusted the wadded-up towel on his forehead.

"Tell me about the man who gave you that money. Is he some kind of priest?"

Desir nodded.

"So you shake down Billy Pearce, and you shake down this guy. Shaking down religious leaders is a niche business model, Mr. Desir. How many other customers do you have?"

"You shouldn't worry about that, my friend," Desir said with a grin. My eyes were drawn to the missing tooth right up front.

131

DJ stopped counting and, with a raised eyebrow, silently asked if he should rough up Desir for giving me attitude.

"I appreciate the concern, but don't worry about me, Mr. Desir," I said. "Now, tell me about Billy Pearce. Rumor is the two of you engaged in a heated exchange of ideas shortly before he was stabbed to death in his own church."

He shrugged. "We talked, yes, but it shouldn't be me you're concerned with. The truth is Billy had wronged a lot of folk around here. Borrowed lots of money too. I'm guessing you come 'round asking about him because he owed you two gentlemen too."

"Wrong," DJ said. "Guess again."

"'The two of you aren't French," Desir said. "Have you come from America with warrants for Pearce? I always suspected that man had a bad history. Probably has a rap sheet taller than me."

"That ain't sayin' much," DJ said.

Desir looked over his shoulder at DJ and bared a couple teeth.

"Whomever we're aligned with isn't your concern," I said, reaching in my pocket. "What you should be thinking about is how well we're doing our homework. For instance, I found this at the murder scene—" I unwrapped the gold tooth and held it right in front of his nose. His pupils went as large as marbles.

"Slow down—wait a minute."

"Did this fall out of your head while you and Billy were conversing?"

"Hold on now!" Desir said.

"Or did it come out when you came back and killed him?"

Desir's nostrils flared slightly. "I killed nobody!"

"Quit the bullshit," DJ replied.

"Look, I was there, collecting. Billy leased that space where his church is through a program the government started, to get folks to use old buildings before they go back to nothing. After Irma, so many citizens left Marigot, and we had so much unoccupied property that good places were going to the rats. But it can't just be any building that gets put in the program, it's gotta be checked out by inspectors and engineers, and only certain ones pass into it.

"Get to the point already," DJ said.

"The point is, I helped Billy. He had his eye on that spot where his church is for a long time, and I helped him get that building for almost nothing, but he had to pay me a monthly fee to stay in it. Understand?"

"And you killed him because he couldn't pay up," I said.

"No! No, never!"

"You can't lie," I said. "You were there threatening him!"

"No, I—" He stopped as if his words had jammed in his throat. "Yes, we argued, but I didn't kill any man. Billy and I had been negotiating for quite some time. My costs had gone up because folks outside the Prefect's Office were closer at the lease grant program, which meant more work needed to happen to get a couple new signatures on Billy's paperwork. I had to pass that cost off somehow. So, I've been in talks with Billy, warning him that if he couldn't pay the new fees, he'd lose his building.

"But that didn't mean anything to Billy. He thought I was raising the price simply because I felt like it. We went at each other for months before his time had come, so I marched down to his office last week to make my last push to impress upon Billy the seriousness of his situation.

"He went hot right away, and, I'll admit, I sometimes get hot too—" He gestured at his missing tooth.

"I heard you swore revenge against him on your way out."

Desir looked at me, then shifted his eyes to his feet. "Sometimes my mouth works faster than I can think, especially when I'm angry."

"You lost control," I said. "Who's to say you didn't lose control again and kill Billy?"

He huffed, clearly frustrated.

"Listen," he said. "The night Billy Pearce was murdered, I was part of a special envoy to Anguilla and I was in the Valley, attending a state dinner."

"How did you know which night he was killed?"

"A contact in the Gendarmerie sent me the report on Billy's murder," he said.

"You didn't have to be there. You could've ordered someone to do it."

"Sir, I happen to strongly believe spilling blood is bad for business. I'd never kill a man who paid me—I fine him through the city most times, and once before I had a man beaten to a pulp for trying to come after my sister, but I haven't had anyone killed. Too much mess, too much to cover for, and more to the point, I wasn't sending anyone after Billy for not paying his dues. I'd simply kick him off the property.

"Frankly, I expect a man to push back at first when I ask for more money, but I know if I give him the proper time to think on it—and Billy had been granted far more time than most—he usually comes 'round.

"And, more specifically in this instance, Billy's girlfriend and her mother witnessed me leaving his church with a bloody mouth, so why would I go back and kill the man like that? I have no desire to go sleep in the piss house over a parasite like Billy Pearce."

Desir was a scumbag, even by his own admission, but I believed him.

"You're such a swell guy, Joe," DJ said.

"Mr. Desir, do you have any way to prove you were in Anguilla the night Billy died?"

"I just told you—" He furrowed his brow in disbelief. "The papers were there. Get ahold of one for Monday, the seventh, and you're sure to see my face in it."

Alicia could check his story, no problem.

"You're running this cheap rent scheme all around town," I said.

"I know it's wrong, but a man has to watch out for himself," he said. "A piece of nice property comes by, I do what I can to buy it up."

"And what about Billy's girlfriend, Shara Bradley?" I asked. "What do you know about her?"

He shook his head. "I never even talked to the girl before. I wasn't making social calls to Billy, and even if I did, she was a kid. What would I possibly have to say to her? 'How was school today? Did you ride your bike over? Is Billy the first man you've ever kissed?' I didn't like Billy Pearce for many reasons, and his being with such a young girl was one of them."

Desir winced and checked the wadded towel on his head, then put it back in place.

"Nobody liked Billy Pearce," he added.

"So we've heard," I said. I motioned for DJ to give Desir back his envelope of money.

He slipped a few bills out, then dropped the rest in Desir's lap, and the guy almost jumped off his seat.

"You're donating money to that guy with the busted-up jewelry stand, man. Consider it your civic fuckin' duty," DJ said.

He and I turned away, going back toward the market where the old man with the broken table was now scooping up bits of jewelry with a broom and dustpan.

"Hey," Desir said to our backs. I figured he was going to complain about the money DJ took. "Why are you two asking about Billy Pearce, anyway? *Does* he owe you money?"

"No," I said. "We're helping St. Martin."

Desir gave us the international male signal of respect—a few approving nods. As if we needed approval from him.

"Well, if you want to know who else had good reason to kill the man, go look for Albert René," he said. "Billy Pearce snaked René's mother into his church and took all the money she had. Took more too, if all the rumors are to be believed."

"Where is she?" I asked.

"At the cemetery, overlooking Marigot Bay," he said.

"She a grave digger or somethin'?" DJ asked.

"No."

She's dead.

"Where can we find her son?"

"René works on his fishing boat. This time a day, I imagine he'd be at the Marigot Market."

CHAPTER THIRTEEN

Returning from Grand Case, DJ and I found ourselves almost back where we'd first set foot on the island. Our day trip had pretty much circumnavigated the French half of the tiny island, bringing us to Marigot Market.

The market consisted of an oval-shaped courtyard that was open on its south end but was otherwise hemmed in by a low, horseshoe-shaped concrete building with a red, clay-tile roof.

The courtyard hosted dozens of vendor stalls, which were little more than canvas sheets supported by steel posts, which were themselves held in place by ropes tied to thick, eye-hook screws drilled into a shin-high concrete wall. Like at the market in Grand Case, I could've picked from any number of handmade jewelry items, Chinese-imported T-shirts with tourist-friendly quips, bootleg media, and hundreds upon hundreds of different medicinal herbs.

That is, if DJ and I had shown up earlier. By the time we arrived in late afternoon, bordering on evening, Marigot Market was nearly buttoned up for the day. A small number of tourists milled between the handful of booths still open, but I got the feeling I was seeing this place at quarter capacity, max.

"Shit, Dep, the man's probably already walked out of here for the day," DJ grumbled. "Maybe we should do the same—I been feeling this sore on my leg, you know, right where Patty cups leg meet, and I think I just gotta get off it for a little while."

"*Wayward's* just over there," I said, bobbing my head to the northwest, where I could see the entrance to the dock between a pair of "I'M WITH STUPID" T-shirts. "You're free to go back whenever you please, but while there's a job to be done, I'm doing it."

I continued into the courtyard, coming to a clearing at the center where concrete paver stones met brick, which met blue glass tile, which met terra cotta cutouts. DJ's leg thumped behind me. Across the courtyard, I spotted an old woman in a folding chair, sitting in a coral-colored canvas hut, alone except for a young woman looking at a painted clay pot.

"I'm going to talk to some locals," I said. "Check around and see if you can get any information."

"Sure, man," DJ said.

I walked across the courtyard toward the coral hut.

"Ma'am?" I asked as I approached.

Her cloudy eyes looked in my direction, but her fingers remained in her lap, where they twisted what looked like dried palm fronds into a human shape.

"Do you know where I can find a fisherman named Albert René?"

"I know him, but if ya' lookin' for good fish, young man, I got a grandbaby up at the dock who can get ya' somet'in' real good."

"I'm looking for René," I said.

"Hmmm, well sometimes I got troubles rememberin' t'ings." Her eyes drifted over to a hand-carved bowl on a table to my right,

138

next to the woman looking at the pot. It was for sale, and I understood what she expected of me.

"How much for that wooden bowl?"

"T'irty," she replied.

"Excuse me," I said to the other customer, as I reached past her and picked up the bowl. Then I took my wallet out and paid the old woman.

"Now, where can I find René?"

"In the big hall behind me," she said. "I seen his crewman, Jean-Phillipe, walkin' 'round, while René hollerin' himself blue at de boy."

"What's René look like?"

"Oh, I don't know," she said. "These eyes, they don't work so good." But they were good enough to pick out a life-size clay cat figurine to my left.

I put my hand on it.

"Sixty," she said.

"A dollar just doesn't go as far as it used to," I said.

"It's a good piece."

"Sure, but for that price, I need you to sweeten the deal. Tell me something else too."

"Yessir, what about?"

"A man named Billy Pearce and his girlfriend Shara Bradley."

"Ohhh, that never be a problem for me, sir, I know about bot' a dem. Mr. Pearce's church ain't too far from 'ere."

"I'm already aware of that," I said.

"Well, he got a young girlfriend, and I know her mama don't approve of the two bein' together."

"I've talked to her," I said.

The old woman looked up at me and shrugged.

139

"Do you have any other information about the girl? What she looked like? Where she spent time?"

"No," she said.

"Didn't you say you knew about both of them?"

"I mighta promised more than I can give," she said. "In truth, I only met Billy Pearce but one time when he stop by to talk about his church."

Of course. Though, I couldn't be too upset at an old lady desperate to make a few extra bucks in whatever way she could.

"Give me a good description of Albert René, and I'll pay you forty for the cat."

"Money first," she said.

"Take a credit card?" I asked.

She grinned as she produced a smartphone with a card reader already attached.

After I'd paid, she delivered on her end of the bargain. She said Albert René was tall with short hair and overgrown arms and shoulders—the sort a fisherman needed to live off his trade. She said if I went into the indoor market and followed the sound of a mean dog bellowing at anybody and everybody who came by, I'd either come across him, or an animal much more agreeable than René typically was.

With my new wooden bowl in hand and the clay cat statue tucked under my arm, I found DJ two booths over, looking at a brass pendant on a twine necklace.

"Lady over there says it's supposed to help protect my mind from evil while I sleep."

"What about that stuff Noubon gave you?" I asked.

"Oh man, you're right! I don't wanna double up so quickly, or I won't know which one's legit and which one's just junk." He put the

140

pendant down and followed me toward the entrance to the indoor market.

"I like the bowl, Dep, but I thought you hated cats, on account of being allergic, and where you gonna put a clay statue on a catamaran?" DJ asked.

"I suppose I fell in love with the statue and didn't give it any thought."

"Cat... catamaran... Now I get it." He looked over at me and grinned. "Suppose you could super glue it to the deck, or nail it down to a counter in the galley. Better yet, go back to the booth where you bought it and make that old lady's day by getting another one. Then, you can add a bowsprit for each hull. Ya already got your figureheads covered."

"Clay wouldn't last against open seas," I said. "But I'll let you know if anything strikes me later."

As we approached the door to the building, a young woman careened into me. She was probably half my size, so she spun off and crashed to the floor, after knocking the clay statue out of my arm. It snapped into two large pieces.

Easy come, easy go.

Stepping over the mess, I went to her and reached my hand out.

"Sorry, sorry, sorry!" she said as she took it and hoisted herself to her feet. It was the girl who had been browsing the old woman's booth. She looked a lot like the pretty local girls featured in tourism pamphlets meant to draw horny, middle-aged men out to the Caribbean. Her hair was long and straight, her skin was smooth as morning bay water, and she had the wide, clear eyes of a baby doll.

"I'm so sorry about your statue, sir!"

"It's fine," I said, picking up each half. The statue didn't break as cleanly as I initially thought, leaving little chips and shards on the concrete paver stones.

"Don't be sorry, sweet pea," DJ said. "I have it on good authority the man didn't want it anyway."

"Are you alright?" I asked, then tossed the two largest pieces into a trashcan next to the indoor market entrance. "You didn't get any of those smaller bits in your hands, did you?"

"No, sir, I'm just fine!" she said, but I could see the tiny nicks in the palm of her right hand.

"You're bleeding," I said.

"It's okay." She started hopping away. Apparently, she was in a hurry.

"Just be careful runnin' around, alright?" DJ said, as she jogged toward a booth. She looped around it and out of sight.

DJ and I picked up whatever we could of the clay shards and collected them in the bowl.

"Still got that nice bowl, at least," he said. "I bet Alicia's gonna love it."

I grumbled and dumped the bits of clay into the trash, then pulled open the door to the indoor market.

DJ and I didn't have to search long before we found a tall man with short hair, built like he crushed live Marlin skulls and fed off the juice that dripped out. He was behind a steel fish-cleaning table, waving a long filet knife over his head, and berating a kid who couldn't have been over twenty years old. Another man, probably around twenty-five, picked up a disposable cooler nearby and made himself scarce.

I started toward Albert René as the kid placed a fish on the cleaning table. René slipped the sharp, narrow blade in and ran it from tail to head, then jammed his fingers in and ripped the fish's innards out, all in the few seconds it took me to get in front of his table.

"Mr. René," I said.

"What?" His voice rumbled like a thunderstorm coming over the horizon.

"I'm looking for information about the murder of Billy Pearce," I said. "Do you know of him?"

René's hand tightened on the fish's body. I heard bones crunch, then he swung it over a small sink next to the table and ran the back edge of the filet knife along the fish's skin from tail to head, plucking out scales and audibly grunting every time he reached its head.

"There's also a girl missing—by the name of Shara Bradley."

Upon hearing Shara's name, René dropped the knife. It clattered into the sink, and he grumbled as he snatched it out, then went back to scaling the fish.

He knew something.

"My partner and I spoke to Shara's mother, Mary, today," I said. "Do you happen to know her? She works over at Mer du Mélasse."

René clenched his jaw. He definitely knew Mary Bradley.

"No," he said.

"But you probably know Billy Pearce."

"Why would you say that?"

"Your name came up in a conversation I had about him."

René slapped the fish back onto the cutting surface.

"I have nothing good to say about that man."

"Nobody seems to," I said. "What do you know about him?"

René scoffed and jabbed the knife into the fish, separating filet from bone. "He's crooked."

"You ain't kiddin'," DJ said. "We went over to his church today and guess what we found? The man had a few grand in cash squirreled away in a vent. Can you believe that? What kinda preacher hides money in his church? Well, I think we all know without me havin' to spell it out."

René offered no reaction.

DJ examined an iced-down table with a couple filets laid across it. The rest had probably been sold or packed into the disposable cooler the other crewman walked away with.

"Only thing I can't really figure about Billy Pearce," DJ continued, "is what he planned on doing with that kinda scratch hidden away? I mean, shit, if it's money you're after, and it seemed like money is what Billy liked, even a bumpkin like me knows you can't just sit on it—it don't do no good to keep cash sittin' there, not doin' a damned thing for you. Why not invest it? You ain't gotta necessarily do it in the stock market. I mean you could help somebody start a restaurant and get a cut, or help a fisherman get a better boat and take your cut through that.... Shit, Billy probably wouldn't have no qualms about loan sharkin', I bet.

"I mean, you gotta put your money somewhere if you want more of it, so why didn't Billy?"

As DJ pontificated about Billy Pearce's lost business prospects, René worked harder with the knife, cutting, cleaning, gutting—the man was being pushed further to the brink with every word from DJ's mouth.

I realized I should help press him along.

"Sure seems like Billy should have done something with it," I said. "You know what pisses me off the most about that, partner?"

"What?" DJ asked.

144

"That money we found belonged to *somebody*. Probably an array of good, honest people contributed to Billy's church because they believed in his message, and they believed Billy would use their money to spread the good word."

"He's a real dogshit person, man. Right off the bottom of a boot," DJ said.

"Regular people on St. Martin gave Billy that money, and it probably wasn't easy for them to simply give it up, but they were willing to sacrifice, difficult as it made their lives."

"That man did a damned shameful thing," DJ said.

"Despicable," I agreed.

René had a fish locked up so tightly in his hand, its eyes were bulging out of its head.

"Pisses me off, just thinkin' about Billy Pearce," DJ said. "And I'm not even from here, but if I or somebody I cared about gave money to that man, I'd want it back as soon as I could get it. And if the man ain't givin', I'd come get it myself, know what I mean? Something like that, I'd do whatever it took to get my cash back. I put my blood, sweat, and tears into getting what I got, and I'll be—"

"Bloodclaat!" René dropped the knife and grabbed his hand. Blood immediately flowed down his wrist and dripped off his elbow.

Being a medic, my first instinct was to help, but as soon as I reached for René, he withdrew.

"Keep your hands away from me!"

"Mr. René, I was a medic in the United States—"

"I don't care what you were!" he snapped. He dropped behind the fish-cleaning table, then came back up with an old T-shirt that he wound around his hand so tight, I thought his fingers would pop off.

"You people come bothering me while I work," he muttered. "And for what? To talk to me about a dead man? A man I never want anything to do with, never cared about, and never want to hear from again."

"Mr. René, we've talked to a lot of people here already," I said. "We know your mother gave him a large amount of money—before she passed."

"That was her choice, not mine."

"I realize," I said.

"I tell her not to give that man anything." He waved the knife around as he spoke, and I was sure to keep an eye on it.

"You're right," I said.

"Anyone with their head on straight knew Billy Pearce was up to no good. He came to Marigot, tellin' people the hurricane was God's warning to us all and that we only had so much time to drop our false idols and fix our misguided ways before judgment come. But I say, what false idols? What misguided ways? He talks about a God with a dead son who come to save us all, but I see no Christian spirit saving me!"

"Preach it," DJ said.

"You want to know who saving me? *La Sirène*—" he touched the flat of his knife to a finger on his cut hand, counting "—*Legba, Damballah, Ezili Dantor*—all the *loa* are watching because my ways are not misguided, I tell you. Billy Pearce was the man pulling people off the righteous path, making them forget where they come from and who got them where they are. So, what happened to that man—I don't care because he deserved it."

"What about Shara Bradley?" I asked. "She's missing. She might even have been killed herself, or worse. Did she deserve that?"

Mentioning her name had an instant effect on René, enraging him. He gave me a look like he was going to plunge his filet knife into my neck, cut out the meat, and sell it as tuna.

I suspected I could push his buttons and get him to say something very stupid, but I had to do it in such a way that I wouldn't become his latest filet.

"Shara was part of it," I said. "She kept Pearce's books, so she knew what was going on. As such, did she deserve to be kidnapped and possibly tortured, raped, or whatever else the people who have her are doing to her right now?"

René spat on the floor.

The young crewman, who, until now, had wisely kept his distance beside a near-empty crate of wahoo, stepped in.

"Sir, would you like some of today's catch?" he asked me. "Captaine René and me can clean and cut up a wahoo steak or two."

"Jean-Phillipe," René growled. "He does not want to buy fish!"

"I was going to buy it for him."

"Giving up *my* catch!" René cocked his hand as if he was about to slap Jean-Phillipe, and the kid scurried away.

"There's no cause to take out your frustrations on the kid, but I understand why you're upset," I said. "No matter if your mother gave Pearce five million or a nickel, it was too much. Every cent that comes to a working man comes by way of his sweat, his blood, the years taken off his life, and it's an insult to see it thrown away on a cheap con artist's promises to a dying old lady."

"Don't you speak another word about her," René said, pointing the knife at me. He held it so tightly, it looked like his muscles were going to burst through the skin from the back of his hand all the way to his elbow. "I didn't have any part in what happened to Billy Pearce and Shara, but don't think you can run your mouth about all kinds of things and not catch a consequence or two from me."

147

"Mr. René, there's a simple way to get us out of your hair," I said. "And it doesn't involve another knife. All you have to do is tell my partner and me where you were the night Billy was killed."

"Do I have to repeat that I have nothing to say to you?" René snapped back. He held the knife still now, pointing it at my chest. "I have no time for men who don't know St. Martin coming by, accusing me of murdering some badwud that nobody wanted around anyhow. And I have no patience for that same man disparaging the woman who birthed me, hear?"

"C'mon, Dep," DJ said.

No, I couldn't leave just yet. Like an old angler who can feel the big fish coming, I knew René had more than he was letting on, and if I could just feel out how to set the hook, I'd catch him, finish this case, and be on my way back home.

"You don't care about your mother," I said. "You let Pearce brainwash her! Now that she's gone, you want to act like you were the world's best son, but you explain to me what kind of son stands by while his mother is tricked by a con artist. Did you even bother to help her?"

He locked his elbow, leaving less than a foot between the knife and my breastbone.

"Walk away," René growled.

"Tell me what you did with Shara Bradley."

By saying that, I knew I was taking my life into my own hands. Lucky for him, René had the wisdom to flick the knife aside before he planted his foot on the edge of the cleaning table and vaulted it, coming straight into me.

I was ready. I grabbed him around the shoulders and tried to get my arms around his neck, but DJ was there and bear-hugged my waist, trying to pull me off. Then, there were other sets of arms in front of me, squeezing between René and me, and as DJ tugged me out of reach, I saw both of René's crewmen pulling him away while he screamed at me in both French and English Patois.

"Jesus Christ, Jerry!" DJ whipped me around, then grabbed me by the back of the neck and walked me toward the exit. "What the hell am I gonna tell Alicia when you're sitting in some hospital bed with your guts in a bucket next to you?"

"Did you see that?"

"I saw you losin' your damned mind!"

"The situation was under control," I said. "I was pushing him."

"Great job, Dep. Real proud of you, you're a credit to the force, and yadda, yadda, yadda, you stupid bastard. What were you thinkin', eggin' on a big, angry, suspected murderer with a knife in his hand?"

I looked back at René, who met my eyes and started hurling curses while his crew fought to keep him from charging at me again.

"You taught me that if we're going to solve cases, sometimes we have to take risks."

DJ scoffed. "Now I get why you were so pissed at me in Puerto Rico."

We walked out of the building and across the courtyard and kept going until DJ and I were on the boardwalk outside Baie de Marigot. Only then did he let go of me.

He exhaled slowly and rubbed his eyes. "Man, it ain't so fun being on the other side of that."

"There's his boat," I said, pointing.

Albert René's trawler, *La Sirène II*, was moored about fifty feet offshore. What looked like all kinds of trash had been fastened to the outer bulkheads. Outside the saloon door there was a rusted, dingy mirror to one side and a mermaid painted on the other, as well as a trumpet mounted above the door and conch shells.

"See that?" I asked DJ.

"I'm seein' a lot."

"Above the door."

He shaded his eyes with his hand. "Oh shit."

"Same thing we saw back at Desir's club," I said.

"Maybe it's just a coincidence."

That didn't seem likely.

A strange design had been painted on the starboard side of the bowl—a crest, or some kind of logo. The top half was diamond-shaped, with a hollow circle drawn in the middle, somewhat resembling a human eye. Below the eye, a triangle pointed down and looked like a platform or altar of some sort.

The way René went on about *loa* and all these symbols on his boat pointed toward a deeply superstitious man. Would it have been past him to play the part of a vengeful ghost in order to murder Billy Pearce?

"Let's get back to *Wayward*," I said. "Albert René looks like a solid lead to me. I want to see what we can do to keep closer tabs on him."

"Sure, Dep."

CHAPTER FOURTEEN

Back aboard *Wayward*, DJ and I filled Alicia in on the day's events and she volunteered to do background on Albert René. While she worked on her laptop at the galley table, I grilled snapper for the three of us in the cockpit. DJ and I ate at the cockpit settee and Alicia had hers while she continued working.

After dinner, I went down to Alicia's and my stateroom and lay back on the bed. I couldn't calm my mind. I kept thinking about the case, of course, but also Arlen. Why had he come to St. Martin? And why now? He'd slithered over to his new private island home and hibernated for the better part of a year.

Knowing I wouldn't be able to nap it off, I hopped off the bed and lifted it up to get at the compartment beneath.

There, in a watertight footlocker, I had stashed a few personal items. I opened it up.

Right on top was a stack of an uncountable number of training certificates from my PJ years for learning how to dive, climb, rappel, jump out of perfectly good aircraft at both high and low altitude, and medical training manuals. Additionally, I had a dozen different pieces of paper that said I knew how to drive just about any personal craft on land or sea. Next to my training certificates, some service medals, and a bunch of other mementos spanning from private high school sports teams to middle school Scouts and even a couple grade school ribbons.

Why I kept all that detritus from the past, I wasn't sure. I pushed aside all these tokens, proving I'd grown up an ambitious, studious, single-minded, upper-class white kid in Newport Beach, California, and came to a photo album.

Most of the pages were empty. In all my years of picking up awards for completing one thing or another, I'd never got one for scrapbooking, but even so, I'd managed to slide a few photos into this album of mine.

And Arlen was in many of them.

I shut my footlocker, let the bed back down, sat on it and put the album in my lap.

The first page had a picture of my sister, Gene, blowing out candles on the cake at her sixth birthday party. I was nine, the same as Arlen's son, my best friend, Jeff, who was next to me, eagerly waiting for my little sister to hurry up and blow out the candles. Arlen was there in the background, laughing about something with my father.

On the opposite page, a picture of all of us camping—me, my father, Jeff, and Arlen. I was about twelve, on my knees next to a campfire, summoning smoke out of logs.

My dad had a pretty good Tom Selleck mustache, Jeff was still baby-faced, and Arlen's hair was the same slicked-back black as it was today. We'd had a great time that weekend in Yosemite. We scared off a bear that night by clanging pots and pans around the same campfire, and the next morning Arlen showed me the best way to bait a hook for rainbow trout.

"Jerry?" Alicia came down the stairway from the saloon. Her eyes went to the photo album on my lap. "I thought you were asleep."

"I couldn't turn my brain off."

By the way she looked at me, she must've sensed there was something wrong.

"I didn't say so earlier, but at the Mélasse today, we didn't just see Mary Bradley," I said. "Arlen was there too."

"You're kidding. Arlen? Did you know he was there when you went over?"

"No," I said.

"Oh, Jer." Alicia put her hand between my shoulder blades and rubbed. "I knew something was wrong when I saw you, but I didn't think..." she trailed off. "What did you do?"

"Nothing substantive, and that's what I can't square up," I said. "Look at me, Alicia. I'm basically a private detective for Armstrong, going every which way across the Caribbean, butting heads with murderers, thieves and assassins, no matter who they are, but Arlen? I just—I know what he did. Even before DJ told us, I knew who the man was, yet when I saw him today, unexpectedly, it was as if he'd slipped past all my defenses, and I was turned into a helpless kid again."

She sat down beside me.

"Why can't I knock him on his ass and pull him into the FBI with a bloody nose? Am I too scared to do it?" I asked her.

"Arlen is practically family," she said. "No matter what he does, there may still be a part of you that loves him like a father."

"Part of me that is too scared to cross him, maybe," I said. "But I used to jump out of airplanes into the middle of nothing, alone. I used to go into active war zones, into hostile territory, alone. I've followed a company of Army Rangers into places where good men only lost their arms or their legs if they were lucky, but am I too scared to take down a man who's clearly the antithesis of everything good and decent? What does that say about me?"

I was rambling. She knew it and leaned her head on my shoulder. She wove her fingers between mine and I felt her pulse against my palm.

"How old were you in that picture?"

She was asking about the camping photo.

"Twelve," I said.

"I remember twelve. I used to idolize my grandmother—she was with the Red Cross in Korea. When she came back to the States, she kept nursing, but that wasn't all she did. She sang in a jazz band, much to my grandfather's disapproval, she smoked cigars, and she ran a successful campaign to be on the city council in Kokomo in 1992.

"Even after all that, when she'd go to a city event or speak at a dinner or something like that, she'd often get introduced as a nurse, which was a guaranteed way to piss her off."

"Grandma took me to this charity ball in 1998," she continued. "I remember everything about it, like the smell of all those perfumes, the way the punch tasted, and going out a couple days before to pick out this blue satin dress with gold accents from L.S. Ayers with grandma and my mom. Grandma wore this black dress with silver embroidery around the arms and neckline—it was gorgeous, and..."

I squeezed Alicia's hand and smiled at her.

"I'm getting off track," she said. "My grandmother spoke at that charity ball, but before she went on, the M.C. introduced her as a nurse. I remember her stomping up on stage, giving her speech, then stomping off.

"As they were clapping for her, I asked her why she was still upset. She looked me straight in the eyes and said, 'Allie, look at me. Am I in scrubs?'"

"I didn't understand until later that she was telling me people are complex, Jer," she said. "It's easy to think we can throw ourselves into a neat little box and live there all the time, but that's just not the way it is. You're not always a PJ, and you're not always a detective, and you're not always the kid that looked up to Arlen. But you're all those things sometimes and they can overlap."

She touched the picture. "It doesn't look like times were always bad with him."

"Not always," I said. "Not in the beginning."

"Not even now," she said softly. "Without his help, we never would've accomplished what we did in Puerto Rico, and Flor Ramos wouldn't be alive. The man has been in your life a long time. Other than Gene and me, he's the only person who's known you longer than a couple of years, and it's not easy to shake someone like that off."

"But I should shake him off," I said.

She slid her fingers out of mine, then brought her hand to my shoulder. When I looked Alicia's way, she kissed me, and my thoughts didn't feel so heavy on my head.

I turned back to the camping photo. Dad was taken by cancer, Jeff had been murdered, and life could never be this way again. I closed the album.

"So what did you find out about Albert René?"

"Let me show you." She led the way up to the saloon. Her laptop was open on the table, next to a half-finished meal of grilled red snapper, and DJ was lounging near the nav station.

"Sleep well?" he asked.

"Like a baby," I said.

Alicia slid onto the bench and opened her laptop.

"I didn't find much about Albert René, the man. He's kept a pretty low profile—no socials to speak of, no criminal history listed online, and I'm not sure he's ever held a mortgage, but I wouldn't be surprised to find a lot of St. Martin's records were lost to Irma." She turned the laptop toward me.

"But AIS data is easy to find, and *La Sirène II* has a pretty good set of it," she said. "Long story short—the boat was out at sea the night Billy Pearce was murdered."

I put my hands on the table, getting a closer look at the screen. The boat's automatic identification system, which uses VHF radio waves to transmit its location to other ships or shore receivers, left no doubt.

"You checked against the date listed in the police report?" I asked.

She tilted her head. "Jerry..."

"Right," I said and crossed my arms. "Well, this might not be as exonerating as it appears. René has a crew on that boat, and any one of them could've taken it out while he was back on St. Martin, carving filets off Billy Pearce. René's boat being out to sea might be a constructed alibi," I said.

"One man knows he's gonna kill another," DJ said, "so he comes up with a cover story. I can see that, but how do we—"

A knock on the side of the hull interrupted him.

By the sound, I knew it was from back near the starboard sugar scoop. We were all on the same side of the saloon, so whoever it was couldn't see us through the sliding door and windows aft.

"Did you two invite someone over and forget?" Alicia asked.

That seemed like a question meant for DJ and we both looked over at him, sitting at the navigation desk.

"Nuh-uh," he said. "Wasn't me. I ain't had a single chance to talk to any women out here. Jerry—you know. You were with me all day."

"You *did* have a single chance—what about the girls at the Mélasse?"

Alicia's eyes lit up.

"Shit, Dep, that was only a minute or two. I'm a fast charmer, but I ain't that fast."

"Hello?" The knock came again. "I can hear you in there," a young woman's voice called.

Just because it was a woman didn't mean the unexpected visitor wasn't dangerous, or even alone. I didn't recognize the voice, so I nodded at DJ. "Back of the chart drawer," I whispered, then jerked a thumb toward the starboard hull. "Go out the deck hatch in the hallway."

DJ knew I kept a 9mm Beretta semi-auto stashed in a secret recess in the chart drawer. The M-9 was the same all branches had issued until recently, so I knew he would be familiar with the weapon.

"On it," he said, grabbing the pistol, and disappearing down the port stairs.

I went to the sliding glass door and opened it, then stepped quickly out into the cockpit, surveying the dock area. There wasn't anyone else around, except the pretty girl from the market—the one who'd crashed into me. She didn't seem the type to come back for revenge.

"What are you doing here?" I asked, moving toward her.

"I wanted to—"

There was a thud on the dock, and she turned toward the sound, eyes going wide when she saw the pistol in DJ's hand. "Oh lawd!"

"Put it away, DJ," I said.

He slipped the gun into his pocket.

"What de hell was dat all about?" she asked nervously. "You gwon shoot me?"

"Forget you ever saw it," I said. "Would you like to come aboard?"

Alicia stepped out into the cockpit behind me. "Hello," she said. "Please excuse my husband and his friend. They may be Neanderthals at times, but they're both sweet once you get to know them."

"What you wanna shoot me for?" she asked, stepping over onto the sugar scoop and ascending the steps. "I run into you at the market, and you two gwon shoot me for dat?"

"Dep can be rude," DJ said, following her, "but he ain't *that* rude. We didn't recognize your voice."

Alicia led her into the saloon, but she kept glancing back at us. "You don' know my voice, so you point a gun at me?" she muttered. "You do dat when you walk down de street? Pointin' guns at strangers for saying mawnin' to ya?"

"Never," I said.

"Probably not," DJ added.

"All I come here to say is y'all don't have to waste yo time lookin' for me no more," she said. "Probably I shoulda stayed gone."

"Looking for *you*?" DJ asked.

"Yeah, lookin' for me," she said. "I'm Shara Bradley."

CHAPTER FIFTEEN

DJ and I were at a loss for words. Shara Bradley, here, in front of us? Things were rarely so easy this early on in an investigation. The kidnap victim never comes knocking on your door, or in this case, the side of the hull.

"You're Shara Bradley?" I asked. "Daughter of Mary Bradley?"

"Dat's de name of de woman who birthed me, yes."

I scratched the back of my head. "How did you find us? How did you know DJ and I were looking for you?"

"The first time I seen the two of you, you was comin' from Billy's church earlier today," she said. "Seemed to me you both were drunk men wanderin' around a neighborhood you had no business being in. Maybe you was lookin' for drugs or women, and I was of no mind to present meself to ya."

"Why were you going back to the church?" I asked.

She sighed and rubbed the knuckles on one hand with the knuckles on the other.

"I did a cowardly t'ing," she admitted, averting her eyes. "De night Billy met his end, I ran away."

"Oh, sweetie," Alicia said, but Shara looked right at me, as if I demanded she explain herself.

"I was scared out me mind, and I couldn't t'ink of not'ing but leaving de church as fast as me legs would take me. I know I'm a fool for leavin', and I shoulda phoned de police or at leas' gone back de nex' mornin' and talk to dem, but ever since dat night, all through me head, all I hear is dat terrible sound—"

She choked up. She didn't have to explain to me, but I needed her to confirm it.

"The sound Billy made," I said.

She nodded. "I never heard a man make a sound like dat in my life."

The poor kid. Even if she hadn't told us, all one had to do was look past those pretty brown eyes to see every muscle in her face was strained with terror and exhaustion. I imagined she hadn't slept much since the murder.

I walked slowly toward her and put a hand on her shoulder. "Nobody blames you for being scared," I said, as I guided her toward the bench seat around the table.

"I sure don't," DJ said.

"Not me," Alicia added.

"Why don't you sit down for a minute and talk to us, Shara?" I asked.

She accepted my invitation, sliding into the bench seat across the table from Alicia, who closed the lid on her laptop. Alicia reached across the table and Shara took her hand.

"I'm Alicia Snyder," she said. "And this is my husband, Jerry, and our friend DJ Martin. I'm sorry if they frightened you. I'm sure you've been through a lot already."

"Shame's hittin' me hard," Shara said. "I never been so scared in me whole life—I t'ought de duppy dat got Billy would get me too."

Nice. She believed in the "Murder-Ghost" theory too.

"A duppy?" DJ said. "Now, what makes you think it was a ghost that killed Billy?"

"I saw it move," she said. "I was in de office, watchin' Billy, and when de duppy came at him, I saw its robes movin' round like its body was wrapped in shadows."

"Billy was in the office with you?" I asked.

"Not when I saw it. At first, we was bot' in de back office when de lights cut out and de front door come crashin' open. I didn't know what it was at first, t'inkin' maybe it was a tree blown down by de wind and hit de power lines before crashin' in de street. Den, when I knew it was de front door bein' kicked in, I tought maybe some drunk come to sleep in the church overnight, but den I see Billy get his gun."

"What kind of gun?"

"Little one," she said, showing the approximate size with her hands. "Anyway, he tol' me to hide in de corner of his office while he went out into de chapel. Billy lef' de door cracked open, so I look out dere, and de chapel was dark as I ever seen a place, but I can just see Billy walking trough and nothing else. Until de duppy come out and—" She swallowed hard.

"It's alright, honey," Alicia said, stroking Shara's hand.

Shara tried to smile at her. "I hear dat sound, and I run."

"Perfectly understandable," I said. "But, if you feel you can tell us, could you explain why you went back to the church when we were there?"

She nodded and grimaced. "I felt guilty 'bout what happened to Billy. I was his woman, and when he need me de mos', I turn and run from him. Knowing I did, it weighed on me, so I went to an *oungan* I know since I was a little girl, Jacques Rosier, an' I tell him what I saw and I ask for his help."

"Go on, honey," DJ said in a coaxing tone.

"Mr. Jacques, de *oungan* I know, say I could stay in his home wid he and his wife and two grandbabies, so I did for a few days, just getting along as bes' I could. I talk to him and his wife all de time, and he keep tellin' me if it was a duppy dere at Billy's church, I got to cleanse de place so it don' claim nobody else. So I can keep it from turnin' Billy into a slave.

"When I feel brave enough to do de job," Shara said, "Mr. Jacques give me a bag with some herbs and instructions of what I suppose to do over dere, and I wen' on my way. Before you say it, I know I shoulda gone to de police firs', but dis felt like de bes' t'ing I could do for Billy, so I wen' to his church to do what Mr. Jacques tol' me. Dat's when I seen de gendarme goin' in, and yellin' at somebody, and I seen de two o' you leavin'."

Her story seemed plausible enough, but I still didn't understand why Shara had come to *Wayward* now, or how she knew we'd be at the Marigot Market.

"And you didn't come talk to us then because you thought we were a pair of drunks on the prowl?" I asked.

"Yes," she said. "But when I saw you askin' bout me at de market today, I believe it could be you work for Joseph Desir—he and Billy got in dis big, big argument just tree nights before, and I know Mr. Desir send people to beat up de ones who don' pay."

"But you still thought it was a ghost that killed Billy?"

"Because I saw it," she said. "It was just a shadow and can't no person move dat quiet and quick."

This ghost nonsense was getting tiresome. I wanted to press Shara on it, but Alicia had lectured me plenty of times before about being too demanding to people undergoing trauma—she liked to say that a gentler hand went far in the civilian world.

I looked to DJ for backup, but he just shrugged. How was I

162

supposed to solve a murder if my partner also believed a ghost did it?

"Anyway, I stay dere, hidin' in an old house nobody live in across de street, waitin' for de gendarme to go before I try to get into Billy's church, but he's dere a long time, and inside dis house is an old couch, and I ain't been gettin' much sleep dese past few days, so I t'ink I'm gonna lay me head down a few minutes while I wait.

"Well, I wake up, and hours gone by. I fell asleep too long. I look across de street and de gendarme is gone, so I get me bag with all de t'ings Mr. Jacques give me, and lookin' at de list of what he tol' me to do—you know, what order to burn what herb and all dat—when I realize de man ain't give me a bowl to burn it all in.

"So, I go down to de market, and I see de old woman sellin' bowls, and when I'm in dere lookin', I hear dis white man sayin' my name. I look over, and it's de same man who come out of Billy's church."

"You could've talked to me then," I said.

"I still ain't know who you are," she countered. "For all I know, you de duppy and you waitin' til night come to take me de way you did Billy. So, I decide I got to find out who you are, for sure.

She leaned over, reached into the bag slung over her shoulder, then slapped my wallet on the table.

"Oh shit," DJ said, laughing. "Man, Dep, she picked your pocket!"

I instinctively patted my jeans, as if that'd save me the embarrassment. Of course, my wallet wasn't there. I snatched it off the table, then checked through to make sure she didn't take anything.

"Jerry Snyder," Shara said, "322 Frenchman Bay Road, Saint Thomas, 00802, US Virgin Islands. You was a policeman yo'self in

California, and I know yo' family got money, but I didn't take nothin' from you, Mr. Jerry. I'm no t'ief."

I closed my wallet and tucked it in my pocket. "But you've got light fingers."

"Jerry..." Alicia didn't like me throwing accusations at Shara. "She's been through a lot."

"I know you saw my address on my license, but how'd you find out I was a cop?"

"I Googled yo name."

Clever kid.

"Honey, have you eaten today?" Alicia asked Shara. "Do you want to take a shower or just lie down for a bit?"

Shara's eyes danced between mine and Alicia's. "I ain't had a t'ing to eat all day."

"I got it," DJ said, rising up from the nav console. "Lemme rustle up some grub. 'Bout time I boiled some of this stuff Noubon gave me, anyway."

He got to work, pulling dishes from the galley cabinets, and hunting around in the fridge.

"So how are you holding up?" Alicia asked.

"I'm okay," Shara said pretty unconvincingly. "Mr. Jacques and his wife done a lot for me dese last few days, but I been puttin' too much on dem. Not only de food and a place to sleep, but all de udduh support dey give me."

"Emotional support," Alicia said.

"I been so tired."

"After being through all you've been through, it's normal to feel worn out."

"I know," she said. "And I know you folk probably t'ink I lost me mind, talking about ghosts and all dat, but I know what I saw."

164

"So, you could see more than just Billy in the chapel?" I asked. "I thought you said it was dark inside."

"He shot his gun," she said. "When he did, de whole room light up and I saw de mon like a shadow, so long and t'in, and I swear he be wearin' loose, tattered clothes, like he clawed out his grave. And I saw he only had one leg."

DJ perked up.

"One leg?" he asked. His hands were working on something below the counter, and even without seeing, I knew he was taking his prosthetic leg off. He held it up for Shara. "Like this?"

She gasped and crossed herself.

"Cut it out, DJ," I said.

He smiled at me as he fitted his leg back over his stump. "I'm just messing with you, Shara. Anyway, some here might be skeptics, but I believe what you're saying. I know a thing or two about ghosts."

"You do?"

"Sure, honey," he said, taking a piece of grilled chicken out of a Tupperware container and dropping it on a plate. "Shit, I'm part ghost myself."

"No," I said firmly. "You're not."

"You don't know what I felt," he said, and I got a feeling another of DJ's ranting tangents, or *rantgents* as I called them, was coming. He often took off on a meandering dialogue that had nothing to do with the case.

"Just because you don't want to believe it don't mean it didn't happen, Dep."

"A phantom itch in your leg isn't a ghost, it's your brain misfiring," I said, knowing as I said it that I should have just ignored him. "And to address the theory you were hammering out earlier today: there aren't any itchy ghosts wandering the world, looking for a good scratch. Can we get back to the case here?"

Alicia shifted on the bench, turning to DJ and arching an eyebrow. "Itchy ghosts?"

I threw my hands up in exasperation. "For the love of... Don't encourage him!"

"Allie, darling, your husband is taking my first-hand research out of context," he said, as he popped the chicken in the microwave and set the timer. "If my leg ain't a ghost, it's about as damned near close to one as a thing can get. I mean, it checks all the boxes, right? Suddenly lost in a time of war, thrown into a burn pit, and probably dug up by some oil contractor looking for a good well. Shit man, ain't you ever seen *Poltergeist*?"

"That was a movie, and they dug up an Indian burial ground. Was your leg part Indian?"

Shara was looking from me to DJ and Alicia in bewilderment.

"Give him a minute," I whispered, as DJ worked in the kitchen. "It's how things work in DJ's world sometimes."

"He cracked," she whispered back.

"My great-aunt used to claim my great-grandma was half Apache, but she also thought Eisenhower was half-alien," DJ said, as the microwave timer beeped. He turned around, scooped the plate out and set it on the counter. "But tell me this: if my itch ain't some kind of spiritual apparition, why did it respond to spiritual healing? Aspirin don't kill cancer."

"The only explanation is that it's all in your head!" I said irritably. "Can we get back to the case?"

"That the best you can come up with?" he asked. "Perception is reality, man. Don't matter if I'm taking a pill or listenin' to the right kind of hum, my brain does what it does, and The Buddha healed me all the same."

Oh, great. Now DJ was taking up Buddhism. I'm sure he'd be able to deliver an enlightening sermon on how all life was suffering just before popping his leg off and convincing some kid he'd been maimed by a land shark.

"The Buddha?" I asked, cringing as the words came out.

"That's what they called the man," DJ replied, holding a fork and knife in his hands and cutting Shara's chicken into little pieces like she was a toddler.

I knew the real reason why even if DJ didn't. He didn't know the girl at all and wasn't about to put anything in her hands that could be used as a weapon. But in his mind, he was a doting father figure.

"Now, I know you ain't given to faith the way some people are, Dep," he launched in again, as he continued cutting. "And for a while there, I wasn't either, until The Buddha sat me down and showed me how to unlock the inside of my own mind, and in doing so, the dude changed my life for the better. I can't swear to understand why it happened or how he did it, but it happened, and he did it, and the next chance I get, I'm gonna track that man down and thank him properly."

"It was a duppy," Shara said softly. "I saw it. It move all obzocky, like it only had one leg, but nobody told it 'bout dat."

"What do you mean?" Alicia asked, leaning closer.

"De duppy walked like he leg was out of joint, ya know? Like de t'ing ain't right."

"So, he wore a prosthetic like Patty here?" DJ asked, lifting his pant leg.

Shara looked up at him, her eyes welling. "I dunno, sir," she said, her lips trembling. "Him walk in a frightful way, like he ain't know how to do it with two legs—like he forgot." She shut her eyes tightly. "I don't like to t'ink on it."

167

CHAPTER SIXTEEN

I ignored DJ's statement that he'd met a man who'd been dead two millennia and concentrated on what Shara had just said. She was an eyewitness to the murder and was not only claiming it was a ghost who did the deed, but one with a bad limp.

"You're saying you saw a ghost walking strangely, as if its leg were broken?" I asked.

"I said it," Shara looked me in the eye.

"You said it," I agreed. "Do you understand this story has layers of improbability stacked one on another?"

"I never believe in no duppy till I seen one," she said. "I ain't crazy."

"I think I'm gettin' it now," DJ said. "Overlappin' truths and all that, because it's me with a phantom leg and a phantom with a bad leg—they call that synchronicity, Dep. A lot of good-brained philosophers spent a lot of their good time trying to figure out what synchronicity really means, you know? Like, on a deeper level? The Buddha told me something about that, and, man, next time I see him, he's gettin' a big handshake."

"You won't be able to do that," I said, unable to resist any longer.

"Will too."

"DJ, you were conned," I said.

He slapped the knife and fork on the counter, looking at me, flabbergasted and a touch wounded.

"The Buddha has been dead for something like twenty-five hundred years," I said.

He shook his head and laughed, then came around and slid Shara's plate of cut chicken in front of her. "You think I'm some kinda goddamned ignorant redneck, that I believe I saw *the* Buddha."

"Those were your words."

"No, man—see this is the crux of your problem, ain't it? You got ears, but you can't hear. I didn't say the man was *the* Buddha, I said he was 'The Buddha.'"

He went back to the galley and got Alicia's electric tea kettle out.

I looked at my wife. "Am I hallucinating? Did he not just say the same name twice?"

She shrugged and rolled her eyes. Smartly, she wanted to stay out of it. And secretly, I think she enjoyed DJ's verbal antics.

"So how did The Buddha unlock your mind?" I asked. "Did he sit you under a tree and make you stay there until your leg-ghost left out of boredom?"

"Now you're bein' disrespectful and condescendin'," DJ said as he filled the kettle. "The man used healing bowls."

"And what was in these bowls? More mystery powder like Noubon gave you?" I nodded toward the small baggie on the counter.

"Nothing in them at all, man. They were sound bowls."

"Sound bowls? Like, uncracked bowls?" I asked. "I figured when you said 'bowl,' The Buddha would be courteous enough to use bowls that were in one piece."

170

"Man, you're being obtuse."

"Nice five-dollar word. Very impressive stuff, DJ."

"Why's he got to get so mean when he feels cornered?" DJ asked Alicia. "Why's he feel cornered at all?"

"Jerry..." Alicia sighed.

I turned toward Shara. "You were describing what you saw in the sanctuary from the muzzle flash of Billy's gun," I said, steering the ship back on course. "That was the only light in the room?"

She turned her attention back to me. "De lights was off, but some come trough de windows in front."

"Good, good," I said. "I know this might be scary, but I want you to close your eyes and try to remember what you saw. Anything silhouetted by the outside lights?"

"Sound bowls make a sound," DJ muttered. When I glared at him, he just shrugged, ignored me, and continued. "It's like music, man. They're these pretty little bowls and you rub the rim of the bowl with a big fat stick that's like twice as big as a Ma Deuce round, and when you do that, it makes a sound. When it makes the sound, I'm telling you it really vibrates down in here." He thumped his chest with a fist. "You can feel it gettin' in your ears and rattling all the way through your body and soul."

"Ignore him," I whispered to Shara. "Think back. Anything you might've seen could help."

"Some of these sounds are good for your heart," DJ continued, unabated, as he paced the floor. "I don't understand it all... Some other sounds soothe the mind, and some help you get over being sick—different bowls treat whatever's ailing ya'. The stuff's real, man. The Buddha even gave me a bowl."

"No, it's not real."

"Jerry needs a heart-healing bowl, big time," Alicia said,

grinning and egging him on.

"I think I'm fine." A note of defensiveness crept into my voice.

"Oh, now, Allie, don't go turning on the man, or we'll lose him for good."

"What's the harm?" Alicia asked, then turned to face him. "You brought the bowl, right, DJ?"

"Yeah, it's in my kit in the stateroom."

I grumbled.

"I'm tellin' you, man, that bowl down there would do you some wonders," DJ said as he poured steaming hot water into a coffee mug. "It's a head bowl, helps me calm my mind and all that, and I know that ain't exactly what you need, but, shit, every little bit helps, right? I mean, I know I'm stressed out with all this stuff, so you got to be feelin' it just a little bit."

He dropped a pinch of Noubon's green powder directly into the steaming cup and walked toward the table. "If you wanna meet me out in the cockpit before we sack out, I'll give you a little demonstration with incense and all that, and I swear to you, Dep, it's gonna blow your mind. Really, what you got to lose?"

My sanity? My sense of self? DJ wasn't exactly Wavy Gravy now, but compared to a year ago, he seemed like a completely different person. I didn't even want to dip my toes into whatever psychic waters he was swimming in, because I didn't want to open my mind so utterly and irreversibly that I had no way to keep out kooky things like believing in ghosts.

"I'm glad you're doing better," I said. "But that's a 'no thanks' for me."

"You sure, man? I got this great incense I'm gonna light up, and I can already feel Noubon's tea, just, like, relaxing me. The good vibes are already wrapping me up." He nodded toward Shara. "If you wanna join me, kid, you're welcome to. Might help you sleep a little better. You can drink some of this stuff that came from our *oungan*."

Our *oungan*, is it? I didn't know if I took more exception that DJ claimed a Vodou priest, or that he lumped me in with him.

She shook her head, mid-chew. "No, thank you."

"What's in that cup, anyway?" Alicia asked, trying to peer over the rim as DJ took a sip.

"Pierre Noubon gave it to me. Said it'd heal my head and help me get to sleep better." He looked to Shara again. "You know that guy? Noubon?"

"No," she answered.

"If you want a second opinion about that duppy you saw, we can take you to him," he offered, at least getting partly back on track. "I was thinking about going to him tomorrow, you know, just getting a cleansing or something like that to keep my spirituality fresh, because, man, after a day like me and Dep had, I wanna make sure I don't have any psychic baggage hanging over me, you know?"

"I really can't," Shara said.

"She doesn't want to, DJ," I said, sidestepping to Shara's end of the table. I put my hand on her shoulder and, looking down at her, said, "You don't have to do anything you don't want."

I noticed the doodles drawn on her jeans—hearts, flowers, little diamonds. They were the same as the stuff drawn in the margins of Billy Pearce's accounting book, which reminded me I hadn't asked about it.

"Shara," I said softly, "when DJ and I went into the back office, we saw a ledger of accounts sitting on Billy's desk."

She seemed to sense the tack I was taking and froze up.

"There are quite a few little scribbles in there like you've got on your jeans. Were you helping Billy do his books?"

"Yes," she said in a mousey voice. Her hand was trembling, so she dropped her fork and looked up at me, the whites of her eyes threatening to overrun her pupils.

"You're not in trouble," I assured her. "We're not the police."

"Hell no, we ain't," DJ said.

"We just want to get a sense of what was going on at the church, and maybe that'll help me and DJ figure out who did what."

"If you say."

"Do you know who Albert René is?" I asked.

She played with her fork, rolling it between her knuckles, keeping her eyes down. "I—well, I don't know him personally, but I know of de man."

"Did you know his mother was a member of Billy's church?"

"I t'ink I heard of a Miz René, but knowin' people's names was somethin' Billy did, not me."

"That's alright," I said. "I only brought her up because we heard a rumor that she made a large donation to the church before she passed, and that her son, Albert, was not pleased about it."

She stopped playing with the fork but said nothing.

"Shara?" I asked. "Do you know something about that?"

"I don't know de man," she said, looking at all three of us in turn. "I know Billy sometimes bothered people 'round de island, but he was a good man dat wanted to do good t'ings for lots of people here. He was puttin' all de money he collected into an account so he could build a newer, bigger church and bring de message to all de folk here dat need hope and when he do it, he was gwon change St. Martin for de better."

The rolls of cash in the vent said something totally different. At least in my mind. Judging by DJ's expression, he was thinking the same thing.

174

"How long you know that man?" he asked Shara.

"About a year, if I had to say."

"You just run into him somewhere and he said, 'How do?' or did your meeting happen another way?"

"A friend of mine bring me to Billy's church a couple times, and I see wid me own eyes how kind and generous he was to de people, helpin' dem get trough deir problems, always findin' de time to listen and to comfort and to offer advice on all de little t'ings people get into.

"One day after service, when I been goin' dere a mont' or so, he come up to me and say he knew by de sight of me dat I had trouble at home. When I ask him how he could know such a t'ing, he told me how his fadduh would hold him down on his bed and whip him wid his belt, and how when he looked at himself in de mirror, he looked just like I looked den."

"Does your mother hurt you?" I asked.

"She don' lay hands on me," Shara said. "She does uddah t'ings dough—hurtin' me widout touchin' me, tellin' me what she t'ink I should be doin' and where I should be goin' and how I'm never gwon be doin' not'ing good wid my life and how it all be a waste for me."

When I thought about it, Mary Bradley did seem oddly disconnected when we spoke to her at the Mélasse.

"What I'm telling ya is dis—Billy connected wit me. He saw me, he show me dat I matter and could do whatever it was I want to do, if I set meself upon it. I know he wasn't a perfect man, but he was a good man to me, and dat's what I cared about."

She went quiet for a moment, as if deciding what to say or not say next. "I don' think he deserve to be killed or cursed."

"Is that what the duppy was? A curse?" DJ asked. "Who cursed him?"

"Hard to know, truly," she said. "Me and Billy find all kinds of curses on de church—t'ings written in chalk and salt on the outside, grave dirt left on de doorstep, old womens' hair. None of dose did not'ing to us but—" she closed her eyes tightly and shuddered.

"That's alright now," DJ said. "You take your time and you talk when you're ready to talk."

She nodded and took a deep breath.

"Billy knew how t'ings work. He wasn't a Vodouist, but he understood dere is power in de t'ings *oungans* and *manbos* do, and he knew dey hadda be treated with caution. We'd always have someone out to cleanse de church after we found a curse, but de last time, when somebody lef' a black *govi* jar sittin' in front of de door, Billy took it, and it called de duppy to him."

"Took it where?" I asked.

DJ and Alicia looked at me in unison.

"My opinion about murderous ghosts hasn't changed, but this jar might prove to be useful evidence," I said. "Where can we find it and what does it look like, Shara?"

"It was a black jar with white *veve* painted on de outside dat I nevuh seen before. Really, it was a pretty t'ing, dough it was terrible. Billy took it inside, sayin' he was gwon use it against whoever put it dere. I t'ought he was jus' messin' 'round—he talk like dat sometimes, you know, sayin' t'ings to get a reaction from me, teasin' me. But den I found dat *govi* in his desk draw, and I knew—"

Suddenly she broke down. Shara buried her face in her hands and wailed while I silently pleaded with Alicia for help.

She moved over next to Shara, putting an arm around her and letting the girl cry into her shoulder while she stroked the top of her head and gently shushed her.

DJ passed a box of tissues over while I stood there, as useful as toes on a fish.

"I showed him de *govi*," Shara finally said. "De night Billy was killed, I opened de draw and he put eyes on de *govi*. I know dat angered de duppy; I brought de t'ing to him. De curse came out 'cause of what I did."

"No, no, no," Alicia said softly as she rocked Shara. "It wasn't your fault, sweetie."

"Not at all," I said. "Curses are just fairy tales."

Alicia looked at me like I'd said the absolute wrong thing.

"Come talk to me a minute, Dep," DJ said, motioning toward the saloon door.

I followed him out to the cockpit and slid the heavy glass door closed. The night air was crisp, and a light wind brought many scents down from the town, the smell of flowers mixed with baked bread. It was dark, but still early. Looking west, out of the bay, there was a thin crescent moon lying almost on the horizon. It looked like a big, puffy spinnaker.

"We should go back to the church," DJ said. "We wanted to drop a GPS on that money in the vent, anyway, right? Maybe we get Noubon, take him with us, and have him do the cleansing Shara was gonna do and he can look at the *govi*."

"GPS in the money?" I asked. "Sure. But the rest isn't worth our time."

"Man, you gotta get outside your own head sometimes," DJ admonished. "Remember what I said about perception being reality? Shara looks at that *govi*, and she knows it's real! Can't ya see that? If we don't do it, she's gonna head to that church and do her cleansing thing, and she ain't in no state to go there and do that—I mean, shit, I know you don't believe in the duppy, but you got to think there's a chance whoever killed Billy Pearce might go back to the church to find Shara."

He was right. St. Martin wasn't a big island, and if the murderer were even somewhat aware that a witness was running around, he'd probably orbit around Billy's church, looking for Shara.

"And checkin' into the *govi* thing ain't a waste of our time; I know you're picking up that Shara ain't telling us the whole truth, not to mention what Noubon's old man said."

"Crazy, blind old man aside," I said, "you're right that we should verify Shara's story."

"Right. So, we do her this little favor. We can earn her trust and I bet she knows all sorts of things about this island and about that man Albert René that'll help us figure out what happened to Billy Pearce."

I had to admit, DJ was correct about the utility in indulging this nonsense. More information about Albert René would be nice, and maybe Shara would tell me a thing or two about that priest in the market who almost had me ripped limb from limb.

DJ grinned. "I can see you're coming around. I just saw lightbulbs come on in both your eyes."

"Let's see if we can get Shara to stay on *Wayward*," I said. "We'll keep her safe, comfortable, and within arms' reach."

"Don't sound like the two of them care to be reunited, but we should call her mom and tell her we found Shara."

"It's the responsible thing to do," I said. "You're persuasive when you want to be, Dudley." I clapped him on the shoulder and slid open the saloon door.

"I told you *not* to use that name, man!"

Alicia and Shara were as we'd left them, though Shara was noticeably calmer. Now felt like a good time to propose a short stay at The *Wayward* Halfway House for At-risk Girls.

"Shara, are you going back to your *oungan,* Jacques, tonight?"

"No, I think he and his wife have shown me enough hospitality for now."

Perfect.

"If you're amenable to it, we'd like you to stay with us on *Wayward* for a time. You'll get your own private stateroom and head in the port hull, and we can arrange to pick up some clothes and other necessities for you, as needed. Here, you'll be safe, clean, dry, and well-fed, and as a throw-in, DJ and I will take care of that whole cleansing business at Billy's church. What do you think?"

"Well," she said, uncoupling herself from Alicia, "it's a very generous offer, Mr. Jerry, but I can't stay here."

"Of course you can," Alicia chimed in. "*Wayward* has five staterooms and can sleep twelve, if we lower this table, so we've got the accommodations. With just four people, we'd hardly see each other."

She smiled at my wife, then looked up at me. "I know dere is room, Mr. Jerry, but I made a promise to stay wid my friend, Ines. Her parents got a house not far from here on Hameau du Pon. I don't want dem worrying 'bout me."

I would've felt better keeping an eye on her, but what was I going to do? Tie her up?

"You can come back here any time you like," I said. "I'm going to give you my contact information, and I'd appreciate yours. Do you know Ines's address?"

"No, Mr. Jerry," she said. "But I can describe de place for you and tell you where to find it."

"Good," I said. "Let's make sure we keep in touch."

CHAPTER SEVENTEEN

I called Mary Bradley as soon as I was sure Shara had stepped off *Wayward*. She answered on the third ring, and I tapped the speaker icon, then placed it on the settee table between me and DJ.

"Ms. Bradley," I said, "It's Jerry Snyder. I'm relieved to be able to tell you Shara is alive and well."

"Who?" she asked.

"Jerry Snyder," I replied. "My partner, DJ Martin, and I talked to you early this afternoon at the Mélasse."

"Ohhh, yes, you boys." She yawned.

"If we woke you up, you have my apologies," I said. "I normally wouldn't call you this late, but we've just made contact with Shara and can confirm she's safe. Turns out she's been staying with your *oungan*, Jacques, since the night of the incident."

"Jacques who?" Mary asked.

"Rosier," I said. How could she not know who I was talking about? DJ appeared to be thinking the same thing as I.

"Yes, Jacques Rosier—de *oungan*. I remember de man now," she said. "De stress is gettin' to me, I t'ink—I'm havin' trouble rememberin' t'ings, but in trut' I haven't gone to him much. Shara was closer to de man. So sorry."

"Ain't nothing to apologize for," DJ said, leaning closer toward my phone. "You been through a lot, Miss Mary, and Dep and I hope knowing that your baby girl is okay is gonna put your mind at ease. The truth of it is, Shara seemed a little frayed herself, and from the way she tells it, seems like she's been through the wringer too. We fed her, and offered her a place to stay on *Wayward*, but she says she's gonna stay with her friend Ines."

"She just left our boat," I added. "We told her to call you when she's settled in."

"Very kind of you two boys, but seems Shara's been alive and well and not called once since she disappeared, so I t'ink she ain't gwon change tonight."

"Whether she does or not, we're gonna keep a close eye on her," DJ said. "We plan on stopping by Ines's house regularly. Ain't that right, Dep?"

"Our job demands we make sure she's safe—we feel she's a key eye-witness in what happened to Billy Pearce," I said.

"She may be," Mary said, "and I t'ank you for watchin' over Shara, but de way she is, you be lucky if even one in ten of the t'ings she musta tol' you be true. De girl enjoy keepin' secrets from people."

"It appeared that way to us as well," I said.

"What else she tell you?" Mary asked. "She swear up and down I been screamin' at her? Tellin' her she a nothin' girl with no good in her head?"

"She said something to that effect."

"Shara up to de same old tricks, playin' off de kindness of good-natured strangers as it suit her, 'xactly like Billy. I wish I could say he put dat in her, but I know my little girl better dan dat, and she been taking advantage of tender-hearted folk long as I can remember.

"I only blame myself for not raising her better dan all dat. I show her all de love a little girl need, and I work dese fingers to de bone, tryin' to give de best to her. I don' know where I go wrong."

I had no wisdom to offer Mary, except that I felt it wiser not to have children, because of exactly what she was describing with Shara.

"Still, it good to know my girl is breathin'," Mary said. "T'ank you bot' for all you done to help me and find Shara."

"Just doing our jobs," I said.

"All de same, you have my gratitude. If dere's anyt'ing else I can do to help you find de trut', you jus' ring me up."

Mary ended the call.

"How much you think Shara lied to us?" DJ asked me.

"I don't believe it was all fake, but of what she told us, how are we to know the truths from the lies?"

"She was a good pickpocket, too," DJ said. "That ain't something you learn in church. And maybe she didn't want to stay here tonight because she's up to something she don't want us seeing."

That possibility existed. But before DJ or I could hash out anything else, Alicia came running up the starboard hull staircase into the saloon.

"Jerry, I just found something very interesting," she said.

"Did René confess to the murder in a Twitter post?" DJ asked.

"We're not that lucky." She set the laptop on the table in front of me. On the screen was a digital map showing the waters approximately forty miles around St. Martin, which included Anguilla to the north and St. Barts to the southeast.

"But we're a little lucky," she continued with a knowing smile. "I've been going over the AIS logs left by René, and I've noticed a very interesting pattern." She pointed at a group of lines that emanated out of Baie de Marigot, then turned in all available directions—south, north, and west. There were dozens of them, and each ended up in its own destination somewhere out in the Caribbean. "These are the voyages taken by *La Sirène* over the last six months or so. They're pretty typical for what you'd expect from a fishing vessel operating out of St. Martin. Nothing suspicious, right?"

Alicia leaned over me and typed something into her computer, then zoomed the map in.

The charts changed. Instead of going out to sea, each line bent northward out of Baie de Marigot, closely following the coast of St. Martin, and each tracked course stopped about a mile into the voyage.

"Is René turning off his boat's AIS transponder?" I asked.

"Looks like it," she said. "I can't imagine they'd have the transponder turn off a dozen or more times in almost the exact same spot, then magically turn on again when they were heading back to Marigot Bay."

I looked up to my wife. "Why would they do that?"

"Could be they're hiding good fishing spots," DJ said. "I know a captain or two who turned off his boat's transponder after homing in on a good spot, just to keep people from pulling up the data the same way we did."

"Aren't the waters on the northeast end of the island protected?" I asked Alicia.

"I think that's right." She sat down on the bench opposite me and spun her laptop toward her, looking it up. "Yep. There's a turtle reserve between St. Martin and a little island off the northeast coast called Isle Tintamarre. Fishing there is illegal."

"If René got cleaned out by Billy Pearce," DJ said, "I bet he's cutting all kinds of corners to make an extra buck or two whenever he can."

"The possibility exists of this being something more serious," I said. "But even if it is illegal fishing, we can use evidence of that crime to compel more information from Albert René."

"So how do we gather evidence?" DJ motioned at the laptop. "Near as I can tell, all we got is a couple ideas with no proof."

"We can get proof. All we have to do is keep tabs on *La Sirène*," I said. "We'll put a location beacon on it. Knowing exactly where she goes is the first step to greater things."

I hopped out of my chair and headed for the starboard hull.

"How you gonna put a tracker on René's boat?" DJ asked, following me down.

"It's dark out," I said. "All I need is the tracker, a snorkel, and some fins to put me on my way."

"Hope you need swim trunks too," DJ said.

I gave DJ an annoyed look.

"Hey, man, it's after dark in the Caribbean—don't let me yuck your yum."

Ignoring him, I went to the bow stateroom, which we'd converted into storage. In the hanging locker, behind a false back, I had a secret compartment with a couple toys like a long gun, some ammunition, and Tannerite kept in a watertight case to keep humidity out. I pulled it out and set it on the bed, getting at the small box in the very back of the compartment—one of two 4G tracking devices with GPS in my possession.

"Is that little toy seaworthy, Dep?" DJ asked, nodding at the tracker.

"We charge this thing up and it can sit passively on *La Sirène's* hull for a hundred and forty days," I said. "I'll put it up near the pulpit, where it should get a decent sat signal. But I suspect René's keeping his boat close to shore, so it should pick up the cell towers. And it's waterproof."

DJ took the box from me and read the back.

"So, we just sit at a computer and watch him go?"

"No need," I said. "It automatically logs for us. All we do is check the data at our leisure."

"Leisure," he said. "Leisure sounds good."

DJ took the tracker topside and plugged it in to let it charge. We decided I'd do the swimming while DJ acted as a lookout with a pair of night-vision binoculars on *Wayward's* bow. It was late, marina traffic was sparse, and René had probably gone to sleep hours ago, but we were better safe than sorry.

About an hour before midnight, the tracker's battery read full, so I kitted up and got ready. In addition to the GPS, my fins, and, yes, a pair of swim trunks, I donned a full-face mask with a top snorkel and built-in comms.

Sitting on *Wayward's* swim platform, my legs dangling in the dark, warm waters, we did a radio check. DJ was somewhere on the bow, out of sight, with a transceiver cable hanging into the water.

I wet my fingers and touched them to the circuit on the outside of the radio attached to my full-face mask. Then, with my other hand, I held the push-to-talk button on the unit. A tone sounded in my ears, signaling my radio was transmitting.

"Jerry Snyder," I said, identifying myself before speaking over the channel, per manufacturer recommendation. "This is a radio test, over."

A second after I let go of the button, another tone sounded, signifying an incoming transmission from DJ.

"This is DJ Martin, bringing you scuba tunes live. Your compadre and number one buddy, making sure you don't get your head taken off by the prop of a midnight booze cruise."

My thumb punched the push-to-talk button.

"Jerry Snyder," I said slowly into the mask, enunciating my name. "End each transmission with over, over."

I checked the small bag fastened around my torso to make sure it wouldn't slip off as soon as I slid into the water. I was also wearing a weight belt with a pouch containing four pounds of lead shot. That would keep my body down and my fins below the surface, compensating for the buoyancy of the dive skin and mask.

The message tone sounded in my ears once more.

"That's a 10-4, Dep buddy," DJ said. "My NV binos are up and running, and the bay's clear by visual. But even these things can't see a narco sub or a shark. Over, over."

I wished DJ would take our comms more seriously.

Alicia tapped me on the shoulder. When I turned around, she kissed her fingers and touched the top of my head.

"Be careful," she said.

I gave her the thumbs up.

"Make your course two-two-zero, Dep-a-roonie," DJ said.

"Jerry Snyder," I said into the radio. "Don't call me that. Over." I twisted the dial on my wrist-mounted compass.

"Oh, you don't like it when I call you that name? Shit, man, that really sucks for you," DJ said. "You're clear to shove off."

"Roger that. Shoving off. Over." I took a breath, pushed away from the swim platform, and engulfed myself in the water. I'd done night dives off *Wayward* before, both with scuba equipment and

187

without, but never in complete darkness with no flashlight or even a lume stick. The last time I'd done something like this was PJ training back in Florida a number of years ago, and just like during those nights spent training, a preternatural sense of calm washed over me.

I was focused; I was ready to complete my mission.

I turned toward *Wayward*, orienting myself, then turned southwest, looking across the hexagonal dock in this small partition of Marigot Bay. Other vessels' lights shone like streetlamps in the dark, open water. The lighted areas attracted small fish like moths to a porchlight. One boat, directly across the hexagon from *Wayward*, had pulled in a pretty good crowd of bait fish, and no sooner had I noticed than a barracuda noticed too. It streaked into the light from the darkness below, then shot back downward like a flash of electricity.

"How's it look down there, Jerry Snyder?" DJ asked. "See Davy Jones anywhere nearby? Over, over."

"Not yet," I answered. "I'm getting underway, over."

I started kicking slowly, in long arcs, careful not to break the surface of the water with splashing or the top of my head. With the six pounds of weight, my buoyancy was perfectly neutral, and I could control the minimal rise and fall of my body with my breathing. Stealth was key here, and no matter how long it took me to swim the two-hundred-yard gap between *Wayward* and *La Sirène*, I would do everything in my power to remain undetectable.

"Can't see hide nor hair of you, Dep. What's your position?"

"I'd estimate I'm ten yards off *Wayward's* bow, over."

"DJ Martin–Man, I know where to look, and I can't even see your snorkel, over," he said.

"How's the target?" I asked

188

"From here, it looks like she's buttoned up for the night and probably full of snoozing sailors," he said, referring to *La Sirène*. "You know, Dep, it just occurred to me that I've got you as a captive audience."

"DJ, no."

"Wait—I'm confused," DJ said. "Is DJ talkin' now, or is this Jerry?"

"Jerry Snyder," I said. "Keep the comms clear, over."

"I'll give that recommendation a good think," he said. "Seems to me that so long as this operation of ours maintains its current course, I can say pretty much whatever pleases me right now, my friend, and there ain't a whole lot of shit you can do about it, over, over."

"Focus, DJ."

"I'm focused as a gambler at a roulette wheel," he said. "You know, I been reading books in my quiet hours and watching these videos on YouTube, and I got a few half-formed ideas on metaphysics that I thought I could use to tickle your brain."

I fought the urge to scream at him—not that my scream would be anything but garbled noise through the radio. I just had to grin and bear it, so I set my attention on long, slow kicks and maintaining a steady rhythm of breathing, picturing the water passing around my body as I glided through, pushed by my fins.

"There's this one guy," DJ said. "Guy named Sadhguru. You ever heard of him? Over, over."

I crossed out of the smaller pocket of bay around the hexagonal dock and into the larger part of Baie de Marigot, where vessels were tied to mooring balls on chains that extended downward, out of the thin light from the surface and into total darkness.

"Anyway, he's this Indian guy, got a real interesting way of talking, got all these temples and shit across the world—real neat guy, all in all."

"Target sitrep?" I asked, trying to get him off it.

"I think I hear somebody listening to showtunes down the way," DJ said. "But you know what this guy Sadhguru says?"

"Yep," I said. "Over."

"No, you don't," DJ said. "He's got this intro meditation video on YouTube I been watching to help me sleep at night, and while he's doing his breathing, he repeats this mantra to himself: 'I am not my mind, I am not my body,' and you know, this whole thing about phantom itches and duppies really got me feeling like I'm closer to that mantra more than ever. Maybe we're all born knowing we aren't flesh and blood and Freudian-type shit as much as we're kind of like air trapped in a bottle, and as the years go on, we start to forget we're the air, not the bottle. Get me?"

"Yup." I had my thumb squeezed so hard in my fist the barracudas must've heard the joint popping.

"I know all this duppy stuff ain't your bag, Dep, but you, like most of the rest of us, only see the bottles walking around, not the wind. But that don't mean the wind ain't there still."

As he talked, I began to hear a buzzing, grow louder.

"DJ, focus! Outboard!"

"What?" he asked. "You're not—shit! Dive, Jerry, dive!"

I inhaled deeply, kicked my feet up, and jackknifed my body downward. Water swirled across my back in an unnatural way, almost perpendicularly, which, I realized after a moment of panic, must've been a prop missing me by inches.

Now a few feet below the surface, I looked up at the underside of a small dinghy zipping away. Then, as the sound receded, I kicked

190

back to the surface. With just the top of my head and snorkel above water, I quickly cleared it.

"Dep?!" DJ yelled over my headset "Gimme a sitrep, man!"

"I'm fine, DJ!" I said, forcing myself not to scream at him through comms. I wished I could've cussed him out, but that probably would've come across as an indecipherable mess too. Instead, I simply said, "I'm unhurt."

"Shit, man, that's the best news I ever heard in my life," he said. "I'm sorry, Dep. I'll do better at shutting my yap and keeping a lookout."

Now you're telling me the best news I've heard all day, I thought, sinking my head below the surface and resuming the mission.

"You got a nice, clear approach," DJ said. "I'm real sorry about you almost getting a new haircut—that tender must've come out from behind one of the larger yachts out in the bay. I didn't see it until it was right on top of you, and I couldn't hear it at all."

Because you were talking to yourself the entire time.

"Probably one of them electric outboards," DJ said. "Those damned things are quieter than a mouse fart man, I swear."

DJ offered no further musings as I closed in on *La Sirène.* I was maybe three meters from the boat before I heard from him again.

"Freeze!" came his urgent voice over the headset.

I froze. I slowed my breathing, keeping only the snorkel sticking out of the water as my body hung weightless.

"Movement on the bow," he said after a couple of seconds. "But it's only a pelican."

With a few quick kicks, my hand touched the hull. "I'm there," I said.

"Still quiet aboard," he said. "But a light inside the cabin came on a few seconds ago. Probably somebody hitting the head."

191

"Moving toward the bow." I kept a hand on *La Sirène's* hull as I came up along the starboard side. At about seventy-five feet long, with a six-foot draft, she was larger than what one typically found in coastal Caribbean fishing operations, which generally consisted of one or two men working from a vessel that was seldom larger than a rowboat and powered by a small outboard. Most of those boats were completely open to the elements and lacked even a rudimentary interior space, never mind sleeping quarters like *La Sirène*.

"You're about five yards from the pulpit," DJ said. "No sign of anybody being aware of you."

I came to the bow and surfaced. There, I kicked slowly with my fins to keep my head up as I looked around. The dock pilings were just a few feet away and I couldn't see or hear anything there. The weight belt made me neutrally buoyant when my head was underwater, but with it above, I was negative and had to keep finning as I unzipped the pack slung across my chest. The only thing inside was the tracker, on which, in the darkness, I had to feel around for the button to activate. Once I found and pressed it, the faint green LED lit up, telling me it was on. The small light was invisible just a few feet away.

Then I peeled the adhesive backing off the tracker and stuck the thing on the underside of *La Sirène's* pulpit. The adhesive was waterproof and vibration-resistant and would stick to any surface. The thing weighed less than ten grams, so there was little chance it would fall off, even in rough seas.

"Signal check, DJ," I said quietly.

A few seconds passed, and through the steel hull, I heard a door slam.

"Connection's good," DJ said. "Get on back."

"Coming home." I started to sink down.

192

"Hold it!" DJ said.

Before I could even ask, I recognized the sound of Albert René's voice. He was on deck, agitated about something.

"René's topside, on his phone," DJ said. "Maintain silence and don't move."

He didn't have to tell me. I stayed there, under the pulpit, confident that the only way René would spot me was if he looked for me. Even then, he'd have to lean over the gunwales pretty far.

As he came closer, his deep, growling voice became more distinct.

"...they accused me of killing Billy Pearce!" he said. "How two men can come here and t'ink they can dig around me and my business while I sit around and wait—I'm not some fool."

"He's turning around," DJ said. "He's going aft. I think you can push off in a few seconds and he won't know you was even there."

Like hell I was just going to walk away from Albert René talking candidly about DJ and me. He was going to say something stupid, and I was going hear it. Keeping both hands on the hull of *La Sirène*, I gently kicked my feet and followed René toward the stern. I couldn't see him, but I could hear him.

"Dep, what the hell are you doing, man?" DJ shouted.

"Quiet DJ," I whispered. I didn't dare say more than that.

"No, no, I'm not going to simply stand still while these two men are running around." René was arguing with whomever was on the other side of the call. "'Cause they got no business asking about me. They're going to ask too much and where does that put us? How can I let them wreck everyt'ing we're trying to do?"

He paused while the other party offered a rebuttal.

"They asked me about Shara!" he shouted, and the participant on the other end of the call must've made a pretty convincing argument, because René answered in a much calmer tone, saying, "No, sir, I can be careful. This does not put our operation into danger. I will not let that happen. I can control—no, sir, there is no need for that. I'll get the job done—they won't be a concern much longer."

A door slammed.

"He's off-deck," DJ said. "Now get the hell out of there while you can, and while you're doing it, explain to me what was so goddamned compelling you risked getting caught?"

I slid beneath the surface of the water and moved slowly away from *La Sirène* and back toward *Wayward*.

"He talked about us," I said. "And Shara."

"Good things?" DJ asked.

"He's planning to kill us."

CHAPTER EIGHTEEN

Concerned about Shara's safety, I convinced DJ and Alicia to come with me over to her friend Ines's house on Hameau du Pon. According to Shara, it was a few houses in from the main street, which ran along the coast.

Seeing as it was after midnight, we had surprisingly little trouble nabbing a ride from one of the cars idling curbside at a nearby bar. It only took the guy three minutes to drop us off in front of Ines's house, which Shara had said would have a half-height concrete wall in front, painted powder blue.

We hopped out onto a quiet, residential street. Other than the car driving off, the only sound was the rustling of a trashcan next to the house, and I only knew it was there because a huge wharf rat jumped off the rim of the can and scurried away when it heard us walking toward the front door.

"Man, I bet Noubon couldn't breed enough cats to kill all the rats on this island if he had a hundred years," DJ said.

"Have you seen a lot so far?" Alicia asked.

"More than I ever thought I would."

Ahead, one of the windows in the narrow two-story house flickered with pale-blue light, a telltale sign of a television left on in a dark room. I pictured Shara sitting on the couch, unable to sleep.

I walked up the steps to the front door and knocked while DJ sat on the half wall, a few feet behind me, and Alicia waited next to him.

Nobody answered the first knock, so I did it again.

"The curtains just moved in that window," Alicia said. "Somebody's home."

I knocked a third time, and still no one came to the door.

"They're in there," Alicia said.

"Shara?" I called to the window. "Shara, it's Jerry—you need to come to the door."

"Maybe it's not her," DJ said.

"My name is Jerry Snyder and I'm a private investigator. I'm here with my partner DJ Martin and my wife Alicia."

"I'm not just his wife, I'm also an investigative partner," she said to the window.

"Yeah, definitely," DJ agreed.

"Shara Bradley told us she was staying here. She said her friend Ines lived here."

The front door squeaked open. I turned to see a teenage girl in her pajamas with her braided hair up in a bun on top of her head. She looked less than impressed to see the three of us there, knocking on her door in the middle of the night.

"What do you want with Shara?"

"You must be Ines," I said. "Can you go get Shara? Tell her she needs to pack all her stuff up and come to the door as quickly as she can."

"Shara isn't here," Ines said. "I haven't seen that girl in two weeks, at least."

"Two weeks?" I asked. "She isn't staying here?"

"Just me here," Ines said.

"Where are your parents?"

"Working. Momma is the bartender at a resort in Simpson Bay and Papa parks the cars. They got some big party going on there tonight, so they gonna be gone at least another two hours."

"And you haven't heard anything at all from Shara?" I asked. "Because I talked to her earlier tonight and she told us she was going to stay here."

Ines cocked her head. "I told you already."

"Do you have Shara's phone number?" I asked. "Can you call her?"

"I been calling Shara for days, but I guess she can't pick up her phone even once for me. I thought she was dead, but you say you seen her?"

"She talked to us today at our boat," Alicia said. "We were all very relieved to see that she was okay, but she told us she was going to be here."

Ines appeared equal parts hopeful that her friend was alive, and annoyed that Shara was avoiding her.

"Shara got to be hiding somewhere, then," she said. "You know all kinds of people got bad intentions for her boyfriend—I been telling her for months that man ain't no good and she never listened to no word I say. They were out to get Billy, I swear."

It appeared to me that Ines wasn't using "they" in a general sense but had someone particular in mind.

"Who was out to get him?" I asked, and that was enough to spook her.

She backed behind the door and tried to shut it, except she couldn't. DJ's leg hit it with a thump, fell into the open gap and stopped the door from closing.

"Ines, please," I said, putting my hand against the door.

"I don't know not'ing about not'ing." She was pushing on the door, apparently unaware of DJ's leg propping it open. "I got to go to bed!"

"Anything you can tell us might help," I said. "We're afraid that someone is going to hurt Shara—we've been all around the island today talking to people, and we know there's some kind of danger still out there."

She stopped trying to push the door closed, and then leaned out so that I could only see her eyes against the darkness behind her.

"You been around St. Martin?" she asked. "What you heard?"

I wasn't about to tell a teenage girl the details of our investigation. I pulled DJ's leg out from the door and tossed it back to him.

He caught it and called out to the girl. "Pierre Noubon said it was a duppy that killed Billy. Shara thought so too."

"A duppy?" she asked.

"Somebody left a *govi* at Billy's church," DJ said. "Shara thought that cursed the man."

"She know who did it?"

DJ shook his head.

"When you went 'round St. Martin today, anybody say anyt'ing to you about The Children of Ogun?" Ines asked him.

DJ and I exchanged a confused look. Ines picked up on it, opening the door the rest of the way, then coming out onto the stoop, next to me.

"People say The Children is a group of people taken over by evil *loa* that don't want to be seen—that don't talk to no *manbo* or *oungan* or nobody else unless they been chosen by Ogun," she said. "The Children do black magic deep underground in a place where the *loa* walk around like anybody else and The Children think Ogun's gonna

198

use them as instruments to bring his righteousness down on those they deem unworthy to be on St. Martin. They said he gonna rise out of the caves to scrub the whole island clean with his iron and his dogs and The Children are gonna dance by bloody cauldrons and eat the people they kill."

I rolled my eyes.

"I know how it all sound," she said. "I didn't believe it neither, but Shara said a year ago that The Children was threatening Billy, that they used to leave grave dirt on his front step, and they put bone dust under the trees across the street from his church, but I never trust a word she said because she's always making up stories about this and that, and everybody knows The Children ain't real. The Children just something people tell their little ones to scare 'em—like a man's dog run away because he left the gate open, but he just tell his babies that The Children take the dog back to Ogun while they all sleep. That kinda thing.

"I didn't believe none of it when Shara told me The Children been coming after her and Billy," Ines said. "Until one day about a month ago, she took me over to Billy's church."

Ines shivered and rubbed her arms. I hoped that signified the end of the ghost story and we could maybe get her to tell us where she thought Shara might be, but my hope was in vain.

"What'd you see?" DJ asked.

"Grave dirt on the doorstep." She swallowed a lump down her throat. "And they made *veve* outside the door, but none like I ever seen before, and it looked to me like they wrote it in ash, not chalk or salt or cornmeal, but ash.

"I was never scared of the ghost stories all the old folk tell, but for a reason I didn't understand, seeing it all there, right in front of my eyes, put a chill in me. I remember Shara opening the door and

199

turning around and looking at me like I been touched in the head, and I t'ink I might've been. I couldn't go inside.

"Shara laughed and kicked the grave dirt aside and she spit on her hand and smeared the *veve*, and I was still there, too scared to move. She asked me if I believed her about The Children now, and I ain't answer until she clapped my shoulder with the ash—was like somebody got a hold on me; my arms, my legs, my throat, even, and Shara broke the hands off me."

I knew Ines was probably feeling the effects of years of psychological conditioning. She'd been told to fear The Children, to fear the things she saw at Billy's church, and she remained a skeptic until she was confronted, when all the right levers were pulled and buttons were pushed to make her believe it was all true.

"Some kinda spirit took a hold on you?" DJ asked.

"DJ, don't indulge," I said. Feeding this girl's delusions was unconscionable.

"Until Shara come and cleansed me." Ines looked at her feet. "I never shoulda doubted her, not even for one second."

"I wouldn't go that far," I said, half under my breath. Anything Shara said apparently warranted heaps of doubt.

"Jerry..." Alicia muttered, then turned to Ines. "Honey, we're just glad you're okay."

"It was Shara that saved me," Ines said. "She knew how. I don't know where she learned it, but she did."

"Did Shara ever say anything to you about an *oungan* named Jacques Rosier?" Alicia asked. "Did you ever meet him?"

"Who?"

"Jacques Rosier," Alicia said. "Shara said she went to him after what happened to Billy, and he was going to help her take the curse off Billy's church—maybe he's the one who taught Shara."

"I never heard of that man," Ines said.

"Maybe you just don't know him," Alicia offered.

"Momma knows every *oungan* and *manbo* on either side of the island. She goes to at least one of them, sometimes two or three, every day she ain't working and she drags me along most the time, and Shara never kept nothing from me. I t'ink I'd know the man if he was real."

"Then where was she staying all this time?" Alicia asked no one in particular. No one could answer her.

"Does your mother know Pierre Noubon?" I asked.

"He's crazy," Ines said. "She only been to him a couple times, you know, to keep up relations and that. Man gave us a cat at least, so I know he can't be all bad, just filled with ideas."

"I like him," DJ said.

Ines politely smiled.

"There was also a priest I met in Grand Case," I said. "Young guy, got a machete tattooed on his neck. Ever met him?"

"No," Ines sounded surprised. "No, never met him. You say he in Grand Case?"

"He threatened me at the market," I said.

"You sure he was an *oungan*, and not just somebody with his head all mixed up?"

"People approached him like he was a priest," I said, "but I didn't ask him about seminary school."

"Can't say I know him," she said.

"I guess your mother has someone new to visit," I said. "Anyway, do you have any idea where we might find Shara? Does she have a hangout? Maybe an old boyfriend or a relative she'd stay with on the island?"

"She wouldn't go back to her mother," Ines said.

201

"I gathered that."

"She don't have much family. Her Papa never been in her life, really, and the way she tell me, he's a military man living in Paris, but she never said much about him."

Would it be better or worse for Shara if she were in Paris right now? Not that it mattered, as it was probably another lie, anyway.

"So, no idea where she might be?" I asked.

"No, sir, not a one," she said. "I wish I could tell you somet'ing, anyt'ing that would find her safe again."

"We'll be around a while yet," DJ said. "So, if something comes to you, you find us and tell us, alright?"

"I will."

Before we walked back to *Wayward*, I gave Ines one of my cards.

CHAPTER NINETEEN

On the walk back to the marina, DJ, Alicia and I worked out a watch rotation—we weren't going to be taken unaware by Albert René. I would be up first for three hours, then DJ would take over until sunrise. Then, while DJ slept and Alicia kept watch, I'd go back to Billy's church and look for any sign of where Shara might have gotten off to. I'd gone without sleep many times and getting just a few hours a day, I could operate efficiently for a week or more.

During my shift, the whole time I sat on the flybridge, not a thing moved around the docks, which I'll admit was a tad disappointing.

DJ took over and I sacked out in the master with Alicia, who was already snoring. I slept like a dead man. I did not get drowsy, I did not drift off, I did not dream. I closed my eyes and the next time I opened them, my 6 a.m. alarm was blaring in my ear.

Alicia was a habitual late sleeper, so I disentangled my arm from hers, careful not to wake her as I slid out of bed. Then, I pulled on gym shorts and a T-shirt and went on my merry way.

Topside, I walked out to *Wayward's* trampoline to find DJ propped in a beanbag with his clothes and prosthetic on, asleep. Next to him lay the night-vision binos we used to keep an eye on *La Sirène*, and on the other side, his singing bowl.

I picked the thing up. It was hefty, and looked to be made of thick brass, which appeared to have been hammered into shape. It was sort of pleasing to look at, I suppose, but I didn't really understand the appeal of the thing. I imagined DJ happily used it as a good prop to strike up conversation with curious girls.

"Any time you want, man," DJ said groggily.

I looked down at my feet to see him smiling up at me, one eye open.

"All you gotta do is ask, Dep, and I'll show you how that thing works and all the crazy shit it can do for your mind."

"Whenever possible, I try to keep crazy shit away from my mind." I turned it over and looked at the mark stamped into the bottom.

"Sometimes a man needs something to flip him sideways, stuff that'd put him so off-balance he's gotta rethink all his assumptions about the world, and maybe rethink how he fits into it all. If you did it, you might even slack off for a couple minutes. Maybe you'd totally forget about work for a second or two."

I tossed the bowl back to him, and he caught it in the breadbasket with a small grunt.

"I happen to like thinking about work."

He laughed and sat up.

"Anything happen?" I asked.

"Not a damned thing," DJ said. "*La Sirène* sat in the bay all night. Didn't even see a light come on."

I looked southwest. "Well, she's gone now."

"That she is," DJ said, looking over. "And we'll know exactly where she goes and when."

"You can sack out in your stateroom for a few hours," I said. "I'm going to get off to Billy's church after the coffee's made."

"I'm ready to hit it with you, man," he said.

"You can't have slept more than a couple hours."

"I've done worse with less." He sat up, stretched, and got to his feet on the trampoline. "What's the shower situation?"

"Freshwater tank's full, hot water tank's only thirty gallons, so go easy. You'd be first up."

"I'll save you some hot water."

Inside *Wayward's* saloon, we found Alicia awake, dressed and with her long blond hair tucked neatly into a ponytail. She was setting up the coffeemaker.

"You don't have to do that," I said as she filled the carafe with water. "I can handle coffee before I head out."

"Head out? No, no, sir. You're not leaving me behind again," she said. "I sat on this damned boat all day yesterday and it practically bored me to tears—I was so desperate at one point, I opened the package on that crochet kit you bought me for Christmas last year."

"I thought you wanted that kit," I said, coming around her in the galley and getting the coffee grinder down.

"Sure I did," she said, "but that was when I was still thinking about going back into nursing and that we'd have quiet excursions on *Wayward*. Remember how we talked about it, before you took on one case after another for Armstrong, and I started helping you? So, we're here on St. Martin, apparently to chase after voodoo ghosts. Which is way more entertaining than crochet will ever be."

I took a deep breath. "We are not chasing 'voodoo ghosts.' And here, on St. Martin, the people who actually practice the religion call it Vodou."

"You sure we ain't chasing Vodou ghosts?" DJ was dumping the water he'd heated in the electric tea kettle last night. His bag of whatever from Pierre Noubon remained on the counter, open and untouched.

"I'm very sure."

"Lotta folks think otherwise, Dep. Might be a chance they're right."

"They're wrong."

DJ shrugged. "I think that remains to be seen."

I grumbled and poured coffee beans into the grinder. DJ started to say something else when I hit the button and his voice was drowned out by the little machine. It was so nice, and so short and when it stopped, so did my moment of zen.

"I said there's more out there than what we can see and hear and all that stuff," DJ repeated without my asking. "You know, you really ought to come meditate with me sometime, Dep. *Wayward's* trampoline, out on the bay here where the water and the wind are both so calm, it's, like, the best spot to be, man. After a few seconds of sitting up there with your eyes closed, listening to the bowl hum deep down into your mind, you start to feel like your body ain't even touching nothing, like you're just floating out into space, and all those worries and cares go with you."

"What worries?" I asked.

"Jerry..." Alicia said into the coffee maker.

"Jerry what?" I took the canister of fresh grounds out of the machine and passed it to her. "What do I have to worry about?"

"Nothing at all," she said. "But you might just try and keep an open mind. If you give meditating like DJ does an honest shot, maybe you'd really enjoy it."

"I'm good for it later," I said. "Right now, I want to get back into Billy's church to see if we can find out where Shara may have disappeared to."

DJ poured water into his mug. "Didn't she mention some abandoned house across the street from the church?"

"That she did, Dudley."

He gave me a displeased look. "I'm getting in the shower. Give me five minutes and don't go nowhere without me."

I took the opportunity to throw on a pair of fresh jeans and a T-shirt and chase yesterday's stink off me with strategically placed cologne and deodorant. Then, I went back to my false-backed locker in the bow stateroom, took out the last of the tracking devices and put it in my pocket. Hopefully the charge from the factory would keep it operating for a couple days. Though, if it died, we could always retrieve it and charge it up again.

When I returned to the saloon, DJ was ready to go in cargo shorts and a loose tank top, with his hair combed back from his face and his long, scraggly goatee bound with a hair tie.

"You didn't have to dress up for me," I said.

"Let's just get going."

So we did. We took three coffees to go, locked up *Wayward* and, since the air was cool and relatively crisp, walked over to Billy's church. The whole way, Colonel Stockwell's admonishment that Alicia wasn't to be part of the investigation kept ringing in my head.

Outside, the church looked exactly as it had when we were chased off by the gendarme. I figured he might've put up a fresh crime scene seal or posted a deputy—or whatever the Gendarmerie equivalent was—to keep people out.

But we found no new tape, notices, or deputies, and the door was still unlocked.

The church's interior was much as I remembered it: small, dark, smelling faintly of burned incense and stale blood.

I turned on my phone's flashlight and walked through the pews toward the office. The three of us got to work, DJ and Alicia fingering through files in the filing cabinet as I took a stack of spiral notebooks off the top of the cabinet and pored through sermons scrawled in what I assumed was Billy's jerky, frenzied handwriting.

When I'd read enough about how I was personally going to Hell when the world ended at a non-distinct, but very imminent time, I set the notebooks aside and decided to comb through the chapel again. At the church I used to go to when I was a kid, all attendees were encouraged to fill out little cards with the names of each family member in attendance as well as addresses. Perhaps Billy was savvy enough to collect all that information. A man in his profession would do well to engage in some targeted marketing—keep in touch with his audience by periodically sending a newsletter to remind them how hot brimstone feels against the soles of their feet.

It was worth a shot. "I'll be out in the main room," I said to Alicia.

She glanced up from a file she held sideways in a folder, studying the contents, and smiled. "Not finding much here."

As I looked through the church sanctuary, I didn't find any cards with address information in the backs of the pews. I didn't find anything notable at all, except a rat in the cabinet on the back side of the altar, gorging itself on a forgotten bowl of stale host. I went through each row, checking under every seat, looking for anything that might be a clue.

Nothing.

So, I went back to DJ and Alicia. As I approached the office, I heard them chatting quietly, but the conversation stopped as soon as I walked in. They were probably talking about me, but it didn't matter—there was work to be done.

"The chapel's given me nothing," I said. "How about you two?"

"If Shara's in some kind of hangout, we didn't find anything about it here," Alicia said. "You guys talked to her mom yesterday, right? She might know something useful."

"It'd surprise me," I said.

"Miss Mary and Shara don't seem to be on the best of terms," DJ added. "She said she ain't really talked to her daughter much."

"I gathered," Alicia said. "Still, it might be worth running down if we find ourselves stuck."

"Sure," I said. Then I noticed the small, black clay jar sitting on top of Billy's desk. "Is that the thing Shara told us about? The *govi?*"

"I imagine," DJ said.

The jar was the size of a misshapen cantaloupe, painted in glossy black, which caught the light shining from my phone in a way that I could only describe as alluring. An intricate white pattern had been drawn all across it like ivy.

"What's your read on this thing, DJ? Is it throwing off bad vibrations or what?" I picked it up and shook it, hearing the rattle of sand and rocks inside.

"Man, you're just bein' mean," he said.

"What? Out of the three of us, aren't you the most aligned to the astral plane? What's your take on it?"

"Honestly, man, that thing spooks me. Just lookin' at it is like somebody stickin' cold needles in the back of my neck, and I think we're better off not messin' around with it."

I turned the *govi* jar, looking closer at the white design on the outside. It was more purposeful and directed than stalks of ivy, and, in parts, looked like straight lines forming a grid of diamonds, and within that grid were blank spaces where objects had been drawn.

209

One looked like a dog's head, and another looked like a rock or a boulder, and when I turned the jar a bit, I saw a machete.

"Well," I said, holding the govi up with one hand, "I just found something interesting."

DJ and Alicia looked at the govi as if it were packed with dynamite. They didn't ask what interesting *something* I found.

"There's a machete on this," I said. "It looks almost identical to a tattoo I saw on that *oungan* in Grand Case."

"The one you asked Ines about last night?" DJ asked.

"You remember him, the murderous one," I said. "I think we should take this thing over to him and pick his brain about it."

"Ain't it The Children of Ogun who put this thing on Billy and Shara?" DJ asked.

"They're a fairy tale," I said. "Something that people are irrationally afraid of, and if I was trying to threaten somebody, I might be the type of guy who takes advantage of that."

"Yeah, but would you draw your own tattoo on it?" DJ asked. "I mean shit, man, that's like leaving a signed confession at a murder scene. Kind of a brainless way to go about it."

DJ had a point; anybody with two brain cells to rub together would know better. There were probably hundreds or thousands of people with a machete tattoo in the world.

"Brains may not have any part in this at all. Perhaps it's an ego thing. Our man could imagine himself a new serial killer and that machete symbol is his calling card."

"Or somebody else is trying to put the machete *oungan* up for something he didn't do," Alicia said.

"Ooh," DJ hummed. "The devious plot twist."

"If that's the case, we ask who doesn't like him," I said. "And if our luck is good, and it happens to be someone who was after Billy, we have a very interesting coincidence on our hands. Could be our friend Albert René has some kind of beef against religious leaders."

"Could be," DJ said. "But do we have to take that *govi* with us? It creeps me out, man."

"Can't confront someone with evidence if you don't have the evidence," I said. "Consider it a test of your spiritual fortitude, DJ— how long can you be in sight of this thing before you've completely lost your mind, or your spirit succumbs to the bad vibes? Can you muster enough positive energy to stop the ghost from popping out and stabbing us all?"

He grimaced.

Before leaving, we stopped by the vent full of money. DJ unscrewed the screws, and we stacked the rolls on the desk. I picked one up and removed the rubber band, then activated the tracker, and rolled it back up.

"We need something to put it all in," I said, holding the roll up sideways. "You can see there's something rolled up in here."

"Just the thing," Alicia said, pulling open the bottom drawer of Billy's desk and plopping a small burlap sack next to the bills.

"Perfect," DJ said, picking up the sack and opening it before thrusting it toward me. "Track or treat."

I chuckled as I dropped the roll in. "Not unfunny, DJ."

We put the sack of money back in the vent and closed it up. If that money moved, we'd know it.

With nothing left to learn or find out, we left, and on the walk back, I smelled seafood on a grill at Marigot market. I wanted to stop for lunch, but DJ and Alicia both said I should stash the *govi* on *Wayward* before making stops in town, so as not to freak out the locals.

I guess that seemed prudent.

We went back toward the marina and as we approached *Wayward*, I spotted a familiar face waiting for us near the starboard hull—the uniformed gendarme who'd chased us out of Billy's church yesterday.

"Mr. Snyder," he said with a heavy French accent, "my name is Henri Lebouc, and I need to speak with you and your friend in private. We can either do it in a holding cell, or here on your vessel."

"In that case, welcome aboard," I said.

CHAPTER TWENTY

Armstrong had close ties with a lot of political figures and law enforcement types and whenever possible, operatives were to further that network by using their own discretion on who to talk with openly and who was only to be a source of intel.

We made it as far as *Wayward's* cockpit before the gendarme started laying into us.

"You two gentlemen have been very busy during your stay in St. Martin."

"We like seein' the sights," DJ said. "There's a lot of pretty places all around the island, and not seein' as much as we can feels like a crime." DJ caught his own gaffe. "Uh, shit, not literally a *crime*, I mean. Just, like figuratively."

"Yes," Lebouc said.

After unlocking the saloon door, I slid open and disabled the alarm, and waited for DJ, Alicia, and the cop to file in before I closed the door.

"Sit wherever you like," I said.

"I'll stand," Lebouc said. "You three sit at the table."

We slipped into the booth around the table, and when I settled in, I put the *govi* in front of me. When I turned back to Lebouc, waiting for him to ask the first question, I caught him looking at it and noticed a hint of discomfort.

But that could've just been me misunderstanding the subtle cues of his body language. He was a hard read, looking like any number of cops I knew back home—bald-headed, steely-eyed, mouth creased from thousands of hours of scowling. Now that I wasn't trying to escape from him, I noticed he and I were about the same height, and he looked like he could make the podium at any triathlon, despite pushing forty years old.

"As I said outside, my name is Henri Lebouc, I am a gendarmerie adjutant." He flashed his badge. "You have been causing trouble around the island. Not only did I catch you two men leaving a murder scene yesterday, I also read a report from one of the prefect's aides that said two American tourists mugged him at the market in Grand Case yesterday, and one of them had a fake leg. What do you two gentlemen think about that?"

I had no thoughts to offer. I was more intrigued by Lebouc sitting us down for a chat. If he was really here to arrest us now, a day after he'd caught us breaking the law, why not do the deed and question us at his station? And if he did mean to arrest us after talking to us here, why come alone? He should have had an overwhelming force with him. Maybe armed officers, maybe not, depending on how exactly St. Martin ran things, but I didn't think he'd come alone to arrest two men.

He wanted to talk. More specifically, I think he wanted *us* to talk because he may have assumed DJ and I knew things he didn't.

"I always heard Grand Case was a pretty safe spot," DJ said. "Real shame the way some people got to ruin it for everybody else."

Lebouc pursed his lips. "This is a serious matter, Mr....?"

DJ looked to me. I nodded back at him. *Give him your name, give him some trust. Let's see where it goes.*

"DJ Martin," he said.

"Mr. DJ Martin, assaulting a citizen and government official of St. Martin as well as intruding upon a murder scene are both very serious offenses."

"Sounds pretty bad," DJ said. "But how many pairs of white guys are out there walking around, anyhow?"

"I caught both of you leaving the church yesterday. Do you care to explain why you were there?"

"It's like I told you yesterday, man, I needed to find the shitter, or there was gonna be an awful mess to clean up, and I didn't come here to sully the beauty of St. Martin. What was I supposed to do? Find a bucket?"

"This is your vessel"— he reached into his pocket, pulled out a small slip of paper and peeked at it— "*Wayward?*"

"It's mine," I said.

"Yes, Mr. Snyder, but is Mr. Martin staying on this ship?" Apparently Lebouc had already done his research on me.

"Yeah, man, I'm crashin' here."

"It is not far from the bars—you said you were intoxicated. Why not simply come back here? Why walk all the way out to the church? And if not that, why not use the bar where you were drinking or one of the many restaurants between here and that church?"

"I liked the scenery at the church better."

"You preferred to relieve yourself at a murder scene?" Lebouc snorted, halfway between laughter and disdain. "No, I don't think you did. I think you have an undue interest, or perhaps it is simply a curiosity for the macabre. Whatever it may be, it is of no concern to me. The outcome will be the same." He reached behind his back and I heard a button snap from his utility belt. He swung a pair of handcuffs around as he came toward DJ.

Lebouc stopped short of slapping them on DJ's wrists, instead tossing them on the table.

"Continue to lie to me, Mr. Martin—and also you, Mr. Snyder, who are lying by remaining silent—and I will charge you with entering a crime scene without authorization, and you will go to prison." He clasped his hands behind his back. "Or you can tell me the truth."

Lebouc may have known my name, but it was clear he didn't know much about us, especially my partner, who, even if he'd recently blossomed into a flower child, never took threats all that well, and didn't appear to be taking this one with aplomb either.

I had to intervene.

"Take those cuffs and shove 'em up your god—"

"Officer Lebouc," I shouted over DJ, quieting him. "You've got a sharp eye for the truth."

"Yes. I know," he said.

"Then you know we aren't tourists."

"What the hell, man?" DJ leaned over the table like he was going to grab me, then stopped when I met his eyes.

"Hear me out, DJ. We've got a man standing right here that might be able to help—if he's the kind of man I suspect he is, and I suspect he wants answers as badly as we do. And for all we know, he might be a friend of the colonel, or he might *become* one."

Lebouc shifted his weight, but like any good cop, his face betrayed nothing.

"We're private investigators working a case," I said.

"Foreign private investigators coming to St. Martin?" he asked.

"Our client is local."

"And you believe I want to help you? Or that I would let you help me?"

216

"For one, you didn't arrest us as soon as you saw us," I said. "You brought us in here, somewhere secluded, to talk, because you want to discuss details."

Lebouc frowned deeper and squeezed his fist, cracking his knuckles. "And what details do you have to discuss, Mr. Snyder?"

I didn't like throwing information to outside parties, but if I let our brewing relationship with Lebouc go sour, he had us for at least one crime, and probably two if he could conclusively prove it was DJ and I who'd roughed up Joseph Desir in Grand Case.

"We found Shara Bradley," I said.

"That's impossible—where?"

"She's alive. She came to us last night. We tried to get her back to her mother, but she wouldn't go. She said she was staying with a friend, but when we went to check on her late last night, she wasn't there and never had been."

"So you made contact with a missing person and promptly lost track of her?" he asked. "That is not good."

"She lied to us, man," DJ said. "Lied to us up and down. It ain't like we could've kept her here on the boat against her will."

"We're still working on locating Shara," I said.

"And is that part of your investigation as well?" He nodded at the *govi* on the table. "You know what that sort of thing is used for by these people, don't you?"

"Yes," I said. "It's a funerary jar."

"Then you understand why a foreigner with one on his boat would not be treated kindly," he said. "You should dispose of it immediately or give it to one of the Vodou priests."

"We plan on it," I said. "We're going to return it to the man who owns it."

"You are? And who might that man be?"

"That's part of our investigation," I said. "I've already given you a piece of information for free, and if we're going to help each other, I'd like a piece of information from you."

"Mr. Snyder," Lebouc said as he came to the edge of the table, "our relationship is not transactional. You realize that I am a gendarme, and that I have authority in the places where you are intruding?"

"You did your research into me," I said. "You probably know I was a law enforcement officer once, too. And DJ and I are both combat veterans. I just want you to take that into consideration before you decide anything. Also, know that I've been in your exact position before, and I realize you wouldn't have spoken a word to us if you didn't need help."

Lebouc planted his knuckles on the table and leaned closer to me.

"This is not a game that we are playing."

I said nothing.

He picked up his handcuffs as he pushed off the table and turned his back to us, moving toward the saloon door, where he stopped and looked across the water off *Wayward's* stern. He glanced down at the cuffs, then, with practiced ease, put them away, and turned to face us.

"Are you aware of the history of Vodou here? In the Caribbean?"

"Not really," I said. "I know it's a melding of African religions and Christianity."

"Many Vodouists in the Caribbean believe their religion helped the Haitians win the only successful slave revolt in modern history," Lebouc said. "There are revolutionary roots in Vodou, and I believe, in the five years since Hurricane Irma, those roots have grown

218

stronger in St. Martin, and they will very soon bear a bloody flower. As a gendarme, my job is to ensure peace and justice, and you can see how a populace in open revolt runs counter to my duty."

"You think Billy Pearce's death has something to do with a coming revolution?" I asked.

"I am uncertain, but I believe this violent political movement may encourage an otherwise good citizen of St. Martin to believe Billy Pierce, and those here like him, represent the corruption of St. Martin and the historical subjugation of her people. And to allow those like Billy Pearce room to grow and live on St. Martin would mean the destruction of the island."

My eyes traced over the machete painted on the black *govi*. Lebouc's theory was compelling.

"So you think arresting Billy's murderer is going to stop the wider movement?" I asked.

"That is not my concern," he said. "I have sworn to serve France and her territories, and I will do all I can to ensure a prosperous nation."

"Heavy shit, man," DJ said.

Lebouc turned toward us and grabbed the handle of the saloon door. "I'll give you room to conduct your investigation, but I'll ask you to please remain in contact with me as you find more information."

"We can work with that," I said.

"Good. If you operate without my knowledge, I will be forced to arrest you, Mr. Snyder, and you, Mr. Martin." He nodded toward Alicia. "Madame, be careful. St. Martin is paradise, but it can be a deadly place."

Lebouc opened the door and left.

219

CHAPTER TWENTY-ONE

After Lebouc left, DJ and I had a lunch meeting in *Wayward's* cockpit while Alicia napped in the master. DJ lay sprawled out on the aft-most section of the settee with his arm over his eyes, and I was seated to port, near the ice chest, finishing the last of the overripe grapes we'd brought from home.

"Man, if we want to find out about revolutionary conspiracies and that type of shit, you know who we ought to talk to?"

"Noubon," I said, as I watched a vessel coming in from the north, beyond the barrier wall.

"Yeah, buddy."

"I won't say he *can't* tell the truth, but considering the subject, any good information we get from him is going to be cut with half-baked conspiracies and rumors. It'd be nice if we could get something concrete on the machete priest, like his name or who he hangs around with before we go to Noubon."

"Desir probably knows the man," DJ said. "Guy like Desir probably stuck his nose in all kinds of business. I bet he could even tell us all about that cop, Lebouc. Like if the guy's on the take somewhere or if he's legit."

"That's a fair bet." I popped a grape in my mouth, then shifted my weight to get a better look at the fishing trawler coming out of the north. "There was a woman running an herb stand in Grand Case that seemed to know a bit about the machete priest too. I don't know if we can get her to talk to us, but if she's around, it's worth a try."

I recognized the trawler motoring back into harbor—*La Sirène II.*

"Could be all this underground revolution nonsense ain't got a bit of anything to do with Billy Pearce or Shara," DJ said. "Might just be a nice little distraction Lebouc told us because he knows we're gonna get his job done before he does and ain't a cop alive that'd let himself be embarrassed on his home turf. Could be he made the whole thing up."

"You're not wrong, partner," I said. "But the way the priest in Grand Case talked, there is likely some form of social unrest brewing. In any case, I think we put uncovering the revolution on hold while we learn a little more about Albert René. Did you notice his demeanor changed when I mentioned Shara Bradley yesterday?"

"I did," DJ said.

"He knows her," I said.

DJ sat up on the bench and pushed himself back until he was propped against the starboard end of the settee. "You think he and Shara got a little side thing going on?"

"I don't know."

"It ain't impossible," DJ said. "They're together, but Billy's in the way *and* Billy took all that money from René's momma, so he kills Billy and gets Shara to help him cover it up. She blames it on a ghost, she disappears for a while, then she goes back to Billy's church to clean up evidence when she thinks nobody's paying attention. Maybe she stashed that money in the vent, too."

"Your theory sounds plausible, except the money. If she put it

222

there, why wouldn't she take it the night of the murder? Or give it to René? Why leave it at the church just for it to be discovered and taken by someone else?"

"Maybe she ain't that smart, or she doesn't have another place to take it without getting in trouble. She's basically a kid." DJ stroked his goatee until another idea hit.

"What if she's trying to pin it all on René?" DJ asked. "Maybe she gets René to kill Billy, and her plan is to hide out, make people think she's been kidnapped or killed by René, then sneak back into the church to grab the money and split."

"If she was going to do that, why talk to us at all?"

"That's easy; she said she wanted us to know she was alright," DJ said. "She wants us to stop looking for her so she can sneak away."

"But if we tell anyone we saw her, she can't sneak anywhere."

"Yeah, but we're just stupid foreigners and we don't know nobody on St. Martin except the *oungan* talkin' about government conspiracies and all that. Maybe she don't think we know anybody at all."

"Well, if we stick to our work, we'll know soon enough." I stood up. "Since *La Sirène* is back, let's check the tracker data against his AIS and see where he goes when he turns it off. We can chase down the machete priest later."

Inside the saloon, the air was hot and sticky. Odd, considering the air conditioning easily cooled the boat if we were connected to shore power or running the genset.

"Leave that door open, DJ," I said.

"Man, it's hotter in here than it is out there." DJ fanned himself as he stepped through the saloon door.

At the same time, Alicia came bounding up the starboard hull steps with strands of blond hair pasted to her forehead.

223

"Why did you turn the air off?" she asked me.

"DJ and I just came in."

"That's hot air." DJ was hovering a hand over a vent. "AC's broke, man."

"Broke? That's impossible—we just had it serviced." I walked over to the thermostat by the nav station. The damned thing had been cranked all the way up. I turned it back to a comfortable temperature. "Somebody must've bumped it."

"You were the last one over there, DJ," Alicia said.

"I know where my hands go," he said. "Most of the time."

"It doesn't matter." I got the laptop out of the nav station desk drawer and brought it to the table. DJ moved the *govi* jar aside, and I set the computer down and fired it up.

"*La Sirène* is back," I said to Alicia, who was slugging down a glass of water in the galley.

I pulled up the tracker map.

La Sirène left Marigot Bay shortly after 4 a.m. on a westward course, then a few miles out, she changed to a northeastern course, and came all the way back to the Anguilla channel, where she followed St. Martin's coast around the northeastern horn and into Cul-De-Sac Bay, within sight of Mer du Mélasse. There, *La Sirène* stayed for a couple of hours, then she took off just after dawn and motored to the far side of Tintamarre Island before coming back home.

That done, I pulled up the AIS data to see whether Albert René wanted his vessel's location known or not. As expected, AIS data for the voyage didn't exist.

"What's it look like, Dep?"

I turned the laptop to DJ.

"No AIS data," I said. "But the tracker says *La Sirène* went all the way around the northern coast of St. Martin early this morning."

DJ moused around the screen, checking times. "She was in that bay near the Mélasse for quite a while."

"That's our first stop."

The three of us had *Wayward* untied within minutes. Hauling the rented Mako center console behind us, we followed the coastline just as *La Sirène* had, with Alicia at the helm, matching our GPS position with the exact course from the tracker, while DJ and I were on deck, scanning the immediate area.

With a top speed of nine knots, we covered the same distance at a slightly faster pace than the trawler had, and came all the way into Cul-De-Sac Bay in a little over an hour. We saw nothing of interest. At least, nothing germane to the case.

I was up on the bow when we first pulled into the bay and I guided Alicia to a sandy spot where we dropped the anchor. Scanning the anchorage and shoreline with binoculars, I found pretty much what I expected—pleasure craft of all shapes and sizes, the people on them and on shore at Mer du Mélasse enjoying the Caribbean sunshine and having a good time.

However, around one of the cabanas on shore, I saw police tape.

"DJ," I called.

He came thumping up from the cockpit.

"Look at this," I said, handing over the binos.

He immediately spotted the crime scene and whistled. "Would ya look at that?"

"Alicia!" I yelled. "We're going to shore!"

"Oh man, Dep," DJ said, with the binos to his eyes. "Guess who I'm looking at right now?"

My subconscious pushed the image of the machete priest to the forefront of my mind.

"Lebouc," he said. "Man's on shore. Seems to be directing the scene."

After Alicia backed down on the anchor and shut down the engines, we locked up the boat and the three of us rode the little Mako to the nearby dock, where we hopped out and walked over to the scene.

Between the thundering bass from the PA at the bar and the gendarmerie cars parked between beach chair loungers, the beach outside the Mer Du Mélasse was an odd marriage of crime scene and beach club.

"Why haven't they kicked all these people off the beach?" I wondered out loud, as we stepped off the dock.

"It ain't obvious to you?" DJ asked. "All these people paid good money to come here, man."

A pair of girls in neon string bikinis ran between DJ and me. Thankfully, he didn't follow.

"They could shut down for an hour."

"Man, you ain't never worked in the hospitality business, and it shows."

"You have?"

"My mom's cousin was in it," he said. "She ran a couple rental houses over in Gulf Shores. I used to help her out over the summers when I was in high school, and man, she had to make the most out of those couple months. Even a week or two with thin bookings had her eating beans out of a can in February. Job usually paid good though, I got to stay on the beach, and there were all kinds of chicks, man."

"So that's where you got your start," Alicia said.

"Oh, no, darlin', I got my start with women long before then. Those summers were the start of my stride." He winked at her, and she laughed and shoved him.

Ahead, a shifting crowd of onlookers watched the police do their work around the private villa. The gawkers were mostly people in swimsuits and flip-flops with drinks in their hands, breaking off from the resort's never-ending bar party to catch the live True Crime sideshow.

"Man, look at all that, Dep."

DJ motioned toward the villa. The outside of it was covered in the same type of ornate scrawlings as were on the outside of the black *govi* jar—they weren't exactly the same, but very similar.

"Those things weren't there yesterday," he said.

"No, they were not."

The three of us weaved through the crowd until we were at the line of police—or gendarme—tape, watching the officers take pictures of the scene, lay out evidence cards and conduct interviews from a couple of the resort staff.

The villa door was wide open, and what I was looking at barely resembled the front room in the villa where we'd visited Mary Bradley for a chat. There was no couch, no coffee table, in fact, no furniture at all—only a large post in the middle of the room, about the diameter of a main mast of a seventeenth- century ship of the line, and this, too, had lots of chalk drawings scribbled across it.

Also, at the foot of the large post was a box of cigars, open, as if waiting for one of the gendarmes to pluck one out. All around the box, beans and grains of rice were scattered and mixed with bits of herbs or leaves.

As I watched, a gendarme came out holding a length of iron chain, which she dropped into an evidence bag held by a colleague.

"Alicia, is that you?"

I knew Arlen's voice the second I heard it. It was like a blow to the back of the head. I turned to see him coming through the crowd with his arms open, getting ready to hug my wife.

"Arlen! So good to see you." Alicia wrapped her arms around him. She was polite to a fault.

"I'm gonna talk to Lebouc," DJ muttered, as he walked in the opposite direction.

"What are you doing here?" Arlen asked her. "Did Jerry drag you out to a crime scene? What an ungentlemanly thing to do to a woman as lovely as your wife, Jerry."

"I'm not here to control her," I said, trying not to turn my attention from the crime scene.

"I wanted to be here," Alicia said.

"Well now, Jerry's a modern man, isn't he?"

"Now, Arlen, don't go teasing him," Alicia said.

"Oh! You caught me." He laughed. "Anyway, I'm just so surprised to see you all out here—what brought you over? Were you thinking of staying at the Mélasse? If you are, you have to let me know. I'm working on a deal for the place, and I'm sure I could get you an outstanding room at a rate that'd make you never want to leave."

"I'm not sure you could do that," I said.

Arlen laughed it off. "No, no, of course not. I know you've got your lives and careers to see to, and it's not as though anyone could ever convince Jerry to stop working, even on an island like St. Martin."

"We all try our best," Alicia said.

"Yes, yes we do. And speaking of work, do you mind if I have a private word with your husband, Alicia? I'd like to talk a little shop with him and, well, I'm afraid I'm still as paranoid as ever when it comes to that sort of thing, and there are only so many people in the world I feel I can trust."

I looked over my shoulder and Alicia checked on me with a twitch of her eyes.

"It's alright," I said. "I'll talk to him."

Arlen smiled at her. "You're welcome to have whatever you like at the bar. They've got an excellent assortment of small batch rums they've distilled here on the island, and if you tell them my name, I'm sure they'll give you the best of the lot, gratis."

"Sure," Alicia said. She looked from Arlen to me.

"I'll be fine," I said.

"Okay," she said, then started toward the bar.

"Don't let Gerard charm you too much," Arlen called after her. Then, as if flipping a switch, his easy-going smile disappeared, and he came up beside me.

"It's funny that we can go almost a year without seeing each other, and now, we've collided twice in two days."

"I've never laughed harder," I said.

Ten paces to our right, one of the resort guests let out a party howl from the hood of a gendarmerie car before upending a yard glass full of beer. Half seemed to get into his mouth and the other half appeared to dribble down his gut and across the hood of the car.

Two officers pulled him down, and, amazingly, let him stumble back toward the bar under his own power.

"Have you ever been to a crime scene as strange as this one?" Arlen asked.

"Never," I said.

He motioned at the villa. "Do you know what happened here?"

"Not a clue," I admitted. "That's why I've come to see."

"What you're looking at is a clash between two different denominations of Vodou," Arlen said, looking toward the villa. "As

229

far as a denomination exists in Vodou, anyway. There is no codified way to worship among Vodouists, so much of the detail is left up to a particular *oungan* or *manbo*. This isn't quite the same as Protestants and Catholics burning down each other's churches, but it *is* very much a clash of ideals."

"How would you know that?" I asked.

"I've been around the Caribbean over the last year, Jerry. I spent a fair amount of time in Haiti, which is the epicenter of Vodou. You can hardly walk ten feet there without tripping over a *manbo*, and even I was welcomed into the congregations there from time to time."

I was amazed that Arlen had such knowledge. I'd been in the islands longer and didn't know much at all about Vodou. Of course, I had no reason to research it, which made me wonder what Arlen's reason was.

"You know," he continued, "real Haitian Vodou isn't at all the bone-through-the-nose thing that most Americans know from movies. It's a religion about healing, about honoring one's ancestors, and about communing with and respecting nature. You see that *veve* on the post in the middle there?"

"The what?"

"The *veve*—the drawing on the post," he said. "That's for a specific *loa*, which is sort of the equivalent of a Catholic saint, but I've never seen a priest say he was possessed by Saint Anthony. Anyway, that *veve* is for the *loa*, Ogun, who is the *loa* of blacksmithing, fire, war, politics, leadership, dogs, and probably a hundred other things depending on who you ask. In Haiti, they say it was Ogun who inspired the slave revolt in the late eighteenth century, and that Ogun guided the slaves through a full-blown revolution."

"So Ogun is some kind of war god," I said, watching the activity around the villa.

"Not a god, heavens no, Jerry," Arlen said. "And it's not just war that he governs. Some say he is a pathfinder, that he's an artisan, and sometimes he's a battle medic or he's a great politician—and there are different aspects of Ogun as well, so whatever he is also depends on which aspect we're talking about."

Arlen cupped his hands over his eyes, blocking the sun, and leaned in, looking closer at the interior of the cabana.

"That's interesting," he said.

"What?"

"That post in there, they call it the *potomitan*. It's a place where the priests and priestesses commune with the *loa*. Usually there are all kinds of different *veve* scribbled across it, but if you look closely at the one inside there, all you'll see are *veve* for Ogun. None for Papa Legba, or *La Sirène*, or any other *loa*. That's not typical."

"I'm getting the impression there isn't much about this whole thing that is."

Arlen cracked off a laugh.

"But you see these *veve* scribbled on the outside of the building?" He motioned at more of the ornate drawings scrawled around the cabana's front door, on the front deck, on the walk outside, and in various other places. "All these *veve* are for different *loa*. There's Sirène "— he pointed at one I recognized from Albert René's boat "—and that one is for Legba. That little boat there is for Agwe, and that strange-looking man next to the door is Gran Bwa.

"The staff said these drawings were meant to deface their *hounfour*—that's what the Vodouists call their temples. Many of the people who work at the resort meet at this villa, where they worship Ogun to the exclusion of all the other *loa*, which runs deeply counter to the beliefs of every other Vodouist I've met. It's very strange."

Very strange indeed, I thought.

"Anyway, tell me what you're doing here again," Arlen said. "Would it have anything to do with the murder of Billy Pearce?"

Shit. Who told him?

"That's alright, you don't have to verbally confirm it to me, Jerry. It's written all over your face."

"Assume whatever you like," I said.

"Jerry, I've known you far too long to not know when you're hiding something." He smiled at me. "And I know that back home, you were a very accomplished police officer. It's a shame what happened to Billy Pearce. I heard his girlfriend has gone missing as well. Her mother works here, if you should ever like to speak with her. I'm sure I can arrange something."

"Thanks," I said. "I'll keep it in mind, but I don't need your help."

"Of course not." Arlen turned and looked at the altar—the *potomitan*—again before turning his gaze back on me.

"Would you care to mention what it is you needed to speak to me about in private?" I asked.

Arlen looked at me and chuckled. "Sometimes it feels like fate enjoys putting me in the right place at the right time to help you. The next time it happens, I hope you can accept the help."

He slapped me on the shoulder and walked off.

I didn't stick around either. I went looking for DJ, and found him next to the villa, behind the cordon tape, talking to Lebouc.

"Mr. Snyder," Lebouc said as a way of greeting me. "Mr. Martin has shared information with me, and as before, I repay in kind. He said you were on the trail of a person of interest, and that is how you came to be here."

232

"That's correct," I said.

DJ tapped Lebouc on the elbow. "Tell him what you told me about René."

"First, I must say I do not ask civilians to assist me in matters of law, but where the law concerns Mr. René, I must look for help from outsiders." Lebouc said. "I give you this information because I want you to continue monitoring him, and you should know who this man is."

"We will."

"He and the crew of *La Sirène II* are suspected of a number of crimes around St. Martin." He nodded toward the villa. "Not only intimidation like this, but assaults, protection rackets and perhaps even murder."

"You think René did this?"

"Mr. Martin said you traced *La Sirène* to Cul-de-Sac Bay early this morning. Members of the staff here say they found the cabana like this when they arrived for work around 7 a.m.."

The GPS data put *La Sirène* leaving Cul-de-Sac Bay an hour earlier than that.

"If René is a suspect for multiple crimes around the island, why hasn't anyone brought him in yet?" I asked.

Lebouc leaned in close to DJ and me, his eyes searching around before he spoke.

"Whenever there is a serious investigation into Mr. René, it is always sabotaged. Evidence disappears, cooperative witnesses no longer cooperate, and things are not done as properly as they otherwise would be."

"He's connected," I said.

"And he's very dangerous," Lebouc added.

CHAPTER TWENTY-TWO

After talking to Lebouc and poking around the crime scene a little more, the three of us took the Mako back to *Wayward* and resumed following *La Sirène II's* early morning voyage.

We motored against the wind out of Cul-De-Sac Bay, on an easterly course that took us toward Tintamarre Island.

Tintamarre was a small, rocky, windward island, about a mile across from east to west with plenty of scrub brush. A large bay on its western end was a popular snorkeling area for tourists eager to spot a bevy of sea turtles. Needless to say, it wasn't for us.

La Sirène had gone along Tintamarre's southern coast, then up the eastern shore, where it stopped for a few minutes, then turned around.

It wasn't long before we'd curled *Wayward* around Tintamarre's east end. I cut the engines, hopped down from the helm and grabbed one of our two pairs of binos—Alicia had the other set, and was already scanning the rocky coast.

"What are we looking for?" she asked.

"Anything out of place," I replied.

The coastline was about forty yards off, and aside from a good-sized cave leading out to a white sand beach, and a twenty-foot-high cliff on the same beach's north end, there wasn't much to look at.

I did, however, see a couple old dock pilings periodically surface in the troughs between the one- or two-foot waves.

"Maybe *La Sirène* really did stop to fish here," DJ said. "Early morning, not far from a coast. If the tide's in like it is now, right here might not be a bad spot to catch snapper. They like rocks, and there might be some deeper spots around, especially if they got caves under the water."

"Doesn't seem like a lucrative area for a commercial fisherman," I said.

"No, but if anyone starts wondering why they came out on this side of Tintamarre, all they got to do is open their holds and say they wanted to try out a new spot. Good alibi."

I set the binoculars down on the cockpit table before climbing up to the helm chair. We may not have found anything worth our time at Tintamarre, but at least tracking *La Sirène* wasn't a complete bust.

I tried to set a waypoint for our trip home, but *Wayward's* chart plotter had other ideas. At the first touch of my finger, the nav screen degraded into an unreadable jumble of letters and numbers.

"Fantastic," I said.

"What's wrong?" Alicia asked.

"The plotter's glitching."

"Glitching? What does that mean?"

"Take a look for yourself," I said as I opened the cabinet under the helm, revealing a bucket of different suntan lotions.

I set that aside and looked at the top of the cabinet, where a bundle of neatly run wires connected into the underside of the helm's instrument panel. I found the one with a white stripe— the power wire. If I disconnected and reconnected it, the system would restart and that might solve the problem.

"I'm goin' up to the bow," DJ said, grabbing my pair of binos.

All I needed was something to push on the little tab at the head of the power cable so I could disconnect.

"Can you get a flathead screwdriver?" I asked Alicia. "There should be one in the toolbox in the port engine bay."

"Sure."

While she went to get it, DJ called my name.

"Dep, come look at this!"

I slipped out from under the helm to see Alicia coming out of the engine bay.

"Disconnect the display's power wire," I said. "It's the one marked with a white stripe."

"I'm on it."

Up at the bow, DJ was pointing at something in the water.

I followed his finger to a black smudge on the clear blue waters. It looked like a frayed line cast off by some other vessel before it came into focus.

"That's nothing, right man? Just some dead seaweed, right? Or like some kind of unraveling rope?"

"It looks like—" I peered closer. Then I saw something that made my heart skip. It wasn't seaweed, and it wasn't rope. It was human hair.

I dove into the water and opened my eyes beneath the surface.

237

The hair was still connected to a woman's body. She was about half the distance between *Wayward* and Tintamarre, and she was wrapped in a red bedsheet, or possibly a toga that wafted loosely around her. Her lifeless eyes were open, staring vacantly out to sea.

Her body was upright, against one of the old dock pilings. I knew she was dead, but I still swam to her as quickly as I could, not even breaching the surface for air when I finally reached her.

She was young—maybe Shara's age, or a year or two younger. Since she wasn't floating, I knew something was holding her to the post. Perhaps someone had tied her there, and I simply couldn't see the ropes due to the loose fabric obscuring her body.

I placed my hands on her waist, or my best guess at where her waist should be, hoping to feel lines cinched around her and tied to the post, but felt nothing. So I put my hands on the post at about the level of her shoulders and began to pat downward until I felt her wrists, and the chains that bound them.

We had bolt cutters on *Wayward*. I could get her free. I surfaced.

"I need bolt cutters, DJ!"

"Is that a person?" DJ called from the deck. "Is she alive?"

"She's dead, but I have to cut her loose," I yelled back. "Get me the bolt cutters!"

Then, a gunshot rang out from behind me. The bullet zipped over my shoulder and splashed a yard or two ahead of me. I should've swum, but all my better sense had flown the coop, so I turned and saw a burst of muzzle flashes somewhere deep in the cave on shore, and more shots ripped into the water near me.

Alicia screamed my name. I regained my senses and ducked underwater as quickly as I could, then swam for *Wayward* like a great white was nibbling at my toes.

More shots broke the surface and lanced into the water around me. The fire continued with every stroke I took and even hissed through the air around me as I grabbed onto *Wayward's* swim platform.

I pulled myself up and heard *Wayward* absorb a bullet, which made me drop as low as I possibly could. I slid on my belly into the cockpit and lay flat against the deck just as DJ stood up and returned fire with the long gun I'd kept in the hidden compartment in the starboard bow.

Alicia was pressed up against the bulkhead near the helm chair, with her Beretta 92FS ready to raise and fire.

"Hold your fire," I said to her as I got to my feet and ran for the helm chair. I hit the button to start the engines and slapped the throttles. *Wayward* responded immediately, jerking forward, and getting us the hell away from Tintamarre.

We all hunkered down as the twin Yanmar diesel engines let out full-throated growls and carried us away. Sporadic fire continued from the beach until we'd put another hundred yards or so behind us.

"Is anyone hit?" I asked, visually checking Alicia.

"I'm fine," she said. "I barely got a shot off."

"DJ?"

He was sitting on one of the chairs at the cockpit table, his head in his hands. He didn't hear me.

I touched him, and he looked up with a start.

"You alright?"

"Yeah, yeah," he said vacantly.

"We're gonna need someone to look at the hull," Alicia said. "I'll check below to make sure we aren't taking on water."

"Good idea," I said, climbing into the helm chair again.

"Is the nav working?" DJ suddenly asked.

"Just as it should be," I said.

"Dep, we gotta get rid of that *govi* jar. It's bad juju, man."

I looked down at him.

"We were just shot at, man, and *Wayward's* had two unexplained problems. I'm guessing she ain't never had much of anything go wrong before."

He'd guessed right.

"I'm takin' that jar back to Noubon," he said. "We can't hang onto that thing any longer."

Maybe I didn't agree with him on principle, but after being shot at, I couldn't come up with a better counter argument for keeping it.

CHAPTER TWENTY-THREE

With the wind at our stern, we deployed the Code D spinnaker, and the northeasterly trade winds carried *Wayward* along at a good clip—nothing record-breaking, but she could sail faster than she could motor. Alicia manned the helm while DJ and I sat in the cockpit and called Lebouc to tell him what we'd found and gone through.

He was disturbed by what he heard, and said he'd get someone over to Tintamarre straight away, and that they would be heavily armed. Lebouc thanked me for the tip and hung up.

I wasn't so sure the person who'd shot at us would be crazy enough to attack the Gendarmerie too, but I'd come across a couple things on this job that had me questioning basic assumptions.

"This shit doesn't make sense, Dep," DJ said, as if he could read my thoughts. "So we got that guy René making a quick pit stop to mess up the *hounfour* in the Mélasse villa, then he goes on to Tintamarre to dump a body—a body that he presumably had on board his boat while he's committing another crime? You think he's just dumb or stupid as hell?"

"I'm not sure what to think, exactly, but I'm disinclined to believe René dumped off the body we found. She was chained to one of those old dock pilings we'd seen, under the water, and doing something like that seems an awful lot of unnecessary trouble. Additionally, if he simply wanted to hide the body, why not dump it at sea? Surely René knows the currents around here, and if he wanted, no one would ever see that girl again."

"Then what the hell d'ya think he was doin' out there?" DJ asked. "I just can't put none of this together."

"In this particular case," I said, thinking out loud, "assembling a coherent theory has been as hard as building a house of cards with my nose. We look for answers and only find more questions."

"Amen to that." DJ opened the ice chest under the cockpit table and took out a can of beer.

"Drinking again?" I asked.

He looked at the can tenderly, brushing a bead of water off it with his thumb before answering. "Nah, thought it was some of Alicia's seltzer."

"Those are inside." I held my hand out for the beer, and he gave it up to me as he walked past into the saloon. I threw it back into the ice chest. I wasn't quite sure why Alicia had bought those cans of beer anyhow. I wasn't a drinker, and she didn't like beer.

I should probably save DJ the temptation and dump them all when we returned to port.

We went the rest of the way around St. Martin, retracing our earlier voyage, and returned to the marina just a few hours after leaving. From there, we took the *govi* straight to Pierre Noubon's house.

He and his father were in the back room with half-a-dozen cats. My allergies spiked the second I dared breathe.

"So you found dis *govi* in Billy Pearce's church?" He had it sitting on the coffee table between the couches. Alicia and I were on one couch, Noubon was on the other with his father wheeled up next to him. DJ lurked behind us, pacing the room like a trapped tiger. "And when 'xactly did you find it?"

"This morning," I said. "Shara Bradley told us it was there."

"You spoke to Shara?"

"I would've told you sooner, but we've been occupied with following leads and avoiding becoming murder victims ourselves. Shara came to our boat last night. When we spoke to her, she was alive and seemed well, but in the ensuing half-day, the situation with her has become more... complicated. We've lost contact."

"She gave us a fake address and disappeared," DJ added. "The girl lied to us up and down."

"I see." Noubon leaned back against the couch, steepling his fingers. "You have come close to much danger. I was afraid of dat happenin', but I knew it to be possible—dat's why I had to get a couple boys from Armstrong—and a woman, too," he said to Alicia.

"Everything seemed under control," I said. "And some would argue that fact remains true, but there are those among us who believe this *govi* jar has brought us a run of bad luck."

"What sort of bad luck?" Noubon asked.

"A couple problems with our boat, but I'm not convinced they were caused by a ghost."

"Yet, you are here wid me, and you have brought me dis." Noubon leaned forward and touched the *govi* with the tips of his fingers.

"There's no need to gloat," I said.

"No, no, I did not mean to." He turned to DJ. "Would you bring me my knife? It's over on top of de shelf in de corner."

DJ brought Noubon a small folding knife, which he then used to pry the lid off the *govi*. The second he opened it up, even I, with my nose ravaged by allergies, could smell the wood ash. He dumped the contents on the table, then, using the tip of the knife, prodded through the mess to separate out a few smaller, ash-covered objects.

"Dis is where de duppy come from," Noubon said. "Where 'xactly did you fin' it in Billy's church?"

"In his desk drawer," Alicia said.

"Yes, close to de man." Noubon picked something out of the ash with his bare fingers. It was small, roundish and about the size of a shooter marble. He blew some of the ash off.

"Christ almighty, that's somebody's toe!" DJ said.

"Your eyes be very sharp, Mr. DJ." Noubon dropped the toe in a small dish.

"Why in the fuck would somebody put a toe in that jar?" he asked.

"Dey hated Billy Pearce very much, I t'ink," Noubon said, as he continued combing through the ash with his knife. "De herbs in here—nightshade and turmeric—dey are powerful binding agents, designed to trap an unwilling spirit in dis jar. And de *veve* on de outside" —he brushed his finger across it— "it is of Ogun. I do not know for sure, but I believe whoever made dis wanted Ogun to forge a prison for a man's *gwobonanj*—de immortal half of his spirit. Dey did not intend to free de spirit, as a *govi* is intended for, but wanted de spirit to serve dem forever."

"And the toe?" I asked

"A *gwobonanj* will always seek a body; de flesh is designed to lure it in."

At that moment, Noubon's old man began to wail. Noubon jumped up from the couch and ran for a teakettle at the back of the room. I expected Papa Noubon to foam at the mouth with another seizure, but no; this was far, far different. He threw his head back and the wail turned into a deeper bellow.

"Papa!" Noubon yelled, trying to break him out of it by calling his name and slapping his knee. "Papa, drink your tea!"

"Nuh offer me tea!" he bellowed. Then the old man swung his arms into Noubon and knocked him aside like he was hollow. "Put me to rest!"

He brought his face forward and looked straight at me. It was like something out of a B-horror flick, and I had to fight to keep from rolling my eyes.

"Kill de red tribe!" he demanded. "Kill de woman and put me to rest on Tintamarre!"

"Let's not get ahead of ourselves," I said.

Papa Noubon growled at me. I don't know if he thought he could intimidate me, or if he were trying to frighten me, but it was all a little much. He must've sensed it wasn't working, and his head rolled back as he slumped in his chair.

"Papa?" Noubon was back on his feet, patting his father's hand, maintaining kayfabe by overselling the act of having to snap his father out of whatever it was he'd been pretending to be in. Papa woke with a deep breath and fell into a fit of coughing.

"Jesus, man, that scared the shit out of me," DJ said. "You ever seen something like that happen before?"

"Maybe in a wrestling ring..." I muttered to myself.

"Many times," Noubon said. "When de *loa* take a person over, it is like dat, but Papa too old to commune with dem now, and much too frail." He rubbed his father's back and his coughing subsided.

"Dere we go now," Noubon said. "You just sit a minute and drink yo' tea, Papa."

Papa nodded and Noubon poured him a fresh cup—the last one had been spilled all over the floor and the cats were lapping it up.

"We got to take that *govi* to Tintamarre," DJ said to me. "You heard the old man."

I wasn't going back to Tintamarre to bury a jar. The only way I'd ever go back to that place was with a small arsenal strapped to my back, and only after the beach had been thoroughly shelled by a battleship.

"I thought you were done lugging that thing around," I said. "Remember what it did to *Wayward?*"

"Who else is gonna put it where it needs to go?" DJ asked. "You gonna send Noubon there, or his papa? You think they're gonna take getting shot at the way we did?"

"The way we handle getting shot at is to avoid it at all costs," I said.

"Jerry, DJ's right," Alicia said. "It's too dangerous for Pierre and his father to take the *govi* to Tintamarre."

Not Alicia too! Was I going crazy? Or was everyone else? I wasn't taking that stupid jar anywhere, and I was slightly offended that my own wife was falling for all these cheap tricks straight out of Miss Cleo's notebook.

"All I want to know is who made that thing," I said, pointing at it. "Not who inhabits it. And when we find whoever made it, I want to ask them some very pointed questions."

"I cannot answer dat for you," Noubon said.

"Fine," I said, feeling perfectly ready to move on from Noubon after this farce. "If you can't tell me, who can?"

Noubon moved back to the coffee table, then used his hand to push the bulk of the ashes and herbs and the whole of a human toe back into the *govi*.

"Dere is a wise old *manbo* in Grand Case who know dese curses better dan me—better dan anyone. She was a friend of my papa's back when dey was younger." He capped the *govi* shut.

"Your mother?" I asked.

"No." He pressed the jar against my chest, and I took it. "She can help you fin' where dis jar come from."

I'm sure we were in for a very compelling show.

Noubon looked me in the eyes, then shook his head. "Mr. Jerry, I don' know what you t'ink dis is, or who you t'ink we are, but I am very confused about why, after what you said happened, and after what you have seen here in my own home, you still don't believe any of dis to be true."

My skepticism was hard earned. At too tender an age, I'd learned through experience not to trust another man's word about what was true, and to only trust my own instinct. And in my gut, I was certain old men did not host trapped souls any more than a clay jar did.

But I didn't want to insult Pierre Noubon, so I kept my mouth shut.

"You will see. Maybe not today or tomorrow or any time soon, but you will see," he said.

"I don't think I will."

Noubon sighed. "I will get Mother Manbo's address for you."

CHAPTER TWENTY-FOUR

The address Noubon gave me took us to a back alley in Grand Case. With the setting sun behind us, our shadows stretched out across the damaged asphalt and spooked a rat from a dumpster, which scrambled for the relative safety of an overturned trash can.

A cold wind blew out of the alley, straight into our faces. The hair on my arms stood up on end, and I squeezed the *govi* a little tighter. Further down the alleyway, symbols had been scrawled on the old stone walls on either side—I recognized the *veve* for Ogun, and the *veve* for *La Sirène*, but I couldn't place the others. I also couldn't make heads or tails of the chalk Xs left on just about every surface.

Even I had to admit that standing at the entrance of this alleyway didn't exactly fill me with a comforting sensation.

"Sure ain't the prettiest place on the island," DJ said.

"We're not here to see the sights," I reminded him, walking in. "Let's just get this done so we can find out where the *govi* came from."

DJ and Alicia let me be the point man for our short excursion into the alley. As Noubon promised, we didn't have to go far to find a small red door with a hand-painted skull. I knocked and a woman's voice answered.

"Come in!"

The room behind the door was dark and small, with a ceiling just a few inches above my head. All around us, against every wall, and sometimes coming off the walls perpendicularly, were steel wire shelves crammed full of bundles of spices tied with twine. Some hung a few inches over the edge of the shelves, contributing to the overall claustrophobic aesthetic inside the room. The air was sharp and thick with spice, almost like you could snap off a piece to chew.

I walked in slowly, taking the first left available to me, where I came to face an old woman wearing a white satin turban, seated at a table.

Even in the dim light cast by the burning candles on her desk, Mother Manbo was clearly more withered and grayer than Noubon's papa. She could've been his nanny, for all I knew. However, unlike Papa Noubon, her eyes were clear and sharp, hinting at keen perception and a vigorous mind.

She did not invite us forward—not verbally but still I felt compelled by her to move closer. It was as if she'd expected us to arrive an hour ago, and we had better get on with our business since we were so rudely late.

As I came toward her, I thought I felt the *govi* vibrate in my hand, but it was probably just nerves.

"What are you doing here?" Another woman stood in an alcove formed by two shelves on my left. I knew her. "I thought you were chased off by Sandley Gaspard."

"You're that woman from the market," I said. "Sandley Gaspard? Is he that priest with the machete tattoo on his neck?"

"It is. Now, please kindly tell me why you've come here." She answered her own question when she noticed what I was carrying.

"Where did you find that? Did you steal it from someone? Why did you bring it here?"

"Pierre Noubon sent us," I said.

She rolled her eyes. "The man is sending us tourists now?"

"Actually, ma'am," DJ said from behind me, "We're not tourists. We're a trio of problem-solvers, but we've been cursed by that *govi* Jerry's carrying, and it's really starting to get in the way of our work here. So, if you could please just like... I dunno... un-curse us or what-have-you, we'd really appreciate it so we can get back to our work."

"Is that so?" She came out of the alcove, looking DJ up and down, then shifted to Alicia. "Are you with them, sister?"

"Willingly," Alicia answered.

The old woman cleared her throat and wheezed.

"Are you alright, Mother?" the woman from the market went straight to her side and started tapping her back.

"I am bothered, child," Mother Manbo said. "Why you t'ink it necessary to t'row yourself between me and every person who walk t'rough dat door lookin' for help? Didn't you come here to be my assistant?"

"You got to manage your hours," she answered. "You can't be wasting your time with every tourist coming through your door. Dese people t'ieving a *govi*, for heaven's sake!"

"Ella!" Mother Manbo barked, and the woman from the market, Ella, stiffened up.

"Dese t'ree travelers just tol' you dey was sent by Noubon. Dey not tourists! Now, I know Noubon ain't so sharp as he used to be, but I don't t'ink he'd let his boy send us t'ree people who ain't gonna help us wid our cause. De man's got enough sense left in his head for dat. Now, tend to dem!"

251

"Yes, Mother," Ella said, setting her attention on me. "Set that down on the table, please."

Mother Manbo smiled and beckoned us forward. "Come now, children. I can't move so much like I used to when I was a girl, catching fish wid de boys. Ya gwon have to help me."

I stepped up to her desk, which was as mystical a thing as I had ever seen. It was hung with ivy and dappled with half-melted candles and there were scales and jars of assorted powders. It looked like something straight out of an Arthurian tale.

"I ain't seen a *govi* like dat one for a number of years." She pulled a tea candle out from a drawer and lit it, then set it dead center on her desk. Light played across her face, highlighting her soft chin and high cheekbones against the darkness around us.

She sniffed the air.

"You can put dat *govi* down on my desk, please, boy."

I set it down, and as soon as I did she grabbed my hand. For a split second, I tried to pull away, but this old woman had a climber's grip, and she must've crushed soup cans for fun. She held onto my hand until, after another moment or two passed, to my own surprise, I didn't want to pull away from her.

"Yes, dere's trouble all around you," she said. "A lost soul, an unsettled tet; family follows you."

Her hands were warm. Her touch had my mind spool back to memories of my mother and walks on Balboa Beach, with the sun just going down past the waves, and the air carrying the comforting cool of the oncoming night.

"Oh, and de duppy!" Mother Manbo said. "A bad one, out for revenge—out to kill de people who took his home. He believe he has kin in you. He say you will want de same t'ings he want. He long for de purity of res', yes, but also family–"

Mother Manbo suddenly broke down into a fit of coughs, letting go of my hand.

Ella came rushing up beside her.

"Mother," she said softly, "you strain yourself too much."

"Is she alright?" Alicia asked.

"I'm fine," Mother Manbo answered. She wheezed and then coughed again before she seemed to catch her breath. "De duppy t'ink de two of you have t'ings in common," Mother Manbo said to me.

"Yeah, they're both stiffs," DJ said.

I had as much in common with a ghost as I had with my fairy godmother.

"Ma'am, I'd just like to know where that *govi* came from," I said. "That's all we came here to do—can you tell us who made it?"

"Dat may be all *you* come for," Mother Manbo said, "but de duppy, he got ideas and t'ings he want to share wid you."

"He can keep his ideas to himself," I said.

"Why dat is? Because you don't t'ink dere ain't not'ing in dis world you can't see?"

"Not a bad guess."

"Well, dere are seen t'ings and unseen t'ings, and de unseen t'ings be as real as any plant or fish or boat. De wind is unseen but it carry you here. Dis duppy, he t'ink you a man who know de loss of family, same as him. He seen into your tet, and say you lost a bruddah, and you got a papa you don't claim."

"Is she talking about Arlen?" Alicia asked, with much more sincerity than I cared to hear.

"Of course not," I said. "Everyone has lost a family member at one point or another. She's just doing a cold read. I used to pull that crap all the time in the interview room back home."

I didn't.

"You t'ink I use some cheap trick on you? For what purpose?"

I shrugged.

"Young man, de duppy is de duppy and I can feel him here jus' as much as you feel me when I was holdin' your hand. He real, he got his mind set, and I don't t'ink dat gonna change no matter if you believe he real, or if you believe he less dan wind howling t'rough de trees. He seen inside you, boy, so now he part of you, and he ain't going nowhere til you give him what he want."

She seemed pretty upset at me, but I expected as much. Mother Manbo had spent a lifetime convincing herself to truly believe all the things she said, and my rationality was an insult to her very identity.

I didn't take it personally.

"What about the *govi?*" I asked.

You ain't gonna hear not'ing but what you wanna hear." Mother Manbo glared up at me. "Fine. Ella, help me make room. Dis hard-headed man gonna fin' out de hard way."

Ella took the scales off her desk and Mother Manbo pushed aside some of the glass jars, then picked up the *govi* and pulled the top off. She dumped it out and sniffed the air.

"Where you find dis *govi?*"

"Know Billy Pearce?" DJ asked.

"Yes, I know de man. He was trouble and he was killed—wait, now, is it dis duppy dat did it?" She breathed in deeply through her nose, closing her eyes, appearing to savor the smell. "Yes, oh yes, it's him! I smell de blood on him. You t'ree really got somet'ing here, don't you? Was Billy Pearce keeping dis *govi* in his church?"

"He kept that thing in his desk drawer," DJ said. "I can't figure how, because we only had it about half a day, and it's already caused us all kinds of trouble. He musta' been itching to get his church burned down or have a tree branch fall and crack his head or somethin', man."

"Dis *govi* carry a powerful curse," she said, then raised an eye to look at me. "If you be given to believe in curses."

"I believe what I can see," I said. "I can't see a curse."

"Yes, yes, I know. And not knowin' 'bout curses mean you know about healing or blessings neider. Yo' frien' dere" —she pointed at DJ—"he know. I can see it on him. You should be like him, and maybe de duppy not attach itself to you."

"There's no duppy attached to me," I said. "And if you really can heal people the way you claim, why aren't there hospitals using powders and prayers?"

"It don' work dat way." Mother Manbo motioned for a jar from a shelf to her left, and Ella went to get it.

"Of course it doesn't work like that," I said. "It can't work like that because it doesn't work at all."

"Take it easy." Alicia put her hand on me, but I hardly noticed it.

"He is just fine," Mother Manbo said, as she pinched something out of the jar Ella gave her and sprinkled it into the *govi*. "I met a million peoples like him, t'inking dey know ever't'ing 'bout de world de moment dey come falling out deir mama. De *loa* don' care wheder dat one believe dem or not— dey dere de same, just as de duppy."

She clapped her hands over the jar.

"You mention misfortune," Mother Manbo said to DJ. "Tell Mother what happen."

"Well, the thermostat went all weird on our boat. And then the instrument panel got all funky, and I said to Jerry, 'is that the first time your boat had problems like that?' and he said, 'yeah-huh,' and, come to think of it, that ain't even the worst of what happened to us. We went out to Tintamarre and we found a girl in the water, but when we went, somebody shot at us—"

Mother Manbo held up her hands. "Stop! Stop a moment now, boy, you're going too fast for my old ears. You say you went out to Ile Tintamarre?"

"Yup," DJ said.

"And you saw a dead girl in the water. Who saw her? You?"

"All of us," DJ said. "Jerry went out to get her, but then somebody got the idea to shoot at him from the beach."

Mother Manbo and Ella gave each other a knowing look.

"Which beach?" Mother Manbo asked.

"That one out on the windward side—you know, by the big cliff. And it's got that cave coming out to it."

"Yes, I know de one," she said quickly. She was thinking about something, her face a blank slate, like there was a live bomb in front of her and she had the wire snips in her hand.

"Mother, I think we better—"

"Yes, we got to finish with de *govi*, and den we talk about de rest," she said to Ella as she capped the *govi*. "Bring de rum."

Ella got a big, clear, plastic handle jug from a cabinet. It wasn't anything I'd ever buy if I wanted a drink. Mother Manbo sipped from the mouth of the jug, then spat it out in a fine mist across the top of the govi. Then, she touched the tea light candle to it and a short, faint blue flame burned on top of the *govi* jar.

"Touch de fire," she said to DJ. "Quickly."

He swiped his fingers across the desk.

"Good, now you, girl."

Alicia made a quick jab with her index finger and yelped when she touched the fire, then laughed at herself for being so jumpy. "I'm fine!"

"Now, you, Mister Seeing-is-Believing, you touch de flame."

"No."

"Jerry, just touch the fire. It doesn't hurt," Alicia said.

"I don't care how it feels," I said. "I'm not touching that."

"You have a very stubborn man," Mother Manbo said to Alicia. "How do you put up with dis all de time?"

"She's incredibly patient and forgiving," I said. "I'm lucky."

"You are too strong-willed."

"It's served me well in the past," I said.

"Oh? How so?"

"When I was in the military, that strong will gave me the discipline I needed not only to survive my duties, but to flourish in my position."

"And what was dat? Did you cart de big guns here and dere?"

"I rescued people," I said. "No matter if they were in the ocean, in the desert, the forest, the mountains—anywhere a person was who needed rescuing, I was expected to go in by myself and bring them out alive. Being ready to do that takes a lot of training. And doing the training takes a lot of discipline and willpower."

"Yes, I am sure," Mother Manbo said. "When you say you was to go in by you'self, you mean you go among you' enemies?"

"In some instances," I said.

She turned to DJ. "And what about you? Was you also a fightin' man?"

"I seen some action," DJ said. "I was a door-kicker until my kicker got kicked straight off me, so I quit kickin'."

"And you?" she asked Alicia.

"No, not me," she said. "I was a nurse."

Mother Manbo seemed to consider our answers carefully. She cupped her chin with her hand and watched the blue flame dance until it had almost danced itself to nothing.

"Noubon's boy sent you to me," she said. "He a good boy who had to do bad t'ings, like so many udduh people."

"He believed you could tell us where this *govi* jar came from," I said, trying to corral her back to the whole reason we'd even come here.

"He don' need me to tell you. De man know where it come from, he just want me to see you."

"So he's just wasting our time? Why would he do that?"

She laughed. I didn't get the joke.

"How long you been here? On St. Martin, I mean," she asked.

"A day and change," I said.

"And in dat time, did you figure who killed Billy Pearce? And where Shara gone?"

"Not exactly," I said.

"Dere a reason Noubon's boy sent you to me," she stated flatly, then snuffed out the last of the blue flame by dropping her palm across it without even flinching. "And dere a reason why he asked Armstrong to help him—yes, I know where you chil'ren come from." She paused and looked at each of us in turn, settling on me. "Noubon's boy didn't ask for your help wit'out t'inking long and hard on it, and wit'out knowing you were needed. What do you know about de Chil'ren of Ogun?"

The Children of Ogun? I'll admit the duppy thing seemed compelling, almost to the point that I'd believe it if I was sufficiently drunk and knocked about the head and neck and tortured into believing it. But I wasn't about to believe a bedtime story like The Children of Ogun.

"You not believe, I know," she said, already dismissing me. "But you two, what you heard about de Chil'ren?"

"They worship Ogun," DJ said. "They're scary, and probably mean. That's about it."

"Dey here on de island," the old woman said. "We seen deir *hounfour*, over at de resort."

"The Mer du Mélasse?" I couldn't believe what I was hearing. "You think that's the place where the mythical Children of Ogun meet up? A resort for drunk tourists?"

"Dey are from stories, yes, but dere *are* people here who claim to be dem," she said. "And dey working out of de Mélasse—Albert go dere dis morning."

"Albert?" I asked. "Albert who?"

"Albert René—de fisherman, got a boat called *La Sirène II* because he los' de original in de hurricane."

My ears were screwing with me. This—no, not René. Not *the* René.

"He killed Billy Pearce," I said.

"Oh? Was it Albert made dis *govi* out on his fishing boat?" she asked. "De man had plenty of reason to kill Billy, but he could not have done it."

"It wasn't a magic ghost from a cursed jar that did it," I said.

"De night Billy Pearce was slain," she said, "Albert was on his boat off Tintamarre, watching de Chil'ren of Ogun in dat cave you saw today. He has been dere nearly every day for de past mont', as have dey."

"If you expect me to believe The Children of Ogun are real, you're going to be disappointed."

"You know not'ing. As I just tol' you, dey a story, yes, but dere be very dangerous peoples on St. Martin who believe dey are de Chil'ren, and if dey believe dat and act as de Chil'ren would, terrorizing good people and forsaking de *loa*, what difference do a children's story make?"

She did have a point. If The Children were behind Billy's murder, it seemed plausible they were a legitimate threat and should be treated as such.

"Alright," I said. "Then tell me about The Children of Ogun."

"To understand dem, you must firs' understand de Daughter of Ogun," Mother Manbo said. "She deir leader. She a terrible, manipulative woman. She trick and lie to de people under her control til dey are believin' it is deir holy destiny to wage war on St. Martin until dey take over de island, unifying bot' halves in Ogun's name, and his name alone. De Daughter will rule as his avatar.

"Mer du Mélasse is already under de Chil'rens' control, as well as Tintamarre, and wid every passin' moment, dey grow in power, 'cause more desperate people, who barely survivin' after Hurricane Irma, turn to de Daughter, believin' she can help make deir lives whole again. It not be long before she begin her revolution, and St. Martin will fall into chaos."

"Sounds less than ideal," I said. "But how is it that a cult took over a resort as big as the Mélasse without anyone noticing?"

"Oh, we try many times to petition for help," Mother Manbo replied, the light dancing across her features. "De local government was crippled in de aftermat' of Irma, and many of de gendarmes and ministers and de like were already followin' de Daughter's teachings. Ella went to Paris to try and beg for help from de French government, but dey did not believe what she told dem, and de Dutch government never cared to talk to us at all.

"In de end, it de powers in charge of St. Martin and deir concern wid deir own money dat allowin' de Daughter to do as she want. So long as de cruise ships come in safely and de resorts fill up round de year, no one wid any real power will care who in charge."

Well, I didn't disagree with Mother Manbo. Still, someone else on the island had to care.

"What about Officer Lebouc?" I said, half to her and half to DJ.

"If he don't care about the cult, he's gonna care about the murder they did," he replied. "They killed Billy, plus they killed some other girl that we don't even know who she is yet. We should bring him in."

"We cannot trus' de Gendarmerie," Mother Manbo said. "It is unfortunate, but we don' know how many of de Chil'ren are in deir ranks, and de gendarmerie demselves only here to keep de island ripe for tourism."

If we couldn't go to the police, and we couldn't count on outside help, it seemed our mission was clear.

"How many people are in The Children of Ogun?" I asked. Then changed my mind. "No, wait, it doesn't matter. We've got a job to do, and we're the only ones who can get it done—Billy Pearce's murderers will be brought to justice."

"I saw an internal memo," Alicia said. "There is someone close by who might be of help."

"Who?" I asked, looking over at her.

"Jesse McDermitt?" DJ answered. "No way, man. He's down on St. Barts for his kid's wedding."

"Yeah, he's out," I agreed.

"Too bad," Alicia said. "Charity Styles is there, too."

DJ's face changed in the flickering light of the candles, softening for a second. Then he looked up at me and grinned. "Ain't the first time we've been outnumbered."

"You two aren't leaving me behind," Alicia added.

Mother Manbo clapped her hands. "Oh, you make me so happy! But de t'ree of you will not be alone—you will go wid Albert."

Right. The guy we've been spying on. Reintroducing ourselves was going to be a hoot.

CHAPTER TWENTY-FIVE

Before we left Mother Manbo, her assistant, Ella, had called ahead to René to let them know DJ, Alicia and I were headed over for a friendly chat. Ella informed us one of *René's* crewmen, Jean-Phillipe, would meet us streetside near the entrance to Baie de Marigot docks.

Ella arranged for a ride with a local who was loyal to the cause, and he took us there without delay—in part because I still had the black *govi*, and the way he looked at it, he made it clear he didn't want the damned thing in his car.

We met Jean-Phillipe in the parking lot across the street from the marina. He was the wiry kid I'd seen wrangling Albert René in the market, and he probably wasn't old enough to buy a beer. He wore an easy smile, and his teeth flashed in the darkness like the Cheshire Cat's.

"Oh, Albert gonna love seeing your two faces," he said as we all piled into his tiny Honda. "If he try to rip both your heads off, don't go taking it personally. The man don't like surprises, and he about to get one that's gonna rile him up good. Maybe if your wife throw a little wink at him, though, he'll calm down."

"She's not doing that," I said.

"If it stops him from killing you, I might," Alicia said from the back seat. "Then again, you've been such a wet blanket..."

"Someone has to do it."

"René is gonna try to kill Jerry, no doubt in my mind." DJ was in the back seat too, riding behind Jean-Phillipe. "The two of them hardly knew each other five minutes and René almost jumped over his fish-cleaning station to clean Jerry's guts out of him too."

Jean-Phillipe laughed. "We say that's a rite of passage. You ain't doing your job if Albert don't try to stick you with his scaling knife at least two or three times a week."

We drove east from Marigot, following winding, patchy roads into the central hills of St. Martin. It was nearing about ten at night, and the jungle out there, spotted with the ruins of houses ripped apart by Irma, looked as hostile and foreboding as any place I'd ever seen.

Consciously, I knew I was tired. But my subconscious would continue driving me forward. Knowing it was half the battle. I'd trained in the worst of conditions, and knew what to look out for, not just in others, but also within myself and my abilities.

It didn't take us long to arrive at our destination—a one-story bungalow, devoid of a roof and front door, and housing only wild brush.

Jean-Phillipe followed a dirt path around the backside of the ruined home, pulling up next to an old Chevy. The Honda's headlights shone on a lone grave marker in the yard, about ten yards ahead of us. A fresh bouquet of flowers was laid at its base and a stick of incense smoldered in front of it, but Albert René was nowhere to be seen.

"Where is he?" I asked.

"I'm not sure," Jean-Phillipe said. "He said he was coming up here to talk to his mama, but—"

Gunshots interrupted Jean-Phillipe. They bashed into the windshield with gut-shaking concussion and instinctively, I threw open the door and rolled out of the car. I hit the deck and scrambled toward the rear of the car. On the way, Alicia landed on top of me.

I rolled out from under her, then pulled her from her hands and knees to lie flat against the ground. "Stay low!" I helped her crawl ahead of me as another round of fire popped into the car. The radiator hissed, a tire sighed, and Jean-Phillipe screamed in terror.

He was still inside.

"DJ!" I shouted. "Where's the shooter?"

"Tree line." DJ was already behind the car. "I'd put him at forty yards off, somewhere between eleven and one o'clock, probably by that outbuilding."

An ambush.

I leapt into the front of the car, grabbed Jean-Phillipe by the collar of his T-shirt and ripped him out of his seat. The shooter took the opportunity to needle a couple more rounds in our direction, and I heard a ricochet bounce off the car's hood just as I wrestled Jean-Phillipe past my seat and out of the door.

"Keep your head down, and crawl behind the car!" I kept a hand on his back, crawling alongside him until we were at the car's back bumper with Alicia.

"Are you hurt?" I asked her.

"No, I'm fine." Her eyes were wide as a barn owl's and she pointed at the truck parked next to us, just as the last bit of DJ disappeared around the corner of it.

"He knows what he's doing," I said, then turned back to Jean-Phillipe, who was sitting against the bumper, holding his forearm and kicking his feet.

"Aw yuh lawd, I been shot!"

"Let me see it," I said.

"You a doctor?"

"Something like that."

With my help, he slowly lifted his fingers off. I couldn't see his wound clearly in the darkness, but as I gently turned his forearm in the moonlight, I saw the faint discoloration of a wet gash about the length of my finger. It wasn't freely bleeding, so it seemed more like a burn than an open wound. My guess was that when I'd pulled him out of the car, the ricochet that bounced off the hood had skimmed over his arm like a rock skipping over the surface of a pond.

More shots rang out and the car shuddered when the bullets hit. Jean-Phillipe yowled.

"It's a burn. Keep your hand off it," I said, pulling off my T-shirt. I draped it over Jean-Phillipe's arm, and he winced, which was a good sign the damage wasn't so deep it affected his nerves. "Just keep that loosely over your arm for now. I'll get you better care as soon as we're out of here."

He gritted his teeth and nodded.

I peeked around the side of the Honda—maybe I'd spot the shooter, or maybe I could see DJ and help him. Then, from the shooter's direction, I heard a man cry out.

"Clear!" DJ shouted.

I stood up.

"Where are you, DJ?" I called into the darkness.

"I'm at the tree line at the car's ten o'clock, right next to that building I pointed out," he shouted back. "Dep, you better get over here!"

"Is it René?" I called back.

"Nope!"

I turned to Alicia. "You two stay hunkered down. Keep watch for anyone else coming from the tree line—we don't know who might be out there."

"Be careful, Jerry."

Staying low, I jogged toward DJ's position. As I passed the gravestone, my eyes picked out his shadowy figure waving at me from the darkness, cradling a rifle in one arm.

"Where's the shooter?" I asked.

"Right there." DJ pointed at the ground with his new rifle.

It took my eyes a moment to pick the man's figure out of the brush but sure enough, there was someone lying belly-up on the ground. His face was obscured by a bush, and I didn't get a good look at him until I shifted next to DJ.

"Officer Lebouc," I said. "Good to see you again."

CHAPTER TWENTY-SIX

Though I couldn't see the man's entire face, a sliver of light played in the blood dripping down Officer Lebouc's nose, and the way he lay on his back was reminiscent of a snarling, defeated wolf with its belly exposed.

"Did you break his nose, DJ?" I asked.

"Might've." DJ motioned toward the ruined outbuilding. "Snuck up on him while he was tucked against that corner right there, reloading his rifle, and I smashed his face into it."

"You are making a very large mistake," Lebouc said. "You two Americans do not understand what it is you are doing in St. Martin—you do not know what is at stake and who to trust! You cannot possibly judge me!"

"We'll see," I said to Lebouc, then turned to my partner. "Do you think he's out here on his own?"

"I didn't see or hear nobody else, and I'm guessin' him being out here trying to kill a couple civilians ain't exactly a department-sanctioned op."

"Definitely not," I said.

"It's some real lone wolf-type shit, Dep."

"But do you think the Gendarmerie would punish him for this? If we turned him in, I mean."

"Man, I don't see them even acceptin' what he did as fact. It'll be our word against his."

"You're right," I said. "We should have Armstrong detain him. After we debrief him."

"Yes, talk to me!" Lebouc said. "Then you will know that you do not understand what you are doing!"

I knelt down and straightened Lebouc's collar for him. The man had bloodied his uniform and accumulated a fair number of leaves and twigs by crawling down here in the dirt. It was disgraceful.

"Officer Lebouc," I said quietly. "After what you just did, you're going to need to give us something *extremely* compelling."

Before he could answer, a man came screaming from the brush behind us. I turned, staying low and letting DJ spin on his heel and point the rifle at the threat.

It was Albert René. His arm raised, he froze as soon as he saw us.

"Hold, DJ!" I shouted.

DJ lowered the rifle.

René's eyes were wider than beignets, and the rock he was holding above his head bounced off his shoulder after he dropped it.

"What in the hell are you two doing here?"

"Do not answer him!" Lebouc sounded possessed. "You must *kill* this man. He is deranged and dangerous and he will kill us all given the chance—he is a terrorist!"

By quick survey of our tactical situation, DJ's rifle likely denied René any chance to kill us, and, personally, I didn't believe he wanted to—at least not out of malice, and not right now. Give him some time, however...

"Officer Lebouc," I said, "DJ and I will handle threat assessments, thank you."

"I saw you try to shoot these men," René said incredulously to Lebouc. "Do not try to act as though you know some truth no one else knows, when you cannot even be honest to people who have seen the truth with their own eyes. Did you also tell them how you have been stalking me for the past three months? Did you know that I found the tracking device you put on my boat?"

"I put no such thing on your vessel!" Lebouc said.

"You lie again!" René stomped toward Lebouc, and I got between them. For all I knew René had his favorite gutting knife in his back pocket, and I didn't want to see it used.

"That's enough. We know Officer Lebouc has credibility problems, and you'll get your turn to air out your grievances with him in a moment," I said to René. "First, I want to hear from Officer Lebouc himself why he was waiting in ambush for us."

"I came for René," Lebouc said. "I know Jean-Phillipe's car, and I thought you were him. That is all. It is an unfortunate occurrence of mistaken identity."

"So you were gonna smoke Jean-Phillipe?" DJ asked.

"That's not a good look for you, Officer Lebouc," I said.

"I told you these men are terrorists!"

"What makes René so dangerous that you're willing to execute him while he visits his mother's grave?"

"He is swine." Not putting too fine a point on his opinion, Lebouc spat in René's direction, but I don't think he hit his mark. "I am a sworn gendarme. I have pledged my life to protect the people of France and her overseas territories. What has he done but try to stand in the way of that?"

"You lying filth—" René started to say.

I held up a hand, stopping him.

271

"Mr. René, I said you'd get your chance. Any further interruptions will be handled by my partner, DJ."

DJ clicked his teeth and winked at him, but kept the rifle lowered.

"So you think killing René and Jean-Phillipe and who-else-knows is protecting France?" I said to Lebouc.

"It is also what's best for St. Martin."

"So I gathered. But what has René done?"

"He is part of an organization that continues to deny the right of self-governance to the people of St. Martin. As Americans, surely you know the importance of a society collectively choosing its own destiny. Men like Albert René want to oppress freedom fighters and intimidate people away from the free and legitimate expression of their religion. What more is there to say?"

There was a lot more to say, I thought. For starters, Lebouc didn't directly answer my question and only spoke in abstraction. And I had a good idea of what sort of "legitimate expression" of religion René was trying to "suppress."

"None of that sounds like the sort of crime that warrants a lead implant in Mr. René's head," I said. "Also, the last time we spoke, you never mentioned terrorism. You told us René is the head of some vast, violent criminal enterprise."

That prompted a cutting laugh from René.

"Not now." I wagged a finger at him, then turned back to Lebouc. "I'm not hearing a strong case for immediate neutralization—and what about these freedom fighters René has his thumb over?"

When Lebouc hesitated to elaborate on his assertions, I figured I had probably already learned about the "freedom fighter" from nearly getting mobbed in the Grand Case market, and also what Mother Manbo had told me.

"You're talking about The Children of Ogun," I said.

Lebouc sighed defensively, and slowly scooted against the wall behind him.

"You can see right through him!" René clapped me on the shoulder. "You can't lie to him, Lebouc! This American is too smart for that!"

"*Connard!*" Lebouc said at René, which elicited a chuckle out of him.

"This man, Henri Lebouc, is known to be a collaborator with The Children of Ogun. I have seen him at Mer du Mélasse, interacting with many people who are members."

Now seemed like a good time to let René have the floor.

"Any idea why he's come to kill you tonight?" I asked

"Yes," he said. "Tomorrow is a holy day for The Children, and they are afraid I will intervene."

"Is that right?" I asked. "And why would they be afraid of that?"

"Because they have taken my daughter, Shara."

CHAPTER TWENTY-SEVEN

With Jean-Phillipe's car shot to immobility, we left the ruins via René's truck. DJ, Alicia, and I —with the *govi* on my lap, of course—rode in the bed with Lebouc, his wrists bound to his ankles by some dock line René had. When we arrived back at the marina, it was nearly midnight, so we took Lebouc onto *La Sirène II* and took her out of the Baie de Marigot, away from prying eyes.

DJ and a third crewman I hadn't met used heavier line to secure Lebouc against a bulwark in view of the bridge. And once we were far enough from land, René left the helm to go join them on deck.

I was at the galley table with the *govi* and Alicia, working on Jean-Phillipe's burn.

"I saved so much money for that car." Jean-Phillipe was at the point of tears. "I been fishing two years to pay for it."

"I don't suppose your insurance has a clause that covers gunshots?" I asked.

He didn't find my question helpful.

"At least we're all alive," Alicia said. "We wouldn't be without your car, Jean-Phillipe."

"Yes, I know, and I am glad for that. But I made plans for my life, see, and that car was the first step."

"Plans?" Alicia asked. "Now I have to know more."

"Well, first we must stop The Daughter of Ogun and get all her followers to see reality again. Then, I wanna start my own business. I wanna build good houses for the people of Saint Martin, houses they can afford. It is something we need bad."

"That's a very noble thing to do, Jean-Phillipe," Alicia said. "Did you hear that, Jerry?"

"Mmhmm."

"Yes, I wanna try and live my life so I can make the lives of people around me better. That is part of the reason why I join Mother Manbo and why I am here with Albert."

"What's the rest of the reason?" Alicia asked.

Jean-Phillipe smiled, as if he was embarrassed to answer.

"Oh, it's something good, isn't it?"

"*Bien sûr*, well, yes—but I am not sure I should say."

"Come on, Jean-Phillipe! You can't leave me in suspense like that."

"I do not wish to cause any problems." He tilted his eyes toward the door.

"Would it cause a problem with Albert?"

"Yes, I think so. Not that he don't approve of me, but..."

Alicia's face lit up. "You like his daughter!" Jean-Phillipe didn't understand that to my wife, coming upon juicy gossip was as riveting as striking oil in the backyard. "Oh my God! Does she know?"

Jean-Phillipe motioned with his free hand for her to quiet down.

"Shara does not know, not yet," he said. "But now I am thinking that I don't wanna be waiting until it is too late to say anything, so I will tell her as soon as we rescue her."

Romanticism was cute, but in my estimation dropping emotional bombs on someone you've just rescued from near death probably wouldn't be the storybook beginning Jean-Phillipe was hoping for. Of course, all that hinged on us locating and extracting Shara first.

"Consider pumping the brakes," I said.

"*Excusez-moi?*"

"Just trust me," I said. "When we pull René's daughter out of whatever she's in, give her time to recover before you start writing love songs to her."

"Jerry!" Alicia slapped my leg, then turned back to Jean-Phillipe. "Don't take it personally. Jerry's never met a dream he didn't want to squash, and I think what you want to do is very sweet."

"I'm just giving him the best shot at succeeding," I said. "But you're free to do as you please, Jean-Phillipe."

"Oh," he said. "Okay."

Maybe I was being too hard on a lovestruck kid, but my advice was well-meaning. Anyhow, the three of us stayed quiet while I finished wrapping the burn on his arm. We occasionally heard muffled voices from out on deck while Lebouc was questioned, and even though I'd told DJ to make sure René didn't lose control, I wondered if I should've gone out there too.

"Jean-Phillipe," Alicia said, "There's something else I've been wondering about, and maybe you can explain it to me."

"*Oui?*"

"Why did The Children take Shara? Is it because they have some grudge against Albert?"

"In part, yes, but there is something else Albert don't like to talk about. He only ever spoke about it out loud once to Mother Manbo. No one else. I only know because I was listening outside Mother's shop. They think I be helping Ella load her baskets with healing herbs for the market."

277

Alicia leaned in and rested her chin on her fist. She was pumping a good barrel of gossip today.

"Albert loves a woman who belong to The Children, I believe," Jean-Phillipe said. "She is the mother of Shara."

Okay, this was a good piece of gossip.

"Mary Bradley?" I asked.

"You know her?"

"We've met," I said.

"If she's part of The Children of Ogun, do you mean to tell us Mary helped kidnap her own daughter?" Alicia asked.

"I do not know if she help. It is possible she try to stop it, but she couldn't. But one thing I know for sure. Tomorrow is the mos' holy day of The Children's holy week—*La Semaine de Fer.*"

"What does that have to do with Shara?" I asked.

"Mother Manbo told us The Children sacrifice girls—brides for Ogun, they call them." He froze, not wanting to say whatever it was he'd nearly said. Then, after thinking a moment, he continued.

"We went to their *hounfour* early this morning— we hope to stop them before they do it," Jean-Phillipe said, tightening his face. "Only, we were wrong about where The Children do... what they do. We go to Tintamarre too late."

La Sirène's saloon fell silent. I was thinking about that poor girl in the water. It was all a fraud, and so she'd had the rest of her years robbed from her for what? The promise of a revolution? The empty hope of spiritual fulfillment? Or was she a sacrifice for the vanities of people threatened by the truth?

"You found the girl." Alicia had reached out and put a hand on Jean-Phillipe's. "Did you know her?"

"No. Probably, she was not from St. Martin. Albert thinks she part of the cult, and maybe they already spread to Anguilla or St.

Barth, or even beyond those places." His hand squeezed around Alicia's fingers. "We have to stop them. Before they kill another. And before they are spread so far we cannot wipe them out."

The saloon door creaked open and in walked René, DJ, and the other crewman of *La Sirène*, a rangy guy in his late twenties introduced as Bartram. I figured he was ex-military of some sort, but he didn't say much, and I thought it'd be presumptuous to ask the man his personal history.

"We need to move on Tintamarre," René said on his way to *La Sirène's* helm. "There is no time to waste."

"Right now?" I asked. "Without any kind of plan or intel on who's over there or what they're capable of? Do you think we should, perhaps, build a plan? Maybe go over the intel you've gathered from watching them? Come up with some—"

René stopped and glared at me. "They are capable of kidnapping and murdering an innocent girl, and they are capable of burning down all of St. Martin to get their way."

"Exactly why we should, perhaps, build a plan? Maybe go over the intel you've gathered from watching them? We should come up with some kind of strategy that ensures your daughter makes it out alive."

"There's no time to plan—we only have time to go!"

"And when we get there, what do you suggest?" I asked. "Should we kill them all or just the ones who give us the most trouble? Or do we only kill The Daughter? And if only her, do you know where we can find her?"

René stepped toward me until his legs were against my knees and he was glaring down at me sitting on the bench at the galley table.

"We must burn their entire island and we must burn their

279

hotel," René said. "We leave not'ing of them, and no chance they ever regain their strength."

"Burn the hotel? And all the tourists sleeping in it?"

"They do not concern me, only The Children do. And they deserve far worse than burning to death. They have brainwashed people, they have twisted Vodou from a way to heal into a way to inflict pain, and they soon come for all of us here tonight. So, either we kill them, or they kill us."

Still, it seemed a tad drastic to burn down a resort full of people. I leaned to the side, looking past René.

"DJ, where's all this coming from? Did Lebouc tell you The Children have a nuke or something?"

"We got a few pieces of information out of Lebouc. Most of it was stuff René had already figured out—like the bit about his daughter and The Children's big holiday bash—but we also learned somethin' new. Somethin' troublin'."

"How troubling?"

"Pretty damned so," DJ said. "The Children been armin' themselves for a while, which René knew from watchin' them over the past two years. But what he didn't know, until a few minutes ago, was when they planned on usin' all those little goodies they been pickin' up all this time."

"You know that now?" I asked.

"Yep," DJ said. "Lebouc said The Children are mobilizin'. And they're goin' on the first offensive of their campaign tomorrow, after dark."

"That is troubling," I said. Then I looked up at René. "Mr. René, burning them all to death has a fair chance of getting the job done, but we should also, perhaps, think of Shara. I have an alternate strategy you might find intriguing."

René folded his arms, continuing to stare down at me.

"If you'd let me stand up, I'll share it with you."

But he wasn't going to let me stand up. He stayed as he was, probably assuming he could intimidate me into murdering hundreds of innocent people.

"Albert," Jean-Phillipe said. "Jerry and Alicia are good people."

René considered Jean-Phillipe's plea for a moment and then said to me, "Fine. Tell your idea."

He stepped aside and I rose to my feet to address our ad hoc crew.

"Believe it or not, this isn't the first time DJ, Alicia and I have been at odds with a cult," I said. "Remember our honeymoon?" I said, turning to my wife.

"I'd never forget it," Alicia said.

"We were attacked by a religious fundamentalist cult, but they lost. What worked for us was hitting the leadership," I said. "Once the leaders were dispatched, the rest of the organization fell apart with minimal loss of life. From what we've learned about The Children, it sounds like everything moves through The Daughter herself. She's their leader in all facets, not just spiritually, correct?"

René didn't want to give me a win, so he hesitated to answer.

"That is correct," Jean-Phillipe said. "The Children look to The Daughter of Ogun as a spiritual guide. She lead their thoughts and also she direct their operations." He motioned to René. "Remember when she go on a sojourn for eight nights?"

"Yes, they ran out of fresh water on Tintamarre and The Children almost tore apart when she wasn't there to keep them in line," René said. "But that was nearly a year in the past and they have gained strength since then—there are leaders other than just The Daughter. Destroying The Children of Ogun may not be that simple now."

"Then we plan for that," I said. "We take out their entire power structure—if the mantle is passed onto the Vice-Daughter, or whatever they might call that person, we neutralize them too."

René shook his head. "No, no, there's no time for that, remember? They're going to try and overtake St. Martin tomorrow night."

"What about the rest of your organization, René?" I asked. "Can you task other teams with taking out The Daughter's lieutenants?"

René threw his head back and laughed.

"What?"

"There is only us," he said. "And Ella, Mother Manbo and Noubon, and a few other folk, but we are the only fighters among them."

"And how many people in The Children?"

"Three-hundred and eighty-eight, at last count," René said.

Well, this certainly altered our tactical situation.

"So it's the six of us against a small army of radicalized and armed zealots?" As a PJ, I was used to being outnumbered and on my own, but I'd never been on a mission that felt quite as suicidal as the one I was working on now. I understood why Noubon was so eager to get outside help.

"If that is a problem for you, then you should leave and it will be three men against an army," René said.

I wasn't leaving. Not when I was on the cusp of bringing justice against murderers.

"Fine. We'll work with what we have on hand," I said. "But it seems to me it'll take more than a few bullets to get this job done."

"It takes fire," René said.

"That isn't quite the sentiment I hoped to foster."

"It is what we have with us," René replied. "You have not been here like I have, but I can tell you are beginning to understand the threat we are facing, and you know that we cannot assassinate one person to save St. Martin from The Children. Their corruption runs deep. They have people almost everywhere, at every level of government, within the Gendarmerie, and all over both sides of the island. If we are to win, we must uproot the greatest part of them and cast it into the fires of oblivion—you do not get rid of a weed by cutting it off in the middle of the stem, it will only regrow."

I barely paid attention while René made his case about why we had to burn people alive—the idea was a non-starter with me. But I did catch the end of his plant metaphor, and that seed blossomed into an idea.

"You're right that we have to destroy the plant," I said. "But the best way to do that is at the roots."

"What?" René wasn't following. Looking around the room, nobody was.

"What are you talking about, Dep?" DJ asked.

"Poison," I said.

"You want to poison The Daughter? Or all of Tintamarre and the Mélasse?"

"No," I said. "I want to poison the idea—the idea of a revolution, of installing The Daughter as a new head of state in St. Martin, of the belief systems from The Children of Ogun taking over. I want to poison everything The Daughter used to brainwash her followers. Like Billy Pearce was doing."

DJ blinked at me. "Are you saying you want to start up a new church?"

"No, DJ. Think of what Billy was doing."

"Preaching?"

283

"Yes, but he was developing a following. And in doing so, he was spreading ideas that were mutually exclusive to what The Children teach. They couldn't have another religion taking resources away from theirs—stealing their potential believers—Billy had to go."

"So you *are* saying you want to start up a new church here?"

"No, I'm saying I want to undermine The Childrens' movement by poisoning the ideas they teach."

"You said that."

"Yes, I know." This notion had flooded into my head, and I wasn't communicating it clearly. I had to stop and think about what I wanted to say.

"Alright," I said. "We know we can't stop The Children from launching their revolution by neutralizing The Daughter."

"Another member of their leadership will step in," René said.

"Right. Taking them all out requires manpower we don't have, and we aren't going to burn down an entire hotel full of people either," I said. "So we can't destroy leadership to stop the army, and we can't destroy the army itself, so what we need to do is destroy the army's morale. In this case, that means showing The Children they've been brainwashed to believe a lie."

"Well, in principle it sounds like a good idea, Jerry," Alicia agreed. "But how exactly do we do that?"

I realized I hadn't a clue. No one did, apparently, because we all stood there and looked at each other, hoping somebody would stand and deliver the answer.

Then, Jean-Phillipe jumped out of his seat. "The sojourn!"

"Sit down," René said. "We have been over that idea, Jean-Phillipe, and it is no use to us."

"No—*Écoutez!* Listen! Do you remember why The Daughter went on her sojourn?"

René scratched his head, trying to remember, then he broke into a smile.

"Her house near Antigua," he said. "Yes, yes! All that money she took from the Mélasse and from her followers!"

"What money?" I asked.

"The stuff her people have been giving her to fund their revolution," René said.

"The Daughter has been building a mansion near Antigua," Jean-Phillipe said. "She tells her people she going on a sojourn about a year ago, but we find out through a contact that really, she meet with a realtor and a builder to start building a mansion on a private island she bought."

Well, now, The Daughter skimming off the top of her cult's war chest to fund the development of her private island certainly appeared to be something that would turn the rank and file against her.

"I take it The Daughter hasn't offered any rooms in her new mansion to house the faithful," I said.

"No," Jean-Phillipe answered. "We think none of them know 'bout it."

"That's good poison," I said. "But we can't expect her brainwashed followers will simply take our word that their leader has been stealing money from the cause. We need receipts."

René nodded, which was the first time he'd agreed with me on anything. I must've really proposed a solid idea.

"Yes, and I know where we can get them," René said. "This information came from a businessman we have been working with. He has been paying us to help expose the cult so he can get their property for cheap, because he is trying to buy the Mélasse."

A businessman trying to buy the Mélasse?

No.

No, no—it couldn't be. Surely there was someone else; it didn't have to be Arlen. I curled my toes in my shoes and braced myself for the answer to the question I was about to ask.

"What's his name?" I asked.

"Arlen Burkhart," Jean-Phillipe said cheerfully.

CHAPTER TWENTY-EIGHT

After bringing Lebouc into the saloon and tying him up in a corner, René took DJ, Alicia, and me back to *Wayward*. We followed *La Sirène* around the southwestern bend of the island, to the Dutch side, Sint Maarten, where we came upon Arlen's custom Amels 180 superyacht, *Heart and Soul*.

La Sirène dropped anchor in the bay, and we tied *Wayward* alongside, then were brought by tender to *Heart and Soul's* stern, where her captain and Arlen were waiting.

Arlen looked as aristocratic as ever with his slicked-back hair, white linen pants, deck shoes, and a tumbler of scotch.

"Well, Jerry, it's always a delight when my friends meet each other!" He was trotting down the stairs from the main deck, then stopped and gave Alicia a hug. "Captain René, however did you come to be acquainted with Jerry and his lovely wife?"

"We're in a hurry, Arlen," I said. "Let's go upstairs and talk."

"Is that true, Captain René?"

"Yes," René said.

"Well, then, by all means let's head upstairs," Arlen said, turning around and leading us upward. "I sometimes get overly excited when guests come aboard—this ship of mine was built for hospitality, and with so few guests aboard, I automatically jump at any chance to show her off."

He guided us into the main deck saloon, which was a large, open room complete with a sitting area, a dining-room table set for twelve, a television, a reading nook, a wet bar, separate up and down staircases, and part of Arlen's private gallery of oil paintings of ships at sea. This majestic, breathtaking, awe-inspiring room on a big boat was all exquisitely held together with steel, tinted glass, mahogany and teak, but as ostentatious as the main deck saloon was, it didn't compare to the upper deck saloon and its baby grand piano.

"Please, have a seat." Arlen motioned to the sitting area, where a couch, a coffee table, and a couple armchairs would invite the typical passenger of *Heart and Soul* to settle into a relaxer from all the exhaustion of being carted around the Caribbean Sea, sampling cultures and cuisines, alike.

I didn't sit. Neither did René.

Everyone else did, including Arlen, who took the armchair at the head of the coffee table.

"It is such a welcome surprise to host all of you aboard my vessel. An absolute delight, truly." He set his scotch down on a side table to his right. "When I thought I heard Alicia's voice over the radio, I assumed that meant I'd died and gone to Heaven." Arlen pointed his most charming smile at her. "I've never been happier to be wrong."

"Mr. Burkhart, we need your help," René said.

"Oh? Whatever could I do for you?"

René looked nervously toward me—was he scared of Arlen?

"Sir," he said, "If it doesn't cause too much trouble, we are going to attack Tintamarre tonight."

"You can't be serious," Arlen said. "Tonight?"

"They have my daughter, Shara." René bunched his fists together but kept his voice calm. "They are going to give her to Ogun."

"Oh, I see," Arlen said. "That whole drowning business."

I was surprised to hear he was already aware that the cult had been stealing young women to bring them out Tintamarre to drown them, and, good and noble a man as he was, he hadn't done anything about it.

"It's such a ghastly thing, isn't it? Drowning little girls— I mean, whoever thought they could get away with that?" He shrugged. "Then again, they have been getting away with it, haven't they?"

"That's why we need to stop them," René said.

"If they have your girl, I suppose it makes perfect sense you'd want to move so quickly against The Children," Arlen said. "But you don't need my blessing to do something like that, Captain René. Your autonomy around St. Martin has long been established—certainly long before I ever came along looking to hire you. I'm only interested in The Children and Tintamarre as they pertain to the Mer du Mélasse."

"How exactly *do* The Children pertain to the Mélasse?" I asked.

"They're the staff, Jerry," Arlen said. "Not *all* the staff, mind you, but nearly all, and the board are all practicing members, and they have a controlling interest through various shell corporations—somewhere between seventy and ninety percent of shares, I estimate. I own four percent."

"So they aren't totally lost," I said.

Arlen chuckled. "You've picked up quite a dry wit in your time down here, haven't you?"

"Mr. Burkhart," René said. "I do not want to interrupt, but we do not have much time, and if we are going to save Shara and finally put down The Children tonight, we are going to need your help."

Arlen opened his mouth as if he were about to say something, but stopped short. He put his finger to his lips and crossed his legs, which was a tell of his I'd learned to recognize a long, long time ago—one that signaled Arlen's belief he was now negotiating.

The man never gave up anything for free.

"I see how our interests may align," Arlen said, "but if you're expecting that I'll pick up a rifle and charge into danger alongside you, you'll be disappointed—and besides, I happen to know Jerry and DJ are *very* capable when it comes to that sort of thing. You'd hardly need anyone aside from them."

"No, sir, that is not what I want to ask you," René said. "What my crew and I would like from you, Mr. Burkhart, is the information about that piece of land you sold to The Daughter, and anything else you might have about the house she is building there."

"That little island outside Antigua?"

"We're thinking if we show her followers what she's doing with their money, they won't trust her anymore," I said.

"Interesting." Arlen pursed his lips. "Well, Captain René, I'm afraid I must respectfully decline your request."

René was in disbelief. He looked like he'd been shot clean through the gut. "Decline?"

"Respectfully," Arlen corrected. "It's just that the information you're asking for is very sensitive and, while it will likely be extremely damaging to The Daughter and her movement, there is a bit of finesse involved in these things. That bit of information has to get into the public sphere at the right time, you see, and I'm not convinced now is the right time."

I expected René to leap across the table and rip Arlen's head off like a gutted snapper's. At least, I would've liked him to.

Instead, René kept his eyes down. His hands were clasped together like he was afraid of what they might do to Arlen if they were free.

"Telling her followers she has been wasting all their money will destroy her movement, it will leave The Children in pieces right away. There is no sense in holding that back!"

"It may do just as you say, Captain." Arlen maintained the detached, erudite tone befitting his social class. He picked up his scotch glass and swirled it gently. "But the idea of the group of you invading the home island of a dangerous cult, then simply waving a few documents in the faces of their most hardcore followers— who have killed and will kill again in service of their system of beliefs—" He shrugged and took a sip of scotch. "It certainly doesn't sound as if they'd do anything but kill you. Certainly, they wouldn't surrender their cause."

"They have to accept the truth!" René shouted.

"No, I don't think so, Captain René."

René ripped his hands apart and launched at Arlen. Disappointingly, his crew and DJ jumped up and stopped him from getting there.

"You're killing my baby girl!" René shouted, as he struggled to get free. "You're putting her to death!"

Arlen stayed in his chair, legs crossed, glass in hand. "Really, Captain René, all of this emotion is completely unnecessary. And you'd do yourself a terrific disservice by harming me."

René broke free of the three men holding him back, not by pressing forward and coming at Arlen, but by turning around and retreating to the doors behind me. DJ, Jean-Phillipe, and Bartram followed him out.

When the door slid shut behind them, I met Arlen's eyes. The heartless bastard gaped back at me in an approximation of genuine human bewilderment. It was a poor copy.

"Well, I'm not sure why he felt that was helpful," Arlen said. "I like Captain René, but he has a real problem with controlling his temper."

"Even you know he's right," I said.

"It's not about right or wrong, Jerry," he said. "You know, one of the best pieces of advice I ever got came from a close friend of mine. He said to never give up anything for free and following that advice has served me unbelievably well."

I recognized my father's own words.

Outside, there was a crash of metal on metal. It sounded like a chair being winged across the deck.

"I'm going to go check on that," Alicia said, as she got up from the couch. She went for the door and patted my shoulder on the way.

"You got this," she whispered.

I supposed it *was* up to me. No one knew Arlen's mentality, his habits, better than I did, and if one of us had any chance of persuading him to do something that might not completely align with his personal interest, it was me.

I waited for Alicia to slide the door shut before I started the delicate dance that was negotiating with Arlen Burkhart.

"You're being an absolute shithead," I said. "Not every contact you have with a human being has to be transactional."

"I'm not sure I agree," Arlen said with a grin. He knew he had me now, and I'd have to give up something to get the information we needed. I doubted there was anyone else in the whole world whom Arlen wanted something from more than me.

"You don't have to agree," I said. "You're getting what you want if we succeed."

"What's that, Jerry? Another piece of real estate? What do I care?"

"Isn't that everything you've always wanted?"

His expression flickered into displeasure before settling into his normal, cold-eyed smile.

"You know as well as I do there's no assurance that whatever little stunt you pull will actually damage The Children of Ogun, let alone scatter them to the winds. What we're really talking about here is an *attempt*, and from my vantage point, it doesn't seem a particularly sound attempt either. You and DJ and Captain René's crew go to Tintamarre and do what? Flash papers around like cops? René knows those people are armed and ready for a fight. Do you think they'll put their hands up and turn themselves in at the sight of you?"

"The plan is to destroy their will to fight," I said.

"Oh, yes, I know that's the plan," he said. "What I'm more concerned about is what happens when the plan goes wrong. Because you and Captain René do have one thing right—the information about The Daughter's real estate deal will be highly damaging to her reputation, but, as I said, only if it is pushed at the right time."

"Then when's the right time, Arlen?" I asked. "After Shara's dead? Or another girl after her? Or when The Children push into St. Martin and start killing anyone who tries to stand in their way?"

"You are so short-sighted, Jerry," he said. "So narrow."

"You're going to let an entire island burn because stopping it doesn't benefit you as much as you'd like."

"Don't be dramatic!" His temper was flaring.

"You're a murderer."

"I am no such—"

"You're as selfish as you've ever been. Maybe more so."

He jutted a finger at me. He was pissed. "That's not fair to me, I've—"

"What? Worked on yourself? Meditated? Seen a guru? That's simply wishing for your problems to go away, and it's not working. You're still doing the same things you did in the past. Maybe it's worse now—you're going to let an untold number of people die to get a business deal done, rather than just—"

Arlen slammed his scotch glass on the coffee table, spilling booze everywhere. "Don't you say it, Jerry! Don't you fucking *dare!*"

He glared at me from across the table, his chest heaving. I had him worked up, but he deserved so, so much more than that.

"Shit, Jerry! Look what you made me do!" He stood up and brushed at the scotch on his pants. "My heart bleeds for Mr. René, for his daughter, for all the girls who have been taken by The Children, and for all the chaos and death they'd cause if I release the information I have when the time isn't right. Do you understand?"

I understood that Arlen was still playing games, and that no matter how mad I got him, he would continue to "negotiate" with me until I finally collapsed in exhaustion or gave him what he wanted.

And I knew what he wanted.

Arlen wanted to be wanted by me. No matter what I said to him, what I did, or how I might feel about the man, in his eyes, I would always be a lanky kid hanging out with him at Yosemite, taking his advice on how to bait a fishhook or what to do when bears came rummaging for food.

He wanted me to be the son he'd lost.

"Arlen," I said, "We need your help. We can't do this without you backing us up."

He tilted his head and looked me straight in the eyes. "Who needs my help?"

There could be no room for doubt. I had to swallow my pride, say it in plain English, and I had to say it directly to him.

"Arlen, *I* need your help."

CHAPTER TWENTY-NINE

After Arlen decided to play ball, we transferred Lebouc from *La Sirène II* to *Heart and Soul*. Lebouc wasn't pleased about remaining a hostage, but his anger was somewhat assuaged when one of the crew members brought him a glass of cognac and Arlen welcomed him as an esteemed guest.

With Lebouc handled, we retreated to *Wayward* to strategize.

Our goals were clear: get Shara out alive and expose The Daughter as a fraud. Solving Billy Pearce's murder had to go on the backburner, but it seemed clear that The Daughter had ordered her followers to do the deed and putting her face-to-face with justice would necessarily mean extracting her from their protection on Tintamarre.

In any case, we were in *Wayward's* saloon with our tools sorted around the room: weapons in one corner, twenty-four-hour rations in another, swim gear laid out on the galley counter and maps spread across the dinette table.

I supplied most of the gear from my various caches in *Wayward*, save a short-barreled rifle DJ had captured from Lebouc that fired 7.62, and an old French FM 2429—a light machine gun that the crew of *La Sirène* must've found at an antique shop.

"How many times have you actually fired this thing?" I asked René.

"Me? Never," he said. "But my bosun, Bartram— the man shot it plenty of times."

Bartram was in the furthest corner of the saloon, checking through my collection of rations, too busy picking out the best ones for himself to be aware of our conversation.

I stooped down, getting a closer look at the light machine gun. With its scratched and abused receiver, worn-out stock, and a barrel that I would hazard to be questionably straight, the FM 2429 wouldn't win a beauty contest. Still, it was a nice piece of history, and we probably wouldn't need it, so I tried not to make too big of a stink about it.

I picked it up by the wooden carry handle, which caused the barrel to snap out of its mounting sleeve and tumble to *Wayward's* deck.

"That happens all the time," René said. "The old barrel got loose over time, but Bartram can fix that, easy."

The threads at the base of the barrel were marred and chipped pretty badly. I'd be impressed if Bartram could fix it in any appreciable manner, and amazed if anyone could fire the gun without the barrel shooting off too.

"What kind of round does this thing shoot?"

"Three-o-eight," René answered.

"I'm afraid I left those and my Garand back at home in my foxhole."

"It's no worry," René said. "Bartram has been hand-loading rounds as we find them. We've amassed a couple hundred back on *La Sirène*."

"Nothing worrying about that statement, at all," I said.

298

"If you don't like it, that's too bad," René said. "My crew and I can save Shara without you."

"DJ and I aren't letting you go in alone."

He appeared satisfied with that answer.

In addition to antique weaponry, René provided the maps. In anticipation of an assault, he, Jean-Phillipe, and Bartram had spent the better part of two years watching The Children of Ogun and keeping detailed notes on their whereabouts and the potential weak points in their compound on Tintamarre.

After getting our gear settled and organized, we gathered around the table and went over René's intel.

"The Childrens' base of operations is in a bomb shelter beneath Tintamarre." Among all the scribblings and notes written on the map, René pointed to a square he'd drawn on the center of Tintamarre in red Sharpie. "The main hatch is here. The only other known entry point is through a cave on the east end of the island that the French began to outfit as an underground dock. They got as far as pouring some concrete and installing a fifteen-foot- wide blast door before they abandoned the project entirely. According to informants I've spoken to in the past, both the hatch and the cave are manned by at least three armed worshippers at all times."

"How many people inside the shelter?" I asked.

"I estimate somewhere between thirty and fifty at any given time, but with their holy week—*La Semaine de Fer*—going on now, they will be closer to fifty in strength."

"And they all live there?" I asked.

"The vast majority of their membership lives in and around the Mélasse. Very few of them live in the shelter year-round. It is mainly The Daughter and some of her closest followers, many of whom are there to train the other members—men and women—for combat."

299

"So they ain't sexist," DJ said. "That's nice."

"How do we get past the guards?" I asked.

"Bartram and I have been talking about that for some time," he said. "It was very wise of Pierre Noubon to bring you here this week. During *La Semaine de Fer*, The Children have a sunrise worship every morning on the east-facing cliffs. If Bartram sails by on *La Sirène* and takes a few shots at The Daughter, they'll send everything they have after him."

"What's he shooting with?" I pointed at the FM 2429. "I hope you've got something more convincing than that."

Bartram grimaced at me. Insulting his gun was like insulting him, I saw.

"It is a good weapon," Jean-Phillipe said. "I saw Bartram practice with it."

"I'm gonna give him a better weapon," I said. "That thing's more likely—"

"If Bart's gonna make 'em chase," DJ wisely interrupted, "what're they chasing with?"

"Small vessels, small arms. Nothing that can do any appreciable damage, even if they reach *La Sirène*, which they can't. She may look like an old fishing tub on the outside, but my crew and I have made some upgrades to her internals. She's as quick as they come."

"Alright. Bartram draws them off," I said. "What do we do once we're in the shelter?"

René pulled aside the map of Tintamarre, revealing a map of the shelter hand-drawn on large graph paper.

"Where did you get this?" I asked.

"I pieced it together from information told to me by a man who used to manage the airport that was on Tintamarre in the sixties— long before the cult moved in.

"Here's the hatch," he said, pointing to a long shaft at the top of the map. "The main shaft goes down about thirty feet, then you come to a big antechamber with a door on either end. You can go eastward, toward their mess hall, firing range, and eventually the cave"— he dragged his finger to the right as he talked, underlining large chambers in the map— "or you can go westward, toward the sleeping chambers and *hounfour*."

"That's their temple thingy, right?" DJ asked.

"Yes, that is it," René said. "Shara is almost certainly being held in the *hounfour*. With Bartram distracting the cult's forces, all we need to do is grab her and head for the entrance."

"With *La Sirène* busy, we can use *Wayward* as our escape craft," Alicia said. "I'll stay as close to the shore as possible."

"No, that's too risky," I said. "You need to be well offshore while *La Sirène* plays rabbit and gets The Children to chase. I don't want anyone accidentally seeing you and forgetting about him."

"Then how're you getting off Tintamarre?" she asked. "Unless the plan is to swim to St. Martin with Shara on your back?"

"She's got a point, Dep. We need a ride back from shore," DJ said.

"If we're worried about *Wayward* being spotted, after I drop you all off with the Mako, I'll sail away from Tintamarre and come back," Alicia said.

"Alright," I said. "But you keep out of sight until the designated time."

"When will that be?"

"Depends on how much time Bartram can give us."

He waved his head from shoulder to shoulder, thinking, but not speaking.

"He can give us as much time as we need," René said. "*La Sirène* can run circles around any little rowboat they put in the water. She can be halfway to Guinea by the time they cast off."

"Take them as far away from Tintamarre as they'll go, but keep them interested," I said to Bartram. "I doubt they'll leave it unprotected indefinitely. They'll come back, and if they do, you keep taking shots at them from *La Sirène's* deck until you're too annoying to ignore. And be sure to keep your transponder on so *Wayward* knows when to come back in for us, even if we lose radio contact."

He nodded.

"That's good with me," Alicia said.

"Good. Now, everyone divvy up gear. DJ can assign weapons and rations while Alicia and I grab a couple backpacks."

"Aye, Dep," DJ said.

Alicia and I went into the port hull, closing the door behind us.

"You don't have to do this," I said to her.

She turned around and cocked an eyebrow at me. "Jerry Snyder, do you think you're *protecting* me?"

"These people shot at us for being too close to their island," I said. "I'm under no illusions we're going to come out of this without getting powder under our nails."

"Then maybe I should make *you* stay back," she said.

"You know I can't do that. Not with Shara on the island, and—"

"A case to solve," she said. "And you should know that I can't sit back for the same reasons."

This woman was unstoppable, and I loved it. At that moment, my hands had no choice but to grab her by the waist and pull her in.

"Don't get distracted from your mission, now." The way Alicia looked up into my eyes, I couldn't have focused on anything else.

I leaned in and kissed her like it was the night after we'd survived that rocket attack on Little Thatch Island. What a honeymoon that turned out to be.

Alicia pulled away, her eyes looking almost phosphorescent in *Wayward's* soft, interior lighting.

"Hopefully the electronics don't break down again," she said. "Since I'm supposed to watch *La Sirène.*"

"I thought we had all that curse business cleansed off us," I said. "By Mother Manbo. That should protect us, no?"

"And I thought you didn't believe in curses."

"When it comes to an op like the one we're looking at tomorrow, I'd pray to any god who'd swear to make it go smoothly."

CHAPTER THIRTY

With our plan in place, all we needed to do was execute.

René and Jean-Phillipe came aboard, and then we motored *Wayward* against the wind around the southern shore of Sint Maarten, then up the coast until we turned east and were about a quarter of a mile off Tintamarre.

DJ and I would go first. We geared up, each of us with a rifle and a pack carrying twenty-four hours of rations, a few extra magazines, a small trauma kit and flashlights. Additionally, I brought my Beretta 92FS, and a larger trauma kit in case our mission took an unplanned detour.

Kitted out for the mission, we boarded *Wayward's* dinghy, piloted by Alicia, and she took us to shore, ordered us to keep safe, then turned around for René and Jean-Phillipe.

Now, standing on a rocky, narrow strand of beach, I looked ahead into the darkness of pre-dawn blanketed over thorny, dry scrub brush and a few respectably sized rocks. When we'd cruised past Tintamarre on *Wayward* the other day, all DJ and I saw were rocks and brush in equal parts, and a handful of undersized trees gnarled by relentless easterly. The sparse vegetation was spread across the dusty island, which was about a mile long from east to west, and I'd guess less than half that length from north to south.

Given the sparse flora, DJ and I only had the darkness for concealment while we waited for René and Jean-Phillipe to join us on shore. So, we both took a knee in the rocky sand, lowering our profiles.

I kept watch, scanning the horizon for any menacing or moving shadows, while DJ slipped off his pack and shuffled the contents around.

"Damned entrenching tool keeps rammin' into my back," he said as he tossed a collapsed shovel into the gravel.

"What'd you bring that for anyway? We were supposed to pack light, and I don't expect we'll be digging into a defensive position."

"I know that, Dep, but I still need somethin' to dig with."

"The prospect of us tunneling out of the bunker is fairly remote," I said.

DJ scooped a wadded-up towel out of his pack and laid it next to the entrenching tool. He peeled a corner of the towel back, and revealed it wasn't wadded up just because he didn't like to fold—he had the black *govi* inside it.

"Where did you get that and why did you bring it with us?"

"I told Mother Manbo what Papa Noubon said." He carefully turned the *govi* in the towel, checking it for damage. "She said if the duppy told us to bury this thing at Tintamarre, we be smart to listen."

"The duppy didn't say that."

"Ah, so you admit!" Even in the darkness, I could see his eyes light up.

"I admit what?"

"You think the duppy is real."

I pretended to see something interesting on the horizon and locked my eyes that way.

"I knew you wasn't a skeptic all the way through," DJ said.

"Shut up and finish repacking."

Before long the dinghy motored into the shallows. René and Jean-Phillipe hopped into the knee-deep water and came up onto shore beside us. Neither man looked particularly comfortable landing on an island while outnumbered by hostile combatants, but René, in particular, appeared surprisingly apprehensive. From the moment he'd threatened to stab me with a fish-gutting knife, I'd assumed Albert René was the type always spoiling for a fight and would relish the chance to spill the blood of the people he hated for kidnapping his daughter. But then again, he might not worry about taking the enemy head-on as much as he worried about his daughter's safety.

"Within two hours, you'll have Shara back safely in your arms," I said to him. "You have my word on that."

He grumbled and stepped around me on his way inland.

"Captain René is starting to like you, I am thinking," Jean-Phillipe said, trailing behind René. I fell in beside him and DJ brought up our rear.

"Is he? It looked to me like your boss is still deciding if he wants to kill me."

"Yes, but that is an improvement, is it not? The first time you spoke his daughter's name to him, he *for real* tried to kill you."

"Fair point, Jean-Phillipe."

Each man had one of my rifles in his hands as we pushed up the rocky shore and into the first patch of scrub. Thorns pricked at the knees of my pants, and the rocky, uneven ground under my boots threatened to break my ankles if I dared set a toe on the wrong spot.

I was careful not to.

Our slow, careful, concealed maneuvers continued inland for another fifteen minutes or so until we came upon what I thought was a long, low boulder, partly overgrown. René crouched and leaned against it, and the rest of us followed suit. With my shoulder now pressed against it, I realized it wasn't a boulder at all, but was smooth and square—a foundation for a long-gone building.

"The way into the bunker is up there, about thirty meters," René said, waving his hand in a northward direction. "We wait here until Bartram gives the signal."

"Right," I said.

Bartram's signal was gunfire. René said he'd open up with that old French machine gun that fell apart in my hands, and I'd reminded Bartram he had my AR with the eighteen-inch barrel, and it was perfect for reaching out and touching our hostile neighbors from the deck of *La Sirène* at about five hundred yards on relatively calm seas. Its range was even longer if he were on steady ground, and longer than that if he didn't care to actually hit them.

I peered over the foundation. Pink light spread from the eastern horizon, and the shadows of rocks and brush and distant trees became more distinct. So, too, did the entrance to the bomb shelter where The Children lived.

As René had indicated, the entrance was roughly twenty yards to our north, between a quartet of hollowed foundations. It was roughly the size and shape of the cellar doors the farm hands disappeared beneath in the opening of *The Wizard of Oz*. However, in place of rickety wood slats, I imagined there was heavy steel.

Suddenly, gunfire erupted to the east. I recognized the sound of my rifle.

"It seems Bartram didn't get that old French machine gun up and running after all," I whispered toward René. "I wonder if it finally disintegrated."

"You don't know that," he said.

Before I could rebut him, the bunker door screeched and clanged open. Two men came out, running eastward in a dead heat, rifles in their arms while their radios crackled with panicked voices.

Too eager, René charged out of our cover and bounded for the shelter door, with Jean-Phillipe right behind him.

"Wait!" I yelled after them.

By the time the word left my mouth, it was too late.

During our planning meeting on *Wayward*, René had told us there would be three guards posted at the shelter entrance and only two had split for the eastern shore. The third popped out of the hatch like a jack-in-the-box, rifle at the ready, as the two men closed on the entrance.

DJ was quick on the trigger and hit the guy just as he fired, but unfortunately, not before. The shooter flipped backward and disappeared.

René ducked against another of the empty foundations, and Jean-Phillipe sprawled to the ground on his belly, kicking up dust.

There was a moment of quiet. The echoes of DJ's shots mixed with the enemy's and disappeared out across the water while we all waited for whatever was going to leap at us next.

Jean-Phillipe cried out in agony.

I sprang from cover and ran toward him. The kid was on his belly, and I could see the wound in the lower part of his leg.

"God, no!" René bellowed and Jean-Phillipe cried.

I slung my pack off, ripped it open, took out my trauma kit and got to work.

"I'm with you, Jean-Phillipe," I said as I sorted out what I'd need. "Hold tight and I can promise you'll get through this just fine.

"Come turn him over," I motioned at René. He and DJ were there in a flash, helping Jean-Phillipe get belly up, and helping him rest on his elbows while they all watched me.

The bullet had entered his shin and cleanly exited his calf, leaving a wound somewhere between the size of a nickel and that of a quarter. I didn't get a clear look at the shooter's weapon, but judging by the size of the exit wound, Jean-Phillipe was struck by a small caliber round and, luckily, by the way it was bleeding in a slow, steady dribble, I knew it hadn't hit either artery, so he wasn't in any danger of bleeding out. However, the shot had likely hit, and fractured, bone, and that couldn't have been comfortable.

"Is it bad?" he asked.

"You'll be okay," I said in my bedside tone as I dug into my trauma kit and got out two squares of gauze, a roll of athletic tape, and some antiseptic solution with lidocaine. "We'll get you patched up and everything will be just fine. You'll be playing soccer again in no time."

I had no idea if Jean-Phillipe played soccer. He'd never mentioned it.

"How bad is he bleeding?" René was cradling Jean-Phillipe's head and seemed more panicked than my patient was.

"It's very light. The bleeding will stop soon," I said, spinning the cap off the antiseptic. "I'm gonna put a little bit of this on the wound. It might tickle at first, Jean-Phillipe, but there's a numbing agent in this solution that'll help with the pain while the antiseptic keeps the wound clean."

I poured it on without warning, and while the stuff fizzed over Jean-Phillipe's wound, he rolled his head back and squeezed his fists through it, but he didn't pass out. Not bad for a kid from St. Martin. I'd seen Army Rangers turn green and black out before I even opened the bottle.

That done, I put the gauze on both sides of his leg and worked on taping him up.

"Jean-Phillipe, as long as we keep that wound clean, you'll recover without any complication," I said. "But I can't guarantee we'll keep it clean out here on Tintamarre."

"We gotta evac him," DJ said.

As if to punctuate his point, rounds of gunfire roared to our east, and boat motors growled into full speed.

"They're still too close to the island," I said. "We can't get *Wayward* here without it being spotted."

"What about Alicia taking the dinghy in?" DJ asked.

"That will take too much time," René answered. He hooked both his massive hands under Jean-Phillipe's arms and pulled him to his feet.

"He can't walk," I said.

But René didn't stop there.

"Hold him up!" he barked at me.

"I'm not holding this man up," I said. "He can't possibly walk with a gunshot wound in his leg."

"He's not walking!" René yelled at me. "Get him on my back!"

DJ and I helped Jean-Phillipe climb onto René's back. As soon as René took his first step toward the bunker's entrance, it became apparent to me that he had no intention of walking back to St. Martin via the bottom of the ocean with Jean-Phillipe on his back. René meant to complete the mission, with Jean-Phillipe riding piggyback the whole way.

"That kinda puts him at a tactical disadvantage, don't it?" DJ asked me quietly. I'm sure René heard him, but he didn't react.

Jean-Phillipe was about half René's size, not a bad ratio, honestly. René had probably hauled in bigger fish by himself, and I had once seen a smaller man than René carry upon his back a larger man than Jean-Phillipe three miles down an Afghani mountain.

"We'll get the job done," I said to DJ. He nodded his approval.

René was able to climb into the bunker entrance without much trouble, and DJ followed behind. I pulled up the rear. As I came to the shelter entrance, I looked over the side at the man DJ had shot. He was sprawled in the dirt, his rifle still in his hands. He was middle-aged with a few gray hairs and wrinkles—far too seasoned to have thrown his life away like this.

As I brought the door closed, I watched the eastern horizon, where gunfire continued to pop sporadically against a backdrop of boat-engine noise. The sky still wasn't quite bright enough to illuminate the fighting, but so long as it continued, I knew Bartram and *La Sirène* were doing their job, so we had to do ours.

A ball of light traced across the darkened waters, moving from my left to my right. It suddenly bloomed into a fireball that, at this distance, appeared no bigger than my thumbnail. But my stomach dropped. I knew exactly what it was.

"*Sirène's* been hit!" The fireball continued to shimmer on the horizon. "It's on fire!"

"What?" René was already halfway down the ladder, but he came bounding back up, pushing past DJ. "How can you tell? How do you know?"

He looked out at the shore, then back at me, and before I knew it, he'd grabbed both straps of my backpack and jerked me close. "Why would you say a thing like that?"

312

"It wasn't my doing!"

"*Espèce d'abruti!*" he shouted into my face. Then, the bunker entrance deteriorated into indiscriminate shouting from René, from me, from Jean-Phillipe. DJ was there in an instant, separating us.

But he didn't need to—I wasn't going to fight René. I just wanted to tell him that in my time, I had seen fireballs. Both those that exploded upon impact and failed to catch, and those that smothered machine and man indiscriminately.

"How do you know?!" René bellowed over DJ. "How do you know?!"

I waited for him to stop.

"He knows, alright, man?" DJ said to René, walking him backward. "This ain't the first time he's seen something like that."

René looked at DJ and grumbled. The two of them separated.

"I don't think Mr. Jerry would exaggerate," Jean-Phillipe said from René's back as René went toward the entrance ladder.

"Where you going, man?" DJ asked René. "Your buddy needs our help!"

René shook his head and started down the ladder.

"Shara needs our help," I said for him. "Bartram knew what was at risk here—the same as all of us."

"Oh, fuck that!" DJ said. "We can't leave the man to burn up!"

"It isn't right, DJ," I said. "And we shouldn't—it isn't tactically sound to abandon our plan and rush out to help Bartram, stiffened enemy resistance or not. However, without *La Sirène* harassing The Children to keep them busy, our rescue mission falls apart. So, how do you feel about playing guerrilla?"

"I feel damned good about it," DJ said without a moment's hesitation.

I slung my pack around and dug out my extra magazines, keeping two for myself. If I had to expend more rounds than that, it meant The Children had gotten Bartram, which meant we were outnumbered, and the mission was sunk anyway.

"Don't get too risky out there," I said, slapping the mags into his waiting palm.

"I'd never do anything crazy, Jerry." DJ laughed as he hopped out of the shelter entrance, then closed the hatch.

I followed René down the ladder.

CHAPTER THIRTY-ONE

I stepped off the last rung of the ladder, joining René and Jean-Phillipe in a large concrete chamber approximately a thousand square feet in size. The lights were on, the TV in one corner was still playing some French movie, and remnants of a hastily exited card game sat on a nearby table.

On the walls, on the ceiling, even on the floor were more *veve*, drawn with chalk or paint or some kind of yellowish powder that looked similar to cornmeal. They all had the same motifs as the other *veve* for the *loa* Ogun that I had seen up to this point—machetes, cigars, and rocks that ostensibly resembled the small piece of iron ore embedded in that ring DJ had found in Billy Pearce's church.

"Are these all for Ogun?" I asked quietly.

"Yes," Jean-Phillipe said. "For him only."

Suddenly, there was a clang behind us, and I spun in the direction of a door on the east end of the room, then raised my rifle, ready to fire the second I saw the whites of any eyes I didn't recognize.

"I'm on it," I said.

I moved toward the door at a deliberate pace, minding my breathing and keeping my cheek nestled tightly against the stock of my rifle. The chattering from the TV deteriorated to white noise as my ears tried to catch any sound that might sneak out from behind that eastern door.

I heard nothing, but that wouldn't give me permission to drop my guard. I continued my slow, sure march toward the door, stopping only when the muzzle of my rifle was a few inches away.

The door was constructed of the sort of heavy steel one expected to find in a bomb shelter or a Navy shipyard. As quickly as I could, I grabbed the handle, twisted it open, and then pushed the door only hard enough to open it a few inches, so that I could see inside without completely exposing myself to enemy fire.

Of course, I didn't immediately spot anyone.

I saw a clean kitchen, stocked with well-used but well-maintained stainless-steel furnishings like a prep table, a pair of stoves and ovens, and a full suite of chef's utensils, suspended from hooks on the far wall. A large pot sat on one of the ranges, waiting to be used, and as I stepped to my right to see more of the kitchen, it appeared a baking tray blotted with uncooked croissants had slipped off the prep table and clattered to the floor.

I pushed the door open the rest of the way, quickly scanned the room once more, then took a step inside.

Nobody tried to kill me, as there was no one to be found. And without any doughy footprints running the other direction or any sign of a hasty cleanup, I could only conclude the sheet had fallen on its own. Probably when *La Sirène* had opened fire on the morning congregation and a general call for help was made over the radio, the pastry chef who had been working here ran off and accidentally left the tray teetering on the edge of the counter, and the tray took a few minutes to work up the nerve to jump.

Or not.

In any case, I had no time or desire to solve the mystery of the suicidal croissants.

I turned back to the main room. René and Jean-Phillipe were already at the westernmost door, waiting for me. René motioned for me to hurry up.

I went through the door behind him. Here, we found ourselves in a long hallway with about a dozen doors on each side, evenly spaced ten or so feet apart. Most were closed, but a couple were left cracked open.

We pushed forward, and I peered into the first open door we came across.

Inside was a dorm-like room with two sets of bunk beds pushed up against opposite walls. Also inside were suitcases and duffel bags; one had been left open and knocked over, scattering clothes and toiletries across the floor. A woven tapestry, similar to what I had seen at Pierre Noubon's house, was hung on the far wall and, same as the *veve* we had seen, the tapestry also appeared dedicated to Ogun.

We pressed through to the opposite end of the hall, through another door and into complete darkness.

I had a light clipped to my backpack strap. I clicked it on.

My eyes focused on Jean-Phillipe a foot or two in front of me, and beyond him a thin post. It looked like one of the structural supports for the shelter, but what it originally was didn't matter, because now it was the *potomitan*—or worshiping post—at the center of The Childrens' *hounfour*.

Like the other I had seen at the Mélasse, this too, was covered in *veve* for Ogun and there were old cigars left at its base and strings of beads as well as a scattering of rice and beans.

"Shara?" René whispered into the darkness.

Chains rattled somewhere ahead.

"Papa?" a faint voice called back.

Even with Jean-Phillipe on his back, René ran for his daughter. I made sure my light followed him, so he didn't trip and break both their necks.

"Oh, my baby girl! *Mon petit chou!*" He squatted down, letting Jean-Phillipe gently slide off, and now that he had, I saw Shara's face over René's huge shoulders as they hugged each other tightly.

René let her go, then planted a kiss on her forehead. Tears were streaming down Shara's cheeks, and he pushed them away with his thick thumbs.

"Are you hurt, baby girl?" His voice was cracking.

"No, Papa, no," she said.

"Have they been feeding you? Have you had a bath?"

"I only been here a day or two, I t'ink," she said.

Stuck in a windowless room, it was probably difficult for Shara to tell how much time had passed.

"We saw each other a little over twenty-four hours ago," I said.

She looked past René, noticing me for the first time.

"Mr. Jerry?"

René put his pack down and ripped it open like an impatient kid on Christmas. While he pulled out a pair of long-handled bolt cutters, I got a good look at Shara.

The Children had placed an iron crown on her head and tied it there with a piece of leather under her chin. She had chains around her wrists, and she was wearing a long, flowing red dress with a lace hem. I'm sure in nearly any other place, it would've been quite a beautiful article of clothing, and proudly worn by nearly any girl her age, but as she was, sitting on the ground with a long, heavy chain holding her to the concrete floor, I doubted Shara found herself enchanted.

"How did you end up down here?" I asked.

"My mother—she saw me," Shara said. "After I talked wit' you, she come wit' some of De Children and snatched me up. She been lookin' for me, she said. I don't know how she find me, but De Children probably got people workin' Marigot Harbor, and dey find me when I come by to you."

"I wish I was surprised," I said, "at the fact that a woman could kidnap and imprison her own child, but your mother is mixed up in all of this."

Shara nodded her head.

"Mary is a damaged woman," René said, as he matched the jaws of the cutters with the chain on the floor. "She lost very many things in the hurricane and while she in her sadness, The Children told her they would save her and all St. Martin, if only she followed them and did what they say, and she listened. She believed the things The Daughter promised. So much so she willing to give up her own girl at that woman's command." René paused and glanced at the chains. "When that woman took my Mary from me. I swore to take everything from her in retribution, but I was almost too late."

He pressed down on the handle of the cutters and when I expected to hear the snap and clatter of a broken chain in front of me, I heard a metallic *tink* behind me.

I turned and my light shone over a small cylinder lying on the floor with a piece of bent metal hanging off it.

Flashbang!

"Cover your ears!" I shouted as I turned away and the flashbang detonated.

Clamped hands and shut eyelids were a paltry defense against the concussive force of one of those things going off in an enclosed space such as the one we were in. I felt the air burst and slap against the back of my knees, forcing me down. My ears rang and I wasn't sure if my eyes had been seared shut or if the lids had been blown clean off.

There was no time to decide before someone kicked me in the back, and my face slapped against the concrete floor, crushing an old cigar.

Before I could regain any sense but touch, I felt my pack stripped from my shoulders before my arms were wrenched behind me and my wrists were bound. Within a handful of seconds, my vision settled from overwhelming whiteness to a soft, fuzzy collage of shapes and shades of gray, and the buzzing in my ears tapered off, but did not disappear.

I was shoved against a wall by probably two or three men. Then they forced me to sit down next to Jean-Phillipe, who appeared similarly stunned into compliance with his hands behind his back.

Just as I had been settled in, the men who were holding me jumped into a dog pile to our left.

René had to be at the bottom. One of his massive legs kicked out and his foot scrabbled across the floor. They had him on his belly, but he was putting up a hell of a fight, even as another man standing outside of the wrestling match ran up and stomped on René's free leg like it was a wild anaconda.

Soon, however, the mass of bodies began to shrink as one man after another peeled off until only René was left lying on his belly on the floor, howling like a rabid wolf with his hands bound behind his back. His big muscles were flexing and undulating, but strong as he was, he couldn't break whatever they'd restrained him with.

Three men picked a defiant René up off the ground and plied him into obedience by battering their knees into his groin and hammering their fists against his head until he sank against the wall like Jean-Phillipe and me.

"I'll cut all your fucking throats!" René screamed. "I'll kill all you fucking bastards! Every one of you! Let me loose and I'll rip your fucking hearts out with my bare hand!"

"Mr. René! Mr. René!" A voice cut above him.

René continued to yell obscenities until the clack of a round being settled into the chamber of a rifle finally got him to shut his mouth.

The machete priest from Grand Case was standing directly in front of René, his finger on the trigger of his rifle and the barrel pointed squarely at René's eyes.

"Mr. René, I've been waiting a long time to do this," he said.

"A long time to do what?" a woman's voice called from outside the room.

I looked at the door and watched her as she strode in, chin high, shoulders back, regal as a queen at her own coronation. She was in a red dress similar to Shara's, with the addition of a red turban atop her head, decorated in strands of pearls and thin iron chains.

The way every eye watched her, the way the room instantly quieted when she spoke, I knew this woman was The Daughter of Ogun.

She walked slowly past Jean-Phillipe and me, coming to the machete priest's side.

"Albert René belongs to Ogun now," she said. "You would not deny Ogun his rightful offering."

"No, Daughter," Machete Priest said, lowering his weapon.

"I know you long for justice against this man. We all do. He has harassed and maligned us for speaking the truth to those who are faithful," she said. "But it is not your place to mete out justice on your own. René will see justice at Ogun's hand, and he will serve Ogun in death."

She turned to me. Her eyes were as stony and cold as any hunk of iron.

"This one will make a fine servant as well."

CHAPTER THIRTY-TWO

I didn't know how long The Daughter and her followers had us chained to the floor of their bunker. We'd been here a few hours at least, or maybe they'd held us here a day. I suppose it could've been ten days, or it *felt* that way.

The mood was going sour. René had been beaten pretty badly but downplayed it. Shara was despondent and every time she reached out to René for comfort, my old buddy, Machete Priest, snapped at them like a crazed chihuahua and threatened, with the help of the other two guards assigned to watch us, to beat René into a fine paste.

But the problems René, Shara, and I faced were simple bothers compared to Jean-Phillipe's difficulties. He was next to me, curled into a ball on the concrete floor, sweating and shivering, muttering to himself in greater quantity, but less conviction, as time passed. If I didn't get him out of here and get his injury treated properly, I didn't think the kid would last through the night—or whatever time of day it currently was.

But I couldn't get him out of here. And as our tactical situation stood, DJ, whom I presumed was still alive, would have to work a terrible kind of magic to smoke out all those blood-thirsty cultists and get us out of our chains and off Tintamarre. The chances of that happening were slim, even if he could tap into whatever curse was behind that black *govi* jar.

"Mr. Jerry?" Shara's voice crept from her corner of the room like a snake-bitten cat. "Is Jean-Phillipe doin' better?"

"He'll be okay," I said, looking Jean-Phillipe over. His shirt was sticking to his back, revealing a bony spine. Why in the hell did I take this skinny kid into a fight? This was no place for him.

"Boy's shiverin'," Shara said.

"That's the body's natural defense for a person in his situation."

"Is it bad?"

"If he were thirty years older, forty pounds heavier, and in poor overall health, yes, I'd say it's bad. However, Jean-Phillipe is still young and still strong, and as soon as he gets food and proper rest, I promise he'll bounce right back."

Neither of which he'd get, so long as we were unwilling guests in this bunker.

"What's wrong wid 'im?" Shara asked. "Did they shoot 'im?"

I looked to René, who averted his eyes.

"He was at the wrong place at the wrong time," I said. "I cleaned him up as best I could, but even with my experience and training, I can't make the dusty ground on Tintamarre as clean as a hospital."

"I'll be—" Jean-Phillipe's teeth chattered. "I'll be okay."

Hearing him lucid startled me. I played it off by gently patting his slimy, cold shoulder. I rested my hand there—a reminder that he would not be alone.

"Yes, you will be. You just hold on. A little time in a proper hospital bed with a cute nurse feeding you chicken soup and changing your bandage, and you'll be back to taking on the world, Jean-Phillipe. None of your plans delayed or changed."

"Can I visit you in de hospital, Jean-Phillipe?" Shara asked.

Jean-Phillipe's shoulder stiffened at the question.

René burst out laughing. At least for a few seconds, before the pounding he'd taken caught up with him. After soothing himself for a moment, his uproarious laughing downgraded to a sensible chuckle.

"What's so funny about that, Papa?"

"It's not," he said, still grinning through a pair of busted lips. "It's a good question, *mon coeur.*"

"I don't know wh-why he laughing," Jean-Phillipe quickly added. His lie was half-convincing, all things considered.

"Ya do too know—" Shara started to say before Machete Priest cut her off.

"Quiet!" he bellowed.

That little man had a big voice and it snuffed out the tiny spark of joy we'd found in this room.

Anyhow, seeing Shara's obliviousness and Jean-Phillipe's bashfulness reminded me how young the two of them were, and how much life they had yet to live.

I had to get both of them out of here and pronto.

But before I did that, The Daughter of Ogun herself deigned to grace us with her presence.

She came in, dressed the same as before, except that her clothes somehow looked crisper and cleaner. Two men with AR-15 rifles flanked her, and, of all people, Mary Bradley brought up the rear.

I shouldn't have been surprised to see Shara's mother make an appearance—her membership in The Children of Ogun fit everything I knew about her.

Yet, here I was, gaping like an idiot upon seeing her dressed the same as The Daughter, minus the strands of pearls and mini-iron chains around her turban—Mary's was unadorned. And on Mary's thinner, more athletic frame, the dress hung looser around the waist and hips, clearly not made specifically for her. It seemed she wasn't granted the use of The Daughter's seamstress.

"Mama!" Shara called to her. "Mama, please!"

Mary didn't look her daughter's way.

"Mama! I need you, please!" Shara begged, but her mother was stone cold. Shara deflated against the wall, her chains clanking.

"What kind of mother hears her daughter crying for help and ignores her?" I asked no one in particular. Then, I looked straight at The Daughter. "You must've promised Mary something beyond imagination."

The Daughter gave me a fiery stare.

"We've brought you a gift," she said to me. She flicked a finger, and one of the guards tossed a singed, mangled prosthetic leg on the floor—DJ's prosthetic leg.

"We've eliminated your comrade," she said. "He was a rambunctious little nuisance, but he fell before The Children of Ogun, much as any other who would defy His will."

"Bullshit he did." I figured DJ wouldn't mind me borrowing a phrase. "There is no reality where any number of your people hunt down our man successfully and live to talk about it. Unless the handful of you in here are the only ones left alive."

"Believe what you want, but in death you will find your friend waiting for you." The Daughter continued to glare at me as she walked closer. There was something about me she seemed to like less than the rest of us trapped in this room. I could see it in her eyes.

"You've been asking about Billy Pearce," she said.

"I have."

"And in all of your efforts, what have you found?"

"That you people killed him," I said. "Which I'm sure doesn't matter to any of you."

"Billy Pearce killed himself," The Daughter said.

"No, he didn't..." Shara said weakly.

"He did, child," The Daughter answered without looking away from me. "Billy Pearce brought about his own death by knowingly tempting the wrath of Ogun, much as you lot have, and found that Ogun has no patience and no love for his enemies."

"Suppose we won't make great slaves then," I said.

She smirked. "What we offer Ogun is his to do with as he pleases. He may smoke his cigars or not, he may drink his rum or not, and"— she motioned to us— "he will take servants and wives as it pleases him."

"Ogun does not want dead girls," René said. "You cannot tie children to a post and let them drown for your—" The machete priest delivered a strong backhand across René's cheek.

"I know perfectly well what Ogun wants," The Daughter replied. "If he was not pleased by the offerings I have made, he would not have extended his hand to us; to lift us out of oppression and imperialism. If our gifts displeased Ogun, he would never speak through me."

"You are running a fucking carnival show!" René bellowed. He caught a boot to the gut for sharing his opinion. He gasped and managed to say, "She's stealing from—" before Machete Priest whacked him again.

I appreciated René's effort to get our message out, but if he was trying to turn the followers in the room against The Daughter, it was better left unsaid for now. Who would believe a few tied-up prisoners?

"What are you fighting for, Albert René?" The Daughter asked. "You have seen so little of Ogun; you understand so little of his will—how can you begin to question the veracity of what Ogun has given us? You came here on the word of a weak, old woman and a paranoid *oungan*. You've been spying on us for years, accusing us of perverting Ogun, and where has it brought you now? You've been cowed by us! You have nothing left! Ogun has cursed you for your sacrilege."

The Daughter approached René. She bent down and lifted his bruised, bloodied chin with two fingers and looked him straight in his rolling eyes until he focused on her.

She pointed at Mary. "Your woman understands. Why can't you?"

"Mama, they gonna kill us!" Shara yelled.

"Death is a necessary step!" The Daughter bellowed. "Shara Bradley, you must see outside your limited senses—outside your eyes, your ears, your mind—understand that you are destined to be honored at Ogun's side from now unto forever! And in eternity, this life will be remembered as you remember a dream in your waking hours.

"But first you must die. To wed Ogun in all his glory, you must seek him in death, and when you are finally at his side, Shara, you will see the other *loa*, the pretenders, bow before you and your new master and all the wives who have preceded you!" Her voice softened and she smiled at Shara. "Do not be frightened, child. His glory will be upon you and surround you forever."

"Mary, you can stop this!" René said. "Mary, look at me!"

The Machete Priest gave René another boot, and the breath went leaping out of him. René wretched and sucked in air.

"Our baby's greater glory ahead a' her," Mary said, as calmly as a doped-up mental patient. "I cannot deny her from it."

"You have to!" was all René could force out.

Mary strode across the room, the hem of her pretty red dress dragging dried beans and rice along with her. She stopped in front of René, just short of being side by side with The Daughter, whom Mary courteously bowed her head to.

"You may." The Daughter magnanimously held an empty palm toward René.

Mary stepped up, bent at the middle, and slapped him. I watched her hand arc across his face, and it was in that moment I noticed she wasn't wearing a ring.

Not a wedding ring (I didn't expect that), but the signet that I'd come to realize belonged to The Children of Ogun—the gold ring with the small piece of iron. Just like the one DJ had found.

The Daughter had one. The machete priest had one. Each guard had one.

But not Mary.

"Ya used to swear ya'd love me forever, Albert," Mary said, waving her finger in his face, "but if dat was de trut', why have you tried to destroy de one t'ing that saved me? Just like dat no-good Billy Pearce, you been tryin' to corrupt our people by steerin' dem away from de one t'ing dat will save us all, jus' because you t'ink you know better dan everyone else."

She straightened up, retracting her finger. "I'm glad to be rid of ya, Albert, just as I was glad to get rid a Billy Pearce."

Did she just—? No.

"Where's your ring, Mary?" I asked.

She jerked her head around to me, confused at my speaking up.

"You lost it at Billy's church, didn't you? The night you killed him."

"Mama?" Shara was as perplexed as I was a minute ago. "But I saw de duppy kill Billy! I saw it! It was wearin' a robe!"

"You saw your mother's dress," I said. "The same one she's wearing now, or one like it. And I've seen a fair number of murders, but never one committed by a ghost."

Shara rattled her chains. "No! Not Mama, she couldn't 'a killed Billy!"

But just as soon as Shara said that I think she realized how foolish a statement it was. She touched the chains on her wrist and followed the one connected to the floor with her eyes.

"You were mean, mama, you were cruel, but I never t'ought you be like dis," she said to her mother.

"De duppy acted trough me," Mary said. "Ogun took me body and imbue me with de duppy's power so I could be de instrument of justice agains' evil."

The way she spoke, it sounded more likely The Daughter had taken control of her.

"You did a commendable thing," The Daughter said, putting a hand on Mary's shoulder. "Mary was unafraid to act when Ogun called her forth. She is an example we should all follow and learn from—all of Ogun's children must be unafraid to act when they are called forth and empowered by him. And with the offering we are about to make, he will empower us all."

The Daughter looked at each of us in turn; Shara, René, me. Then, her eyes stopped on Jean-Phillipe.

"Except for that one," she pointed at him. "His sickness will curse us, and his weakness displeases Ogun."

She motioned at Machete Priest, who, behind her, pulled a handgun from the belt around his red pants, pointed it at Jean-Phillipe and fired.

Shara and René screamed and cursed. I was paralyzed. I couldn't have moved if Machete Priest pointed his weapon at me. I couldn't believe they would kill a man, kill Jean-Phillipe who wanted nothing but to help his neighbors, so... *casually.*

"It's time. Pick up Shara and the two men," The Daughter said. "Ogun is an impatient *loa.*"

CHAPTER THIRTY-THREE

The Daughter and her entourage of guards, plus Mary Bradley, left Jean-Phillipe's body where it was, and led us out of the bunker's *hounfour* with our wrists chained behind our backs and our feet in shackles linked together by a very short chain. I was at the end of the line, with a pair of guards flanking me, René was ahead of me, and Shara was at the head of the column, being led in her chains by The Daughter, with Mary walking alongside.

The bunker appeared as empty as the first time René and I had gone through it. I hoped that meant DJ had shot the vast majority of The Children of Ogun to pieces. A grim thought, I know, but Jean-Phillipe was fresh in my mind.

We went eastward, through the common room, through the kitchen, through a shooting range and armory, and then past more private quarters and bathrooms and all the rest of the necessities a small army would need to survive underground for an extended period of time.

Beyond all these areas was a large steel door, which, from René's map of the bunker, I knew opened to the cave. We proceeded through the door and up steel stairs toward a catwalk over a dry dock—basically, a large concrete trench about fifteen feet wide and ten feet deep, dry except for glistening droplets of condensation that snuck in every time someone opened the exterior door.

Above the dry dock, our parade moved across the steel catwalk which, ahead of us, dog-legged right. I couldn't see what lay beyond the turn, but I could hear the persistent murmur of surf surging and receding.

We turned the dogleg, and the catwalk faded into steps, which took us down into a familiar cave. Ahead, I noticed fire flickering against the night sky. At first, I thought they were faraway bonfires, or, more hopefully, the small vessels of The Children's ragtag navy alight on the water, but as we got closer, I realized they were torches. And these torches surrounded people standing on the beach, all of them dressed in red, all of them armed.

"All glory to Ogun!" The Daughter shouted as we left the cave.

The people on the beach erupted into cheers and shouts and drumbeats. The sound of the drums was echoed and amplified by the cliff face to the left and they danced like they weren't all brainwashed nuts and just a nice group of armed partiers enjoying local music on a Caribbean night, ready to watch a few folks ritualistically drowned.

Once she reached her crowd of followers, The Daughter took Mary by the arm, and the two of them rushed forward from our parade and melded into the group, dancing and clapping and rejoicing like the rest.

Machete Priest remained at the head of our column. The crowd separated for us, but Machete Priest halted our procession and a handful of men came out of the rabble holding iron weights about the size of coconut shells, which they clipped onto the chains between our ankles with carabiners. They attached four onto my chains, and I don't know how many onto René's. Then Machete

Priest resumed the march, the men with the iron weight filing in alongside us, and we moved steadily off the sand and into the water.

Aside from The Children following behind me, I was the last one into the surf, and as soon as the water reached up to my knees, the tenor of the beach party changed. The drums beat faster and harder and howls began, chasing us into the water, and getting more furious and crazed the further we marched.

Firelight from the beachside torches played on dock pilings in the water ahead of us. At first, I couldn't see the furthest one over Shara's iron crown, but I remembered it. And I was sure that, like the girl I'd found, Shara would be joined to it while awaiting her otherworldly groom.

Then I saw it. The piling was only visible between the crests of waves. Mercifully, she wouldn't last long.

In front of me, seven or eight men were wrangling René. He tried to put up a fight, but he was so bruised and broken, he was lucky to have walked under his own power.

The Children lifted him up and were getting his arms over the top of another piling. Their aim was to slip the piling in the gap between his arms and his back, and they did it with less trouble than they apparently anticipated from René.

Then, hands took hold of me. I don't know how many men had me—enough that they were able to wrap their arms around me and lift me off my feet, and no matter how much I fought and kicked and tried to bash heads with the iron weights hanging off my ankle chains, I couldn't stop or even slow them down.

After a moment, they had me fastened to the dock piling. Behind me, the howling and the drums hit a thundering, ferocious pitch, and the sounds of both were almost impossible to tell apart.

335

The waves slapped my chest, the same with René ahead of me, and beyond him, the waves crested over Shara's head, though her iron crown remained firmly in place.

She sputtered and coughed in the trenches between waves, but it wouldn't be long before the sea denied her those short breaths too. She started to scream and cough. She was losing herself.

"Stay calm!" I desperately yelled up to her. "You have to control your breathing!"

She couldn't hear me. Not even if I was right next to her, would she have been able to listen to me. Shara was dying, and if she took my advice, she'd only prolong her suffering.

"Just hold on, Shara! Stay calm!" I yelled.

"Be quiet!" René barked at me.

"If she breathes—"

"*No.*"

"DJ's out there," I said. "He can save us. He *will* save us."

"I said shut your fucking mouth. Let my daughter die in peace."

There was nothing I could say to that. René had the right, as Shara's father, to demand quiet.

And, so, I stayed quiet while Shara coughed sea water. She didn't want to go; she was a fighter.

"*C'est bon, mon coeur,*" he said, his voice hitching. "*Respires l'eau de mer*—breathe in the ocean."

I didn't speak as I listened to the drums beat. I wouldn't say a word when The Children cried out in joy for Ogun. I offered no contradictory instructions for Shara as she gurgled and coughed and finally released a sigh cut short by the waves, giving in to her father's wishes. I remained silent while the sea rose over her iron crown.

René wept softly for his little girl.

Behind me, the drumming and cries reached a new pitch. The Children must've seen Shara's head was completely submerged and they were awash in pure jubilance at the certainty that Ogun had his newest bride.

Then gunshots echoed off the cliffs.

I thought it was celebratory fire from the beach until I spotted a muzzle flash on top of the cliffs to the left. Lead was raining onto the beach.

The drumming tapered off slowly—some of The Children probably hadn't realized they were being shot at straight away. But, within a few seconds drumbeats were swallowed up by the roll of concentrated, overwhelming small arms fire. I couldn't turn to the beach to see, but every man and woman there with a firearm must've opened up. I could see the cliff, at least, and the pieces of rock being sheared off by bullets and ground to gravel and dust before they even hit the water.

If that was DJ up there shooting down at the beach, he was pinned now and would be dead soon.

"*Sirène!*" René screamed.

I turned my eyes from the cliffs and looked straight ahead.

La Sirène came steadily out from behind the rock, and her bow was engulfed in a dazzling light. For a split second, I thought they'd hit her with another rocket, but when I heard the bullets snapping over my head in time with the bursts of light, I knew it was Bartram and his old French machine gun.

He must've bolted the damned thing to the gunwales. It hurled flame and lead, and the screaming from the beach took on a newer, more blood-curdling tenor.

Bartram must've been devastating them. Weak, inaccurate return fire shot well over the top of *La Sirène*, and only for a second before the shooter either ducked for cover—of which there was very little on that flat beach—or was mowed down with his comrades.

I was so mesmerized by Bartram and his machine gun laying waste to the cultists, I didn't notice DJ was already at Shara's piling, pulling her free.

"Here!" René yelled as soon as Bartram stopped firing. "Pull the boat up! Come closer!"

Within a couple of seconds, *La Sirène*'s engines growled and she lurched into the bay.

I could see the damage to her was extensive. She was listing port, and she'd had her top blown right off—the saloon was missing a roof and most of its starboard bulkhead. The back half of *La Sirène* was black as coal, too, but she was a tough little boat and kept swimming.

Bartram expertly pulled her just short of DJ and Shara at the front piling. He ran to the starboard side and reached over, pulling at her limp body, but he and DJ managed to get her up out of the water and Bartram pulled her aboard.

They helped René next, getting his arms over the top of the post. He and DJ were able to unlatch the weights on his ankle restraints. He hobbled to *La Sirène's* stern, where Bartram waited with a pair of bolt cutters while DJ helped me get free.

DJ plunged below the surface of the water, and I felt the weights come off my ankles before he resurfaced.

"They tried to tell us you were dead," I said. "I knew it was impossible."

"Not all of me," he said. "They got Patty, though—my best leg. I woulda been up on that cliff faster if I had it." His eyes darted toward Shara.

DJ helped me get my arms over the top of the piling, then we both got to *La Sirène's* stern, where Bartram waited. He handed DJ the cutters and he disappeared. I felt the chains on my ankles move, and a moment later, my hands fell free and I scrambled onto the platform to help my partner out of the water.

How he'd managed to move around and inflict as much damage as he had, hobbled on just one foot, then escape and swim out to rescue us was beyond me.

René was hunched over Shara's body on the foredeck, furiously pumping her chest with his hands, despite his wrists still being manacled. She'd been underwater a long time. Too long. I didn't think she had a chance of coming back to us, but I wouldn't tell a father not to try and save his daughter.

Then she coughed.

René rolled her over and she hacked up seawater. Before she'd gotten all of it out of her system, he threw his arms on her, overjoyed, as she continued to cough.

I couldn't believe Shara was alive.

CHAPTER THIRTY-FOUR

After Shara was up and conscious, she, René, and I retreated to what was left of the saloon while Bartram helped DJ out to the starboard deck so the two of them could keep eyes on the beach. A counterattack seemed unlikely to me. The kind of accurate, concentrated fire Bartram was able to send against that unprotected beachhead had likely put an end to any serious resistance from The Children.

In any case, I set up a triage station on what remained of the kitchenette bench. Shara only needed monitoring—she might still have seawater in her lungs, she might not—so I had her take a seat while René took the edge of the bench.

René needed the most attention, as, from the parts of him I could see, he looked like a well-loved GI Joe. His face was an exhibit of the different sizes, shapes and colors of contusions the human body was able to produce under diverse circumstances, and his left shoulder, normally rounded under his large deltoids, had gone square; a telltale sign it'd come out of socket.

I didn't have my trauma kit, but DJ's pack was hanging by a strap over a piece of bent steel jutting from the wall. I got it down and opened it up. The towel with the black govi was missing, but DJ's first aid kit was still there.

I unzipped the kit and laid it on the table next to René.

"You some kind of doctor or something?" René asked as I pulled out gauze for a nasty cut above his right eye.

"No, but I've had some practice with field medicine."

"Eh? What's that mean?"

"I can patch up wounds and tell when a man's shoulder is dislocated," I said, nodding at his shoulder

"Good enough for me, then," René managed a weak, uncharacteristic and extremely unsettling smile. I assumed he must've been cracking up, but then I noticed Shara's delicate fingers holding his right hand.

"Thank you, Jerry," he said. "For all you done."

I didn't accept gratitude very well, and having it come from Albert René was a shock to my system. I managed not to bristle. I stayed on task, peeling a square of gauze apart, then taped part of it above his eye.

"I mean it," he said. "Thank you."

DJ hobbled in, using a boat oar for a crutch and noticed his open pack.

"I had to borrow your kit," I told him. "I noticed the govi was gone."

"Yeah," he said with a shrug. "I buried it up on that cliff. Figured the duppy would help me out if I did."

"*La Sirène*, this is *Wayward*." Alicia's voice suddenly crackled over the radio.

I jumped up and ran for the mic, which was only partially melted out of form.

"*Wayward?*"

"Jerry! Oh my God, are you alright? What happened?"

"Plenty of things," I said, looking at René and Shara. "We've got Shara—she's okay, and I'm okay."

"How're René and Jean-Phillipe?"

Jean-Phillipe? I couldn't break the news to her now. Not over the radio.

"It's a long story, my darling, and it ends with me holding you tight. Did Arlen come through for us?"

"Oh, yes!" she said. "He went *beyond* the call of duty. He released a video of The Daughter walking around her new island and inspecting the mansion she was having built."

"Who's seen it?"

"It's all over the island, Jerry," she said. "I've been in contact with Pierre Noubon, and he said Arlen also released information about The Daughter's banking assets to the local news. Every penny she's stolen from her followers is there in black and white, and she's spent most of the money The Children donated on herself—including the house and a Mercedes."

If the mansion didn't show her followers she was a crook, a luxury car in the Caribbean was frivolous by any standard.

"What's the reaction been?" I asked.

"The Mélasse practically shut down when the news hit. Her followers there are refusing to work, and the government is finally getting involved.

"Noubon told me a lot of the employees have been gathering at the Mélasse, demanding that someone arrest The Daughter and put her on trial. They think she's going to show up there."

No way would The Daughter have the gall to show her face to those people after being exposed.

"Well, if we find her, we'll know who to bring her to, at least," I said.

"Is she still on Tintamarre?"

"Maybe. Maybe not. Truthfully, I think she's dead," I said, "but if she's still alive, one can almost be certain she's executing a long-held escape plan and may have already left the island."

"I'll keep circling Tintamarre," Alicia said. "Turn the radio up and leave it there. If I see her, I'll call out."

"Acknowledged," I said.

I spent the next two hours cleaning up René as best I could. I went through nearly all of DJ's trauma pack and a partially singed first aid kit Shara found aboard *La Sirène*, but I had his worst cuts covered and, after a lot of cursing in French plus a strong yelp, I got his shoulder back in place. I used an old T-shirt as a sling for him.

"You'll need to see a doctor at your first opportunity. Get a facial x-ray," I said. His nose was certainly broken, and by the swelling, I'd wager he had a hairline fracture to his right eye socket. "And it'd be wise to have someone do a chest x-ray, too. Your rib bones probably look like broken glass."

"Yes, Jerry," he said.

"And rest up while you can—now, even," I said. "Few things will help you heal faster."

But René was already looking past me, through the big blast hole in the saloon wall, past DJ and Bartram, and out at the aftermath of the bloody massacre on the beach.

"We'll have to wait until dawn to see if The Daughter is out there," I said.

"Do you think she's out there?" The way René said it with quiet concern, I knew he wasn't talking about The Daughter. He was thinking of Mary.

I turned away from the hole in the wall, fixing my attention on retying the knot in his sling for... reasons. My eyes met Shara's. She,

344

too, was staring out at the beach with an expression on her face that appeared a mix of guilt and hope.

"The two of you seem awfully concerned about her," I said. "Considering everything she did."

"You are married, yes?" René asked.

"I am."

"And do you love her?"

"Of course," I said.

He nodded toward the beach. "I still love *her.*"

"I'm not sure how—" I was temporarily at a loss for words. "Can you ever forgive Mary for what she did?"

René swallowed and grimaced.

"I couldn't forgive 'er," Shara said. "But I can let de past be de past, if she want to make it so."

"Then so can I," René added.

I knew they'd feel differently later, but I didn't dare ruin the moment.

"*La Sirène,* this is *Wayward.*" The radio crackled with Alicia's voice.

I was on the mic in an instant. "Go ahead, *Wayward.*"

"Something's going on at the Mélasse," Alicia said. "I've been monitoring radio traffic and the cops are saying the employees have cornered two women inside one of the cabanas."

"It *has* to be The Daughter," René said. "And Mary!"

I wasn't as sure as René, but I think our presence there was warranted.

"*Wayward,* we'll meet you there," I said into the mic.

"I'll wait for you," Alicia said. "*Wayward* out."

I called Bartram and DJ back in and filled them in on the situation. DJ theorized that if The Daughter wasn't among the bodies on the beach, she probably went back to the Mélasse to rally what was left of her followers, but it didn't sound like she'd been successful.

Bartram manned the helm and had us back into Cul-De-Sac Bay, looking at the Mélasse, in practically no time.

We were about three hundred yards off the beach, in the channel between Pinel Island and Petite Clef, but even at night, from this distance, it was impossible not to see the mass of humanity that had gathered around the defaced cabana—the Childrens' *hounfour* at the Mélasse—and there was no mistaking their intention to knock the door in and drag out whomever was inside. When Bartram slowed *La Sirène*'s throttle, we heard the mob's shouts echoing across the water.

Wayward was about halfway between *La Sirène* and land, waiting for us, as Alicia promised. We came alongside, lashed on and everyone transferred from *La Sirène*, save Bartram.

"They definitely have The Daughter trapped inside that cabana," Alicia said as she pulled our trailing dinghy to *Wayward*'s stern for boarding. "I don't know who she's got with her, but the gendarmes make it sound like it's a hostage situation."

"It's Mary," René said. "I know it is."

I was willing to entertain that idea for René's sake, so I let Alicia take René and Shara to shore first. DJ and I watched from *Wayward*'s cockpit—me standing on the deck, and DJ in the helm chair, since standing was a bit of a challenge to him currently. We watched René and Shara disembark near shore and run up the beach toward the mass of people, but even with our night-vision binos, both of us lost sight of them when they slipped into the crowd outside the *hounfour*.

"You think Mary Bradley's her hostage or her last holdout?" DJ asked me.

"I'm afraid to find out," I said.

Alicia came back to *Wayward's* stern with the dinghy, and DJ and I boarded. We crossed the water with the throttle wide open, but by the time we were within a hundred yards of shore, the crowd parted.

They had The Daughter. Specifically, a group of four or five men had The Daughter by her arms and legs. Even from that distance, we could hear her screaming and see her fighting to get away.

They reached the edge of the water and threw her face down into the surf. She began to lift her head up when a gunshot rang out, and her body went limp.

The Daughter of Ogun was dead.

"Where's Mary?" DJ shouted over the wind.

I didn't see her on the beach. For the sake of René and Shara, I hoped Mary's absence didn't mean she was already dead inside the *hounfour*.

Alicia didn't slow the dinghy until we'd beached it beside the dock. She cut the engine and DJ stayed aboard while Alicia and I scrambled toward the *hounfour* together. I led the way, shoving through bloodthirsty revelers cheering and dancing, basking in the victory of apparently putting their worst mistake behind them.

We cleared the crowd and stumbled into the *hounfour*.

René and Shara were there, holding Mary. She was unharmed and teary-eyed.

"I'm sorry to de both of ya," she said. "I been an awful mother, a bad woman, and I been lookin' so hard everywhere for happiness, I been blinded to what's in front of me. I done so much *wrong*."

Her eyes met mine. She knew what I'd come to this island to do, and that I wouldn't stop now.

"I have to atone and repent for my sins," she said, more to René and Shara than to me. "I have to confess what I did."

347

CHAPTER THIRTY-FIVE

That night, Mary Bradley turned herself in to the authorities and confessed to the murder of Billy Pearce. We were all held too, of course, but since we had dealt with the biggest existential threat the government of St. Martin had faced since the Dutch and the Spanish went head to head over ownership of the island in the 17th century, we were let go with the explicit understanding that no one would talk about The Children of Ogun or what happened on Tintamarre.

I didn't like it, but I supposed with Mary Bradley confessing to the murder of Billy Pearce, we had achieved our mission's objective.

A week later, under a clear, blue Caribbean sky, DJ, Alicia, and I attended Jean-Phillipe's funeral at the cemetery on the south side of Marigot Bay. Also present were René, Shara, Bartram, Pierre Noubon, Ella, and Mother Manbo, who conducted the ceremony.

René had told me Jean-Phillipe's only family was a half-brother who lived in Texas and couldn't make it, so I felt obligated to help remember a promising young man I'd known a little longer than a day.

Now, nearing the end of the ceremony (I assumed), Mother Manbo chanted in French and wiped ash across the top of Jean-Phillipe's sarcophagus while Noubon beat on a large drum and hummed along with her.

Their rituals were quite pleasing, and, I think, were I given to religion or mysticism, I would've seen the appeal in the spiritual healing power of Vodou.

After the ceremony concluded, as Alicia and I left, arm in arm, my phone rang.

It was Arlen.

"Jerry," he said before I got a word in. "How was the funeral?"

"Peaceful," I answered. "You should've been here."

"In that graveyard on the bay, was it? I intended to attend, but a surprise meeting came up, and well—Listen, don't walk back to *Wayward* too quickly."

I stopped. "Why not?"

"Something very unsettling is about to happen, and I'd like to speak to you on *Heart and Soul* about it," he said. "If you turn to your left, you may see her about a mile and a half offshore."

"Are you watching me?" I asked.

"No, not me. Not directly, anyhow," he said. "I know it's very rude of me to spy on you, and we can address that when you come aboard to chat, but believe me when I say there's something I positively need to explain to you, and I think you won't want me to delay once you see what it is."

"If it's so urgent, why can't you explain it to me now, Arlen?"

"As I said, it hasn't happened quite yet."

Suddenly, an explosion rocked the bay and a fireball sprouted and grew toward the sky. Smoke and fire mushroomed upward, and pieces of debris sailed through the air and then arced into the bay like pebbles tossed by a giant.

It was pieces of *Wayward*.

"I didn't do that," Arlen said. "But I believe I know who did."

Also By Wayne Stinnett

The Jesse McDermitt Caribbean Adventure Series

Fallen Out
Fallen Palm
Fallen Hunter
Fallen Pride
Fallen Mangrove
Fallen King
Fallen Honor
Fallen Tide
Fallen Angel
Fallen Hero
Rising Storm
Rising Fury

Rising Force
Rising Charity
Rising Water
Rising Spirit
Rising Thunder
Rising Warrior
Rising Moon
Rising Tide
Steady As She Goes
All Ahead Full
Man Overboard
Cast Off

The Charity Styles Caribbean Thriller Series

Merciless Charity
Ruthless Charity
Reckless Charity
Enduring Charity

Enduring Charity
Vigilant Charity
Lost Charity
Elusive Charity
Forced Charity

www.waynestinnett.com

Also By Stewart Matthews

The Cready Marsen Mystery Series

Repo Man   The Captain

The Detective Shannon Rourke Series

Chicago Blood   Chicago Lies
Chicago Broken   Chicago Creed
Chicago Betrayed

The Barrett Mason Series

Matador   Ghosts
Tyrant   Wardogs
Jackal   Red Star

www.smwrites.com

If you'd like to receive my newsletter, please sign up on my website:
WWW.WAYNESTINNETT.COM.
Every two weeks, I'll bring you insights into my private life and writing
habits, with updates on what I'm working on, special deals I hear about, and
new books by other authors that I'm reading.

The Gaspar's Revenge Ship's Store is open.
There, you can purchase all kinds of swag as well as autographed
copies of Wayne Stinnett's books.
WWW.GASPARS-REVENGE.COM

Visit Stewart Matthews's website at
WWW.SMWRITES.COM

Made in the USA
Monee, IL
18 November 2022

18080649R00201